THRILLER UNGER, L
Unger, Lisa,
Last girl ghosted /

11/11/2021

LAST GIRL GHOSTED

LAST GIRL GHOSTED

LISA UNGER

WHEELER PUBLISHING
A part of Gale, a Cengage Company

LIBRARY OF CONGRESS CIP DATA ON FILE.
CATALOGUING IN PUBLICATION FOR THIS BOOK
IS AVAILABLE FROM THE LIBRARY OF CONGRESS.

ISBN-13: 978-1-4328-9131-2 (hardcover alk. paper)

Published in 2021 by arrangement with Harlequin Books S. A.

Printed in Mexico
Print Number: 01   Print Year: 2022

For Jennifer Manfrey
Because you're a total badass
and the first person I'd call if
I needed to get rid of a body.

∎ ∎ ∎ ∎

PART ONE:
GHOSTED

∎ ∎ ∎ ∎

Disguised since childhood, haphazardly
assembled
From voices and fears and little
pleasures,
We come of age as masks.
Rainer Maria Rilke

PROLOGUE

MIA

Mia Thorpe drove, the road ahead of her long and twisting. Dark. She'd been driving on and off for two days, was stiff and bleary-eyed from the trip. She'd stopped last night at a motel for a fitful sleep, half-waiting for word from Raife that didn't come. *Don't worry if you don't hear from me,* he'd told her. *Cell phone service is spotty. Just follow the directions. I'll be there when you get there.*

She believed him. She trusted him. She did.

She'd lain on the hard, uncomfortable mattress in a motel room that smelled like cigarette smoke and industrial strength cleaner. Each time she'd managed to drift off a passing car would cast its headlights on the wall beside her bed, shining through the too-thin curtains, waking her. She doubted if she'd nabbed two solid hours.

She was on the road again before the sun rose.

9

"I think I love him, Mom," she said out loud. Though her mother was long gone, Mia was sure she was still listening.

When Mia was six years old, she wanted to change her name to Princess Rainbows. She knew that it was possible to change her name because her dad told her that when she was grown up she could change her name to whatever she wanted. But while she was still his little girl, he would very much like her to keep the name that he and Mommy gave her.

A name is like a gift, he told her. *We gave it a lot of thought and picked something we thought was as beautiful as you are.* Mia Belle Thorpe. *And technically, isn't Belle a princess name?*

That was true. But there were three other Mia's in her class, and one other Belle. And a Bella and an Isabella who liked to be called Izzy. Mia Belle Thorpe wasn't like Mia with the red hair who frowned miserably at her corner desk, and cried all the time. She wasn't like the Mia who was really good at math and always shot her hand up like a rocket when it was time to volunteer to solve problems at the board. And she definitely wasn't like shy Mia who was pale as an egg and never spoke at all, was frequently absent.

She was Mia, herself. She didn't want to be

10

one of four Mia's in the room. The teacher, to avoid confusion, took to calling them by first and last names. Mia Thorpe. She remembered hating that. She couldn't even say why.

Maybe it started then, this idea that she had to assert her "specialness."

Her mom always told her she was special — that she was pretty, and smart, and a ray of sunshine. *There's no one like you, little star. You're my special girl.* But how could that be true if there were three other Mia's in her classroom alone? Mia Belle Thorpe was pretty sure then that no one else in the world was named Princess Rainbows.

Around this same time, she discovered the wild pleasure of slamming doors in anger. So after another argument erupted, over her afternoon snack where she'd listed all the ways in which having the same name as three other people had annoyed or inconvenienced her that day, her mother ended it by saying: *Mia Belle Thorpe, we will not discuss this further. You are not changing your name to Princess Rainbows. Now please go do your homework.*

Mia had stormed up the stairs, and slammed the door as hard as she could, making, it seemed, the whole house vibrate with her misery. She lay on her bed weeping, and must have fallen asleep because when she woke up, the afternoon had turned to dusk. The light in her room was an unfamiliar gray.

She and her mother rarely argued. Mia might get very mad at her dad for being bossy, or for tooting, or for trying to help with math when he really had no idea what he was doing. But her mother was soft and sweet, rarely said no, always knew how to fix anything that was wrong, and consistently smelled like flowers. And when Mia woke up, she felt regretful for storming off and slamming the door so hard.

The house was quiet when she left her room. Which felt odd. Because usually she heard her mom in the kitchen — cooking, or talking on the phone with a friend, or listening to the radio while she made dinner. There were all kinds of familiar noises in the house. But silence was not one of them.

She crept down the stairs. It was easy to apologize to her mother; she knew it would be accepted with hugs and a kind conversation about why things couldn't be the way Mia wanted them to be. There would be some consolation prize — maybe a cookie, or a concession on another matter of conflict.

But when she entered the kitchen, she found her mother lying on the floor. One of her mom's red velvet flats had fallen off her tiny foot. And it looked just like she was sleeping.

Mom, she said, sitting down beside her. *Mommy. I'm sorry.*

But her mom didn't stir, and Mia lay down beside her, rested her head on her chest. She knew that something was horribly wrong. But she pushed it so deep, squeezed her eyes shut and held on tight. She was sleeping. She'd wake up very soon.

That's where her father found them when he came home from work, not long after. The sound of his wailing would stay with Mia for the rest of her life.

It's not your fault.

This was the single phrase she heard most often after that day. From her father, from therapists, from aunts and uncles. But Mia knew how much her mother hated when she slammed the door. Truth be told, that's *why* she slammed it harder than she had ever had before. And so no matter how many times people told her it wasn't her fault, she knew that it was.

Mia's mother had asthma; they'd recently had to change her medication. She'd ignored warning signs — shortness of breath, dizziness. She'd had a heart attack. No one's fault, not really. But Mia knew that being upset *could* aggravate her mom's asthma.

She wasn't upset, her father, Henry, told her. *She called me after you fought. She said,*

Princess Rainbows is at it again. We thought it was funny, cute. She wasn't mad at you. She was never mad at you.

Mia didn't believe him.

And while she loved her father, it was true that she loved him somewhat less than she loved her mother. It was also true that a very special kind of light that her mother brought into her life, and into her home, went dark. Though there was still light, it wasn't anything like the light that came from her mother's love. And her father, who had always been goofy and funny and full of laughter, with big appetites, and grand ideas, and big plans for day trips and vacations, seem to deflate, go pale and quiet.

The world should have ended. It did end for Mia and Henry in all sorts of ways.

It just didn't for anyone else. They both went on in that unfamiliar gray light together with the person they loved less than they had loved her.

It wasn't until years later, in rehab for the first time, that Mia Belle Thorpe worked to unpack this moment of her life. How everything that went wrong later for her, started there; how every moment after was colored by the loss of her mother. She was special after that. She wasn't math Mia, or shy Mia, or grouchy Mia. She was Mia whose Mommy had died.

Mia Belle meant *my pretty,* or *my dear one.* It was special because it was the name her mother had given her. She wished she could tell her mother that she knew that now.

Now.

Now, the farther she went on the dark road, the more of herself she left behind. All the people she'd been — the pampered little girl, the child who'd lost her mother, the angry teenager, the addict, the recovering addict, the person struggling, always struggling to find the specialness she'd seen reflected in her mother's eyes.

You were special to her. You are special to me, her father told her. *That's the only special anyone needs to be.*

She'd left everything that tethered her to her life behind. She hadn't called her father to say goodbye. He didn't like Raife and he didn't understand their relationship, so there was no point in fighting about her plans. After a while, she'd send him a letter, explaining.

She imagined that it would be a relief to have some distance, for both of them. Her father had a girlfriend now; she seemed nice, had reached out to Mia multiple times. But no. Just no. Maybe if Mia and her father had some space from each other, from the memory of their shared loss, they could each be happy

15

for a while. She loved her father. But it didn't make her happy to be with him. She strongly suspected that he felt the same way about her.

Let's leave the toxic modern world behind for a while. Maybe not forever. But for now, I know a place where we can be free. That's what Raife had said to her when he issued his invitation.

It sounded right to her.

On this dark road, with just a burner phone she'd picked up at a drug store, all the chatter had gone quiet. There were no social media notifications, no constant pinging announcing the ugly news headlines, or junk emails. No endless texts from friends with memes and plans for the evening. There were no podcasts. No Siri to ask about the weather — or whatever.

The car she'd picked up in the lot, as Raife had directed her, just had an AM/FM radio. As she drove, the stations she could receive changed. A country music station faded away into static. She cast about and found some classic rock station with a mouthy DJ that eventually devolved into white noise, too. For a while, all she could get was a Christian sermon filled with fire and brimstone. She listened for miles, just because she found that she was afraid of silence.

She had the map he'd left her, figured how to use it. He'd marked on the map where she should stop for gas. No cameras. Pay cash.

But slowly, she learned to let the quiet wrap around her. Finally, the nervous chatter of her mind quieted, as well.

She hadn't seen another car for hours. Above there were only stars and stars and stars, until the light of the rising sun brightened the sky.

She didn't know the place she was going. Or how long she would be there. But she knew that for the first time in her life, she could taste freedom.

ONE

Now

Modern dating. Let's be honest. It sucks.

Is there anything more awkward, more nervous-making than waiting for a person you've only seen online to show up in the flesh?

This was a mistake. The East Village bar I'm in is crowded and overwarm with too many bodies, manic with too many television screens, the din of voices, somewhere music trying in vain to be heard over the noise.

I'm early, which has me feeling awkward and waiting on something I'm not sure I wanted in the first place. I started off standing by the door, half-planning to leave, then finally made my way into the fray and slipped into an open place at the bar.

And here I sit on an uncomfortable stool. Waiting.

I should go.

19

My order of a seltzer water has earned me the indifference of the pretty, tattooed bartender with the hot pink hair and magnetic eyelashes, and she hasn't been back since briskly placing the tumbler in front of me. She has a point. There's no reason to come to a place like this — a hipster watering hole at happy hour — unless you've come to have a drink. One certainly doesn't come for the atmosphere. But it's important to keep a clear head.

I've never been here before. My best friend Jax suggested it, an old haunt of hers. Crowded, she said, anonymous.

Safer to meet a stranger in a crowd, right?

Safer not to meet a stranger at all? had been my reply.

A worried frown. *And then what? Never meet anyone?*

Would that be so bad? Solitude. It's not the worst thing in life.

It was Jax's idea. The whole online dating thing.

Robin, my childhood friend, who is basically Jax's opposite, was against it. *Love,* she said, *is not an algorithm.*

Truth.

Anyway, who's looking for love?

Only everyone, Robin would surely say.

I take a sip of my icy sparkling water and

glance at the door. A roar of laughter goes up from the big group at the table in the back. I keep my eyes on them for a moment, watching. Three women, four men, young, well-heeled, coiffed and polished — coworkers maybe? Relaxed, easy, comfortable. The opposite of how I feel. I notice that my shoulders are hiked up. I force myself to relax, breathe.

The man beside me is uncomfortably close, his shoulder nudging up against mine twice, now three times. Is he doing it on purpose? I turn to see. He's bulky, balding, a sheen of sweat on his brow. No. He's not even aware of me. He's on his phone, scrolling through pictures of women.

It's that other app, Firestarter, the one just for hookups. It tells you who is in your vicinity, looking for a brief, no strings connection. There are people all around him, an attractive brunette alone at the end of the bar, also staring at her phone, a group of young girls — students judging from the New School sweatshirt and the pitcher of beer — at a high top right behind him. He's on his second scotch at least, I determine by the empty glass next to his full one. But he just keeps scrolling through the images on his phone, looking and looking.

Strange. The world has become a very

strange place.

Venturing another glance at the door, I watch a group of three young men walk in, floppy hair and skinny jeans, unshaven, one of them sporting that giant beard some guys seem to favor these days. It's like he has a bush on his face. But there's something virile about it, too, isn't there? Very *Game of Thrones.*

This will be my third meeting from the dating app Torch, which according to Jax is the *only way* that people meet these days. She set up my profile, helped me figure out how to scroll through the guys who had posted their photos. Jax likes them buff and dumb; me, I'm partial to geeks. Bookish men in glasses, people who read and think, who hike, meditate.

Needless to say that's the minority on Torch.

My first date was with Drew, an actuary and a Russian literature enthusiast. We met for sushi, got a little drunk on sake, and I spent the night at his place, a Lower East Side walk-up. I snuck out in the morning while he snored loudly.

As far as Jax was concerned, this was a successful outing. But it left me feeling a little hollow. Not sure if I'd been used, or done the using. He didn't call, and, the sad thing was, I didn't even want him to.

My glass is empty. I catch the bartender's eye and point. She gives me a curt nod.

"Another seltzer?" she says, taking my empty glass.

I press a twenty across the sticky bar and her demeanor changes palpably. She works for tips after all, and I'm taking up valuable real estate for a soda water drinker.

"Thanks," I say when she hustles my drink back, this time with a generous twist of lime.

My second Torch hookup was with Bryce, a yogi and a meditation instructor. He was — very flexible. We went to a vegan place in SoHo and spent the night together in his minimalist Williamsburg loft. He called once, twice, three times.

I feel a connection, he said in this text.

I didn't.

I'm ashamed to say I never even answered him. Jax assured me that this was the way of it. People *expected* to never hear from each other again.

Look at it this way, said Jax. *You've gotten more action in two weeks than you have in two years.*

Sadly, she's right.

Another glance at the door, which is disappearing in the growing crowd. Really. I'm gonna go.

Tonight, I'm waiting for Adam. A technology expert with a penchant for Rilke and Jung.

This guy? said Jax in dismay.

True, the grainy picture on the screen was not flattering — heavy brow, nose too big. The text was minimal to the point of being curt. Dislikes: shallow people. Likes: solitude. Personal mantra: Everything in NYC is within walking distance if you have enough time. Closing with: "You are not surprised at the force of the storm." Only a Rilke geek would know that line and what it meant. It hooked me in a way the others hadn't.

Who are you, Adam? I'm more interested in seeing you in the flesh than I should be.

But maybe you're not coming. It's still five minutes before our scheduled time, but probably I'm about to be stood up.

I text Jax: This is the last time.

Is he a dick? It seemed like he would be a dick. You can usually tell.

Hasn't shown up yet.

How early were you?

A half hour.

24

I am treated to the eye roll emoji. Just chill. You never know. Have another seltzer, you lush.

I'm about to text her back when the door opens.

There you are. I know you right away.

There's a strange clench in my solar plexus at the sight of your face. A rush of recognition. From the photo I saw, yes. But something else. You're taller than most of the men in the room, broad, muscular, in a charcoal blazer over a dove-gray T-shirt. Standing a moment, looking uncertain, you run a large hand through the thick mane of nearly shoulder length, jet-black hair.

He's here, I text Jax quickly. Gtg.

Is he hot?

Are you? Hard to say. Your nose *is* too big, eyes weirdly black at a distance. When you scan the room, your gaze meets mine. I smile but don't wave. Maybe not hot in the classic sense. But something that has been dormant within me awakens.

That moment, it freezes. Everything around us pauses, seems to wait a beat. I feel my breath in my lungs as you push toward me through the crowd.

Just as you reach me, the guy in the next

seat miraculously leaves and there's a space for you to slip right into it, and you do.

I like your smile; it's a little lopsided, sweet.

"Beauty and the beast," you say, by way of introduction.

I blush stupidly. "Adam?"

We shake hands. Your grip is warm and solid, gaze intense.

"Nice to meet you, Wren." Your voice is deep, almost a rumble. Then, after a quick assessing glance around the bar, "Is this the kind of place you usually like?"

There's a gleam of amusement, mischief in your eyes.

It's weird. You're *so familiar,* as though I've known you for years. A light clean scent wafts off you, the late autumn chill from outside still lingering on your clothes.

"No," I admit.

"Then why choose it?" It could be confrontational, peevish. Instead, it's purely curious.

"I didn't. My best friend Jax — she thought it was a safe place to meet a stranger."

Your eyes linger, searching my face for I'm not sure what. Then, "Is there a safe place to meet a stranger?"

"Maybe not."

Your smile deepens, and you lift an easy hand. The bartender rushes to do your bidding, coming quickly from the other end of the bar; you're that kind of guy I think. A natural air of authority. People rush to do your bidding. You order a Woodford Reserve on the rocks, then look to me, inquiring. I shake my head, lifting my glass.

"But we're not strangers, are we?" you say when the bartender has left.

I feel a little rush of uncertainty. "Are we not?"

You rub at that powerful, stubbled jaw. "It definitely doesn't feel like it."

"No," I admit. "It doesn't."

When your glass comes, you lift it to me and I clink it with mine. The smile on my face is real, all my nerves and tension dropping away.

"To strangers who somehow already know each other," you say. Your tone is easy, posture relaxed. You're comfortable in your own skin.

"I like that."

"So do I."

We're shouting at each other over the din. You talk a little bit about your work in cybersecurity. I tell you that I'm a writer — which is the truth but not the whole truth. We are leaning in close to hear each other.

My throat is starting to ache a bit from yelling.

Finally, you say, "Should we just get out of here?"

"Where do you want to go?"

Is this just going to be another Torch hookup? Because I've decided I don't want to do that again. Maybe it's the way of it now, like Jax says. But if it is, then I'd rather be alone.

"Anywhere but here," you say.

We don't go back to your place or to mine. We just start walking, which, when the weather is crisp and the city sky is that velvety blue, is my favorite thing to do. We wind through the East Village to Lafayette, passing Joe's Pub and Indochine. We cross Houston, wander through the garish lights and shuttered shops of Chinatown and end up on the Brooklyn Bridge, that lovely relic of Old New York.

We log miles and sometimes we're talking about your childhood — lots of travel, about mine — isolated, unhappy. But sometimes an easy silence settles. And it's the silences that excite me most. The ability to be quiet with someone, there's a delicious intimacy to that. In Brooklyn Heights we stop at a quiet bar near Adams where low jazz plays, and people talk quietly, huddled together in cozy alcoves in the near dark.

"This is more like the kind of place I like," I say.

"Me, too."

You talk about work again. You own a cybersecurity firm, are new to the city after traveling extensively since childhood — first for your father's work, then for your own. Various locations in the US, Europe, and Asia. I take in details — the expensive cut and material of your jacket. The manicured nails. How you stare when I speak, listening intently. You wait until I'm done talking, take a long beat, before answering or commenting. How you haven't touched me, not even casually, though we're very close together.

"I have an early morning," I say finally. I don't want to break the spell between us. But neither do I want to get glamoured into doing something I'll regret. It's too easy to give in to the natural impulse. Better to cut things short.

If you're disappointed or offended, it doesn't show. You look at your watch, a white face, with black roman numerals. Analog in a digital world. For a technology expert, a man who owns a cybersecurity firm, you haven't even once looked at a phone.

29

"Where do you live?" you ask.

"Right around the corner actually."

"Can I walk you home?" You lift your palms, maybe reading my expression. "That's it."

I nod. "Sure."

Outside, you offer your arm and I loop mine through. It's funny and antiquated, but totally comfortable to stroll through the pretty tree-lined Brooklyn streets arm in arm like this. Your warmth, your strength. It's magnetic. I feel something I haven't felt in a long time. We walk in silence, pressing close. Finally, we get to my brownstone.

You look up at it, then to me. "All yours?"

I nod, a little embarrassed. I bought it when it was a total wreck and have been fixing it up for years. But, yeah, it's a pretty big deal to have a place like this here.

"I thought you said you were a writer." Everyone knows that writers are usually broke.

"I just got lucky with this place."

Your smile is easy and knowing, no judgment. "There are a lot of layers to you, Wren Greenwood, that's what I'm getting."

That's very true.

"There are a lot of layers to all of us, Adam Harper."

You stare off into the middle distance for

30

a moment, then back to me. "So — look."

Ah, here it is. The brush-off. I knew he was too good to be true.

"I'm not great at playing games." You run a hand through your hair; in the glow from the streetlight, it sheens blue like blackbird feathers. I've already picked up that this is something you do when you feel uncomfortable.

You clear your throat and I stay quiet. You go on: "I like you. And I don't want to have some soulless Torch hookup tonight."

Okay. Wow. Not what I was expecting. Again, I opt for silence, my default setting.

"So, can I take you to dinner tomorrow?" You glance at your watch again. "Well, tonight I guess?"

Somewhere down the street there's a swell of piano music coming from one of the other brownstones. I hear this often, and it never fails to give the night a magical quality. The air is cool, though tomorrow is supposed to be a scorcher. Global weirding, go figure.

Jax would tell me to say I had to check my schedule.

But Robin would tell me to be myself.

"I'd love to," I say, not into games either. "Where and when?"

"I'll pick you up here at seven?"

I nod. "Perfect."

You start to back away, hands in pockets, and I can't stop smiling.

"Good night, Wren Greenwood."

"Good night, Adam Harper."

Finally you turn and walk briskly away. Then, you're gone around the corner.

Torch. It *is* shallow and soulless, a poor facsimile for human connection. But maybe there's something to it after all.

I walk up the stone steps and let myself in with my electronic keypad, step into the silence of the home I have made, locking the door behind me. The air still smells of the soup I cooked earlier. It's always a relief to return to the nest. For me, there's a tension to all encounters, even the good ones.

The truth is that I haven't really been with anyone seriously since college, and that was an embarrassingly long time ago. Let's just say I have intimacy issues, trust issues.

Maybe I should have said what I was thinking: *I like you, too, Adam.*

On the other hand, we don't know each other at all and maybe that's how you end all your dates, easing the parting by scheduling the next encounter, one that will never happen.

Maybe, Adam, you won't show up tomorrow and I'll never see you again.

So it is with the modern dating ritual.
Could go either way.

TWO

"So . . . hot or not?"

When I come downstairs the next morning, Jax is already in my kitchen, making coffee. I didn't sleep well, my slumber plagued as ever by vivid dreams, mostly bad. I'm not surprised to see her. She has the door code and I heard her come in.

From the look of her, inky curls wrangled into a tight plait, dark skin flushed, T-shirt damp, she ran from her place in Chelsea. She's a super miler, runs like a fiend — inside on machines, or outside through the city, over bridges to outer boroughs. She runs like something's chasing her, fast and powerful, never, and I mean never, tiring. On the rare occasion I join her, she leaves me gasping in her dust.

"Hot?" I venture, slipping onto a stool at the island.

The kitchen is a work in progress, original appliances on their last legs, walls un-

34

painted, light bulbs hanging from the ceiling waiting for their fixtures, cabinets in the middle of being refaced — doors gone, stain stripped. The guy I had working on the cabinetry has mysteriously disappeared; it's been two weeks.

Just a text: Hey, got called to another job. Be back to you soon.

Will he come back? There's no way to know. It's possible I've been ghosted by an extremely talented and bizarrely cheap but massively unreliable carpenter.

Amid the ruin, a brand-new gleaming espresso machine and milk frother hum and hiss. Let it not be said that I don't have my priorities straight.

"An answer should not sound like a question," says Jax, in response to my uncertain statement.

She sounds *just* like her mother, Miranda, who over the last eight years has become like my surrogate mother. But I know better than to say so. Jax pours almond milk in the frother and presses the button. The aroma of espresso, already in cups, wafts on the air.

"It's a reductive question," I say. "Hot or not? What are we — internet trolls?"

She pins me with her stunning green-hazel eyes. Jamaican mother, British father, Jax always says that she's a true American girl. Her ancestors hail from all over the world, but she is Brooklyn born and raised. So, New Yorker first, everything else second.

"He's not still here, is he?"

She looks past me, her gaze traveling down the hall toward the stairs.

I shake my head, gratefully take the cup of coffee she hands me over the quartz countertop that sits, not properly secured yet, atop the unfinished island. "I told you I wasn't going to do that again. No more Torch hookups."

She shrugs and lifts her eyebrows, as if this is some unreasonable assertion, takes a sip of her coffee. "So what happened?"

What did happen? *Something.* I felt *something,* which I wouldn't have said about my last encounters.

I woke up thinking about you, Adam, wondering if we are really having dinner tonight.

"Nothing," I tell her. "We talked, we walked. It was — nice."

"Did you take a picture?"

I laugh at this. Jax lives online. It's 8:00 a.m. and she's probably already posted on Instagram about her morning run. I keep a much lower profile. "He wasn't the selfie type."

36

"Okay," she says, drawing out the syllables. "What type was he?"

"I guess the type I'm going to see again. He asked me to dinner tonight."

Raising her eyebrows again, this time in surprise, she slides into the seat next to me and we drink the strong coffee in companionable silence for a moment. She's scrolling on her phone. Glancing over, I see that she's pulled up your profile.

The picture *is* unflattering. You're better looking in person.

Her frown tells me that she doesn't approve of you. "What about the other guy?" she asks.

"Which one?"

"The literary one. You said he was nice, you know — talented." She laughs, moving her shoulders, mock sexy.

I find myself staring at her; I'm often a bit enthralled by her beauty — her high cheekbones, gleaming eyes, full lips. My friend doesn't think she's beautiful, but she is.

"Drew," I say, remembering him — nice body, thick head of dark hair, bedroom eyes. I don't remember thinking he was *talented.* Our night together was serviceable at best. "He didn't call."

She tips her head to the side, considers this. "You didn't call him either."

"Exactly. There was nothing there," I say, thinking that will be the end of it. But she's still watching me. "What?"

Jax looks for a long moment at your picture, tugging at her braid. "This guy. He just seems — too serious. I just want you to — you know — have *fun*."

As far as my friend is concerned, Torch hookups need to be light and easy — night-club dates, weekend trips to Miami Beach, champagne brunches that end back in bed. That's her. Not me.

She looks at me like she wants to go on, but then presses her mouth shut.

"What?" Instantly defensive in the way that you can only be with people who know you too well.

She lifts her palms. "I'm just saying. Don't get hooked into one guy, date around a little."

Date around a little. She uses the app as a catalog of potential hookups. I'm not sure she's seen the same guy more than twice. This is the way of it. Swipe left. Swipe right. The pool is big and shallow; if reality doesn't measure up to socials (and when does it?) — block, unfriend, delete, *move on*.

The idea — her idea — was for me to get *out there*. Stop working so hard. Live a little,

38

let loose.

"What are you worried about?" I bump her with my shoulder; she reaches for my hand and gives it a squeeze. "He probably won't even call. I'll never see him again."

"Hmm," she says. "What about *this* guy?"

She holds up a picture, an extremely fit man with a goatee and slicked-back hair flexes his muscles and stares suggestively at the camera. We both break out laughing.

"Uh," I say. "Pass."

There's a tapping at the window over the sink, and I look up to see a blackbird there. He gazes inside, inquiring. I've been leaving seeds for him. There's a postage-stamp-sized backyard behind my town house and I've filled it with plants; the blackbird has made a nest I think in the gutter over the back door. I walk over to the sink and look out at him. His body gleams blue in the morning light.

And just like that, I'm back there.

My father's house. Big and rambling, run-down and with a list of problems we didn't have the money to fix. Isolated on a huge tract of land that had been in his family for generations. The house where he grew up, and where he moved our family when I was ten for reasons I couldn't understand at the time.

39

I put my fingers on the glass, and remember the foggy window in the old kitchen, the warm, nutty scent of oatmeal on the stove, my mother humming softly, my brother Jay sulking, angry about something — everything. There was a blackbird that visited that window, too, attracted by seeds my mother left. *Birds are the messengers of the universe,* she used to say. *They sing its song.*

"Wren."

I startle back to the moment, to Jax. "Earth to Wren. Where did you go?"

Home, I think. *I went home.*

"My point is," Jax goes on. "Just take it slow. See him again if you want. But date a few other people. Have some fun, you know. Things don't always have to be — so heavy, so serious."

She's talking about my work, our work, but more than that. She's talking about me.

I watch the blackbird peck at his seed. He cocks his head at me, then flaps away into the gunmetal-gray sky.

THREE

I wait near the corner of Seventy-Ninth and Broadway, leaning against a light post, people watching. It's rush hour, the sky a bruised blue and the winter air biting.

A flustered young woman clutching a big tote and wearing a bright red coat races past, leaving a waft of perfume. *"Are you out of your fucking mind?"* she shouts into her cell phone, face pulled taut with anger. Then a svelte man with salt-and-pepper hair, dressed in a slim black suit seems to glide past, lost in whatever he's listening to in his AirPods. The placid expression on his face tells me he's on another wavelength, lifted out.

A river of traffic moves slowly in each direction, horns bleating pointlessly, intermittently, manhole covers rattling, busses hissing to a stop. A taxi driver shouts angrily out his window in a language I don't understand.

41

As I stand on the busy city sidewalk, maybe a hundred people — more — every color, nationality, gender variation — a beautiful, chaotic mosaic of the world we live in sweep past me. I let the energy wash over me, listen to three different languages being spoken. Shabby or stylish, rich or poor, conservative or wild, a mingle of everything a person can be. That's what I love the most about this city, it's acceptance of all the layers of humanity.

And that's just the surface — what's underneath is impossibly deep, rich, complicated. I can almost hear all their voices — their worries and fears, hopes and dreams, the problems that keep them up at night. That's what I do. I help people solve their problems. My superpower is listening.

I glance at my watch. I'm early as usual. And I'm starving — as usual.

According to my favorite food blogger, the best pizza in New York is in New Jersey, at a place called Razza. Of course, the snobbish New Yorker in me is sure that this cannot be true. Is there anything better outside New York? Still, since we've basically been on a food tour of the New York area since we met three months ago, we consider ourselves obligated to find out. Hard duty ahead of us tonight, to head out of the city limits. But we'll bear up.

I *guess* we're a "we"? What do you think, Adam?

Since our Torch date, there hasn't been a day that we haven't seen each other. A meal, a coffee, a midday assignation at the art cinema, a stroll through a Soho gallery, a walk along the High Line, wherever. Each outing is usually just a preamble to long nights (or short, stolen afternoons) of lovemaking — sometimes gentle, sometimes desperate, always leaving me moved, spent, shaken.

Things have happened fast. Too fast, according to Jax. Robin doesn't like it much either. She has always been a worrywart.

Wren, what do you really know about this guy? He's, like, taking over your life.

I'm getting *to know him. That's what a relationship is.*

Robin is just jealous. Ever since we were little, she hasn't liked competition for my attention.

What Jax wanted — for me to be lighter, have more fun, get out more often — she was right. The truth is: I'm happy. Does it sound weird if I say I'm happy, maybe for the first time?

Another few minutes pass, I gaze up and down the street looking for your towering

43

frame in the crowd. I'm embarrassed to say that I don't remember the company name. Black Vault? Locked Box? Something like that, evoking security. You told me. You said it was a black awning, gave me the street address. But I quickly forgot it since we agreed to meet on the corner. Should I poke my head into one of these nondescript office building lobbies? I'm sure I'd know the name if I saw it on a directory.

No, better to wait on the street. Keep a little distance.

Though we have seen each other almost every day since our Torch meeting, we *are* taking it slow. I don't know much about your work, just the broadest strokes; much of it is confidential because of its nature and the kind of clients who need private cybersecurity.

We have not met each other's friends.

Jax is full-scale nagging, but I'm not ready. As for my work, well, all you really know is the boilerplate, that I am a writer and that I have an advice column, written under a pseudonym, that has done *surprisingly* well.

And all those layers you intuited on our first night together. Well, most of them are still intact.

But, like I told Robin, that's what a relationship is, right?

44

We reveal ourselves in layers. Over time.

Or — depending on how things go, not at all.

"Hey."

There you are. Right in front of me, looking uncharacteristically flushed, a bit ragged.

"You're a million miles away," you say gently, leaning in for a kiss. "Sorry to keep you waiting. Client issues. I texted."

Maybe you did. I'm not the best steward of my device; it's buried deep in my messenger bag. I dislike that buzzing, ringing little tyrant. I'm always squinting at my texts, that little keyboard. I usually just wind up calling instead of texting back. *Nobody calls anymore,* says Jax. *It takes too much time.*

I hate that cold, stripped-down way we communicate now. I want voices, the nuances of meaning inherent in tone. Better yet, I want to look into eyes and touch skin, to feel connection. I wasn't raised with technology, not the way others were. My father — he wouldn't even let us have a television. No computers, no video games, no cell phones.

You're an analog girl in a tech world. It's one of the things I like best about you, Adam said when I confessed this.

So even though you would rather text,

45

Adam, you call. Because you know that's what I want. I like that about you, your consideration. On the nights we are not together, sometimes we talk for hours, lingering on the line even when we've run out of things to say.

Tonight, with the bright white sun tipping below the buildings, there's something off about your demeanor. Instead of giving me the laser beam of your attention, your gaze is diffuse, eyes scanning the street all around us, like you're looking for something.

"Everything okay?" I ask.

You focus in. Those black eyes in the textured landscape of your face — heavy brows, wrinkles at the corners of your eyes, stubble, a slight scar on your pronounced cheekbone.

"Just — a hard day. Sorry."

Seems like there might be more to it, but rather than press, I say, "I'm starving."

"Me, too. Let's eat."

We take a cab to Jersey City. Decadent.

Me? I'm frugal. Subway, not taxi. Chicken, not lobster. Macy's, not Neimans. But you, Adam, you hate the crowds, the crush, the unreliability of our city's massive subway system. You'll walk if you can, cab it if you can't.

From the quiet interior of our taxi, the

46

crowded streets pass by in a crawl, then a rush, as we hit the tunnel. In the dark, we make out in the back seat like prom dates, everything disappearing but the voyeuristic eyes of the cabbie in his rearview mirror, the traffic noise, the hum of our speed through the tunnel.

And then we arrive to a neighborhood of low buildings. It's one of those not quite gentrified areas, that funny blend of gritty and chic that places in the city are sometimes, trying to be one thing, but really something else underneath. Like all of us.

Inside the small, warm space, we order multiple pies just to get a sampling. Then we wait, chatting mostly about my day. I pretend not to notice that you are edgy in a way that's new to me. That you keep looking behind me, toward the door as if you are waiting for someone to arrive. Finally, one by one the steaming pizzas arrive.

It's heaven — dough fluffy yet crispy, creamy, oozing cheese, freshest tomatoes, a hint of hot honey. Divine slivers of prosciutto, explosions of garlic.

Oh, God. I'm in love.

"I like that you eat," you say, watching me with a now-familiar intensity, like I'm a puzzle you're working.

For a moment, I'm embarrassed, glancing

down at the nearly devoured pie beneath us. But you're right; I eat — passionately, unapologetically. We have a shared passion for great meals.

"Food is life," I say. "If you don't like to eat, you don't like to be alive."

Your smile, it turns your very serious, nearly brooding face boyish and bright.

"Amen."

We eat until we can't, ask them to box up the rest. Food, the sensory pleasure of eating art, for us, it's a kind of foreplay.

Back in Brooklyn, we crash through the doors of my town house, tearing at each other's clothes as we climb the stairs. We've been to your place a few times, but we generally default to mine. Your place in Chelsea is cold — all modern lines and stylish but hard furniture, like a museum. It's elegant, well-designed, but void of personal details.

It's like you don't even live here, I said when I first visited you there.

I guess I don't, you said. *I travel a lot. I'm not here that much.*

"Then where's home?"

Something strange crossed your face, and I wondered for the first time and not the last if there were as many layers to you as

48

there are to me. You tapped at your solar plexus. *Right here, I guess.*

I found that oddly sad but didn't say so.

My place is the opposite of yours, messy where yours is neat, warm where yours is cool. Big furniture, bought for comfort, pillows and throw blankets for maximum softness. Like the fluffy white down of my comforter where we find ourselves now. It ensconces us.

Our lovemaking has changed over the last week. What was gentle, exploratory, considerate — is this okay? Are you okay? — has become urgent, hungrier. There has been a shift in its pitch, a change in vibration.

Your arm around my back is powerful, your breath on my neck a growl, deep and desperate. Then you're so deep inside me that I let out a cry, half pain, half pleasure. You don't stop. It's wild and raw as we wrap around each other, and I come alive with desire, with pleasure.

You breathe my name. *Wren. Oh, God. Wren.*

I hear your passion, your helplessness; it's an echo of my own. Each time we make love I feel like I know you better, as if you've revealed another layer of yourself without saying a word.

When we're done, and we are only our

49

breath and the darkness, I think you've drifted off to sleep. But then you shift, close your arms around me, and whisper, "Tell me something you've never told anyone else."

Up to this moment, I've measured everything I've shared with you. I've given myself over in pieces, slivers of truth, layers of self, curated memories, only the most banal likes and dislikes. But there are things I've hidden. It hasn't been necessary to bare all; relationships these days rarely last. I can't afford to give all of myself away to someone who may ghost me without a moment's notice.

Does he know? Jax asked when I confessed how much I liked you.

No, I told her.

When will you tell him?

Now, I think. This is the moment. Tell now or it becomes a lie, something I've hidden. So, in the warmth of your embrace, in the dark of the hours after midnight, I tell you something I've never told anyone else.

FOUR

"Can I see you tonight?"

You always ask this, nearly every morning, as if it's not a foregone conclusion.

"Of course," I always answer.

You're already dressed in fresh clothes from your overnight bag. When I woke just a little while ago, I heard the shower running. Glancing at the clock, I saw that you were running late and that I had slept in. It was a long night with us talking and talking, until finally I must have drifted off. The memories, the things I've told you, they cling. I regret it in the light of the day. The night made me feel safe. In the morning glow I feel exposed. Shame, it tingles all over my skin.

"I want to ask you something tonight," you say, fastening your belt at your trim waist.

"Ask me now."

You shake your head, smile wanly. "Impa-

51

tient thing."

I roll over on my side, prop myself up on my elbow, and watch you as you pull a brush through your wet hair, your large frame filling the mirror over the dresser. Your hair is thick and wild, the envy of any woman. But when you look at your reflection, it's with a critical frown.

"Where and when?" I ask.

"There's a place I want to try in the Village. I'll text you the address."

When you come to sit beside me on the bed, you smell of sage and mint.

"Thank you," you say.

"For what?"

"For sharing yourself with me. You won't regret it."

"Run while you can," I quip with a confidence I don't feel.

You kiss me long and deep, then reluctantly pull away, hand lingering on my hip.

"I'm late," you say with a groan. "See you tonight."

And then you're gone, and I am alone with my confession, my past, all the voices in my head.

I spend the day working, my escape hatch, the place where I bury myself and all my own problems. The day passes quickly. You don't call at lunch, but around two in the afternoon I get a text with the address, a restaurant I don't know.

My stomach flutters with butterflies, as if it's our very first date. Maybe in a way it is. Because now you know.

What do you want to ask me, Adam?

I arrive at the restaurant, butterflies reaching a crescendo.

The space is dark and glittery. Private booths and candlelit tables. A golden buddha sits in the center of a dark fountain where lotus flowers float. I look for you, but I don't see you.

It's not like you to be late.

The host with big dark eyes and chiseled features, dressed impeccably in triple black, is smiling, and I can see in his face that the dress I'm wearing — new, a rare frivolous purchase — was the right choice, highlighting my cleavage and brightening my eyes.

"You're the first to arrive. Can I show you to your table?"

"Yes, please."

His eyes linger.

I'm nothing special to look at. I mean, I'm *okay*. But I'm not in love with my legs. And my hair has a life of its own when it rains. I haven't mastered the whole makeup thing. In a city of beautiful, stylish, glamorous women, I usually have a whole urban warrior look going, mainly jeans and leather jackets, T-shirts, and Doc Martens. I'm not one to thread or wax, pluck and manicure, starve and preen. *A natural woman,* you said. *Rare these days.* I took it as a compliment.

But this dress, a royal blue wrap, clinging, long, really highlights my assets.

Why am I dressing up for tonight? I don't know.

If he's going to break up with you, at least he'll see what he's missing, said Robin unhelpfully as I got ready. She'd lounged on my bed, just as she always has — at ease, sure of herself, ready for anything.

At the table, I look at the menu.

Wow.

Very pricey.

You always pick up the check. Which at first, I didn't feel comfortable with. We struggled over the bill. *I'm old school,* you told me. *At dinner, the guy pays. It's just gross if you don't.* But I grew to love this about you. Your generosity. Your kindness. You give without asking anything in return.

I keep glancing at that door when it opens — a young couple laughing, an older gentleman with a baritone voice. I'm hungry — of course. The waitress comes to ask if I'd like a drink. But I'll wait for you. Those butterflies, they've turned into crows.

Moments from last night keep coming back to me.

You've been through so much, you said, your voice heavy with compassion. *You're a survivor.*

There's more. Layers. There's always more to us than what we say and show. But I have shared everything I can. I am exposed enough.

So, after I got your text, I zipped out to a boutique I love and bought a new dress. Retail therapy, not usually my thing. I can see the appeal though, a new skin I've slipped into. Something bright and fresh.

The door opens and a tall, stunningly chic woman with dark skin and a magnificent black wrap breezes in. She sits at the bar, is joined shortly by two Asian men in crisp charcoal gray suits. They lean into each other, conversation low and intense.

You won't be long, I tell myself. You're on your way.

White tablecloth.

Orchids in a vase.

The low hum of voices, flute music. I wait.

It's half past the hour. Definitely not like you.

Finally, I dig my phone from my bag.

55

Oh.

Three missed calls. I try to call you back, but there's no answer. An unpleasant throb in my center. Fear pulses. I know that bad things can sneak up on you. One moment life seems solid enough, predictable, and the next your whole world gets pulled out from under you and you're floating in space. Zero gravity.

I text: Is something wrong? I tried to call you back.

A few more minutes pass. People enjoy their meals, oblivious to the thumping of my heart. My waitress keeps glancing over at me. Other servers zip past, carrying trays of food — the aroma is heavenly, but it barely reaches me.

Finally, after ten more minutes pass, and you don't call, don't answer my calls or texts, I gather my things.

You're not coming.

Something is wrong.

FIVE

Rising, I draw looks, leaving my sweating water glass, dropping my crumpled napkin on the table. The back of my throat is tight, heat rising to my cheeks. Shame. It lives in the pit of my stomach, curled like a snake, waiting to strike and sink its fangs.

It was too soon to have told you. We didn't know each other well enough. I have buried my ugly past for a reason. It was years before I told Jax. And even she doesn't know all of it.

But you.

Isn't that what love is? We *want* to show ourselves, don't we? Hoping against hope that when we do, we will be loved for exactly who we are, not who we were expected to be.

"There's been an emergency," I say to the waitress who comes to see what's wrong, why I'm leaving. "I'm so sorry."

The waitress, the host, they're so kind and

accommodating. Which hurts. Kindness sometimes hurts me. I can't explain that.

On the street, I try again to return your call, but there's just the recorded message: *I'm sorry. The person you have reached has not set up a mailbox.* Strange.

Your place is not far. It's probably faster to hoof it than get a cab and crawl through traffic. Anyway, the walk will calm me, clear my head.

The city can be a kind of forest; you can bathe in its sounds if you let yourself go quiet inside. The horns and voices, the rumble of the subway under your feet, there's a kind of rhythm to it, a peaceful disharmony. There's a stream, and if you enter it, it carries you — lights changing from *don't walk* to *walk,* people clearing a path. I enter the stream, and it only takes me twenty minutes to walk from the East Village to your place in Chelsea.

By the time I reach your building, I am sure there's a simple explanation for why you've stood me up after I revealed the darkest thing about me. After I whispered it to you in the dark, and you held me. *I'm so sorry,* you said over and over. And I felt seen, heard, understood.

The clean white entryway to your building has no doorman, just a slick monitor and intercom. Twelve B, the only buzzer without a name beside it, is stiff and white under my finger.

Why should strangers know who lives in 12 B? Just another way people neglect their security, you said.

That's your job. Security. Selling security systems to companies and individuals. You install cameras and silent alarms, motion detectors. You educate about cybersecurity, set up firewalls, encrypted websites. You've told me about the way con artists, criminals, and hackers can worm their way into systems to steal, to sabotage, to subvert. You're passionate about it. I like people who are passionate about their work. It was one of the first things I liked about you.

No answer. I press the buzzer again.

Finally, "Hello?"

I am taken aback by a female voice, young, cautious. Now, her face swims on the screen. She's pretty with dark skin and ringlet curls. For a moment I can't find my voice. Who is she?

"Is — Adam there?" I ask, my throat dry.

She shakes her head. "There's no one here by that name. Sorry."

I hear a child's voice. "Mommy, who is it?" She moves off camera and when she returns, she's holding a small child — a boy in a red shirt — who reaches out with a chubby hand to the camera, blocking the image with his palm. There's a caged bird in my chest, wings flapping in panic. Who is this woman? This child?

I clear my throat, collect myself.

"This place belongs to — a friend of mine," I say. "Is he there?"

I check the buzzer again. This is the right place. I've been here twice — once for dinner. Once I spent the night.

After that, we were mainly at my place. In fact, I haven't been here in months. Your place — it's cold. I tick back to my time here with you. Couches stiff, bed too hard. No food in the fridge. Your clothes hung like soldiers, filed and pressed, ready to go into battle. No pictures. Even your bathroom — a single deodorant, toothbrush, toothpaste, floss. One bar of soap in the shower. Certainly no sign of another woman, a *family*.

"Is he there?" I ask again when the toddler moves his hand away.

"No," she says. She's seems like a nice person, a mom type with a patient voice and understanding eyes. "Oh, this is just a vacation rental. I am here with my family this week. Sorry."

I don't know what to say. It's clear by her

wide-open expression that she's telling the truth, or she's a very accomplished liar — which most people are not. Again, I glance at the doorway, the buzzer, the intercom. It's the right place, the place we were together. I'm sure of it.

"Thank you." Because what else is there to say?

"Good luck finding your friend," she says, and the screen goes black.

A glance at my phone reveals that there are no more calls, no answer when I try your number again. Another text:

I'm sure there's a good reason that you stood me up. Call me. I'm not — worried or anything. Not freaking out. At all.

No little dots pulse, telling me that you're about to answer. Of course, you've disabled the read-receipt option on your messages. So, I don't know if you've gotten my message. I feel the throb of unhappiness, such a familiar emotion. The helplessness of a lost connection. People only stay in your life if they want to. So often, they just go away. And there's really nothing you can do.

I stand helpless on the street, ticking through my options. Wait and see if you show up here? No. Try you again? No.

Another call to you and I've veered into hysteria. You've stood me up. There's a woman and child in the apartment I thought was yours. It occurs to me, in just this moment, that we have no friends in common, no one that you know who is known to me, as well. There isn't someone who I could casually call and say: *Hey, have you seen Adam?*

Is that weird?

Standing awkwardly on the street for another minute, I stare at my silent phone. And then because my options are few, I just go home.

When I get down to the subway platform, the train is idling in the station. I slip into the seat next to an old woman reading a Bible. In general, I seek to sit next to people who have books in their hands, or people who are writing long hand in a notebook, or just staring off into space. Those types of people seem safer, kindred somehow. The train pulls from the station, then races, wobbly, squealing. Not packed but crowded enough, it winds its way to Brooklyn Heights, and I exit at Borough Hall.

On the street a cold front seems to have moved in quickly and definitely. It's grown downright frigid as I make my way home. This dress is way too thin.

Why did I not wear a jacket?

Where are you?

I bow my head and walk quickly. Brooklyn has a different rhythm than Manhattan. It's slower, easier. But there's still a pulse.

For a second, I imagine that you are sitting and waiting on my stoop. *I lost my phone,* you'll say. Or: *you won't believe what happened.* And we'll go inside my brownstone — which in every way is the opposite of your place — and I'll pour us each a glass of wine and light the fireplace in the living room. And you'll tell me what happened. And there will be some very good reason why there was a strange woman in your place, claiming that it was a vacation rental. And the incident will be forgotten as we make love.

I can feel your skin, my fingers in the thick of your hair, the way you hold me, hold my eyes, make me feel things — a hunger, a falling, a desire so intense it's frightening.

But you're not on the stoop. Inside, the house is dark and silent.

I flip on the downstairs lights, lock the door behind me. The place, the home that I've built, is a comfort. Dropping my bag by the door, I sink into the soft embrace of my couch and pull the cashmere throw around me, still holding my phone in my hand. The

63

screen gives back nothing.

I'm not sure how long I stay there, curled up, waiting for word from you. A long time. I must have dozed off, because the vibrating of my phone startles me awake.

Something's happened. I have to go. I'm sorry, Wren.

I don't understand, I type quickly with my thumbs.

I know. I'm sorry.

Just tell me what happened.

But an error message comes back, telling me that my text could not be delivered. I sit there and stare at the red, trying again and again to reach you.

I flip on the television for a distraction. An impossibly coiffed, plastic male face delivers the news. He doesn't look real. *Is* he real? I wonder. Maybe he's one of those avatars, a computer-generated image of what a newscaster *should* look like. But no, on my high-def television I can see the cake of his makeup. The news is all bad, of course. A virus is sweeping through China at an alarming rate, images of men in hazmat suits spraying down some kind of plaza fill my large screen. The stock market, which has been a come-one-come-all party for the last few years has started to slide. There's a big red zigzag to show the downward trajectory of our wealth. A plane has crashed in the Middle East, all passengers lost. Now, a fiery wreckage fills the screen. "The new aircraft model," the newscaster says, voice low with disapproval, "had known mechanical issues. An investigation is underway."

Even though I don't want to, I hear my father's voice. A newscast like this one would have him thundering about how the world of men was about to fall. How humans were a virus in the body of God, and eventually we would be ejected. He used to thump his fist on the table when he really got going. I hear the china rattling.

A pall settles over me, as it always does when the news makes my father's ranting seem sane. My phone stays stubbornly dark.

There's an almost physical twinge in my solar plexus, the severing of our connection.

I don't know how I know this. But my whole body aches with the certainty.

You're gone.

Six

Then

The air in the old minivan was thick with misery, the trailer on the back thumping and squeaking behind us, threatening to break away. I turned to watched it swerve and lurch, thinking of my stuffed animals and books piled into boxes inside, imagining what it would all look like scattered across the highway if the trailer got away from us, went crashing off the road.

I'd stopped crying, tears dried up as the hours on the road passed, after the town I knew as home receded in the rearview mirror, and soon there were only trees and sky, the long and winding road to nowhere. The radio station we were listening to faded into static. I'd told my friends I was moving but I hadn't said when, because I didn't know. We left in the night; I never got to say goodbye. That is the core problem with being a kid; the adults in your life make decisions and you are carried along in the current of their choices. Avery. Grace. Sophie. Would they wonder where I'd gone and why I hadn't really said goodbye? I asked my mother.

"We'll send everyone a note when we get where we're going. They'll understand. People move all the time. It doesn't mean you're not friends anymore."

How could you be friends with people you might never see again?

I tried to reach for my brother's hand, but he pulled away, turning against the window, looking out, his face a mask of sullen adolescence.

"The best thing about this place," said my dad from the front seat. His eyes caught mine in the rearview mirror. "Is the land."

"It's gorgeous, Luke," my mother, Alice, agreed, her voice taking on the false brightness reserved for doctor's visits. "So peaceful."

He reached across the seat for her, rested a hand on her thigh.

"The world of men is failing," he went on. "Where we're going, we'll be free."

"The *world of men* is not failing," said Jay. "*You* are. You lost your job, our house is in foreclosure, and there's *no place else* for us to go."

I felt my whole body stiffen, heard my mother draw in a breath. If we were sitting at the kitchen table, it would have been a moment of ignition. A leap, a chase, a beating if my father could catch Jay. My brother was growing bolder as he grew in size. He was fast. Faster than our father usually these days.

"Shut your mouth, boy," my father said easily, instead. He was driving; he was sober. He was a different person than he was after a few beers, or when he was hungover. "I could fill a book with what you don't know."

Jay scowled, fell silent.

"Little bird knows the truth," he said, catching my eyes again. "Don't you?"

My mom turned to me and smiled. She was a golden beauty with glittering sea glass blue eyes, kindness etched into her face. I was her accomplice in calming my father, telling him what he wanted to hear so he didn't get angry.

"It's our family home," I said. "It's where we belong."

And in doing so, I betrayed Jay. He shot me a venomous look, and I moved as far as I could away from him in the car. I didn't have the words to tell him that I was doing it for him as much as for mom and me. When my dad hit him, I felt every blow.

68

"That's right," said my father, eyes shining. "It's where we belong."

It was dusk when we finally arrived, pulled up the long gravel drive. The house hulked ahead. It looked as if no light had ever burned inside its windows. The trees around us were inked lines, hiding shadows.

Houses are like people. They have memories, and energy. They wait. They wilt from neglect. They sicken and decay. They haunt, and they are haunted. This house was a too big, rambling old place, populated by restless ghosts and bad memories. It seemed to rise out of the trees as we grew closer.

Its windows were eyes. Its eaves, arched brows raised in dark surprise.

The land, acres and acres of it, I'd come to learn, was a forest of ill-conceived ideas and broken promises.

But when my father got out of the van, his face was lit with a smile I had never seen. Even Jay seemed to shift off his cloak of unhappiness, as he exited and reached high in a stretch.

My mother got out and went into Dad's open arms. Jay stood beside them, and when I came to join them, he dropped an arm around me, looking down. It was an apology for being such a jerk in the car; I accepted as any acolyte would, shifted into him, glad for the warmth and strength of his body.

It was just the four of us then, standing on the edge of an uncertain new life.

"Do you hear that?" my father asked, face bright. I shivered and pressed into Jay, wrapped my arms around my middle.

"Nope," Mom said after a moment of listening. "Don't hear anything."

"Exactly," he said with a laugh. "You don't hear *anything*."

Just the wind in the leaves on the trees all around. The smell of pine.

He released my mom and clapped his hands together once, the sound echoing.

"We'll have to get the generator running tomorrow," he said. "Tonight we'll make a fire out back for cooking — good thing we grabbed those groceries and firewood in town." Even at ten years old I was thinking about the case of beer, knowing without the words to say it that exuberance, like depression, might lead to drinking. And drinking could lead anywhere.

He jogged up the steps to the house, my brother at his heels.

My mother turned to me and smiled. I saw hope in the light of her eyes, in her wide smile. I wanted to feel what she felt.

What was wrong with them? Were they

70

seeing something I couldn't? My mother grabbed my hand and squeezed, pulled me toward the house.

"This is a place where your father can heal," she whispered. "A house that's been in his family and now belongs to us with lots of land. Think of it as an adventure."

Adventures were supposed to be fun. My heart felt like a stone.

"It's an *adventure,*" she said again, as if repeating it would make it true. Her eyes glimmered with joyful tears.

"You'll see," she said when I stayed quiet. "We're going to be happy here."

I let her lead me inside.

SEVEN

Now

The morning outside my window has dawned gray and drizzly. There's no bird at the window, just the tap of rain. My neck is sore from sleeping on the couch.

After a fitful night, I am groggy and unmotivated. I pick up the phone. Nothing from you or anyone. The battery is running low.

Wrapped up in the cashmere throw, still wearing my dress from last night, I can see the tops of trees through my window. Even in Brooklyn there's birdsong in the early morning, but I don't hear it now. I pull the blanket over my head, squeeze my eyes closed. Maybe I'll just stay here for a while. Maybe all day.

But after a while my caffeine addiction kicks in, so I pad to the kitchen and brew some coffee, still tethered to my phone.

While the coffee brews, I call Jax and tell

her what happened.

"What a dick," she says when I'm done.

"What do you think happened to him?" I'm still thinking about one of your final texts. *Something's happened. I have to go. I'm sorry, Wren.*

"Sounds like pure bullshit to me," she says. "Like he's making up some kind of intrigue to disguise the fact that he's a coward."

She's running on the treadmill, her voice breathless, the sound of her feet falling heavily, the whirring of the belt loud on the line. "*All* men are cowards. If he hadn't disappeared now, he would have later. Or he'd have cheated. Or had a secret gambling addiction. Whatever."

Jax doesn't like most men. Her father left when she was young, and Miranda raised Jax and her brothers alone, working two jobs and always struggling. On the other hand, Jax doesn't like most women either. In fact, I think I'm one of three people she likes.

"Maybe," I concede. Because to be fair, neither of us have had the best relationship luck.

"Let's face it." Her footfalls slow; the treadmill whirs to a stop. "We're better off alone. Why don't you and I just get married and call it a day?"

She's said this before. But since neither one of us is gay I don't know how it's going to work out. Maybe it would work out fine. Maybe in the end a solid friendship is all any of us needs. I find myself smiling.

"Can I get back to you on that?" I say. It's not a new conversation.

"Sure." She has a smoky, sexy voice, perfect for her podcast. "And, hey, you know what? It's *okay.*"

"Yeah," I say, not feeling it. At all. "Of course."

She's still breathless. I hear her guzzling water.

"Let's go out tonight," she says finally. "Dance, drink, meet someone else. You know, *old school* like they used to do it before dating apps."

I can't think of anything I want to do less.

"Not tonight," I tell her. "I think I'll stay in and sulk."

Her laugh is throaty and deep. She can always get me to go out and she knows it.

"We'll see about that," she says before ending the call.

I have deadlines, so I push my worry and disappointment deep inside, and I get down to it, carrying my coffee into my office. I sit at the desk that used to belong to my mother, and tilt back in the ergonomic chair

74

I bought to save my aching back. I pop open my laptop and try to focus. But, of course, I obsessively check my phone and my email.

Maybe I'm overreacting.

Your job, it *is* a *little* mysterious. You can't always talk about your clients and what you do for them. What if you got called away suddenly, couldn't discuss it? That's possible, right? Maybe it has nothing to do with my late-night confessions.

But the morning winds on and no word from you.

No, the truth is that I've been ghosted. I can already see myself fading into a shimmering mirage, you disappearing, a dot on the horizon.

I guiltily ignore a call from Jax's mother, Miranda, who, along with Jax's older brothers, is the closest thing I have to family. She sends a text instead: Call if you need to talk. Men. Believe me. He's not the last Coca-Cola in the desert. She includes a bunch of man emojis. Always careful to be inclusive, they are of all colors and professions — one blond, one brunette, one Black, one Asian, a guy with a mustache, a detective, a doctor, a beefeater, a punk. One of Miranda's gifts is to make me laugh; like my call with Jax, Miranda's text lightens my mood. What would I do without them?

Near lunchtime, I lose an internal battle and start scanning your social media platforms. You rarely post, just the occasional news article about security related matters. There's nothing new on any of them.

Click, click, the colorful Torch site fills my screen and another series of clicks brings up your profile. Nothing's changed there either, just the same minimalist information that drew me to you in the first place. Your profile photo is so different from the other images — men with bare chests and flexed muscles, holding up big fish they've caught, or leaning on expensive cars, some holding hunting rifles, others running marathons. Posing in this ultramodern forum but sending the most ancient messages without even realizing it: I am strong; I can defeat predators; I can provide.

Not you. Yours is a just a grainy image of you staring intently into the camera, daring the viewer to look away. Somehow now, you don't seem real. You're a fiction I created. Nothing ties us together except the tenuous code of our meeting.

I take a couple more passes at your various outlets.

Social media stalking. It isn't pretty.

Okay. Back to work.

■ ■ ■ ■

I call my column and podcast *Dear Birdie.*

Come here, I tell my readers, *and bring the thing you can't bring anyplace else. I have seen it all, walked unimaginably dark passages, and I will use what I've learned there to help you navigate the horrors of being a human on this planet. No problem too big, too ugly, too strange, too terrifying. Bring it. We've got this. And you're safe as long as you're here.*

It started as a blog I launched just after college, then grew bizarrely in popularity. In less than a year, I went from relative obscurity to having a kind of cult following, largely thanks to an article that ran after the death of a famous advice columnist, naming Dear Birdie as one of her younger, hipper heirs.

Major advertising money started pouring in as the blog grew and grew. After a while of publishing it on my own, an editor contacted me, asking if I would like to move it to the *New York Chronicle* — for the web and the print edition. The offer was good, much higher than I would have imagined; people who are reading little else apparently are still desperate for advice anywhere they can find it. I could hardly refuse.

Later, I started recording a podcast, which also became wildly popular. The success of it surprised everyone — most of all me. Now there's talk of a television series, short fictional vignettes from some of my most popular installments. The money has been — significant.

And the real me, the person behind *Dear Birdie,* remains anonymous, unknown.

I don't do interviews; I don't make appearances. For a while only my editor, Liz, Robin, and Jax knew my real identity. Now, we have a growing staff and more people know that Dear Birdie is Wren Greenwood. But they've all signed nondisclosure agreements and want to keep their well-paying jobs. We're a relatively young team so we haven't had to deal with firings or disgruntled employees leaking my secret.

Actually, even *you* don't know about *Dear Birdie,* Adam. Another layer. One, luckily, I chose not to peel back.

Now, there's a staff at the *Chronicle* that vets the emails that *Dear Birdie* receives. When the blog was at its most popular and I was doing it alone, I was overwhelmed by the sheer volume of despair and horror, misery, hope, kindness, fear, true love, mental illness, heroism, rage. It was a deluge of humanity in which I almost drowned.

Robin always worried about this aspect of my vocation. *Is this wise? Haven't you been through enough?*

"Sometimes helping others is how you help yourself," I told her. That was true at first.

And sometimes they pull you under, she warned.

That had been about to become true before the *Chronicle.*

Now, my editor chooses, using whatever editorial criteria she applies to making sure we cover relevant topics, not too dark, not too light. It's a gift, to cull and curate misery. Left to my own devices, I'd choose the most desperate, those with the most to lose, those about to be lost.

I'm the lifeline and I still want to help the people most desperate to reach Dear Birdie. After all, I'm usually their last resort.

The woman who was afraid her in-laws were poisoning her. Her hair was falling out.

The girl looking for her father who disappeared. She suspected her stepmother might have killed him, and that she might be next.

The mother who thought she saw her dead son in a crowd, and can't stop following the man, even though she knows it's not her son. The stranger had taken out a restraining order against her.

I worry about them. Sometimes I dream about them. Does that ever happen to you? Do you have dreams that you are not in, in which you are only the observer? It's probably just me.

Pulling myself together, I sort through the emails my editor sent. My deadline for the column is tomorrow. And I am a punctual person; never late. Everything I turn in always perfect, no typos, no awkward sentences. *Perfect,* is my editor's most common response. *As ever.*

I'm not going to let a breakup derail me.

I do what I always do. I print up the letters Liz has sent. I make a stack, close my eyes, and shuffle, picking at random. Then I start to read.

Dear Birdie,
I am a widow. My husband, the love of my life, died four years ago. And at the behest of my children, I recently started dating again. I have to be honest, at first I was just going through the motions. I think we only get one great love in our lives and I've already had mine. But my kids worry that I'm lonely, so they set me up on one of those dating apps. I'm

80

still youngish, attractive enough — I think. I went on a couple of dates. But, no. Is it me? Or have people just become boring, self-involved, empty? I thought it was a lost cause.

But then I met someone. Someone smart, funny, kind — he made me laugh. He made me feel something. I felt like I could be myself with him. I felt something I haven't in a while — hope that there was still time for love.

But then, one night, he called me and said he was in trouble. He traveled for his work, and he was stranded overseas. He'd been robbed, lost his wallet. He was in the hospital. Could I wire some money? I did, of course. We'd been seeing each other for a while; he was always a gentleman, very generous with gifts. He always paid for everything. I didn't hesitate. I thought the sum was high, but I'm financially comfortable and I knew he'd pay me back.

I guess you know where this is going. He disappeared. Once I wired the money, I never heard from him again. All of his online profiles disappeared, even the one on the dating app. His phone was disconnected. I went to what I thought was his house. It was an

Airbnb. He never lived there.

I'm so ashamed. How could I be so stupid? Of course, I didn't call the police. Or tell my children. I mean, what a fool! I went online. This is such a common scam, and I, a lonely, financially secure widow, am the most common type of mark. But now the world seems so dark, and I feel so alone. His lies. I believed every single one. I did tell my best friend, and she thinks I should pursue it. Call the police. Hire a private detective. She wants me to "take my power back." Whatever that means. But I feel so hopeless and sad. I'd rather just try to forget. Dear Birdie, should I track him down or just put this behind me?

Sincerely,
Forever Alone?

Funny how the universe works, isn't it? Many times, the letter I choose has some connection to something I'm grappling with in my own life, at least figuratively. But this one hits a little too close, and I feel a rush of anger on behalf of this woman.

Dear Forever Alone,
First, you're no fool. Those of us who take a chance on love are brave and

hopeful. Love hurts; sometimes the loss and disappointment can be truly crushing — which you clearly know. I think you are a hero for trying to get out there again after your husband's passing. Many people after experiencing loss just close themselves off to love. But not you! You marched bravely into the fray. And please don't give up. While there are many scam artists and predators out there, of course, there are many more good and honest folks who want the same thing you do — friendship, companionship, a little romance. So — don't give up!

Yes, the sweetheart scam is a common one. And you are certainly not alone in having fallen for it. Unfortunately, it's the good and openhearted people, those with the most to give, who are the most vulnerable. Because they think everyone is as honest as they are. This man — he's a coward and fool. And beyond that — he's a criminal. I think I know what your friend means when she says she wants you to take your power back. And I agree. I think you should file a report with the police at the very least. And if you are so inclined, and have the means, I think you should hire someone to track him down. We have a private detective to whom we can refer you, no charge. It might not be possible; con artists tend to be very good at covering their tracks. But it might be a worthy exercise. And in the best case you might get some justice and prevent him from robbing someone else — of their money and their hope for finding love.

Stay strong. Stay hopeful. True love is out there waiting for you.

With warmth and respect,
Birdie

When I'm done with my letter, I polish it, rework it, think about it a bit more. A tweak here, there. As I hit Send, a sigh moves through my body, a kind of release. I feel much better than I did before. Which is often the case, and very much why I started doing this in the first place. I am also imbued with a sense of purpose, my own words ringing back to me.

You know what, Adam? You don't get to just slink away into the shadows.

You don't get to ghost me.

EIGHT

Sitting in front of the fireplace in my living room, I call your phone again. This time, it doesn't ring at all. Instead, there's a harsh three-note tone, and a recorded message informing me that the number has been disconnected.

Disconnected? No.

A few more tries convince me that this was not a misdial on my part.

A gully is opening in my center, as I open up your *Fake* book page again — only to find it gone. I hit refresh a couple of times; it was still there this morning — just a couple of hours ago.

But now, bold white type on a gray screen announces: This user is no longer active.

My fingers travel clickety-clack across the keyboard. Back to Torch.

We joked that your profile on the dating site was a kind of nonprofile, designed to scare away anyone not on the same wavelength. There was that unflattering selfie where you look brooding and your nose seems too big for your face. It is, in fact, too big for your face — in an oddly attractive way.

What does that say about you, I wonder? you pondered on our second date. *That you found my not-trying-to-the-point-of-being-antagonistic profile appealing.*

We'd just had burgers at the Shake Shack in Madison Square Park and were sitting on a bench outside the playground watching the city kids play and run and shout.

I really like Rilke? I offered, sipping on my chocolate shake.

You have a way of looking at me that is unnerving and exhilarating at the same time. It's like you're searching me with your eyes. You demand my gaze and then look deep. You're present. So many people aren't. *People are sleepwalking,* my father used to say. I hate it when I agree with him.

You sipped at your shake, turned your gaze away. A mischievous smile played at the corner of your lips. *Your type — brooding depressives who want to be alone.*

I shrugged. *I thought you were being ironic. I mean — you did go to the trouble of putting yourself out there. You must be looking for* something.

You chuckled a little, gave an affirming nod. Then, you put out your free hand, and I put mine in yours. We laced our fingers together. We hadn't kissed yet. Somehow it felt more intimate than any other encounter I'd had in ages, including my recent hook-ups.

We're all looking for something, aren't we? I said. You never answered, but your smile deepened. Cast in the patina of what has happened — what *has* happened? — the memory of that moment darkens. What *were* you looking for exactly?

Now your profile — your nonprofile — is gone, too.

I'm chasing a shadow; you slip further into the ether.

My heart is thumping when I'm done looking for you, my throat dry. New fears start to crowd into my head, pushing and jostling against each other.

You spent a lot of time here at my place. I trusted you as I took a shower, ran errands. You had access to my files, my computer. The letter Dear Birdie just read and answered rings back at me.

His lies. I believed every single one.

The sweetheart scam. Wouldn't that be something? If *I* had fallen for one of those. Me — the one who knows too well all the

87

horrors of which people are capable.

I quickly get online and check all my financial accounts, but there's nothing missing. Most of my *Dear Birdie* money is invested with a small private firm. My father thought the stock market was the ultimate con. But I've done well enough.

So even if someone hacked into my checking account, they would only get whatever was there, enough to cover monthly expenses — which are surprisingly low for a homeowner living in Brooklyn. The house was paid for long ago thanks to *Dear Birdie*'s success. And, again, it must be said, I'm cheap. Or *frugal.*

Everything above basic costs goes directly to my accountant, Marty, for saving and investing. He's an old guy, a New York City lifer, a Depression-era thinker, so he admires my supersaver tendencies. *Nothing you buy will make you feel as good as money in the bank.*

I grew up without much. I also know what it feels like to lose even that. So, yeah, I hold on, I guess. Or maybe I don't want to get used to having too much. I don't know — it's complicated.

Or maybe it's my father's voice: *The more you want from the world, the more it holds you by the throat.*

As I sit with my web browser open, news items flash in little banners at the top of my screen periodically. I can usually only read the first half before it disappears.

Virus spreads, Chinese officials warn world that —

Oxycodone deaths reach an all-time —

Stocks tumble on news of —

Australian fires rage, claiming hundreds —

Each little banner is a lure, drawing me away from my task. But I block them out.

Where else to look for you?

I tick back through all the places we've gone, the things we've done, what you've told me about yourself. Then I remember your apartment where a strange woman answered the door.

Oh, this is just a vacation rental. I am here with my family this week.

I open the vacation rental website she mentioned and search the listing by address.

Click, click, click. After scrolling through a few apartments, there it is.

Chic, modern Chelsea two-bedroom with stunning views, the headline enthuses — *walking distance to almost everything!*

I scroll through the photos. The bed where we made love for the first time. The kitchen where you cooked me one of the best meals I've ever had — a spicy Chilean sea bass with roasted garlic new potatoes. We drank wine, a bold and fruity cabernet, and laughed and laughed. It felt like love, almost right away. Not what I was expecting — loose connections, fun, but brief encounters. This was more.

Clicking through the pictures on the listing, I see the bathroom. We showered together in the huge steamy stone and glass affair, very stylish. Subway tiles, marble countertops.

In retrospect, it looked very obviously like a vacation rental. Something stiff and cold about it.

The owner's name and contact number are listed at the bottom of the page. Joe is a "superhost" apparently, and his listing boasts that he'll get back to you in under an hour. So, I send him an email.

Dear Joe, This might seem odd, but a friend of mine is missing. His last known address is your Chelsea vacation rental. I am attaching a photo. Do you recognize him? Did he leave contact information? Thanks so much for your help.

Then I wait. There's no phone number to call — there so rarely is these days. No person waiting on the other end to answer your questions, your thoughts and concerns in real time. Warmth replaced by so-called efficiency. The silence around me expands.

Finally, an email comes through, its chime startling me — my editor.

Perfect. See you in-studio later.

In-studio to record the *Dear Birdie* podcast, where Jax and I read three different letters out loud, then discuss. One broken heart, one dark mystery, one lighter, funnier question about modern etiquette or social navigation. Jax takes the hard-line. I take the softer approach. We sometimes have a third — one of our therapists or a private investigator — to offer some practical advice when needed. Nuts-and-bolts type stuff.

I have to admit I'm the most surprised of all by the runaway success of the column, the podcast. Even the television option looks promising. There are just so many people out there lost in this modern world, looking for a connection. Dear Birdie gives that to them, even if they are among the majority who never write or leave a voice message.

Even if they're just out there alone reading or listening.

My doorbell rings. I'm so lost in thought

that the sound moves through me like a Taser. I practically leap off the couch where I've curled myself up in a ball, and race to the door. I don't even look before I swing it open, so sure that it's you with flowers, with words that explain this weirdness. You'll wear that crooked smile. We'll laugh about it all.

But it's not you.

It's a man I don't recognize with icy green-gray eyes, close shorn blond hair. He stands at an angle on the stairs, halfway up as though he's moved back down after ringing the bell to keep a polite distance. Leaning against the railing, one hand in the pocket of his bomber jacket, he offers a low-wattage smile.

"Wren Greenwood?"

I move back behind the door a bit. He doesn't move forward to close the distance I'm trying to create between us. So far, no one has tried to find out Dear Birdie's true identity, but I'm always afraid that the day will come. The tsunami of mail, some of it from regulars, can get dark. Some people are grateful, but some are angry. Many benefit from the advice I have to give, but a few hate me, blame me for mistakes they have made based on how they interpreted my words. There have been a few death threats. We all agree that it's better if Dear Birdie remains anonymous.

"Can I help you?"

He takes out a tattered brown identification wallet from the back pocket of his jeans. Holding his ID out to me, he says, "My name is Bailey Kirk. I am a private investigator licensed by the state of New York."

"What can I do for you?" I say, wary. He puts the wallet away and moves forward to hold out his phone.

"Do you know this man?"

Curiosity pulls me from the safety of my house to look more closely at the image there.

My breath leaves me when I see that it's you, Adam.

Your hair is different, shorter and maybe a little lighter. Your skin is tan, as if you've been on vacation. You look relaxed, happy in a way that is unfamiliar to me. I wonder where you were when this picture was taken. I'm jealous in a weird way that I am not there with you, that I never saw that look on your face in real time.

I step back from the stranger. I've already forgotten his name. This time, he does come up a stair, moving closer. I haven't answered him, but a knowledge has passed between us. *You wear your heart on your sleeve,* my mother always said. I could never hide anything from her, from anyone.

"Can we talk, Ms. Greenwood?" he asks. He lifts a palm. "I don't have to come in. We could walk to that coffee place on the corner."

He nods over toward the shop where I stop most mornings when I'm heading into Manhattan. His manner, his tone, is gentle, polite. But he stays rooted, that smile unwavering. There's something steely to him, something solid. He's not just going to go away. I feel frozen, uncertain, blood rushing in my ears. When I still don't say anything, he goes on.

"My client has hired me to find this man. He was dating my client's daughter when she disappeared nine months ago."

He taps on his device and holds out his phone again.

This time there's a willowy girl with faceted hazel eyes, a smattering of freckles, a bounce of golden curls. Her smile seems somehow radiant and sad at once; her gaze almost imploring. She's your type; I can tell. She and I don't look alike; if she seems sun-kissed and bubbly, I am cool and quiet. My hair is dark, my eyes a deep blue. But there's something about her that I know I see when

94

I look in the mirror. What is it?

My heart is thumping again, dread finding an acidic home in my belly.

"I'll just get my coat," I say. It comes out like a whisper. He nods and moves off the steps and stands on the street, waiting — arms folded, legs akimbo.

"Take your time," he says. I wonder if he'll start walking toward the coffee shop. Grabbing my phone from the couch, my bag and coat from the hallway foyer. I think I should text Jax to say what's happening but then I just don't. I lock the door and turn to find him still standing there.

"Shall we?" he asks.

I stay, hand on the knob.

"Bailey Kirk with the Turner and Ives Agency," he says easily into the awkward silence, as if he suspects I've already forgotten. "I'll wait if you want to check my credentials."

That picture of you. So far, I haven't admitted that I know you. In fact, I haven't said much at all. I could just go back in, lock my door, and refuse to talk to this guy. He's not a cop; he has no authority over me or anything.

He starts walking slowly, a glance back at me to see if I'm following. I hesitate, considering my options. Finally, curiosity gets the better of me. I move down the stairs and follow him.

NINE

The coffee shop is overwarm and crowded
on a weekday midmorning, populated by
Brooklyn creatives with AirPods, open
laptops, and man buns. There's even a guy
in a flannel shirt with one of those full
beards that looks like a bush is growing on
his face. I am really eager for that particular
trend to die.

Bailey Kirk asks for my order. Triple
espresso almond milk latte, I tell him, and
he gets in line with a nod, waving away the
ten I offer. I find us a table by the window,
my hands shaking. The aroma of the various brews are heavy on the air, cups and
spoons clink, voices are low, the frothing
machine hisses. I shift into my seat, watching him.

Who is this guy?

Different from the other people around
him. Focused, where others are diffuse. He's
powerful, broad and tight bodied, where

people around him seem loose, soft. He approaches the counter and speaks softly to the barista. She smiles the way young girls do in the presence of virility. He says something that makes her laugh. Then he turns to look at me, maybe to check if I'm still there. And I'm embarrassed to be caught watching him, look away.

Again, I remind myself: *You can go. You don't need to talk to this person.*

I only glanced at his identification. Really, it could have been his gym membership card. Grabbing my phone, I enter "Turner and Ives" into the web browser; a slick, mobile-friendly site pops up featuring the faces of two stern-faced but not unattractive older women and the bold words: **Integrity * Ethics * Success.**

The firm specializes in, according to their boilerplate, insurance fraud, police investigation support, cold cases, missing persons.

I click on "Staff" and there he is, Bailey Kirk, unsmiling with that searing gaze. Former NYPD homicide detective, graduate of John Jay College, he is the firm's "top investigator" with a nearly 100 percent success rate.

It's the "nearly" that interests me. Failure is much more interesting than success; it tells you so much more about a person.

What is a *success rate* exactly when you're talking about detective work? Cases solved? Lost people found? Bad guys caught?

I flash on the image Bailey Kirk showed me, the pretty girl he said you were dating.

Who is she?

For that matter, who the hell are you?

The man with whom I've been sharing my bed, my body, my life for the last three months. It's not very long; I know that. But it feels long. In this modern age, it's a serious relationship. Not a hookup. Not a "situationship," which Jax says is someone you hook up with regularly but from whom you don't expect more than sex and some laughs. I expected more than sex and laughs. You did, too, right?

And what does this detective know about you? Curiosity keeps me rooted.

The truth is that I only know what you've told me. Your name is Adam Harper. You're turning forty in February. You're from Upstate New York, originally, though your family traveled most of your life because your father couldn't hold a job. Your parents are divorced. You're not close to either of them. You're totally estranged from your brother. You are a cybersecurity expert, with an engineering degree from MIT. You can cook. You can be a workaholic. You don't snore. In fact, you barely seem to sleep at all.

I still feel you on my skin.

The things you told me were supported by the odd detail — your tattered and worn MIT sweatshirt, your passion for a great meal, your knowledge of the web and its back alleys, the fine lines around your eyes, the tension in your shoulders when you talked about your family.

There were no moments where I doubted the truth of what you said.

All the places where I would go to dig deeper now — your social media feeds, your dating profile — are gone. There's nothing at all to connect us, except this stranger. No friends in common. No neighborhood bar where we might bump into each other.

Bailey Kirk doesn't glance back again to make sure I'm still there. He knows I'm hooked. Of course I am. I met a man online. He disappeared. He wasn't who I thought he was. How many letters has Dear Birdie received about just this thing? My brain is in overdrive, revisiting our conversations, the intimate moments we shared. Was there an off note, something that should have been a red flag? No. There's nothing.

The detective comes to our table with the coffee, seats himself, keeping his black bomber jacket on. A scent wafts off him, something soapy and clean. There's a day of stubble on his jaw, a golden blond roughness. His image on the website is airbrushed. In real life, he has fine lines around his mouth, a furrow on his brow, the slight bruising of fatigue under his eyes.

"So, you met him online, right?" he says, starting the conversation.

He slides the coffee over to me; he has ordered the same for himself. It's scribbled on his cup. Is it a mirroring thing, a technique to put me at ease? Or maybe he has a dairy intolerance and a caffeine addiction like me.

I nod. "On Torch."

He gives me a look — a kind of amused eyebrow lift.

"Isn't that more for just hooking up?" he says.

"It can be," I say with a shrug. "I wasn't really looking for anything serious."

That's what everyone says these days. It's true and not true, right? Deep down everyone's looking for love, aren't they? When did we forget that it's the only thing we really want?

"What *were* you looking for, then?"

They — those experts who seem to know everything — say that online dating is the biggest change to the mating ritual in a millennium. Once upon a time, your dating pool was limited to a small group of say fifty-to-a-hundred-plus people. It was an intimate, if somewhat shallow pool — your neighborhood, town, school, church. The first big change was the rise of agriculture and the growth of cities and towns. The pool got bigger, but ways to connect remained somewhat consistent in that you had to meet someone somewhere, or through someone else you know. Close tie connections — family, friends, geography.

Then, enter the internet and the rise of dating websites, and that pool grew to essentially everyone else in the world looking for — whatever. Sex. Love. The fulfillment of whatever other appetite, need, desire.

Some might view this is as a positive thing — this new era of choice, of plenty. But the truth is that these loose tie connections are almost never lasting. There's no social obligation to treat people well. You're not going to find yourself sitting in the church pew next your Torch date's grandmother on Sunday. So, when you're done with someone, you can potentially discard him, and realistically expect to never see him or anyone he knows again.

Now, I suppose I can add myself to the

ranks of Dear Birdie's lonely hearts, badly burned by a soul-crushing online-dating encounter.

Of course, I knew all this before. We all do, don't we? But when Jax started pushing for me to get on Torch, it *had* been an embarrassingly long time since I dated anyone, *touched* anyone. I guess you could say I was lonely. Does it make me seem desperate to admit that? Lots of people are lonely.

"Just a good time maybe," I answer finally. It doesn't ring true, and the corners of his mouth tick up in the slightest shadow of a smile, something kind, knowing.

I have my phone in my hand, keep refreshing my email, wondering if I'll hear back from Joe the superhost. I don't know what the regulations are. Maybe he won't reply to my query. Or he'll say he can't share that information. But probably it's just up to him, right? The internet is like the Wild West. Anything goes. The rules change all the time.

"So how does Torch work?" he asks, though he must know. Doesn't everyone?

"You make a profile, answer a questionnaire, post a picture," I tell him. "Then you get on the app and you scroll through. Double click if you like what you see. Move on if you don't. If it's a match, meaning if the person you like likes you too, you can connect with that person via the app."

He takes a sip of his coffee, glances around the room.

"How many people have you met this way?"

"Not many. Three."

"Three," he repeats. It's neutral. I don't feel judged.

Another shrug, a sip of my latte. It's the perfect temperature. "I'm picky." I don't really like that word; it sounds superior, arrogant, so I correct myself. "Or I guess I have a type."

"What was it about it this guy?"

His body language tells me that he's relaxed but alert, those eyes scanning the room, resting a moment, then moving on to the next thing. Analyzing, evaluating.

"He was different," I say. My conversation with Jax rings back. She said he looked too serious. But that's what I liked about him. What she didn't say, and what I know she was thinking, was that he looked just a little like my father. Not so much physically, just something in the eyes, his aura.

"Different how?" Now Bailey's gaze comes to rest on me.

"Everyone on there was posing and posturing. Most of them seemed shallow and just looking to get laid. There are a lot of really stupid people on Torch — all abs, no substance. He was like the opposite of the typical Torch guy."

"All substance, no abs."

I smile. His tone is flat, but I pick up the teasing energy. It's gentle, looking for humor in a bad situation.

"Something like that."

He takes a drink from his cup; I do the same. He has an interesting face, those fine lines adding character, a thoughtfulness to his gaze, a full mouth. He smiles, but his eyes are serious, watchful. I try to guess his age. Early forties maybe? No wedding ring. I see some ink peeking out from the cuff of his jacket, wonder what kind of tattoo he has under there.

"What did he tell you his name was?"

I almost don't want to tell him, still clinging to you, to the idea of us that I thought was the truth. Was that not your name? If you lied about that, then — what? You're a stranger. A stranger in my bed, in my heart. How many different ways have I said a name that wasn't yours? In query, in laughter, in pleasure.

"Adam Harper."

He nods, eyes still scanning the room.

He's not writing anything down, which seems weird. That's kind of what you would expect a PI to do, right? Have a little notebook or something.

"When did you see him last?" he asks.

"Look," I say. "What is this about?"

He sighs, leans forward a little. I see a little more of that tattoo, but I still can't make it out. "My client's daughter, Mia Thorpe, has been missing for nine months. She was a troubled girl, vulnerable, when she met this man on an online dating app."

He pulls up another photo on his phone and lays it on the table between us.

There you are again, Adam Harper. Looking like someone else. Someone lighter, happier, younger. Your skin glows, warm and golden. I ache to reach out and touch you.

"My client thinks that this man — who Mia knew as Raife Mannes — has something to do with what happened to her."

"Thinks."

"Mannes, too, has disappeared."

A man walks through the door of the coffee shop wearing a surgical mask. I've seen this before, more and more in fact, especially on the subway. I heard on the news that some people believe the virus from China is heading this way. The sight of people wearing masks makes me uncomfortable. Do they know something I don't? About the air, about a sickness in the air? Or is it that they're sick, trying to protect others? My father would surely have a rant about this. The end-time wouldn't come with a bang, he promised, it would sneak in subtly, curling and silent, a poisonous gas.

No one else seems to notice the man in the mask, everyone staring at a screen — phones, laptops. Some people are having low, blank-eyed conversations with no one, speaking to a person they hear in their earphones. In fact, we're the only two people it seems, sitting across from each other, talking to each other.

"Okay," I say, refocusing my attention. "So, you say this man Raife, who I know as Adam, was dating Mia, who you said was *troubled*. Mia goes missing. So does Raife. And your client — Mia's father — hires you to find her or him or both."

"That's right," he says.

"I don't like that word — troubled."

"Why is that?"

"Because it implies that there was something wrong with her. Aren't we all troubled in one way or another?"

He seems to consider. "It's not a judgment. Some of us are more vulnerable to predators than others, wouldn't you agree?"

"Predators." The word makes my skin tingle.

"There are people who take advantage of vulnerabilities to get what they want."

I can't argue with that. "Is that what you think he is? A predator."

I glance down at the picture, remember the feel of your arms around me. The truth is, I've never felt so safe or loved as I did when I was with you. How can you not be the person I thought you were? There must be some mistake.

"All I know is that a woman is missing, and so is the man she was dating," Kirk answers. "That he was not who he claimed to be. That all her accounts have been drained. And she left her father, her friends, her apartment, and phone behind without a word."

I search for something to say, but all the words jam up in my throat.

He goes on, "Then nine months later, his profile is back up on Torch under another name."

You and I, Adam, we *had* the talk about exes. You told me about your high school sweetheart. Your first real love, a British girl you met while you did a year abroad in London. You did mention someone else — there was a woman more recently, one with emotional problems. You said that the breakup was ugly, protracted, hard. That you hadn't been with anyone since. You made it sound like a couple of years. I told you about my college boyfriend, not everything, the few dates and hookups I've had since. Embarrassing, I guess. Most women in their late twenties might be married, have children, or serious partnerships. Or at least they've had serious relationships that ended. Not me. You're the first person I thought I might be able to share myself with, all my layers.

You are not surprised by the force of the storm. Rilke. That was the line that hooked me in.

"So how did the trail lead to *me*?" I ask.

"That's my job," he says. "I'm a *detective*. And you should know — everyone should know — that privacy is a thing of the past. If you have the right connections — and I do — anybody's information is for sale."

"That sounds like a lecture, not an answer."

He finishes his coffee and places the cup on the table. There's a thing he does with his hands, make a fist of one and cups it with the other hand, squeezes.

"I have a couple of Torch profiles, so do other people at my firm," he says. "We've been watching for his photo to come up. I think this is how he operates. He finds women on online dating apps."

I don't love the way that sounds. *I think this is how he operates.*

"Women? There are — *others.*"

He doesn't answer. "When his photo came up finally, it was pretty easy to find his matches — with the right connections at Torch."

"How many matches did he have?" I'm curious. You told me that I was the only one you'd picked from that sea of pursed lips and offered cleavage. You said it was my eyes, blue, glowing against pale skin and jet hair. Hypnotic — that was the word you used.

Kirk offers that enigmatic smile again. "Just one. He only chose you."

I'm restless, anxious, sit forward in my seat.

"How could you even get that information?"

"I work for a pretty powerful firm. They throw a lot of money around."

Is it that easy? I wonder. Is everything in this world about money? Dad would say yes, of course it is. The root of all evil.

"What about me?" I venture. "How many matches?"

How shallow, right? You'd ask too if you could. Wouldn't you want to know how many people thought you were cute. Again, that flicker of amusement.

"You only liked three people and they liked you back," he says. "But, for the record, you had tons of potential matches. But it seems that you only chose a handful of men, including our friend. Picky, like you said. Or — you have a type."

Our friend. But you're not my friend, are you, Adam? I don't even know your name, your real name.

I'm not sure why, but everything comes out in a rush — about last night, how you stood me up, how I went to your place and discovered it was a vacation rental, the cryptic text you sent. Of course I keep to myself what I revealed to you.

Kirk asks for the vacation rental address and I give it to him, telling him also about my email to Joe the superhost.

"Has he gotten back to you?" he asks.

I pull my phone from my bag and check my email. "Not yet."

I keep my eyes down, swiping again and again with my thumb, waiting for an answer.

"So, the last time you saw Adam?" he prompts, bringing me back to the conversation.

"Monday," I say. "He spent Sunday night with me and left for work in the morning."

We made love before the alarm went off, both of us half asleep, my secret in the air all around us. Your eyes gave me everything I needed — passion, understanding, comfort. You weren't afraid or distant. If anything, you seemed closer, your arms wrapped so tight around me, so deep inside me. I still feel you.

"Where did he claim to work?" Bailey asks.

"Uptown."

"Company name? Address?"

I shake my head, a little embarrassed. You've told me, of course. Or did you? "I don't remember. Something to do with forts or locks or vaults."

There's a bit of skepticism etched into his brow.

"You've never been to his office?"

"Just the other day for the first time. I didn't go in, just waited for him outside."

Just like the apartment, I realize. I'd been to the Chelsea place just often enough that I had a mental model of where you lived, just enough that I didn't question the truth of it. It was too early to have met your coworkers, to have accompanied you to the office Christmas party. After all, you hadn't met any of the people I work with. In fact, I hadn't even introduced you yet to Jax.

"Where was that?" His tone is patient, coaxing.

"Uptown. Seventy-Ninth between Broadway and Columbus. Maybe?"

"Address?"

"No. Sorry."

"Feel like taking a ride up there with me? See if you can find it."

I check the time. I have to get to the studio. "I can meet you later," I say. "I need to work."

He doesn't ask me what I do or where I work, just offers a nod. How much does Bailey Kirk know about me, I wonder. The thought makes me a little uneasy. I have imagined myself as hidden, private. *Privacy is a thing of the past.* Was that true?

"What time can you meet?" he asks.

"I can be there by four. Corner of Seventy-Ninth and Broadway."

"Okay," he says. "It's a date."

How does he know I'll be true to my word? Maybe he doesn't need to know. Seems like I was easy to find, in spite of my believing otherwise. How many times do I enter my address to have something shipped, or for a membership to this or that, thinking it's private, secure, protected? What

113

information did I provide Torch? Oh, wait, I didn't. Jax did everything. But she's the only person more careful with my secrets than I am. Other than Robin.

Or maybe Kirk can see that I *want* to meet him, that I'm hooked, into him, into you, into the missing girl already. After all this is my beat — people and their problems. Maybe he can see that I want to know what's happening, maybe more than he does.

We exchange numbers, and I feel his eyes as I exit and head for the subway. Before I head underground, my phone pings. An email from Joe the superhost. The message is brief. Just a phone number and a single sentence. Please call me.

TEN

"Dear Birdie," I say into the mic.

These recordings used to take place in a makeshift studio in my apartment. But since moving to the *Chronicle* there has been a serious upgrade. A soundproof room, a long high table with multiple mics, big comfy chairs and wide headphones that sit on my head like a big hug.

Today, Jax sits across from me. Her hair is in a wild pile of inky curls on top of her head wrapped in a brightly printed scarf that matches the pattern on her dress, which is basically a muumuu. She rocks it with her tall frame. Effortless glam. How does she do it?

Jax is an influencer. Her brand is: Change Your Life! Take Charge of Yourself and Create Your World. Bad habits? Break them! *Here are ten easy ways how.* Unhappy? Grow up, woman up, and stop believing the stories someone else told you about your-

115

self. *Write your own story!*

Her advice plays very well with a certain set. She has her own podcast, regularly appears on mine, and has a big book contract. *Stop Giving a Fuck About Everyone Else and Start Living Your Life for YOU.* Or something like that. I'm helping her write it, because Jax is a verbal, visual person — sound bites and perfectly staged photographs. The act of writing, for her, is an act of torture — she procrastinates, rages and rails against the page. The chapter we're currently working on: No, You are NOT Destined to be JUST LIKE YOUR MOTHER!

I really hope that's true.

Her book, like my friend, is smart and funny, and full of solid advice for young people struggling to find themselves. Jax is a strong voice, a warm touch. She tries to live her own advice.

And we have Ben with us, today. A family therapist, Zen Buddhist, with a seriously chill vibe. He softens out Jax's hard edges; she's much gentler when he's in the studio. He sits, hands folded, mouth in a peaceful smile, her energetic opposite in gray shirt and khakis, light brown hair going gray, kind eyes. I've suspected for a while that they might like each other. There is a lot of staring and light touching. They are yin and yang.

I clear my throat and say again, "Dear Birdie."

My podcast voice is not my real voice. My real voice is girlish and soft. I channel another part of myself in the studio, and my voice comes out smoky and soothing. Dear Birdie is not Wren Greenwood. Dear Birdie is cool and calm, knowing, patient. She's wise and careful. Wren Greenwood, obviously not so much.

I read the letter that I answered earlier. Jax and Ben are both miked up, waiting.

"That's rough," says Jax when I'm done.

"There's a lot to unpack here," says Ben.

"I think her friend is right," I say. "I think she owes it to herself to seek some justice. Even if she doesn't get it. Just the act of trying will help her to reclaim some of what he's taken from her. And I'm not talking about the money."

"I agree," said Jax. "People like this guy — they count on you shrinking into the shadows, letting your shame keep you silent. That's how they get away with it again and again. I'm thinking — just spitballing here — hit man?"

We both laugh. "Maybe not that extreme," I say.

"Looking for justice is one thing," Ben puts in gently. "Looking to harm someone because they have harmed us is another."

"But that's a kind of justice, isn't it?" says Jax, leaning forward, challenging him as she so enjoys doing.

"There's no justice in doing harm, no matter what the crime," Ben says.

"We can stand up for ourselves without harming others. We can speak our truth, and ask people to make amends, and still behave ethically," I offer.

Jax shakes her head vigorously; this is a push-button issue for her. "And the bad guys run amok, because the good guys don't want to *do harm*. I mean look at the world. The bad guys — they're winning."

"But that's *how* we keep being the *good* guys," says Ben. His smile is serene, loving.

We go around and around like this for a while, until finally I conclude with the answer I penned earlier. I'm sure we'll get lots of mail about this one.

We have a couple of other letters to address — a woman who can't move on from grief and has given in to agoraphobia. Here we talk about fear, and how the world moves on, even when we can't, and how to navigate that disconnect. Ben talks a bit about immersion therapy and finding someone who can help her to reenter the world one step at a time. We refer her to a counselor who specializes in grief.

After that we go light, discussing a letter from an older office manager who works with a passel of millennials and her inability to understand emoji use. *If I don't put a smiley face emoji or some hearts in my texts, people think I'm mean!*

"Language is fluid," I say. "Every year there are new words, colloquial changes. Over time words that mean one thing come to mean another. Emojis, like it or not, are part of that state of change. It might seem silly. But would it kill you to send heart eyes to express warmth and goodwill?"

Ben makes an affirming noise.

"Or you could simply tell your staff that emojis are not your thing," says Ben. "Then plan a gathering so that you can all get to know each other better. Have some real-time conversations, so that people can hear your voice in your other communications more clearly."

"Or," says Jax. "Just pick one signature emoji — the smiley face, or even the three hearts smiley face, and use that. It can be part of your brand."

It all runs over me. In the studio, dwelling in Dear Birdie, all the rest of my life is gone as if it doesn't even exist. I forget all about you for a while. I am lost in other people's problems, helping them navigate a world that it seems like we're all struggling to understand. I am reluctant for the session to end. But end it does.

"You doing okay?" Jax asks, as she pulls on her coat to leave. "Did you hear from him?"

I shake my head. I consider telling her about Bailey Kirk, about the missing girl. But I'm not ready to "unpack" it yet, as Ben would say.

"I guess I've been ghosted."

"I'm sorry, honey," she says, pulling me close. She smells like tea tree; her embrace is full of love energy. I let that flow though my body.

"I'm okay," I lie into her shoulder.

"I know you are," she says, pulling back to look at me. "You're wonder woman. Meanwhile, why don't you talk to Jason? Take your own advice." Jason is the private detective to whom we refer some *Dear Birdie* letter writers, a tech genius who practically lives inside a computer.

"Yeah. Maybe," I say. "Anyway, Adam didn't take anything from me."

She puts a hand on my shoulder. "Didn't he?"

Jax and Ben leave together, and I'm alone in the studio. The production team on the other side of the glass is already at work on editing the session. I like this warm, windowless space. All sounds muted, lights dim.

I check to make sure the mic sound is off, and then I call Joe the superhost. He answers after one ring.

"This is Joe." An old man's voice, gravelly and gruff.

"Hi, this is Wren. I left a message about my friend."

He issues a mirthless laugh. "Yeah, well, your *friend* owes me about $5K."

"How's that?"

"He rented my place for a long weekend," he says. "Sent me the money via wire transfer, nice and easy. When he asked if he could stay for another week, I said yes. It was slow and I didn't have anyone in the calendar."

I hear sirens in the background. Joe clears his throat.

"Okay," I say.

"He told me he'd wire again, and I wasn't too worried about it because he'd done as he said he would the first time. But a couple of days went by. Finally, some money came through — but a fraction of what another week would cost. This went on for about

121

two weeks — he didn't pay. Didn't vacate. Finally, I sent someone to kick him out. But he was already gone."

The words rattle around my brain. This doesn't compute with anything I think I know about you.

"When was this?" I ask.

"A couple of months ago, now." He's clicking on his computer. "He checked in October 1. I sent someone on November 1 to get rid of him, but he was gone."

Where have you been living all this time? In your office? Another rental somewhere? Is that what you do — just move from place to place?

"Did you file a police report?" I ask.

"No," he scoffs. "The police don't give a shit. New York City is not a vacation-rental-friendly town. People don't like it. But, you know, this is my retirement income."

"What name did he give you?"

"Adam Grove," he says. "Surprise, surprise, not his real name. Some people only take credit cards because of this type of thing. But I try to trust people. Or I did. From now on, it's credit cards only, pay up front, no refunds."

"I'm sorry this happened to you," I say. I realize I'm using my Dear Birdie voice.

There's a surprised silence on the line.

"I hope you find your friend," he says after he blows out a breath. "If you do, tell him to pay an old man what he owes, and he can have his things back. And as for you, young lady, take my advice. I think you should spend your energy finding some new friends."

A little glimmer of hope. "Have his things back?"

"I have a box of junk he left in the apartment. I thought about trashing it but then I decided to hold on to it."

"Do you mind if I come by and take a look?"

An old-man sigh. In spite of his gruffness, I can tell Joe is a nice guy — I don't know how. Something about his tone.

"Look," I say, when he doesn't answer, "I'll pay what he owes you."

I didn't plan to say that. And it's kind of a crazy thing to do. But it just came out. Something about our discussion on ethics and doing no harm. I feel responsible that you hurt this man. Why is that?

"And why would you do that?" he asks.

"Because I can," I say. "And it's not fair what happened to you. I'll bring cash."

Another silence. Finally, "You got a deal, kid. What time?"

I check the time on my phone; there are a

123

couple of hours before I have to meet Bailey Kirk. "How about now? Where's the box?"

"In my storage unit on Tenth Avenue. I'll meet you there in an hour."

After we end the call, a text comes through with the address of the storage facility. I'll have to get to the bank and across town in an hour.

In New York City, there's only one way to get anywhere fast — but it means taking your life into your hands. Citi Bike.

ELEVEN

Then

"Let's go."

Jay roused me from my light slumber by touching me on the shoulder.

The strange room was golden in the rising sun. I'd barely slept, dreaming of my friends, my old room, my English teacher Miss Penny who told me I was an "exceptional writer." The ache for all of it was physical, something I felt in my stomach, in my heart. A spiraling case of homesickness. Even though this was our home now.

"Where?" I asked, not eager to move from the warmth of my bed.

Are we running away? I wondered. Maybe I could live with Grace in her pretty house. It seemed possible; but then I thought of my mom and I was rooted to this place, this new life. *Buck up, buttercup.* Mom's famous pep talk.

"I found something in the woods," Jay said

with a note of intrigue. "I want to show you."

He moved over to the door frame, waiting. The room was plain, just a bed, a dresser, a small closet.

This was my sister's room, my father told me when he carried my boxes in the night before. *Bigger than your old room, right? Make it yours. Do whatever you want to it.*

An aunt I'd never met. They were estranged, my mother said. Didn't get along. Then my aunt died. So I was sleeping in a dead girl's bedroom, sort of. At least that was the story I had been telling myself, imagining her creeping, pale and stiff out of the closet, or from under the bed, scaring myself silly until my mother scolded me to pull myself together.

Jay was already dressed. I climbed out of bed and he waited while I pulled on my jeans, sneakers, leaving on my unicorn pajama top. I followed him down the creaking stairs and out the front door where the morning was alive with birdsong, bright green with leaves, and a velvety coolness in the air. We walked along a thin path in the woods until we came to an old tree house that sat rickety looking in the thick branches of a tall oak.

"Is it safe?"

"Probably not," said Jay, with a shrug. "That ladder won't hold my weight. But you can get up there. Go check it out."

I tugged on the rope ladder that hung from a hatch in the floor of the tree house. It felt solid enough. I was never a girlie girl, always half tomboy. I had to be if Jay would have anything to do with me. He taught me to throw a ball, to make a goal in soccer, to ride a bike, to walk off a skinned knee, not to cry like a girl when I was mad.

I climbed on the bottom rung, bounced a little to see if it would hold. When it did, I scrambled up.

Oh, it was magical. Sun streaming in from the roof slats, smelling of wood and leaves and rot, a worn old mattress in the corner, a stack of books swollen with moisture, a table with shells and feathers. All of it grimy, neglected, obviously having been abandoned for years.

"What's up there?" Jay called from down below.

Nothing. Everything. What was it that I found so wonderful? It was a secret space, a place apart from the world where all time stood still. I could hear the birds singing, the wind pushing the leaves around. And for a moment I understood why my father loved this place; I was washed over with a sense of peace.

The floor felt solid enough. I vowed to clean it, care for it, and make it mine. I wanted to stay up there forever. But finally Jay called me down.

"What's it like?"

"It's perfect," I told him.

He glanced up at it, the sun and the wind playing on his white blond hair.

"Good," he told me. When he looked at me, his eyes were serious. "When things get bad, that's where you go, okay?"

I didn't have to ask him what he meant. Last night had been peaceful enough. We'd cooked our dinner on the fire my dad made out back — hot dogs and beans in a skillet. He'd even taken out his guitar, sang a love song he'd written to my mom. But Jay still had a fading purple bruise, a faint shadow on the edge of his jaw, from a few nights ago when a similarly peaceful moment turned ugly.

"And don't come back until I come to get you."

I nodded my agreement, stayed silent. He dropped an arm around me for a moment, and we both looked up at the tree house. Then he shoved me away lightly, rustling my hair.

There was movement in the leaves. At first

I thought a person was there, stone still and watching us through the trees in the dappled light, someone tall and bulky. I grabbed Jay's arm. But he just smiled, put a finger to his lips. Then I saw it was a deer, a doe. She stared at us with dark, glassy eyes, then bounded away into the forest.

TWELVE

Now

What are we looking for when we look for love?

What did I hope to find with my posting on Torch?

Why did I choose you?

I'm thinking about this as I whip through traffic in my usual reckless, kamikaze style — bobbing and weaving, playing chicken, skating past opening car doors, and finding narrow alleys through stopped traffic.

On a bike, the city is a blur of car horns and changing lights, throngs of people and doorways, alleyways, parks, windows. I am in the middle of it all, and totally alone all at once. I get stern lectures from Miranda and Jax, both requesting that I forgo my Citi Bike habit after Jax's older brother Pete was hit by a car, laid up for nearly ten weeks and still in physical therapy. I've had a couple of wipeouts over the years, some pins in my elbow to show for one, a scar on my leg from the other. Both times I was wearing a helmet, but not today.

I earn an angry shout from a guy for passing too close as he waited to cross. I lift my hand in apology, still thinking about dating and love and how messed up it all is these days.

But meeting someone online isn't *so* different from picking someone up in a bar, is it? Or a chance encounter in a park, or show, or anyplace where people gather. It's just a bigger playing field, right? After the initial connection, however inorganic, isn't it all the same? There's a meeting. If there's chemistry, a connection, then there's another meeting, a slow peeling back of layers, a gradual revealing of different parts of the self.

My father would have thought this modern way was just more evidence that the end of the world was coming. That people are getting further and further away from each other, losing their humanity, their ability to connect — in spite of imagining themselves more connected than ever through their devices.

The envelope of cash I have stuffed inside my pants is pressing uncomfortably into my abdomen as I ride. I can't remember the last time I had so much green. Or any at all. Money, too, has been reduced to an electronic affair mostly. The swipe of a card, numbers on a screen, bills spit from a machine, if you need cash at all.

I'm old enough to remember before we were swallowed by the digital age, before our lives were controlled by screens and devices. I remember ticking clocks and paper money, ringing phones attached to the wall, doors that locked with a key, doorbells without recording cameras. You remember that, too, Adam. We share a nostalgia for the analog.

After returning the bike to one of the racks, I walk the rest of the way to the storage unit, a great behemoth of a place that spans an entire city block, a whole universe devoted to storing people's junk that they don't care enough about to use, but which they're not ready to purge. Hoarders. For a second I flash on the house where I grew up, but I push it away hard. I can't afford a trip down memory lane.

Come home, Robin said this morning. *Just come home.*

I hate to keep breaking her heart. But I don't want to go back there right now.

As I walk, people scurry past, a couple of them wearing masks like the man in the coffee shop. Just like that SARS, or the bird flu, there's apparently a strangely named disease from a faraway place that won't impact us much at all, I'm sure. But people are always ready to give in to panic; me, I tend to underreact. My father would accuse me of being "worldly," which to him meant that I dwelled in the material. That I suffered under the delusion of permanence, that I erroneously believed that the things I could see and touch had any meaning at all. He'd see those people wearing masks as a sign, the white horse of the apocalypse — pestilence.

It's almost as if because I shared my past, spoken words out loud, that I've given my father permission to invade my thoughts. This is why I've buried it all so deep. To speak of it is a conjuring, thoughts and phrases, unwanted memories coming back as alive and vivid, so near. I should never have told you. I had constructed my life so that I never had to. I could have taken it to my grave, so to speak. Too late for regrets, though. What's done is done.

There's a narrow old man standing by the entrance to the facility, hands in the pocket of his peacoat, a plaid cap, chunky shoes. He's not quite as tall as I am, rubs at his jaw as I approach. His face is a landscape of

133

lines and shadows.

"Joe?"

He nods, sticks out his hand and I take it in mine. It's papery and warm. He holds me with his gaze, taking measure it feels like. Whatever he sees, he offers me a slight smile.

"I'm Wren."

"You're younger than I thought you'd be."

"I'm older than I look." Not quite thirty, I look younger. I still get carded. I crave gravitas, the respectability that comes with age. But it seems elusive.

He nods again and then turns to head inside the gate. I follow him through a labyrinth of concrete hallways, punctuated by metal door after metal door. When we get to number 39, he comes to a stop. He bends to unlock a padlock, and hauls the door open with a clanging that echoes off the long passage.

I'm tense, my shoulders aching, wondering what pieces of yourself you might have left behind. A powerful waft of moldy damp air makes my sinuses tingle.

Joe flips on a light. The space is orderly, rows of boxes carefully marked: tax documents, bedding, Marty's artwork, Millie's clothes, photographs, letters. There's an old wingback chair, a dresser, a steamer truck, a standing lamp. I feel the urge to start rifling through. The detritus of living life, how it collects, how we hold on to it, how it defines us. It tells a story, and I love the stories people have to tell. I feel a craving to understand Joe, know about the life he's lived. But there in the center of the room, there's a single unmarked box.

He bends down for it and hoists it up. It looks light; there can't be much in there. But I am greedy for it, for any piece of you.

I take the money from my pocket in a thick white envelope.

"You said five thousand?" I say.

He frowns, takes a step back. "Are you sure you want to do that? Cover your boyfriend's debt. You were my daughter? I wouldn't let you bail out some deadbeat."

I look down at the cash in my hand. He has a point.

"I'm not doing it for him," I say. "I'm doing it for you."

He smiles, eyes crinkling. I can see he's amused, trying to figure me out. "You don't even know me."

He's right on some level. But I think how we treat any one person is how we treat the world, how we treat ourselves. If I can right a wrong, it's far more valuable than the sum of five thousand dollars. Maybe it restores

Joe's faith or maybe someday he pays it forward. This is why, I think, people bring me their problems and ask me to solve them. I'm always going to try to fix and help.

"Please," I say when he doesn't take it. "I'm happy to do it."

Finally, he reaches for it. I notice a tremor in his hand. "Thank you, young lady."

He hands me the box.

"Do you mind?" I say.

"Go ahead." Joe takes a seat in the wing-back chair.

I sit on the floor with the box and start to look through it. Your watch — large white face with Roman numerals, black leather band. I admired it once for its simplicity. You said it was your grandfather's, given to him by your father, that it meant something to you. Why would you leave it behind? Probably just another lie.

Your favorite hoodie is light and soft in my hands — a lovely navy blue cashmere garment that cost a mint. You are one of those stealth wealth people, dressing down in items that don't look like much but are unaffordable to most. I put the garment to my nose and take in the scent of you, feel my body tingle. For a second I'm back with you, in my bed, that last time we were together. Your skin. Your arms. The silk of

136

your hair between my fingers. I look over at Joe, embarrassed, but he seems lost in thought himself, stares off into nowhere.

A slim black Moleskine falls open in my palms. All the pages are blank. I flip through once, twice, hoping for any scribble on any page. Nothing.

The Mont Blanc pen is shiny and new, another simple, elegant instrument with its white star top and gleaming back shaft. It is sturdy in in my hand. I'm a writer so I can't resist taking off the cap and putting the nib to paper. Who are you, Adam Harper? I write in careful script.

Finally, there's a shave kit — straight razor and badger brush, neatly packed in a leather pouch. I remember this from your bathroom, noticing how everything you owned was an *object,* something chosen for its design, curated. None of these items tells me a single thing I didn't already know.

Disappointment and frustration do battle in my chest.

I'm certain the box is empty, but I peer inside one last time.

And that's when I see the thing that makes my heart stutter and the ground beneath me spin. It's a newspaper article, more than a decade old, folded and creased. Not a copy. Not a printout. The actual newsprint article from the paper. A familiar face stares at me from the grainy images; ink transfers to my fingers.

"Everything all right?" asks Joe, startling me.

"Yes," I lie. There's acid in my belly and up my gullet. "Everything's fine."

"Find what you were looking for?"

"I think so."

He rises and offers me a hand to help me up. I accept and he's surprisingly strong. I stow your belongings in my messenger bag while he watches, leaving the empty box. My whole body is shaking. There's a ringing in my ears.

"You look like you've seen a ghost," Joe says with concern.

I have. I have seen a ghost. I see her every time I look in the mirror.

THIRTEEN

I grab another Citi Bike and hoof it uptown, happy to lose myself in the exertion, tempting fate and earning angry bleats from drivers — who as a rule hate people on bicycles. They must resent our freedom, while they sit trapped in boxes, nowhere to go, snaking through this crowded city, time standing still.

Every nerve ending in my body is buzzing. Mentally, I tick through your possessions. The watch, the hoodie, the shave kit, the pen, the notebook. And the thing I almost missed. The article. The ground I thought was solid beneath my feet is quicksand. I'm sinking, nothing to grasp and keep me from drowning.

Again, I return the bike about a block away from my next meeting, and walk the rest of the distance, still reeling, trying to put pieces in this puzzle together.

139

I thought I was sharing the darkest part of myself.

The thing I'd kept hidden from almost everyone.

But you already knew.

How?

It doesn't seem possible. With help, that history has been long buried. What happened to my family happened long ago, in a small town. Media coverage was blistering, but over the years so many other, more audacious horrors have captured public attention. Our ugly story has all but faded completely from public memory, thanks to short attention spans and the endless catalog of horrors that parade and preen like performers at a carnival show.

The event is there if you know what to look for, if you dig deep on the internet into horrific crimes and events. But it's long gone for the most part. It hasn't been rediscovered by a crime blogger or true crime podcaster, brought back to life for those who like to safely wander into darkness and see what's there.

I even hired someone — a search engine fixer, someone who manages what people find when they enter your name into Google. Now, when you enter the name I use, you find my carefully curated social media presence, my website, a listing on the New School alumni page. A bland, forgettable presence. There's no connection from my past to Wren Greenwood, no connection from Wren Greenwood to Dear Birdie.

I have been careful, eager to escape my past and protect my present. Just, apparently, not careful enough.

Bailey Kirk is waiting on the corner, leaning easily against a lamppost as the river of city dwellers flows by him. He doesn't see me, at first. It's interesting to watch people when they don't know they're being observed. As he was in the coffee shop, he's relaxed but alert now. He watches people as they pass, neutral, nonjudgmental but seeing. He's not staring at a smartphone, or blanked out, lost in thought, seeing nothing. He's present, a rare thing. He catches sight of me and lifts his hand in a wave, which I return.

What does someone with resources like Bailey Kirk know about me? Should I tell him about my visit with Joe, the box of your belongings? No. I think I've decided that the quicker I get away from Bailey Kirk, the better off I'll be. Maybe.

"I wasn't sure you'd come," he says, as I approach.

"I keep my promises."

We fall into step, walk up the busy sidewalk past a deli, an unmarked metal door, a posh residential lobby, a few shops, a small vegetable market. I wasn't really paying attention when I was here the other day, having no intention of going into your office. So I'm not sure of the address, but I remember that you said there was a black awning. But as we walk, I'm not sure which building it was. I didn't see you come out.

We walk down the other side, and back again, not speaking. He hasn't asked about the vacation rental or whether I've heard from Joe, so I don't offer up the information. I'm still not sure about him, what he knows, or what I'm ready to share.

Finally, I come to a stop under an awning that we've passed already.

"Maybe this is it," I say.

"You've never been here before," he asks. There's skepticism in his tone.

"No," I say, feeling defensive. "We were taking things slow."

He holds the door open for me and we walk inside. Glancing around the lobby, which is unremarkable in both size and atmosphere, Kirk's eyes finally come to rest on a camera mounted in the far corner of the lobby, a round white eye with a blue lens. There's no doorman.

A directory on the far wall lists company names and there it is: Blackbox Cybersecurity. Eleventh floor.

I point to the listing, white plastic letters plugged onto a black board. "This is it," I tell him.

He calls the elevator, still having exchanged the bare minimum of words. While we wait, I feel his eyes on me. When I look over, he doesn't look away. I can't read his expression.

"Are you okay?" he asks. There's a kindness to the question that surprises me.

"Yes," I lie. "I'm fine." The truth is I'm scared of what we're going to find upstairs.

When the elevator arrives, we both climb on. My shoulders are tense, pulse racing. Maybe there will be key-card security and an abrupt end to this errand; in fact, I'm hoping for it, aware that my heart is stuttering with dread.

But when he presses the button for the eleventh floor, the elevator starts to move. We stand awkwardly side by side as the red light travels, illuminating one number after the next with a pleasant ding. He is close, barely an inch between us, though there's plenty of room for him to be farther. I am aware of his heat, of his scent. A kind of warm sandalwood, maybe.

The ride seems long, the elevator slow.

What will we find when it opens?

Will you be sitting at a desk, diligently working, embarrassed for me to see that you haven't disappeared at all? That you're just done with me?

Maybe you'll bluster with embarrassment. Maybe you'll rage. Perhaps you'll cut and run from this detective who has questions about a missing girl, someone you dated. How will you answer the thousand questions I have?

Will it be a busy office? Posh and populated with smart people sitting behind big computer screens. Maybe it will be gray and run-down, flickering fluorescent lights, rickety furniture.

But it's none of these things. It's just an empty space, lights out — a reception desk, a small room filled with a scattering of white, modern desks, and ergonomic swivel chairs, some file cabinets. We step into the small foyer, and the elevator doors close behind us. Quiet, the aura of abandonment hums.

"You're sure this is the place?" asks Kirk, with a frown.

"No," I admit. "I'm not."

"Hello?" he calls out, but his voice just bounces around the empty space.

144

He walks into the main area, starts looking in desks. Not knowing what else to do, I follow, feeling like an interloper.

The desktops gleam with newness; slim drawers clean and empty. Everything seems unused, one of the chairs still with remnants of shrink-wrapping. There are no personal items — coffee cups or framed pictures. Even the wastepaper baskets are pristine. I lose myself for a time, looking for any other little piece of you. I'm wearing your watch. It's far too big for my wrist. When I put it to my ear, its ticking is loud, a beating heart.

We open closet doors, peer into an empty conference room.

I've been tingling since I saw that article, felt the newsprint against my fingers. I run from my past, want nothing to do with the person I used to be. She's dead and gone. For the first time in a long time, I can feel the darkness breathing on the back of my neck, a hand reaching from beyond the grave.

I've escaped her darkness into the life I've built in the light. It's a little lonely, sure. But at least I can help people, have friends, an adopted family thanks to Jax, a home. Dear Birdie would say: *You can choose and create the life you want. You are the author of your reality.*

That reality was enough for me before you. Before you awakened a hunger to be known.

Inside my bag, my phone is vibrating. I ignore it, but no sooner than it stops, it starts again. Glancing around for Bailey Kirk, I don't see him, but hear footsteps, the sound of cabinets opening and closing in a room behind a closed door — probably a break room.

The phone keeps vibrating, and I reach in to dig it out as I keep walking, coming to a stop by a desk in the only office with a door, its back wall a floor-to-ceiling window. The number is unknown, but I answer anyway.

"Hello?"

There is only silence on the line. Then the sound of someone breathing. I clench the receiver, pull it closer. "Who's there?"

I look through the glass to the office building across the street.

There, in the window, is a large dark form. I know the shape of your shoulders, the way you carry yourself — tall and a little stiff, your movements slow and careful like you're afraid to cause yourself pain.

Is it you?

"Is it you?" I say out loud, moving closer to the window. But the dark form there moves away. I put my hand on the cool glass.

I hear something. The rumble of a voice in static. But I can't make out the words.

"Adam."

The light goes out across the street. The line goes dead. My breath leaves me.

"Hey?" Bailey's voice startles me, making me jump and spin to face him.

"Woah," he says, lifting a hand. "Sorry. Find anything?"

I shake my head, all my words jammed up in my throat.

"Who was that?" he asks.

"It was him. I saw him," I say. "There. I think."

He frowns at me, looks out the window as if to see what I was staring at. But there's just a busy office like this one might have been. People going about their business, their lives, a whole other universe. The window where he stood is dark. There *was* someone there. Wasn't there? But it doesn't make sense. How? Why?

"You saw him? In the office across the street?" he asks.

"He's — gone." There's a note of despair in my voice that shames me. I see a flash of empathy — pity? — move across his face.

We look at each other for a moment and then both bolt for the street, not bothering with the elevator, jogging down eleven

147

flights of stairs, our footfalls echoing loudly off concrete walls. We burst through the metal door that leads outside.

Bailey runs into traffic, holding out his hand, drivers stopping short, leaning on their horns in protest. I follow. On the opposite sidewalk, I scan the street, up and down, looking for you. You're taller than most people. If you're here, you'll be easy to pick out of the crowd. I want to see you so badly, run after you and grab your hand, ask you what the hell is going on? But I don't see you. Just a street full of strangers. Other strangers.

It's not hard for Kirk to gain access to the eleventh floor — with his ID and the swagger he has about him. He seems to have a way of getting people to do what he wants, including me.

A burly, middle-aged security guard escorts us up in the elevator to a posh advertising agency — all gray and white, with large screens showing slick ads for beauty and clothing, models preening, glossed lips, shiny cascades of hair, flowing fabrics. There's an ambient soundtrack playing that reminds me of a South Beach hotel, low, soothing electronic beats.

Everyone seems impossibly young and well-coiffed.

I twist at my hair, glance down at my distressed jeans and leather jacket, my cross-body bag. My urban warrior look. Jax calls it my bike messenger look, which sounds somewhat less cool though probably closer to the truth. But I haven't mastered fashion the way she has. I can't rock a muumuu on a nearly six-foot-tall frame or slip my elegantly thin form into a long black shift that clings to my perfection.

Bailey shows your picture around, but no one recognizes you, glancing up from their screens disinterested, heads shaking. I walk into the space and venture to the place where I think I saw you. People sit at silver laptops, talk into head pieces; there's a hum of voices, ringing phones. Some stare as I walk by, a raggedy stranger in their well-heeled midst.

I find my way to an empty office. From the window, I can see the place where I just stood across the street.

What's happening? What kind of game is this? Something comes back to me, a memory I don't want. I push it away.

I hear Bailey's voice; it's measured and calm. *I'm searching for a missing girl.*

He enters the room and I turn to him; the security guard is still shadowing us. He has a serious face, lots of worry lines in his brow. Wedding ring. Looks like the kind of man who commutes on the train to work, lives in the outer boroughs, married, lots of kids, watches the game on Sunday. He's getting impatient, seems suspicious now of our errand.

"What was the name of your firm again?" he asks.

"Turner and Ives," Bailey answers. I make a mental note to research them further.

"Are you sure it was him?" asks Bailey, coming up close.

I am, but I'm not. The encounter has taken on a strange patina.

"I don't know," I admit.

"You don't know what you saw, what you heard?" I see why he has the furrow in his brow; it deepens with his frown.

When I don't answer him, he puts an arm around my shoulders, starts shepherding me toward the door. It's an oddly manly gesture, one I'm sure some women wouldn't like. Like he's the strong one, and I'm the fragile waif who needs to be helped away. But there's something about his scent, about his aura. Or maybe it's me. I am shaken and confused. I let him move me toward the door.

"Let's go," he says. "You look like you've seen a ghost."

"That's the second time I've heard that today," I answer.

He frowns at me again, but there's a glimmer of amusement in his eyes. His gaze is as clear and green as a river, rushing over me, through me. We leave with no answers, no closer to you, only more questions.

FOURTEEN

Then

Rewilding.

That was my father's word and what he wanted for us, why he moved us out into the middle of nowhere. He wanted us to disconnect from the toxic modern world, and return to nature where we belonged.

After Jay showed me the tree house, he went back to ignoring me. So while my mother tried to get us settled, cleaning, stocking the kitchen, unpacking boxes, and my father, Jay at his side, worked on repairs, I lay on the stiff bed in the unfamiliar room and quietly wept — missing my life back home, my friends who I had no way to contact, even my school.

When the tears dried up, I explored the house. The master bedroom, which now belonged to my parents, had been my grandparents' room. There was a big brass bed, and a rocking chair beside a window with a view of the trees. Jay had the room that belonged to my father. Old model airplanes hung from the ceiling, some football trophies on a shelf. In the desk drawer, I found a picture of someone who looked like Jay standing on the porch, looking smart in a suit, his arm around a pretty girl in a flowered dress.

"Who's this?" I asked my mother, bringing it to her.

"That's your father," she said with smile. "Wasn't he gorgeous?"

I couldn't reconcile that boy — carefree, smiling — with the man he was now. It seemed impossible.

There were lots of pictures, albums stored in a chest in the living room. My father pored over them, sharing stories about his childhood, people long passed. But I didn't really listen. And the people in the pictures looked pinched and joyless, hardened by life and circumstance. They looked like the kind of people who would yell at you if you made too much noise.

Then I discovered the study, a room with just a desk, a big chair, and shelves and shelves of dusty books. Books about trees, about flowers. Volumes about birds, and local fauna. There were guides on tracking, hunting, storing and preparing food. There was a big book about guns, about bomb making, about survival. *Bush Craft 101. The Survival Medicine Handbook. When the Grid Goes Down.*

Sitting in the creaking chair, I disappeared into Emily Dickinson, Robert Frost, William Carlos Williams, Yeats, Thoreau. And, of course, Rilke. I was a gifted reader. Even if some of the concepts eluded me, the words resonated.

Alone and isolated, I read and read — learning about the land we lived on and how to survive the end of the world, about the fearsome beauty and gifts of nature, and the magic of words.

Each night at dinner, my father wanted to know what we had discovered about the property that day.

I already knew that silence wasn't an option. Jay went on about the barn with tools, an old graveyard. Jay told me not to talk about the tree house, so instead I talked about the dolls I found under the bed, the owl I saw in the tree outside my window, staring at me with the wisdom of ages. About the books in the study.

"Those were my father's," he said. "He was a big reader, like you."

The way he said it, I wasn't sure if it was a good thing or a bad thing.

"Try to get outside," he said finally. "Let the land talk to you. There's only so much you can learn from books."

I just nodded. There was no arguing if you didn't want to earn his wrath.

In the photos we had in our old house, my father was smooth faced, with a square jaw and a smile in his eyes, striking in his uniform. But out here, his hair was wild, his beard growing in. His eyes were often flat, or distant, or staring at something none of us could see.

"Give it a chance."

"She will," said my mother, always eager to head off that moment when he lost his temper. She put a hand on my arm.

"I will," I said, eager to help her. "It's pretty here."

The words, spoken in fear, tasted dry on my tongue.

He nodded his approval, eating the stew my mother made. "Even food tastes better out here, doesn't it?"

We all agreed. Maybe it was even true.

The next morning, when the sun was barely lighting the sky, he pushed into my room.

"You're not spending another day with your nose buried in books, kiddo," he said. His form was dark, filling the doorway.

155

"Come with me."

I dressed quickly — jeans, a hand-me-down sweatshirt of Jay's, my Converse Chuck Taylors, red and broken in just right, like all the cool kids at school. Usually it was my brother following behind Dad, me watching, feeling both left out and relieved. But that morning I followed him outside.

He sat on the porch step and I sat next to him.

"Listen."

"To what?"

"Just listen."

As we sat there, and the sun rose painting the sky pink, the trees came alive with birdsong. I'd come to know their individual calls: the melodic trill of the scarlet tanager, the buzz of the black-throated green warbler, the *cock-a-ree!* of the red-winged blackbird. The wind made its own music rustling through the leaves, whistling in the eaves.

My father ran a hand through his hair, then dropped it heavily on my shoulder.

"That's what we're supposed to hear, not the blaring of an alarm, street noise, sirens, television chatter. This is the real world. Everything out there is fake, toxic."

I felt something shift inside me. A thing that had clung and resisted, railed and

156

raged, let go. A breath that I had been holding released.

"Today, I'm going to teach you how to garden."

That morning was the first time I glimpsed her, a girl in the woods. As I followed my father to the patch of land he'd cleared for the garden where we would grow our own vegetables, I caught sight of her in the trees. She smiled at me, but when I raised my hand in greeting she turned and ran.

"I saw someone," I said, rushing to catch up with my father. His big strides put him far ahead, me always scrambling to keep up. Jay was as tall as he was now, not as big or strong. But they walked in step, side by side when they were together. "In the woods."

"I didn't see anyone," said my father, looking behind us.

"A girl."

He shook his head. "Just a rabbit probably."

Wild wheat-colored hair, tiny, a tattered flower-printed shirt over jeans, dirty. I thought to argue, then bit my tongue.

"There *are* other folks nearby," he said. "People who choose to live the way we want to, keep to themselves. You'll meet them soon enough I imagine."

This thought cheered me, too. Other

people. New friends, maybe.

He looked behind us again. "But for now, it's just you and me, kid."

The rest of the day passed in a blur of effort — helping to finish clearing, hoeing, aerating the soil, hauling water from the creek, planting seeds, and seedlings he bought in town. The sun was warm, but the air was cool in the shade, the day breezy and fresh. I was sweating with effort, dirt under my nails. But somehow it didn't feel dirty or hard, somehow that dirt felt cleaner than anything else I'd ever touched.

At lunch, we sat under the shade of a big oak tree and ate peanut butter sandwiches, and apples my father had packed in his rucksack, drank water from his metal canteen. I noticed that he was still wearing his dog tags, the metal flashing in the sunlight. He was right. Food did taste better here.

"You're a hard worker," he said. "That's good. I know this — isn't easy. But you're strong."

I swelled with pride, looked up at him and ventured a smile, which he returned. We didn't know each other, not really; we were strangers just starting to understand each other better. He'd been deployed for most of my life. Jay had had much more time with him. When I looked in his face, I saw my brother, but I didn't see myself.

I wanted to say something, but instead I just stared at him, taking in the hills and valleys of his face, the straw of his beard, the shine in his eyes. He didn't seem to mind.

In the afternoon after he'd finished his studies, Jay joined us, and the work went faster. I couldn't shake the feeling that someone was watching me. Kept glancing through the trees, hoping for another glimpse of the girl I was sure I saw. But I didn't see her again, not that day.

We were out there working until the sun started to dip; then we walked back to the house, a rare moment of harmony and well-being. We ate a big, peaceful meal together. And I thought as I helped my mother clean the kitchen that maybe my father was right. That this place was where we belonged.

That night I slept dreamless and deep.

FIFTEEN

Now

Bailey and I ride the train to Brooklyn, sitting close but not talking. Silence. I guess that's his thing. He has insisted on escorting me home. I suppose I should be offended. After all, I don't need some guy to get me safely to my doorstep, do I? I've been taking care of myself for a good long time.

But tonight as the sun dipped and the sky turned to tiger stripes of black and orange, and a cold wind blew, I found I really didn't want to be alone. So I didn't stop him from following me to the subway, or getting on the train with me.

Now, as the train rumbles us home, I keep flashing on that form in the office window. But it wasn't you, was it? How could it be? My mind is playing tricks on me.

It wouldn't be the first time.

The same question is on a loop in my head: *Who are you?*

Bailey's shoulder presses against mine. There's a draw to him, a comfort in his physical presence. I don't shift away, and notice that he doesn't either.

A muscle works in his jaw; his foot taps. These must be his tells for when he's deep in thought. His phone keeps buzzing in his pocket; I notice that he doesn't pull it out to see who's calling.

"So," he says finally, the train still racing and jostling. "I'm trying to understand this. Your phone rings, a call from an unknown number, and you picked it up."

"That's right."

"You thought you heard a voice, but you can't be sure."

I don't say anything, nodding my assent. Across from us, an older woman in a heavy coat reads a paperback with the cover ripped off. Her shoes are scuffed; the bag on the ground between her legs is packed with random items, a doll, a newspaper, a colorful shawl. I wonder what her story is. Everyone has a story, a problem, a question.

"You thought you saw someone in the building across the street," Bailey goes on, snapping me back to *my* story, *my* problem. "Someone watching you. You thought it might be Adam."

Again, just a mute nod. His recounting of events makes me seem wobbly, unstable.

"You know that doesn't make any sense, right?"

I bristle. What is it with this guy?

"That's what happened," I say, sounding peevish even to my own ear. "It doesn't matter if it makes sense to you."

That earns me another worried frown. He's doubting my sanity. Maybe he thinks I'm just another *troubled* girl, like the one he's chasing. But how can I explain to him a moment that seemed real to me, but not to him. I can't. Perception is a head trip, very personal.

At my stop, Bailey follows me onto the platform, falls into step beside me. As we wind through the streets and near my house, there's woodsmoke in the air, indoor lights are glowing. The piano music again, carrying tinny and distant on the air. It's one of the things I like about my neighborhood, that it seems small, a quaint patch in the teeming morass of the city.

On the steps, I say, "Do you want to come in?"

Mostly just to be polite. Mostly.

He'll take off, I'm sure, back to whatever it is that private investigators do — following, watching, digging deep into the dark, back alleys of lives, seeing what people are trying to hide, finding what's been lost.

He looks around uncertainly, up, then down the street. Then he surprises me with a quick nod, climbing up the steps, waiting as I unlock the door. Inside, he hangs his jacket next to mine on one of the hooks in the foyer. When I slip off my shoes, he does, as well.

"Coffee?" I ask.

"Thanks," he says.

As I brew the coffee in my construction site of a kitchen, he walks around, inspecting. It doesn't bother me. He looks at pictures I have on the wall. A grainy of photo of Jay and Mom standing by a tall oak holds his attention for a while. He touches the windowsills, the wainscoting, looks at the set of German knives I keep in a block on the countertop.

"This is quite a place you have here."

"Thank you," I say, even though that could mean a lot of things coming from someone like Bailey Kirk. It doesn't necessarily sound like a compliment.

New Yorkers are always interested in real estate — how you found your place, how you can afford it, walk-up or elevator, doorman or not. Owning a town house in Brooklyn Heights? Not just a single floor but the whole damn thing. That raises eyebrows. It's like deep space — mysterious and difficult to fathom — how anyone makes enough to afford to live well in this city.

What are you, a Saudi prince? you asked when I brought you here for the first time.

"How long have you lived here?" Bailey asks now.

I froth the almond milk, pour it into the coffee, hand him his cup. He nods his thanks. I remember that he likes it the same as I do.

"About three years now," I say. "It was a wreck when I bought it — still is. I've been fixing it up slowly. It's not nearly done."

I lucked into this place, alerted to a distressed property auction by a Realtor friend. Still it took almost everything I had, and I spent the first year living in an uninsurable property that was on the verge of being condemned — with lots of company. Roaches, rats in the attic, even a stray cat in the yard who has since moved on. I spent all my free time watching YouTube videos, figuring out how to fix and repair, finding people who could do the things I couldn't. I like it, fixing a broken, neglected thing, making it whole. Now, it's mine, clanging pipes, and uneven floors, middling paint job, and all.

It feels like you. That's what you said about it, Adam. *Warm, embracing, elegant but not fancy. Charming but not cloying.*

You seemed to fit right in here — you sank into the couch, took over the kitchen. And the bedroom. Oh, yes, you were a master in the bedroom. That's where we spent most of our time — and in the soaking tub, and the big shower. Just thinking about you brings up heat.

I wait for Bailey to say what people usually do — *it must cost a fortune.* Or more boldly, *how can you afford this place?* But he doesn't say anything like that, just gratefully drinks the coffee I gave him.

In the living room, I make a fire. Bailey sits on the window seat, looks outside to the street. I figure he has more questions, otherwise why would he be here? But he doesn't ask them right away. When the fire is crackling, I stare into the flames for a minute, just sitting there, holding my coffee.

I try to make sense of what's happening but can't. The things Bailey Kirk has told me, the picture of you that looks like a stranger. I can't fit those things with the man I've known these last few months. Who are you, Adam?

You lied. You're a liar. You're someone

totally different than I believed you to be. I've lied, too, hidden things — important facts about myself and my life. But what I felt for you was true. The time, my love, it was real. The first rumble of anger vibrates beneath my shock and sadness.

"Adam left some things in the apartment," I say finally. "The vacation rental host gave them to me."

Bailey's eyebrows lift in surprise. "What kind of things?"

I tell him about my conversation and meeting with Joe, share with him the contents of the box I found. I take each thing out of my bag and place it on the coffee table, lining them up neatly so that I can look at each thing. Kirk sinks into the seat beside me on the couch. We sit with our legs touching, looking at the items spread out before us.

Your hoodie. The notebook. The pen. The shave kit. I take the watch off my wrist, lay it down.

Not the article. I don't have to share that, do I?

Why do we trust this guy? Robin. She's a shadow, a trick of light, a tiny little wisp of a thing, with spindly legs and straw for hair. Her shins are covered with cuts and bruises, her jeans torn. She's a bird, a squirrel, a rush of leaves taken by the wind.

Robin, my childhood friend. She's as real as anyone is to me. Maybe she's even more real than you are, Adam. It's just that I'm the only one who can see her.

I don't answer her now, not with a stranger in the room. He already thinks I'm unstable.

Why *do* we trust him? I don't know. Maybe we don't.

"Can I take these things?" he asks. "The lab back at my firm. We might be able to get some DNA evidence. Of course, it's been through a lot of hands."

I am reluctant to give any piece of you up. But I nod. I want to cling to these things, especially the sweater. But I should know better. We don't get to keep anything.

He must see it on my face.

"I'm sorry," he says, his voice soft, deep. "I know he hurt you."

I wave him off, feign nonchalance. "He was just a guy I met online."

You trust him because he looks like Jay. Just like Jay, says Robin.

Yes, the golden hair and grayish green eyes, the coolness, the mettle, that way of a guy who fixes and finds. She's right. Robin is a keen observer.

Bailey flips through the pages of the notebook. Will he find something I didn't see?

167

He comes to the page with my handwriting on it, holds it out to me. I probably shouldn't have done that. Tampering with evidence or some such, right?

"I wrote that," I admit. He just nods, keeps paging through the book.

"Will you tell me about Mia?" I ask. "Your client's daughter."

He glances up from the empty black Moleskine, and those eyes. Yes, he looks just like Jay. Too much like Jay. I look away, feeling the breath in my lungs.

"What do you want to know?" He puts the notebook down.

"Her story."

He sighs and leans back, seems to consider. Then, "Mia? Her mother died when she was young and, according to her father, she never really got over it. She struggled with depression, then addiction in high school. Then an eating disorder. She got help finally, went to rehab. Her father, he stood by her, did the right things. She went to college, seemed to have her act together, wanted to be a writer. She started a blog, was having some success."

Sounds a little too familiar. Do you have a type, Adam Harper? Adam Grove? Or is it Raife Mannes? How many names do you have?

168

"Then a friend encouraged her to try Torch. She started dating here and there. Nothing serious. Hookups, really, according to her father. Which he didn't love, but she was a grown woman."

He leans forward, picks up the pen, turns it this way and that, then places it carefully back on the coffee table.

"Not much Thorpe could do, really. And then there was Raife — or Adam. Or whatever his name is. Her father said that she changed almost overnight. He thought she might be using again. She abandoned her writing, dropped out of school. And then, she was just gone. And Raife Mannes, he turned out to be a ghost — all his profiles disappeared, his cell phone disconnected, his address a fake. My client hasn't heard from his daughter in nine months."

Bailey leans back in his seat, rubs at his temples. "This was my first lead in a while. I hate to have to tell him that the trail is cold again."

"What do you think happened to her?"

He shrugs, drains the last of his coffee. "Do you know that people just walk away from their lives all the time? I mean like thousands of people, usually men, walk out on jobs, on families. They cash out ac-

169

counts, and shift off their life like an old skin."

I know all about that, yes, I think. But say instead, "Did she do that? Cash out accounts?"

"Her accounts were cleared. By her? By someone else? I don't know."

He lifts and replaces the notebook, the watch.

"What about you? Did he take anything from you?" he asks.

"No," I say. "I checked."

"Keep checking."

I nod my agreement.

"What about her phone? Her blog? Her social media? Her credit cards?" I press.

I know a thing or two about finding the lost — those people who walk away. Dear Birdie hears about them all the time. From the children looking for parents, the wives looking for their husbands, the lonely hearts who give their money and their love away. More people walk away than are taken, I think. That's what Jason, our consulting PI, has told me. More people abandon the life they built than are wrested from it. It's not a crime.

You should know, says Robin. She's over by the fireplace now, squatting, poking a stick into the flames. I ignore her.

170

"We found her phone, her purse, and her wallet in her apartment," Bailey goes on. "She hasn't used a credit card, or posted on social media, or on her blog since she disappeared."

"Do you think she walked away? Or do you think he . . . hurt her?"

You were gentle with me, Adam. Respectful. Loving. Kind. You wouldn't hurt anyone, would you? Not like that. You're not a monster.

But now that you're gone, it's as if you were never really here. You could have been anyone, I knew so little about you.

But no. Our last hours together, as we wrapped around each other in the dark. Wasn't there a knowledge there, an intimacy that went beyond your name, your job, your address? I'm sure there was. At least for me.

I almost tell Bailey about the life *I* walked away from, about the article I found and how it means that you knew about me before I told you. I nearly reveal my secret identity as Dear Birdie.

Why would I do that? Reveal myself to this man I barely know.

Of course, I don't. It's not relevant to this, to his hunt for Mia Thorpe, for you.

Are you sure about that? asks Robin.

171

Stop being a brat, I think. She shoots me a look.

I never told you about Dear Birdie, Adam. I would have eventually, I suppose. But I just hadn't pulled back that particular curtain yet. There are so many layers to me. But maybe not as many as there are to you. Are you a killer? A predator?

What would you have taken from me if you hadn't run from Bailey Kirk?

Because that's what you did, right? Somehow you discovered that Bailey Kirk had caught up with you. You ran. You had to.

"It's possible she walked away. It's possible he hurt her," says Bailey into the silence that has grown between us. "But there's no evidence — no blood, no body, no trace of either of them. All Mia's money is gone. She had quite a bit. Enough to live somewhere cheap for a while if that's what she wanted."

Where would you go? South America, I suppose. Mexico? Where could one live cheaply and anonymously? There's a man I know. He wrote a book about how to disappear completely and never be found. He's been on the show. *There are all kinds of reasons people choose to leave their lives behind,* he said. *Some of them are understandable — debt, affairs, unhappy marriages,*

172

escape from justice. Others are personal. You may never know why.

"You said there were others," I say.

Outside a siren wails up the street. It's loud since we're at street level. He waits to reply. Then, "Other women missing after meeting a man on Torch, yes. Two others that I know of since starting the investigation into Mia Thorpe, from my contact at the dating site."

"Him? Adam?"

"The pictures are not the same, unless the photos are very old, unless he's changed his appearance dramatically, or he used other images from his profile, but there were similarities in the information. Rilke poetry, a kind of ironic, anti-dating-site vibe, bookish, dark."

"Do you have the profile pictures?"

He takes his phone from his pocket and I see that there are five missed calls and eleven unread texts. How can he stand it?

He opens the photo app and shows me. The pictures are grainy, lots of movement and blurred lines. In one, a thin young man stands by a lake, turns away smiling. It could be you — as a teenager, thinner, happier. In the other, a young man with floppy brown hair, mirrored sunglasses perched on a large nose, and a full beard stands on a

173

subway platform. I see the shade of you, though either photo could easily be someone else. But I might have picked either of them from a Torch lineup. I feel the same electric jolt I felt when I first saw your image on the app.

"Where were the other women?"

"Mia Thorpe was from Philadelphia. Bonnie Cartwright was from Chicago. Melissa Farrow was from a town in upstate New York called The Hollows."

A finger traces down my spine. The Hollows. A place I know too well.

"Do you know it? The Hollows?" he asks when I don't say anything.

I shake my head, not trusting my voice. I feel the heat of his gaze. When I look at him, his slight smile unnerves. How much does he know about me?

He doesn't press, just goes on.

"All of them with troubled pasts — Bonnie the survivor of a school shooting, Melissa orphaned after a fire killed both her parents, raised by her grandparents. Mia lost her mother, struggled with addiction. They were all young women of some means. Bonnie received a big payout from a lawsuit. Mia had a trust from her mother's family. Melissa inherited her parents' life insurance policies. All struggled in the aftermath of extreme trauma — PTSD, addiction, psychotic breaks. When they disappeared, their money went, too."

He's watching me, carefully now.

"So, what about you?" he asks. "Is there something dark in your past?"

I bristle. "I don't fit your profile, Detective."

"No?"

"I'm still here."

A shrug, a nod. "True enough."

We sit a moment, engage in a brief staring contest where I lower my eyes first. He takes a card from his pocket and puts it on the table in front of us. I shift away from him on the couch. A little more of that tattoo reveals itself through the cuff of his long sleeve tee. It looks like a vine with thorns, but I'm not wearing my glasses.

"Maybe he's not done with you," he says.

Something about the way he says it makes me go cold inside.

"If he gets in touch with you again," he says, "I hope you'll give me a call. Whatever you think he is, whoever you think he is, I'm betting you're wrong. Don't protect him."

I try for a dismissive laugh, but it comes out a little too loud.

"He was just a guy I was seeing," I say. "It

175

wasn't that serious. He took nothing. He ghosted me. That's what you get for meeting a guy on Torch, right? It's like you said. Most people only want one thing from sites like that. Casual hookups. Sex. When it's over, it's over. I'm the idiot for thinking it was more."

Why are you lying? Robin asks. *I think he's trying to help you.*

Bailey sees my eyes drift over to the fireplace, and his gaze follows mine, then comes back. The worried frown again. Do I seem unstable to him? *Troubled,* like the missing girls? Maybe I am.

"Look," he says, "he used a fake name. He lied about his work, his address, all his profiles have been deleted. His phone was disconnected. He wanted something from you and didn't get it. Yet. My guess is that he's still circling you. That he'll reach out."

I remember one of your final texts. *Something's happened. I have to go. I'm sorry, Wren.*

Something's happened. Bailey Kirk happened. It's obvious.

"Or he knew how close you were to finding him," I say. "That must be why he took off, right? And now he's gone for good."

Bailey presses his mouth into a disappointed line and gets to his feet, moves

176

toward the foyer, taking those pieces of you.

I'm glad he's leaving, and part of me wishes he would stay. The night ahead seems dark and long. And there's a light that comes from Bailey — something strong, upright, good. He's not like you; everyone has layers but I don't think he's hiding anything, nothing rotten anyway. We lock eyes again, and I'd be lying if I said there wasn't some electricity there. I look away first.

"You know," he says into the quiet. "For your sake I hope you're right. Maybe your Adam Harper made me somehow, knew I was on his trail, and he's far from here, not looking back."

But I wonder if Bailey's right. You wanted something from me that you didn't get. Didn't you know that all you had to do was ask? I'm one of those desperate lonely hearts that I'm so good advising. I'd have given you anything. Followed you anywhere. What were you going to ask me? To come away with you? Is that what you asked them?

"But for *my sake,* for Mia, for Bonnie, for Melissa, I hope there's another thread I can pull. Maybe these young women walked away from their lives. Or maybe they were taken, hurt. Maybe they can still be helped. That's what I'm hoping, Miss Greenwood."

177

Is it me? Or does he lean on the name?

"I hope so, too," I say. "I hope you find Mia and all of them, that they're well and safe. That Adam is not the reason they're all gone."

Outside another siren, this one distant, the bleat of someone's horn and an angry shout.

"When you're ready to open up about whatever you're hiding, please give me a call. I can help. You can trust me — Miss Greenwood."

You can trust me. Can I? Can I trust anyone?

I look down at the card and put my hand on it, give him a weak nod, stay quiet.

I think he wants to help you, says Robin. *He wants to keep you safe.* Sometimes she's angry. I can hardly blame her. I failed us both.

The footfalls of his boots echo on the hardwood floor, then he exits the town house, closing the door softly behind him. When I head to the window to watch him walk up the street, he's already gone.

While I'm standing at the window, my phone buzzes. There's a text from an unknown number.

Don't believe what he tells you about me.

There are more layers to my truth than you can imagine.

The missive sends a little jolt through me, and I fumble with the phone to text back.

Who are you? I type quickly.

Where have you gone?

Who's Mia?

Explain this to me. Make me understand.

Please.

I walk out onto the stoop, the cold wind whipping around me, causing me to shiver.

Are you nearby? I text. Are you watching me?

I think I can feel you, scan the street for shadows, dark forms in doorways, behind trees. But the block is mostly empty, just a couple of kids walking up the opposite side, burdened with big, heavy school backpacks but laughing at something.

Why are you doing this?

I try to call the strange number but it just rings and rings. No voice mail picks up.

No answer to my texts ever come.

Finally I go back inside, a hollow in my center.

SIXTEEN

If I can't find you online, Adam, maybe I can find Mia Thorpe. I sit on my couch and pop open my laptop, enter her name into the search bar.

It isn't hard for me to find her, at least the digital trail she's left in her wake.

Between her Facebook page, her Instagram feed, her blog *Mia Writes,* she's laid bare, more or less, for all the world to see. I scroll through her Facebook profile — the expected collection of happy snapshots — girls day at the beach, martini night, birthday parties. On Instagram, she's artful — staged shots of books she's reading, the view from her window, lots of café shots with cups of coffee and treats, her own line drawings, which are elegant and yet somehow childlike focusing on subjects like birds and flowers, simple landscapes, some abstracts. Her preferred filter is Clarendon — a brightening, prettifying sheer over the life she was living.

But these are just glimpses, moments staged and curated. The surface of Mia, what she wants the world to see — someone young and pretty, light and carefree. In her blog, she goes deeper. The last entry is an essay called "The Dark Doorway." And in it, she writes about her battles with depression.

I feel like when my mother died, she took with her the Mia I saw when she looked at me. I could never find that girl in my own reflection. To Mom, I was special — bright, powerful, beautiful — her angel. To the rest of the world, I was just a girl. Small for my age, shy, passingly pretty, smart enough. Just Mia.

Some days, the despair is like a dark doorway. It stands open, waiting. If I walk through it, I know I won't come back.

I know the feeling.

I look for pieces of you in her feed. But you don't show up among the people in her life — all young and attractive, like her, bright, laughing, and full of life. I search for your shadow in the crowds on the dance floor, at parties. But you're not there. She doesn't mention meeting anyone, doesn't post a selfie with her new beau. Her posts in each feed end around the same time, more than nine months ago. No more artsy Instagram shots, no more nights out with friends, no more essays about grief and despair.

I find her on Torch by searching through the site by age, height, hair color, gender, and poetry for preferences. It takes a while; there are a lot of girls in the world that match the shallow parameters I'm searching. But finally, there she is. Her profile image is grainy; she looks off camera with a slight smile, wears a fuzzy white sweater, her golden curls a glittering cascade down her shoulders. No bikini shots or suggestive phrases, promises of no-strings encounters.

I'm looking for friendship first, then the love that could grow from that.

Mia and I would have been friends, had we ever met. It seems that you have a type. Though Mia and I don't look alike, I feel the connection. There's something kindred. Another soul looking for a way into the light from darkness. I think about the other women Bailey Kirk mentioned, all survivors of trauma, forging a path to normal.

I search through Mia's friends on Facebook and Instagram, thinking maybe I'll find you among them, or some link or lead to you. But no. If it were easy to find you, I'm guessing Bailey Kirk would have done so already.

Finally, I scroll through the comments friends left after Mia disappeared.

Where are you, Mia?

Please come home! We miss you so much!

We love you, honey. Please come back to us.

Don't do this, Mia. We can't go through this again. Please let us know you're okay, sweetie. I love you.

That one gives me pause. So — Mia has disappeared before. I try to click through to that profile, someone named January Crandall. But the account is private, not allowing friend requests. I think about messaging someone else — there are a couple of people who comment more than others, are featured most in her images.

But then I don't know what I would say.

I'm looking for my boyfriend, who disappeared with Mia? What can you tell me about her, about them? Weird. No one would answer that. I certainly wouldn't.

Scrolling back through Mia's essays, I find one about her struggles with addiction — pills. She doesn't specify what, just that she was prescribed something for anxiety and took too much, found she couldn't get through a day without it. Started getting more pills from a dealer, someone she thought was a friend.

The combination of whatever I was taking, it messed with my sleep, then my reality — until I didn't know what was real, what I was dreaming. Maybe it was the best thing, though. It forced me to get help for all the things beneath the addiction.

Bailey mentioned this. You also told me that your ex had problems.

If there is one thing I know about addicts, it's that they are prone to disappearing. This gives me a glimmer of hope. Maybe you didn't have anything to do with her disappearance. Maybe you're not the man Bailey thinks you are. Maybe there are, in fact, more layers to your truth than I imagine.

It's late when the doorbell rings. I startle from sleep, nearly knocking my laptop to the floor. I must have drifted off as I chased Mia Thorpe down the rabbit hole.

She invaded my dreams. I chased through the acreage of our property, branches hitting me in the face, stumbling, the way I chased after Robin that last night, following her because she knew the way, and my father was right behind us. He always had the advantage on that property. Robin loved it best. But he had been born in the house, grew up tromping though the woods. He knew it better than anyone. Its trails. The tunnels. The trees with all their hidey-holes. We never had a chance.

When I finally catch Mia, grab her by her bony hand, she turns on me, a ghoul with wild eyes and sharpened teeth. *He's mine,* she hisses.

The doorbell rings again. Then I hear the sound of the key code being entered.

It's after midnight. You have the code I remember. I never changed it.

Bailey's words echo back: *What if he's not done with you?*

I don't know what scares me most — that

185

you are or that you aren't.

I walk to the door that leads to the foyer, peer around the frame. There's someone there, coming through the outer door. Who is it? On my doorstep in the night?

But it's not you.

It's Jax. I step out into the hallway as she bursts into the space, her breath ragged, grabbing me into a tight embrace, then releasing me and heading in. She fills the senses with bright colors and the pleasant mingling of her perfume, her shampoo, something else like cinnamon that is just her.

In the living room, I see that she is crying, that her hair is coming loose from the scarf, that her dress is ripped at the collar. Jax doesn't cry. Alarm rockets through me.

"What happened? What's wrong?"

I take her back into my arms and she clings to me.

"I hooked up with some guy," she says.

"On Torch?"

She shakes her head. "Instagram," she says. "He was a follower. We started talking."

I take her red cashmere coat, her Louis Vuitton tote that cost more than a used car.

"He spammed me," she says, sitting on the couch. She takes the scarf out of her

186

hair and her dark tresses cascade around her shoulders. "About a week ago he followed me on Instagram, started liking all my posts, made some intelligent comments. He said he was a family therapist. It seemed like he was *on the path,* you know. And — he was hot. When he DM'd me, I gave him my number. We've been — talking."

Talking is kind of a big deal. It's not messaging. It's not texting. Voice contact is for real.

"I met him tonight. We had dinner. It was nice. Then we went back to his place. And he got — aggressive."

"Did he hurt you?" I say, touching her dress. I turn on the light, so I can see her skin. But she doesn't look hurt. No marks or bruises. Her hands are shaking. She's shivering a little. I put a blanket around her shoulders.

"I felt mauled, pushed. I told him I was gonna go. He tried to *keep me* from leaving his place." She pauses, takes a breath, touches her shoulder. "He *ripped* my dress."

I reach for her again. "Are you *okay*?"

She puts her head into her hands as I rub her back.

Then, "I'm okay." She looks up, eyes filled with tears.

The volume and texture of Jax's beauty

cannot be captured with words — her glowing skin, glittering eyes, spectacular cheekbones. Her real name is Jasmine. She calls herself Jax because she would *not be named* after a Disney princess, but she has that kind of cartoonish prettiness, as if someone drew the perfect her.

"But I *felt something* you know. I thought he was a good guy. I thought that this was the *real* thing. But as soon as we got back to his place, he was on me."

She wipes at her eyes angrily, pulls back her shoulders. "I — shouldn't have gone back with him. I thought we were just going to have a drink."

I put up a palm.

"Woah. Just because you go back to someone's place doesn't give him the right to expect more than you're willing to give."

We hear this a lot, women blaming themselves for being assaulted. *I shouldn't have gone back to his place, his hotel room, his car.* The truth is a nice man, a good guy, never forces himself on you. When you want to leave, he lets you. He accepts whatever disappointment he might feel, treats your feelings with respect. He lets you set the pace. I remind her of this advice we have to give, often, to all different kinds of women. There are really good men out there; and they know how to behave. When a man tries to force himself on you, doesn't let you change your mind, or leave — that's assault.

"I know, I know," she says. "But — how could I have been so wrong about the kind of man he was?"

Good question. I'm asking myself the same thing.

I thought *you* were a good guy, Adam. Smart and funny. A hard worker, into your profession, a considerate lover, a good cook, a listener, a friend. We laughed and shared ourselves. We spent Sundays in bed watching classic movies. I made you French toast. It wasn't any good, but you ate it anyway, offering praise and enthusiasm for my effort.

Maybe we're all so confused these days about what's real and what isn't, what's authentic, what's fake, that our instincts for the truth have been dulled.

That's what my father would say.

Jax's phone pings. She holds it up. I see a picture of a guy with a goatee and smiley eyes, dark skin, kind smile. " 'I'm sorry,' " she reads aloud from the text that comes through. " 'Please forgive me.' "

"Don't answer," I say.

She puts the phone down but keeps staring at it. It pings again.

" 'I misread your signals,' " she reads. She gives me a look, grabs the phone.

"I liked you," she says aloud as she types with her thumbs, red nails blazing. "That doesn't mean I wanted to sleep with you right away. We could have talked. Had a drink. Seen each other again. You didn't have to jump me the second I was in your door."

She hits Send.

Nothing comes back. We both sit there, staring at the pulsing dots. Finally, another ping.

" 'You're a tease,' " she reads, eyes flashing with anger. "Oh, no, he *did not* just say that."

"God! Really?" I say. "Fuck this guy."

We block his number, then get online on my computer, and block him from all her socials. And just like that, he's gone. Ghosted — can't comment on her feeds, can't call her. He officially doesn't exist.

When we're done, we sit on the couch and she cries in my lap while I stroke her hair. The fire is just embers, and the room has taken on a chill the way old places will. Things seem dark and sad, empty.

"Okay," she says, sitting up. "Pity party over."

"Right," I agree, squeezing her hand.

"Now, you," she says, tracing her lower lids with manicured fingers, fixing the smear of mascara. "Tell me everything."

"Nothing to tell," I lie. "He's gone. I haven't heard from him."

She squints at me. "No. There's something else going on. What is it?"

I want to tell her about Bailey, about the article, about the office, the missing women and the connection to The Hollows, the town where I spent part of my life. But I know if I do, she'll be all up in it. She'll be on the phone with Jason, our private investigator; the thing will come alive with her energy and heat. I need to be alone with it for now. I need to think.

"Really," I say. "Sometimes people just leave us. It sucks. It hurts. But you can't hold on to someone who wants to get away. You have to move on."

"You sound like Dear Birdie."

I shrug. "I am Dear Birdie."

"You don't have to handle everything alone, you know." In other words, she knows I'm keeping things from her. And like any good friend she's letting me keep my secrets, knowing I'll spill it when I'm ready.

"I know."

I make her some tea and take her upstairs to my guest room, give her a pair of clean

191

pajamas, turn on the light by the bed. The room is cozy and comfortable, soft blankets and big throw pillows. She's slept here many times; I often think of it as Jax's room.

"I guess I was lonelier than I thought," she says, climbing into bed. "I thought this was the *real thing.* Not just some Torch hookup."

"I know the feeling," I say, sitting beside her. Smart women, both of us. Successful. Good people. Kind. Loving friends. Why is this so hard?

"Please tell me what's going on," she says. "Wren, please. Tell me."

I hesitate again, but she takes my hand and squeezes.

"We're in this *together,* right?" she says when I stay silent. So, I give her the abridged version — that your profiles have disappeared, that a detective is looking for you. That you might not have been who I think you were.

"So, *who is he?*" Jax whispers when I'm done.

I flash on my dream, chasing Mia though the woods. On another night, it might have been Robin. Every now and then when I catch the person I'm chasing, it's a younger version of myself.

"I have no idea," I have to admit. The man

192

you were with me might simply be a fiction. Someone you created — or I did.

Jax looks young and frightened in the dim light of the room. She's not the powerhouse she usually is, the ass kicker, the influencer, the woman-up guru with all the answers. She's just my friend. Someone who needs my comfort and love as much as I need hers. Someone who, at the moment, is as lost in this crazy modern world as I am, as all the people who come to us for advice.

I have no idea who you really are, Adam. But I am going to find out.

I tuck her in and kiss her on the head like a child. She's asleep before I leave the room.

I change and get into my own bed, turn on the television.

More bad news. That virus, it's spreading from China to Europe. There's talk of a lockdown, borders closing for containment. Wildfires rage out of control in Australia. The honeybees are disappearing, no one knows why. When did the news become worse than any dystopian fiction we could imagine?

As I open my laptop and dig into the virtual lives of Melissa and Bonnie, I find myself thinking that maybe my father, the end of the world prophet, the doomsday prepper, had it right after all.

SEVENTEEN

Bailey Kirk walked up the street quickly, aware that Wren Greenwood might watch him go. He found his way to the truck he had parked around the corner and climbed inside. The interior was cold; it had been sitting all day. He cranked the heat and rubbed his hands together until the cold air from the vents started to blow hot.

He checked his phone. Five voice mail messages to which he didn't want to listen. Eleven texts he didn't bother to read.

He scrolled through. Mostly they were from Nora. A couple from Diana. His bosses. He was in the doghouse.

Three were from Sabrina:

Hey, what are you doing tonight?

Netflix and takeout?

So — what? Are you ghosting me? She

194

finished it with a ghost emoji.

He typed in what he hoped was a not-too-curt, but clear response: Not ghosting you. Out of town. Call you tomorrow.

Sabrina. She was a nice girl, sweet and funny — a superhot redhead with a big laugh, and a bombshell body. But their encounter had been a mistake, the result of too much to drink and not enough foresight after a company happy hour. He'd been trying to disentangle himself ever since.

He watched the screen, little dots pulsing.

Whatever, B. No biggie.

He wondered how to respond and then didn't, deleting the text chain, as he did with all nonprofessional communications on his phone. He was often confounded by modern communications, relationships, how they worked and didn't work. The only thing that really made sense to him was the job.

When Bailey Kirk was sixteen, his mother, Lauren, lost her engagement ring — which she'd been wearing every day for the twenty years since his father, Matthew, proposed.

She knew it had been on her hand in the morning when she was cleaning the breakfast dishes, because she'd noted how it caught the light streaming in from the kitchen window, casting rainbow shards on the wall. She'd taken Bailey and his younger sister, Ellie, to the high school they attended — there was no bus. She'd gone to the grocery store, done some laundry, then went out to prepare the fallow garden for spring, which the groundhog had just predicted was coming early.

The ring was loose. She'd lost a bit of weight lately thanks to cutting out carbs and going from two glasses of wine in the evening to one and sometimes none. She was never a thin woman; she was strong and fit, a powerful tennis player, a yogi, a walker. She was always looking for a way to cut this or that, lose this or that.

Bailey Kirk thought his mother was the most beautiful woman in the world. So did his dad.

You're perfect, his dad told her often and loudly. *Kids, your mom is perfect.*

Far from it, she'd demure, smiling.

She had glittering brown eyes that always smiled, soft skin, warm arms always waiting to hug and hold. She had a heady laugh that filled Bailey with happiness when he earned it through his jokes or his antics. She made a killer banana bread. She got mad. Bad grades, messy room, back talk, broken curfew, dirty clothes on the floor — you were going to get a tongue-lashing. But there was no anger, not really. Never yelling. Rarely was there even punishment — which was probably why he never really learned to clean his space. He'd just pile all the mess in the closet or under the bed, knowing what she couldn't see, she wouldn't go looking for. Now, a grown man, he was neat to the point of being fastidious. But then, he was an unapologetic slob.

By the time Lauren was making dinner that night — a one-pot baked ziti with ground turkey that everyone liked — the ring was gone. She was still wearing her wedding band. But the engagement ring with the big two-carat diamond was not on her finger.

She went upstairs. There was a ring dish on a shelf in her walk-in closet where she put the engagement ring and matching platinum wedding band, also studded with diamonds, when her hands were swelling. She didn't think she'd taken it off, usually took off both when she did. The dish was empty.

The world came to a grinding halt, dinner stalled, homework interrupted.

"Guys, can you help me?"

She was shaky, had tears in her eyes. The

three of them — Bailey, Ellie, and Mom — moved through the house, the car, the garden, looking in all the nooks and crannies, under the mat in the car, between the couch cushions. Ellie looked through Mom's purse, her drawers. In the garden, Bailey took the rake and scraped through the soil his mother had just turned and aerated. About an hour in, Mom started to cry. Just sat on the couch and wept. Both Bailey and Ellie stopped to sit beside her and wrap her up in their arms, the way she had done for them so many times over lost friendships, or bullies, or homework frustration.

"Don't worry," Bailey said. "I'll find it."

And it was that day, that moment, where he discovered an obsession for finding things that had been lost. There were only so many places where the ring could have gone. They didn't have cleaning people; he and Ellie were too old for sitters. Their older brother, who might have been a suspect in darker days, hadn't been home in almost two years. There were no strangers moving through the house that day — plumbers or electricians or whatever. So, it hadn't been stolen. The ring was loose, but not that loose. So, Bailey deduced that there were only so many conditions under which it might have fallen from her finger without her noticing.

Matthew was handy, and he'd taught Bailey how to do things — like change a tire, fix a running toilet, unclog a drain. Bailey didn't always pay attention, his mind on other things like video games and soccer and the weird feelings he had about certain girls who used to be his friends with whom he'd played hide-and-seek and caught toads in the creek behind his house, but who now smelled like flowers and wore lip gloss. But sometimes he *did* pay attention to his dad's instruction, because he liked to understand how things worked, little everyday mysteries solved.

He got his father's toolbox and went to the kitchen. The pipe under the sink had a dip. If the ring went down the drain while his mother was doing the dishes that morning, there was a chance it was still sitting there. He turned off the water to the sink, got the wrench, and removed the pipe. He dumped the contents into his hand, while Ellie and Mom looked on hopefully. There, in a revolting glob of soapy grime, was his mother's diamond ring.

She sobbed as he handed it back to her. It wasn't the ring. It wasn't its cost or its value. It was her husband, his father, and her love for him, and their history and their memories, and the way she cherished that glittering symbol of Matthew's love. His father could have bought her another ring, but there was no way to replace that one, how it held all the energy of their life together. Bailey was a kid, just sixteen years old, and he was confused about the world and people and himself a vast majority of the time. But he saw that, what the ring meant, and understood it with a shining clarity. Some things were not *just things,* not just dead material items with a dollar value and nothing more. Some things were like people. And everything, everyone, had to be somewhere.

And ever since that day, Bailey Kirk didn't like questions without answers. He didn't like items that were lost and could not be found. Because whether you were aware of it or not, there was always an answer. One indisputable truth about what happened and why. And the lost, they were always somewhere. There was no sucking vortex in the world where rings and watches and keys and *people* fell through and were removed from existence. The world, and the spaces contained within, were finite. There were only so many places to go. Only so many things that might have happened.

People weren't things, and when they went

missing, there were more layers, more possibilities. Inanimate objects didn't conspire to stay gone or hide from those searching for them. An object didn't have a reason for leaving its life behind. But still, the number of possibilities were finite.

He kept a picture of Mia Thorpe in the visor over the drivers' seat of his truck, and he reached for it now.

There were other missing women that he was concerned about. But Henry Thorpe was his client. And Mia was the precious child that he had lost. And there was a certain energy to that. Bailey was connected to Mia through Henry's grief. There was a gossamer strand from her being to his, a spider-silk tether that he could shorten millimeter by millimeter until they were face-to-face.

He moved the truck and found a spot up the block and across the street from Wren Greenwood's home, her stoop and lower level windows visible. He put his seat slightly back, and settled in, watching.

Time wound on and he dozed off a couple of times, startling awake, but he wasn't worried that she had left. That house, cozy, with an understated luxury, was her nest. He was betting she didn't leave unless she had good reason — work or friends or love. And he'd left her with food for thought. He'd be willing to bet that she'd spend the rest of the night on her laptop — searching for answers about Mia Thorpe and the man they had in common.

Adam Harper.

Raife Mannes.

Also, possibly Timothy Johnston.

Maybe Cliff Jensen.

A ghost in the machine. Maybe a con, a thief. Maybe a killer. Bailey had never seen him in the flesh; the guy was always one step ahead — which had Bailey wondering about a couple of things. All he was to Bailey was a series of digital images, the one thing that three missing women had in common. The one *person.* The women had lots of *things* in common — traumatic pasts, a certain amount of wealth, a willingness to look for love online. They were all fragile in some ways. He thought of Mia as someone who had been broken by grief, glued herself back together, only to be shattered again.

There was a pattern to all of this, something that connected them all, some missing piece that would lead him where he needed to go. But the pieces floated, never quite clicking. It was confounding. The client was desperate. His boss, who he called X, just to be a dork, had checked in earlier that day.

"So where are we with this?" Nora wanted to know. It was her firm, founded by her and her partner Diana. Both of them came to the work from careers in the FBI, moving into the private sector for the money and the freedom it allowed them. They were both badass — killers on the range, technical wizards. Diana knew kung fu; she bested him at the gym time and again. Nora was a relentless interrogator. He didn't bother trying to bullshit her. Ever. Nora Turner and Diana Ives; he'd worked for them for almost ten years.

She knew where he *was with this*. Nowhere. He diligently filed his daily reports via their encrypted website.

"I need a few more days," he told her. "I have a lead. Maybe."

She was quiet for a moment; she was probably reading his report as they spoke. "This Wren Greenwood? Not her name. But okay. What does she know?"

"I don't think she knows anything."

"So."

"But I think she'll lead me to him just the same. And when I find him, I find Mia."

"You're sure."

"I am."

"You don't think poor Mia is just back on drugs, holed up in a crack house somewhere."

"I don't."

"Or that she took off with him, or someone, or just wanted to get away from her helicopter father."

There were a hundred reasons why he thought not — some of it to do with her blog, her Facebook posts, the pictures he saw online, in albums in the Thorpe house, posts she left on friends' pages. Mia was on her way to wholeness, to a full and happy life — until she met Raife Mannes. She had a pattern to her engagements, a rhythm to her life and movements. She wasn't heading back to drugs.

When Bailey closed his eyes, and dug deep, he knew that wasn't what happened to her. He didn't have to explain that to Nora. She knew how it worked, the pursuit of lost people. Ten percent of it was nuts-and-bolts tracking. Ninety percent was energy — when you'd been cut off electronically anyway. When there was no cell phone, no credit card charges, no camera footage from gas stations and tollbooths, from doorbell cameras. When you had to get old school.

"I can give you a couple more days," she

said. "But without a real surge forward, I am going to have to tell Henry Thorpe that her trail is cold and stop taking his money. It's not right to keep stringing him along, giving him false hope. That's not what we do here."

That was true. The first and last word at Turner and Ives was *ethics.*

"Okay." He never bothered arguing with either one of them.

"Bailey, you know —" she started.

"I know, X. Sometimes lost stays lost."

"And people need to grieve that fact."

"Right."

A sigh, some tapping, then, "We have other cases that could use your talents. There's only one Bailey Kirk."

"Just a couple more days."

"Okay."

"Thank you."

"And stop calling me X."

End of call.

He knew it too well, that sometimes lost stayed lost. He'd learned it all kinds of hard ways since the day he found his mother's ring in the drain. He *was* estranged from his brother; they all were. After years of trying to reel him back from addiction, help him to manage his mental illness, they finally had to let him go. No one knew where he was. Bailey knew his mother never stopped looking. But Bailey had.

When lost wants to stay lost, sometimes you have no choice but to let it go.

He sat. He had a gift for that, sitting and breathing, being totally present, the watcher. The world came alive — he was aware of his breath, the squirrel running up the tree to his left, the glow of Wren's lights, the light that came on and went off on her neighbor's third floor, the man walking his little dog, talking on his phone, the man who rode by on his bike, music blaring from a speaker, the laundromat owner pulling down his gate for the night.

Then at ten minutes after midnight, he watched a slim form move hurriedly up the street and climb Wren's front stoop. For a moment, a brief electric flash of hope, he thought he might get lucky. Adam Harper returning in the night. He checked his glove box for his gun. A 9 mm Glock sat flat and dark in the mess of napkins, and papers, a crushed pack of cigarettes, some packs of Black Jack gum. A Snickers bar, a tangled mass of headphones. Well, maybe he had not grown fastidious exactly. His mom would be mad. *Bailey! Clean that up!*

He looked back at the stoop.

No. It wasn't Adam Harper — Bailey

would have to think of him as that moving forward. It was the best friend, another pretty, smart, young professional woman who, from what he'd gleaned, for some reason didn't seem to get the dangers of online dating. From her body language, he'd say she was in crisis. She let herself inside. And then everything was quiet again.

He waited. All night. Wren Greenwood was it, his last connection to Mia Thorpe.

So, when she left her town house early in the morning, the friend still inside, Bailey Kirk followed.

■ ■ ■ ■ ■

PART TWO:
REWILDING

■ ■ ■ ■

I want to unfold.
Let no place in me hold itself closed,
For where I am closed, I am false.

Rainer Maria Rilke

EIGHTEEN

MELISSA

Melissa Farrow had always, always been fascinated by fire. She loved the way it danced on the air, twisting and writhing, reaching and flickering. She didn't understand why more people didn't seem to notice what a tiny miracle of science an open flame was. Only under the right conditions could it be made, could it survive. It was fragile; the slightest breath could extinguish it. It was a roaring destructive beast, able to fell buildings. Her father could snuff a match with a calloused thumb and forefinger. But if the flame from the stove or the fireplace found its way to your skin, to your clothes, it would devour you.

The first time her mother caught her with matches, she was trying to light a pile of dead leaves her father had raked into the corner of the yard. She was ten and she wanted so badly to see those leaves go up in a tower of flames, a bonfire like the one she'd seen on the beach during a family vacation to the Jersey Shore. A great tower of light reaching into the starry sky, roaring and crackling, but so safely contained that people moved close with marshmallows on the ends of long sticks to make s'mores. She remembered how her mother held on to the collar of her shirt as she and her father inched closer, reaching out their sticks.

Be careful, Mom said, her voice tight with worry.

She's okay, her father said gently, looking down at Melissa.

Melissa wasn't afraid at all. The sound of it, a kind of wind, the heat on her face like a mask. At night sometimes she dreamed about it.

There was a big box of matches in the drawer in the kitchen. Her parents used them to light the fireplace, candles on the dinner table, or when the pilot light went out in the oven or the furnace.

The matches in a blue box were thick, with big red heads. A simple, quick strike, an expert flick of the wrist and the end ignited, a tiny dancer, a miniature explosion.

Melissa took the box. Her father was at work; her mother was on the phone. She'd been thinking of that pile of leaves since the weekend, imagining what it would be like in flames, how it would smell. She wondered if there were marshmallows in the cabinet. There were. She took the box, the bag of marshmallows. She'd find a stick in the yard. That was the real way, her father said, not those fancy, extra-long skewers they gave you at the hotel.

Out in the yard, the air was cool and the sky was a bright blue. She was off school because of some teacher in-service day and parent conferences that night.

She stood in front of the pile, and took a match from the box. Even the box was nice, a tidy thing that opened like a drawer. She struck one, two, three. Nothing. She wasn't fast enough or something, the match heads crumbling into dust with her clumsiness.

Finally, it worked. It was more like a strike, quick and sure, than a drag the way she'd been doing. And there it was. A perfect little flame, happily come to life on the end of the stick. The potential of it — all the things it could do, all the forms it could take.

Melissa!

Her mother. She dropped the match and it snuffed out in the wet grass.

What on earth? Are those matches?

The look on her mother's face was so surprised, so quickly edging to anger and fear that Melissa started to cry.

213

"I wanted to roast marshmallows."

But that wasn't the truth of it. She wanted to watch things burn. Because it was amazing how fire could reduce a solid thing to dust. It literally changed things from one form to another. And that was a kind of miracle.

Inside she got a lecture about playing with matches, and how fire was a thing that could quickly get out of control, how it raged, and could kill her, destroy their house, their neighbors' houses. She knew that, of course. She was sorry, she said. Her mother comforted her as she cried. *It's normal to be curious about things,* her mother said. *But fire is not a toy.*

She was sorry. She was sorry that she hadn't had the chance to watch those leaves burn. That her mother was scared and angry. That she was in trouble. But she still wasn't scared. And she didn't love flames any less.

Melissa rarely thought about that day, that first day when she tried to start a fire. Because what came after it was so life-altering, so world-changing that that first afternoon was lost to her memory. It came back to her now though, as she drove away from the city, from the life she'd built from the ashes of her childhood.

How quickly it all got left behind. He'd said that was how it would be, but she wasn't sure she believed him. He told her, *Once you ditch that phone, everything that you think tethers you to your life will fall away.*

Cash. A burner phone. A map — a real paper map! — marked where she should stop for gas, to spend the night. Places that took cash, that didn't have cameras.

It's not forever, he told her. *Think of it as a life reset. When we come back, we'll be stronger, free from the prison of this modern life.*

She'd used cash to buy the car from the used lot he'd sent her to. It was older, not like her Range Rover that had Bluetooth, and a navigation computer, linked to her phone so that her email literally popped up on a screen in the dashboard.

She was nervous at first, edgy, leaving everything and everyone behind. But he was right, the farther she got, the less real it seemed. She'd never been away from her phone for so long — with its endless texts and news alerts, it's pinging, ringing, vibrating. In the first hour on the road, she must have reached for it about twenty times.

The road was winding through towering pines.

She reached for the radio and turned it on, spinning the dial — the dial! — until a station came in. The news. Fires were raging in

California, people having to abandon their homes in minutes as flames raced toward their communities. Also, after years of drought, Australia, too, was battling giant blazes that were destroying homes, nature, animals.

Still, she felt a kind of thrill in her heart when she thought about fires raging. Something she never shared with anyone until she told him. Fire. It was a natural occurrence. It was the planet's way of cleaning away the old, fertilizing the soil, making way for new life. It was only a tragedy because we had built too many homes, done too much damage to the natural world. Because we stood too close to the flames. Even the animal populations would regenerate, if not for all our abuses. People rage and blame the fires for all of their destruction. But people are to blame.

Melissa drove and drove, getting sleepy, and wondered if she should pull over. She hadn't stopped at the roadside motels he suggested. Instead, she'd pulled into campsite parking lots and slept in the car, used the restrooms, cleaned up with water from the sinks. She didn't like motels; she preferred to be in her own space.

She kept driving. She didn't think she had much longer to go. But how could you really know without a nav computer telling you your exact arrival time?

The fire that killed her parents. It was purely an accident. That box of matches; Mom just put it back in the drawer and told Melissa not to touch it again. Melissa was a good girl, a straight-A student with lots of friends, and a soccer superstar. She was not the kind of kid who went to detention or earned the wrath of her teachers. And her parents never had reason to punish her for anything. She never got her iPad taken away, or grounded like so many of her friends. So when her mother told her not to touch the matches again, she had every reason to believe that Melissa would obey.

It was really Priss who couldn't let it go. Priss had been her friend for so long that Melissa didn't even remember herself without the little girl that lived under her bed. Even her parents accepted Priss as a permanent fixture of their lives. She even got a present at Christmas. Priss was there when no one could play, when she was scared at night, when her parents argued — which wasn't that often but really bad when they did.

What had her parents argued about that night? Money. What exactly about money, Melissa couldn't even remember. Something her mother, Jessie, had bought, not discussing it with her father, Ramon, first. He had a bad temper, and Mom wasn't one to back down either. It started over dinner where they kept their voices tight and controlled because Melissa was there. But when she went up to do her homework, their angry voices wafted up. It went on.

When her mother came to say good-night, Melissa could see that she'd been crying, her eyes red, her smile fake.

"Are you okay?" she asked her mom. Sometimes her mom came and slept on the floor of her room. Tonight might be one of those nights.

"It's okay," she said. "Married people argue sometimes."

"About money."

Her mother offered a little laugh, pushed a wisp of hair away from Melissa's eyes. "Arguments are almost never about the thing they're about."

Melissa understood that, and didn't.

"But it's okay. We'll work it out. We always do, don't we?"

Priss was under the bed, had been since Melissa had come up to do her homework. As she got older, she saw Priss less and less often.

After the yelling died down, and Melissa lay in her bed, Priss wouldn't stop talking about those matches. Not that she talked exactly. It was kind of like an idea in Melissa's head that

218

was there because it was in Priss's head. Later, she would try to explain this to the battalion of doctors she saw, until she realized it just made her seem strange and she should stop talking about Priss and her ideas altogether.

Downstairs, Melissa took the matches from the drawer in the kitchen and brought them to the living room where she thought she would light the candles.

Honestly, that was the last moment she remembered clearly. She knew that the flame caught on one of the drapes, and that it went up with a horrifying whoosh, a terrible exhale of breath. She remembered that she didn't scream, because she was so afraid that she would get in trouble. The fire, just like her mother had warned her, leaped from one thing to the next. She just watched, mesmerized by its acrobatics, its swiftness, its unapologetic swallowing of everything it touched. Both her parents died that night from smoke inhalation. Melissa was rescued by firefighters. And she never saw Priss again.

Apparently there was something about the construction of the house, something faulty in the drywall that turned it into a tinderbox. And there was a huge life insurance policy, which Melissa's grandparents were careful to save and invest for her.

No one ever blamed her exactly for what had happened. A terrible mistake, the shrink said, an accident. But sometimes when she thought Melissa wasn't looking, her grandmother watched her with such a look of sadness and confusion. What would it be like to raise the grandchild who accidentally killed your only daughter? Melissa would wonder later when she was older, had years of therapy, was less myopic. But both her grandparents were gone by then.

When she met Jack on Torch, she had no living immediate family, a loving circle of friends — who all had their own families now — some distant second cousins who sent cards at Christmas. But the truth was that she was terribly lonely — obviously. There would be no other reason to enter into the morass of online dating.

The world, it's a chaos, he said. *Can't you feel the precipitous decline?*

All you had to do was turn on the news to know that it was true. Most people were sleepwalking, anesthetized by their games, social media, sports obsessions, permissible upscale addictions like food and wine. The world was coming undone, and most people were more interested in cute cat videos.

I have a place we can go. Not forever. Just a break.

Of course she said yes.

She popped the lid on the cola can she had in the center consul. It was warmish, but it was the blast of sugar and caffeine she needed.

Melissa kept driving on the dark, winding road. It couldn't be much longer now.

NINETEEN

Now

I've barely slept as the sun rises, the light through the blinds painting my bedroom pink. I draw in a breath, reach for my phone. No more texts from you. I'm relieved — and bereft.

My laptop is still open beside me, and when I reach for it, the screen comes to life with a picture of Melissa Farrow. Another beauty, different from Mia, from Bonnie, from me. But something similar, a thread between us, something in the aura. She has lush brown curls and smoky eyes filled with longing, the tattoo of a raven on her shoulder, a goth who dresses all in black. She is nowhere but Instagram. If she had a profile on Torch, and I'm guessing she did, it's gone.

Her feed is simple, mostly black-and-white images of city views, strange objects — an armless doll in a trashcan, an abandoned shoe in the street, a stray dog curled around a litter of puppies in a cardboard box — or isolated trails, vistas. No words, other than her bio. *You create yourself in ever-changing shapes/unsung, unmourned, undescribed/like a forest we never knew.*

Unmourned. Rilke again.

Her final posts are the ones that have hooked me. They are portraits of places I know well. A graveyard. A wooded trailhead. An old house abandoned and fallen into disrepair. A simple chapel.

Her last images are of The Hollows, the place where I grew up, where my father grew up. I guess in some ways, it's home.

I shower and dress — jeans, black cashmere sweater, boots, my leather jacket. I throw some clothes, toiletries in a knapsack, pack up my laptop.

Down in the kitchen, I brew a triple espresso. I drink my coffee by the window, looking for my blackbird friend. But the seed on the sill is untouched and he doesn't come.

Are we going home? Robin wants to know. Today she wears Jay's sweatshirt, torn jeans, and scuffed sneakers. She's not there, this ghost of my childhood. But she is. I don't answer her. She lingers by the door for a moment, then fades away.

223

I think about waking Jax, telling her the whole ugly story. But she'll want to go with me and I need to be alone. Or it seems as if I should take on this journey alone. So I leave her a note instead:

I'll be back. Take care of Dear Birdie.

She'll know what to do.

I slip out the door, set the alarm, and head toward the garage where I keep my car.

The truth is that since Bailey Kirk said it yesterday, maybe before that, when I found the article among your things, I knew I would have to go back there. That I would have to go home.

My breath comes out in white clouds as I move quickly up the street, huddling against the chill, passing the other pretty stoops, then turning onto the busy commercial street. It's already hopping at this early hour, people clutching coffees and cell phones, heading for the subway, joggers, moms with strollers, yogis with mats in slings across their bodies.

A guy with dreadlocks and a blue jumpsuit has his earphones in and doesn't say a word as I hand him my ticket. He disappears to retrieve my car from the mysterious depths of urban automobile storage, then returns with it to hand me my keys.

"Hey," he says, watching me with a look I can't read. "Be careful."

I shake my head. "Sorry?"

But he turns away, goes back to his tiny office. Was he talking to me? Or was he on the phone talking to someone else? I keep looking in his direction for a moment, the words echoing. When did even the simplest exchanges become so confounding?

Maybe it's me.

It's definitely me.

I get in my car, close the door, feel the quiet leather interior ensconce me. It's a cocoon. My shoulders ease, breath comes easier. I pull out into traffic and start to drive.

A car, you said. *How does that work with your whole Miss-Frugal-I-take-public-transportation thing?*

It doesn't, I guess. We're all full of little inconsistences, aren't we, Adam?

But when it all becomes too much, sometimes I need to get out of the city — not on foot, on bike, or on the train. When my many secrets, the noise inside and outside my head, all the desperate people out there who need Dear Birdie's advice are a wave threatening to wash me away, my vehicle becomes a life raft, a little ship I get in to float away.

Dear Birdie,
I found my birth mother through one of those genetic testing services, but she doesn't want to meet me. She's kept me a secret all her life, has a new family, other children. I feel so alone, knowing that I have a family who might never know me. What should I do?

Dear Birdie,
I can't forgive my father for driving drunk and being responsible for the accident that killed my mother and my brother. He's in jail and I can't bring myself to visit him even though we're all we have left.

Dear Birdie,
I can't shake this feeling that my life isn't my life. That I'm a fraud and all the things I post on Instagram are just a shallow version of who I should have been. And my relationships are all weirdly competitive and I hate my job. Do other people feel this way? How do I find my true self?

Some of them I can help. Some I can't. Accepting the difference is the hard part.

I know there are happy, well-adjusted people out there. People living authentic lives that have meaning and purpose. People who have deep and healthy relationships, weathering life's many blows with strength and faith, coming out the other side of pain and tragedy stronger and wiser, with more compassion for themselves and others.

But Dear Birdie doesn't hear from those people. Ever. People come to her for help. And having walked a dark terrain, she is uniquely qualified to guide people back toward the light.

Isn't she?

Sometimes. But she's not feeling it on this gray misty morning, where winter is settling into the air, and you've disappeared, and the past is digging itself out of its grave.

Today, I'm as lost as everyone else. Maybe *I* should write a letter to Dear Birdie.

Dear Birdie,
I have run away from the darkness of my past and created a successful life. But there are so many layers to me. The person I was then. The one I am now to do my job. There's the person my few friends know. And then, there was a man

227

I thought I could love, who is also buried deep, not who I thought he was at all. In fact, he might be a monster. Just like my father.

Are we all just layers of secrets and lies?

Or is it just me?

I feel like a fraud, a ghost in the haunted house of my life.

What I should I do, Dear Birdie?

What would Dear Birdie tell that lost soul? She'd say: Sounds like the universe is telling you that it's time to peel back all the layers and expose the truth, speak it loud from the rooftops. You'll never find yourself unless you're willing to *be yourself*.

I've always been better at giving advice than taking it.

Now I'm on the Henry Hudson, heading north. As the city recedes from my rearview mirror, I am awash in memories of a place and time I have sought to forget.

My father.

In my early life, he was just a uniformed picture on the wall, a talking head on a computer screen. Then, he was suddenly back in our lives, in our home — a tired man at the kitchen table, a sleeping form in my mother's bed. *Shh, Daddy's resting.*

The house.

A rambling, ramshackle mess set on twenty acres in a town that sounded like something out of a horror movie: The Hollows.

My mother growing thinner by the day, weaker.

She snuck into my bed some nights and held me close, the way I used to do with her when I was little and afraid.

One night, when things had been especially bad, she whispered, *He was someone else when I first loved him. He'll heal. This place will heal him. He'll be that man again. You'll see.*

Now I know. He needed help. But he didn't get it and we all paid the price.

Why didn't you know how sick he was, Mom? It's a question I can't ask her.

I am deep in the ugly twist of my memories when the phone rings. I press the button on my dash to answer. He doesn't wait for me to say hello.

"I wanted to check in on you." It's Bailey Kirk. "How are you doing?"

"I'm fine," I say briskly.

Who is this guy? I thought perhaps I'd seen the last of him. I remember I gave him my number, and really wish I hadn't.

"Sounds like you're driving," he says. "Where are you headed?"

229

"Out of town for a few days," I say. "I need to get away."

There's music playing in the background of the call. Jazz. A mournful saxophone, tinny and distant.

"Not doing anything stupid, right?" he says. "Like looking for your friend."

Am I looking for you? Or am I running away from you? Maybe both.

I opt not to answer Bailey, am about to hang up. Then, "So is Wren Greenwood your real name?"

It's not. It's not my real name, the one my parents gave me. It's my legal name, the one I gave myself.

"Of course it is," I lie.

There's a silence. I am gripping the wheel so hard that my knuckles turn white. I force myself to relax.

"Because it's funny — that's the name on your driver's license."

A dump of dread in my belly.

"But it's *not* the original name attached to your Social Security number."

An ache begins behind my eyes. Silence. That's best. But he continues.

"Your profession on ConnectIn is listed as a freelance writer. But I can't find a recent byline anywhere."

Wow. He's really going deep.

230

"And that town house of yours? I know you bought it in a foreclosure auction. But how many *freelance writers* can afford a town house in Brooklyn Heights?"

I think about how to respond. I don't want to tell him about *Dear Birdie.* How because of the volume of followers, big advertising money started to flow in, more than I thought possible. When I moved it to the *Chronicle,* they paid me very well and continue to do so, because it's one of their most popular columns and podcasts. That I've saved and invested, made more money from the money I've earned. That the house is worth far more than I paid for it. I am not wealthy, but I have done very well.

"I don't know what to tell you," I say easily. "Family money. I've been lucky."

Partially, that's true, too. There was a sum, a small inheritance from my mother's side of the family that paid for school, expenses, gave me a solid financial head start. Like everything in my life, what I tell Bailey is partially true. Layers of truth and lies, mingling like colored sand, creating shades and hues. All of it true. None of it true.

"It's none of my business, of course," he says. "Curiosity is an occupational hazard, I guess."

"You're right," I say. "It's none of your

231

business who I am or where my money comes from. It has nothing to do with Mia Thorpe, your client's daughter. The girl you're trying to find."

He makes an annoying clicking noise. "But the answer to that lies with a man you both dated."

"Maybe," I concede. "But I did a little digging into Mia Thorpe."

He sighs. "Goddamn Google. Everyone's a PI these days."

"It seems to me like she's disappeared before."

Now, it's his turn to go quiet.

"I scrolled through her Facebook page, the comments from her friends begging her to get in touch, to come home, saying how worried they all are."

"Yeah?"

"So there was a comment from a woman who said something like, 'Please don't put us through this again. This time, let someone know where you are.' So, did she? Disappear before?"

"She did."

"And where was she?"

"I told you last night. She'd checked herself into rehab, a posh place out west. But that was for six weeks and her father knew she was there. This is very different."

"Addicts disappear," I say. "That's a common behavior pattern."

"And you know this because . . ."

"Because everybody knows this."

He clears his throat. There's a lot of background noise. It sounds like he's driving, too. "Not because you're used to giving people advice?"

Shit.

"Don't worry, Dear Birdie. Your secret is safe with me."

An electric wave of alarm. He just outed me as Dear Birdie. They don't call private investigators dicks for nothing.

I summon my grown-up voice. "You know what, Detective Kirk. Back off."

"Wait —"

I end the call, hands shaking. He's the first one to dig through my layers and find the truth. It seems to have taken him approximately twenty-four hours. Of course, as a PI he has access to resources that the average person doesn't. But still. I press my foot to the gas, adrenaline pumping. I feel naked, exposed, and a little angry. When the phone rings again, I don't answer it.

The city falls away, disappearing from my rearview mirror, as do all the selves I am when I'm there.

TWENTY

Then

"Come here, little bird."

My father's voice was just a croak, emitting from the dark of their bedroom. I paused in the hallway outside his door. The echoes of the fight he and my mother had the night before still seemed to bounce off the walls.

"It's okay. Come say good morning to your old man."

I moved to the doorway and stood there. The room smelled faintly, not unpleasantly, of sleep and cigarettes.

"Closer."

I walked into the room over the creaking hardwood floor and stood beside the bed. The blinds were pulled, but sunlight streamed in from the edges, casting the room in a buttery yellow. He was shirtless, thickly muscled, tattoos on his arms. His sandy hair was a wild tousle.

He reached for his pack of cigarettes, then looked at me and put it back. "I shouldn't smoke."

"It's bad for you," I ventured.

A rare smile. "You're right."

He rubbed at the crown of his head. "Where's your mom?"

"She's working."

She worked in town, just to bring some money in, at the local grocery. Every time I saw her leave in the rattling pickup, I worried that she wouldn't come back. But she always did, smuggling contraband to us, things from our life before — Cheetos and Snickers bars, Oreos, and Goldfish crackers.

He nodded, a frown wrinkling his brow. His face had so many shadows, could pull into so many different masks. Gentle, tired like he was now. Dark and angry as he had been last night when he and my mother fought. Peaceful when he played the guitar. Blank, hollow like he was just before his rages.

"Are you hungry?" I asked, eager to keep him as he was.

"A little," he said with a shrug. "Can you cook?"

"I can make oatmeal. Would you like some?"

He nodded. "That would be nice, little bird. Then we'll go out. I want to show you something."

After breakfast, we walked through the woods, down a winding path that was barely there, cleared by Jay and my father. I had to nearly jog to keep up with him. As we walked, my father delivered one of his sermons.

"When the global financial collapse ends society as we know it, and the sky turns red with flames, people like us will be the survivors. The world will belong to us."

"When? When will the world end?"

I wondered about my school, my teachers, the friends we'd left behind. What would happen to them when the world ended? And how *could* the world end? It didn't seem possible — the air, the earth, the sky, the birds — all of it here long before us.

"It's already ended. Humanity just hasn't gotten the memo."

"What's a memo?"

Another chuckle. "Never mind. Here we are."

We had come to stand before a squat cinder block building with a large metal door. It was jarring to come across it in a place of nature, all hard angles among the curve of trees, the swish of the wind, and drop of leaves.

"What is this place?" I asked, putting my hand on the cold metal door.

"It's something my father built," he said. "It's a bunker. A safe house."

He took a ring of keys from his pocket and unlocked the door. We stepped inside and climbed down a narrow flight of concrete steps with the outside light guiding our way. At the bottom, he unlocked another door.

He walked inside and turned on a battery-powered lantern that hung from a hook on the wall.

I followed him, my heart thumping, throat dry. There were two cots, a table with four chairs, a tattered plaid couch, piles of books and games, and what looked like endless rows of shelves stretching into the dark. The air was moldy and dank.

"Who lives here?"

"No one," he said. "Right now, we just use it to store the things we'll need later."

He went deeper into the space with the lamp, and I followed him past rows of canned goods. I recognized some of the jams I'd made with my mother, her careful handwriting on the labeled jars — blueberry, strawberry, grape. Cans of tuna, sardines, beans, and beans and more beans

— black, baked, pinto, garbanzo, navy — stood in tiny organized rows. Yams, apple sauce, peanut butter — giant tubs. Sacks of rice were stuffed into plastic containers. Rows of batteries, jugs of water. It seemed like enough to last a lifetime. Where had it all come from? Some of it was covered in dust; other items seemed new.

My father unlocked another door. Inside this deeper room, he held up the lantern.

I drew in a breath. Weapons. Bows and arrows, all manner of knives from serrated hunting knives to machetes. And an enormous stockpile of guns — semiautomatics, rifles, assault weapons, pistols, and rounds and rounds of ammunition. My throat went dry.

"Why do we need so many guns? Guns are for killing."

A heavy hand on the crown of my head. "Because in the end, only those who can defend themselves will survive, little bird."

"Defend against who?"

I looked up at him, sure that he was going to say something like aliens or zombies, the diseased undead.

"Each other."

Something about the way he said it, the flat quality to his gaze made my whole body tingle.

That night I would dream of zombies and the sky turning red, running from a faceless demon through the trees, a demon who turned out to be my father.

Now, as I pull off the highway, the roads get smaller and smaller, until I'm on the one that will lead me right back to the place from which I am forever running.

The newspaper article I found in the box of your things is yellow and creased, lying on the passenger seat.

On the radio, David Bowie sings about the starman in the sky.

A sign by the side of the road reads: Welcome to The Hollows.

I pull onto Main Street and drive though the pretty square.

The Hollows is a picture postcard of a town, one of those places where people from the city come for the weekend to visit pumpkin patches, and pick apples, and drink cider, watch the leaves perform their wild color show of gold and amber, flame red, and bright orange. Quaint, they might call it. Peaceful. Bucolic. The tony boutiques selling local crafts and art and wool blankets from sheep up the road, the yoga studio bright and spare with white oak floors, the upscale coffee shop with its cold brews and gluten-free scones will seduce. It's the kind of place urban dwellers long for when they imagine that simpler life.

But that's not what I see when I come here. There's another side to The Hollows. One a casual weekend visitor might not see. Bad things happen here — more than other places. A simple internet search will confirm that I'm not being dramatic. Bad things certainly happened to me here.

Something inside me is tight, my shoulders tense. I remind myself to breathe as I move out of the square and The Blue House Inn rises on my right. It's a big Victorian house painted the color of the sky, turned charming B and B.

I park my car in its small lot and head inside. On summer weekends, I might have called ahead, knowing that it would be booked. But the season has passed, and a gray ceiling has settled over the town. The trees have shed their leaves, leaving black branches reaching into the sky. Besides, there's always a room for me here. The proprietor and I have a long-standing relationship.

Darkness begins to fall around 3:30 p.m. in the winter months. Why does it always feel colder here? A damp chill makes me shiver as I take my luggage from the car.

But when I enter the lobby, a little bell announcing my arrival, the space is warm and cozy, with a fire crackling. Wingback chairs and an overstuffed couch, oil paintings of area landmarks on the wall, shelves and shelves of books. The head of a deer hangs over the hearth, eyes glassy and confused at the way of things. Why do people think it's okay to do that, to hang the heads of dead animals on the wall?

The bespectacled young woman at the check-in desk looks up from her phone, surprised that anyone has come in at all. There's a textbook and laptop beside her. When she puts her device down, I can see that she's on Torch, sorting through the catalog of hopeful faces. I want to warn her off, but I hold my tongue. No one appreciates unsolicited advice. We all like to learn our lessons the hard way, don't we?

"Is room 33 available?" I ask. It's the largest room, one with a sitting area, a fireplace, a desk by the window.

She pushes up her glasses, offers a wry smile. "*Every* room is available."

"I'll need it for a few days at least."

Tucking a strand of her long, auburn hair behind her ear, she tells me that there are no guests on the calendar, enters my name when I give it into the computer.

"You've been here before," she says. "Is your information the same?"

I confirm that it is and after some keyboard clicking, she hands me a gold key.

"You can stay as long as you like," she says. "Just let us know when you're ready to check out."

Thanking her, I shoulder my bag.

"Can I help?" she asks. She glances back at her phone, eager I'm sure to get back to the addictive activity of boy shopping.

"Thanks. I can manage."

I walk through the sitting room and down the hallway, floorboards creaking, the scent of lilac in the air.

Inside the room, I set up my laptop, charge my phone, put my overnight bag in the closet. Flipping on the switch that lights the gas fireplace, I stare into the flames for a moment.

I put Dear Birdie and Wren Greenwood into their respective boxes.

I log into Tor, also known as The Onion Router, a way to log on to the dark web. A place where you go online when you don't want to be followed.

Because there are two different internets. The one we all know and can't live without. The shiny, frenetic mess of every person you've ever met, and all the information you need, and every single thing you want to buy. There are the bright, candy colors of social media sites, and coupon clearing houses, and places to store your million photos — and edit, and print, and make a mug! It's a confessional. A world news hub. A cookbook. A radio. A television. Your portal to the universe where every question that has ever been asked, has also been answered with varying degrees of accuracy.

And then there's the strange, ugly, netherworld of the dark web. That's where I'll find the person who can help me find you.

Twenty-One

I follow Robin through the dark. She runs like a rabbit, impossibly agile and swift. *Wait,* I want to call after her. But I have no voice; terror and exertion have taken it. I have a stitch in my side; my throat is sandpaper. There are footfalls behind me, someone crashing through the forest — bigger, even clumsier than I, groaning. I stumble, fall and skin one knee, scramble to my feet again and keep running.

Up here.

There she is in the tree house. Her face is a tiny moon in the dark sky of the window.

Quick, before he sees you.

I scramble up, silent and fast. It's minutes before he goes hulking past, roaring in pain and anger. A monster. A bear. The boogeyman. My father. He heaves and pitches, my name a wail in the night. But he never looks up, lurches away.

His voice grows fainter until the forest

swallows it. Silence. Just my ragged breath. Robin sits on her haunches in the corner, legs stick skinny, hair a tangled nest.

We created a nature table in the tree house — especially beautiful leaves, interestingly shaped rocks, a bird's nest and some broken blue eggs, an owl pellet, a snail shell, a big black feather, a piece of wood charred by lightning, a tiny skull probably belonging to a mouse.

This is a crow feather maybe, says Robin, pointing to the shining bent thing. She's trying to distract me. She's not afraid of him like I am.

"That seems right," I say, my voice shaking, my breath still shallow. "I've seen lots of crows lately."

They're smart. Did you know that? They remember people, hold grudges. They're thieves — especially of shiny things. They eat anything. They're survivors like us.

She hands me the feather. It glows blue-black in the moonlight.

You'll be okay, she whispers.

We lie on our backs and watch the starry night through the slats in the roof, hearts beating. Somewhere an owl hoots, mournful and wise.

I wake, drooling on my keyboard, with a

blistering headache and a terrible longing. I can feel and smell those woods, that tree house.

How can you be homesick for a place you hated?

My computer is pinging. I log in and the screen comes to life.

Think of the dark web as a kind of night market, a place where you might buy any type of illegal paraphernalia from guns to drugs, hire any kind of services from hit men to hookers, and do so without being tracked by the any of the things that track you on the World Wide Web. This is where I found the man who helped me become someone else, at least online. You're never supposed to contact him again unless it's an emergency, but I've logged on to his site and opened a chat box.

I'm found, I wrote, and identified myself by the code name he gave me long ago: lost-girl. I fell asleep waiting.

Now there's a curt response: Not my problem. No guarantees in this business.

I opt for honest begging: Please help me.

What do you want?

What do I want? Good question. I found this man when I was trying to create an online presence for Wren Greenwood, effectively burying my past in a digital grave. I thought it meant that no one would ever connect my past to my present. But it obviously didn't work. So what do I want from him now?

Hello?

Can you help me find the man who found me? I type.

He found you? Now you want to find him?

Another good point. I think about just dropping this. But no. If he can help, I need him to. So, instead I type, It's complicated.

That's a pretty common relationship status these days.

Can you help me?

Hard to say.

What do you need to find him?

The red cursor blinks. I wonder if he'll just disappear and never answer me again. He — I think it's a he? — and I have never met. I don't know his name, what he looks

247

like, where he lives. But he helped me construct an online past for an identity that wasn't mine. Now, if he doesn't answer me, there's really nothing I can do.

I wait, foot tapping, agitation growing. Outside the sun is setting, the sky a morose steel gray. I'm so tired. It feels like midnight. But the clock says it's only 3:30 p.m. Shit. *Dear Birdie.* I have to call Jax.

I sweat it out another ten minutes, watching the screen. I'm about to give up on this when he answers: Send me everything you have on him. I'll see what I can do.

He gives me an email address that is just a series of numbers and a server name I've never seen before.

Thank you, I type.

Don't thank me yet. And this is not a freebie.

Of course.

He names his price and it's high. My desperation must be palpable. And I don't bother negotiating.

I type: Fine.

Bitcoin, please.

He provides a Bitcoin address. I have no

idea how to deal with Bitcoin. I'll have my accountant do it, assuming *he* knows how. Then, I experience a moment of clear thinking, fingers traveling across the keyboard.

I'll pay when you find him, I try. I may be desperate, but I'm not stupid.

Half now. Half when I find him.

Fine.

When I get the money, I'll get to work.

I send him everything: Adam — the name I knew and the one Bailey Kirk gave me — the name of your company, all the photos I have, the defunct links to your disappeared social media and Torch pages, the address of the vacation rental you passed off as your apartment. The names of the missing women. Everything you told me about yourself even though most of it is probably lies. Even lies have a pattern.

When I'm done, I sit a minute feeling like I'm standing on the edge of the digital abyss into which you've fallen. I found you online, and, now that you've disappeared, I only have your electronic footprint to follow. I've hired a person I have only ever communicated via the dark web to help me.

What are you going to do if you find him?
Robin wants to know. She's over by the fire,
a shadow in the corner.

"I haven't gotten that far," I tell her.

Maybe you should let him disappear.

She's right, of course.

Another ping: I'll be in touch.

How?

The chat window closes.

I send an email to my accountant and ask
him to transfer the Bitcoin. I know I'll get a
phone call, probably pretty quickly.

Then I call Jax.

"You will not believe the level of my
productivity today," she says by way of
answering. "You would be proud."

"Really?" I say. "Because when I logged
on to Netflix, it looks to me like you've been
binge-watching *Buffy the Vampire Slayer*." I
didn't log on to Netflix. I just know her that
well.

"Well," she says. "That, too. BUT — I did
Dear Birdie all by myself. I wrote a THOU-
SAND words on my book. AND I did my
nails."

"Back up," I say. "You did *Dear Birdie*?"

"Easy, girl, I didn't send to Liz. I was waiting for your call."

"Okay," I say. "Read."

I look at my email and see that she sent the *Dear Birdie* missives about an hour ago. I could easily read them myself, but I like to hear the words out loud.

She reads the letters and her answers: a hoarder who wants to change since her husband left and her daughter won't see her; a young man who feels brokenhearted because women reject him and he wants an expensive, painful surgery to fix his weak jaw hoping that will help; a woman complaining that her millennial employees are all lazy and self-involved.

Jax reads her answers and I have to say, her responses are almost word for word what I would have written, but with her own special butt-kicking flair.

Get some help, sister, she writes to the hoarder, after offering some information on the psychology of hoarding, suggesting therapy, and offering words of support. *Clean up your house and bring your family home.*

Love is a head trip, she tells our incel. *When you work on yourself from the inside, find your authentic groove and live your life from that place, you'll attract the right woman, the one who will love you for who you ARE, not how you LOOK. Do NOT go under the* knife. *I guarantee that's not going to help you.*

Then, some love for millennials who get a bad rap a lot of the time. *Maybe they just have a better work-life balance. Maybe if you started going home at five occasionally, you would resent them less. After all, didn't people fight for the eight-hour workday?*

I make a few tweaks in the shared document. But mainly, I leave them as is.

"You could be Dear Birdie," I tell her when we're done and have sent the file off to Liz.

"No, thanks," she says. "I don't think I can do this every day, Wren. It's hard. People — are in so much pain."

"Some of them," I say. "Yeah."

She heaves a sigh. Then, "The mauler, as I have come to think of him, has been texting me all day."

"We blocked him."

I hear her open the refrigerator, rummage around. She's only going to find lettuce, some stale pizza, a half-eaten container of Thai Amazing Chicken, which was somewhat less than amazing. There's a cheap bottle of white that's been in there for ages.

"I might have *unblocked* him?" she says.

"Jax."

"Do you *not* go to the grocery store?" she asks. "Maybe — is it possible — that I overreacted. Maybe it was a misunderstanding?"

I can't believe what I'm hearing. "Oh, my God. He *ripped* your dress."

"I think — it was an accident?"

I let silence be my answer to that.

"I know," she says after a beat. "I *know*. I'll block him again. I will."

More silence from me. Then, "You're not thinking about seeing him again."

"No," she says. But she sounds wishy-washy. "No."

I can hardly judge her. Here I am, chasing after you. A liar at least, maybe far worse. Why?

"How could I have been so wrong about someone?" she asks, echoing my own feelings. Her voice softens when she's sad.

"Sometimes we see what we want to see," I say.

Another deep breath. "Where are you?"

My accountant is calling on the other line.

"Jax," I say. "I have to go."

"You know I can track you, right? Find My Friends?"

Oh, right. I forgot about that. I can track her, too.

"And, I'm *not* stalking you? But. I know you're up there. What the hell are you doing in that place?"

"I'll call you back."

"You hate it there, right? Why do you go back?"

She's still talking as I click over to the other call.

It's my accountant's assistant, a young-sounding, soft-spoken guy named Lyle. I convince him that I haven't lost my mind, don't have a gun to my head, and after some weak protesting about how Marty is not a fan of Bitcoin transactions, he agrees to make the payment.

"You're sure everything's all right, Ms. Greenwood? This doesn't seem like you."

"I'm fine, Lyle, really. This is just — one of those things."

What does that even mean? The words taste as disingenuous as they are.

"I know Marty would like to talk to you, Miss Greenwood," he says. "You know the stock market is in a bit of tumult these days. He wants to discuss making some changes to protect your investments."

The stock market. My father would stroke out. The ultimate con, the devil's game of corporate greed. But Jax's mother Miranda taught us both how to save and invest. *Work for your money, and then make your money work for you. That way you never need to rely on any man.* That made sense to me. When I think about my own mother, I remember

254

someone trapped by her circumstance, in my father's thrall, without the means to make a life for us without him.

"Just tell him to do what he thinks is best," I say.

"I know he really wants to have a discussion with you. Is there a good time?" he presses.

"I'll call and make an appointment next week."

Surely my life will be back to normal by then.

"Miss Greenwood —"

"Thanks, Lyle. I have to go." Rudely, I end the call while he's still talking.

Now, all I have to do is wait for my dark web contact to get back in touch. Like he's not just going to take my Bitcoin and disappear forever.

I have a few errands to run while I wait to see if I'll ever hear from him again.

TWENTY-TWO

Trees bend in the stiff wind. What's left of the afternoon light is leaking from the sky as I pull through open gates up the paved drive. Passing a small structure on my left that has the aura of abandonment, with foggy windows and a small porch covered with leaves, I wind up the path, driving slowly. The gloaming of a northern winter afternoon is the perfect time to visit a cemetery — if you're looking for atmosphere. The shadows of the gravestones are long; the last of the day's light white and sharp on bare branches.

Gravestones stand in careful rows, some tall, some squat. Some are monuments to the deceased, some statues, small stone houses. The metal fencing is down in places, not being kept up, it seems. I imagine teenagers sneaking in here and getting high, romping among the dead with the careless laughter of people who think they'll never die. Some of the graves are overgrown, untended, others tidy with flowers carefully placed.

After parking the car, I remove the orchids I picked up at the market on my way out of town. The wind whips at my jacket, my hair, as the temperature drops and the sky dims. I stay on the path between the graves.

I don't mind the dead. And I am not afraid of ghosts. The living are far more dangerous. There's no one else around — no other parked cars, no one kneeling at graveside. Silence. Solitude. As far as I'm concerned, these are good, not frightening, things.

The ground is cold and hard through the soles of my boots. When I get where I'm going, I kneel to clear the fallen leaves from the first headstone.

My mother, Alice. Not quite forty years old when she died.

Then, Jay. We'd just celebrated his eighteenth birthday the month before.

I push away leaves and branches, thinking a rake might have been helpful. Not that I own a rake. In the detritus, a cigarette butt pops an unnatural white. Probably nothing, a million ways this tiny piece of trash might have found its way here.

But I imagine someone standing over Jay's

grave smoking. My father was a smoker. There was always the faint smell of tobacco on his clothes, on his breath, an ashtray overflowing with butts on the back deck. He'd lean on the railing, looking out into the woods, smoking, lighting one off the other. Camels, no filter.

Try to cut back at least, my mother would beg.

I will. I will.

Did someone stand smoking over my brother's grave?

Robin would say, *Look at the ground. It will tell you everything you need to know.*

I search the ground around me. But whatever story it might have to tell eludes me. It's so deserted here. Hard to imagine it any other way. I'm one of a very few left to mourn my brother and my mother, to miss them, to visit.

The last grave is the one I dread the most. Robin, just fifteen.

There's an angel engraved on her headstone, the only flourish among the three stones. Otherwise, they're simple — just names and dates, simple type, clean black borders. Nothing else, no words about who they were to whom. A simple stone remains the only marker of a life.

I clean up as best I can without tools, pull

some weeds. Lichen has made its home in the nooks and crannies of the headstones.

When I'm done, I place orchids at each site. They're wilting, already preparing to return to the earth.

When I'm done, I'm left with a familiar hollow feeling.

There's a pointlessness to this errand. It's a superficial, going-through-the-motions activity that doesn't make me feel any closer to them. Their remains might be here but I don't believe that their spirits are, floating above, watching. I can't bring myself to speak — to tell them about my life, catalog all the ways I miss them, how I regret a thousand things that can't be undone. Instead, I just stay on my knees, feeling the cold and wet soak through the fabric of my jeans as the sky grows slowly darker. Someone looking at me from a distance might think I was praying. I'm not.

A harsh, startling call carries over the air and I look up, heart jumping, to see a shiny black crow on the tilting fence. He's huge, must be more than a foot tall, chest wide, great black claws gripping the fence.

Caw! Caw! he says. He watches me with his timeless beady black eyes. Time to go.

I rise.

"Get lost." I don't like crows. I move

closer to him, trying to menace him into flight, but he holds his ground, unafraid. A bit cheeky, it must be said, staring boldly, offering a wing flap to show who's boss. Some cultures see the crow as the symbol of death. Some say he carries the soul to the afterlife. Others still see the crow as a symbol of transformation. When he shows up in your life, get ready for change.

Caw! Caw! Caw! I imagine that he's laughing at me, feel an irrational wash of anger.

That's when I catch sight of something. A shift in the shadows between the trees that line the edge of the property.

There's someone there. Tall. Broad. He's watching me, takes a step forward.

"Hey," I yell.

I should run the other way, back to the safety of my car. But I don't; that's not me. Instead, I move closer.

"Hey!"

Is it you, Adam? Are you following me?

A pair of headlights cut the gloaming, startling us both. A car moves slowly up the winding road in my direction. When I turn back, the shadow shifts and disappears.

Again, another moment when I should retreat, back to my car to get away from the person in the woods, whoever it is in the car winding up the drive. Instead, I follow the shadow in a run, crossing the clearing, and push through the trees and step into the dark of the forest as the white sun dips below the horizon.

TWENTY-THREE

In the game of chase, Robin always won, and I was always left breathless with a stitch in my side, calling after her, hearing the sound of her laughter growing fainter and fainter.

Wait, I'd breathe, the word disappearing into the oak and elm, the humid air.

"Wait!" I call now, my voice loud, sharp in the trees. "Stop!"

Adrenaline is rocket fuel. My heart is an engine.

He's heavy and loud, running far ahead of me. I'm in decent shape; a fair runner these days. The Jax influence. I'm not like her; I can't lose myself in the exertion of my body, a super miler who doesn't ever seem to need to stop or rest. She buries me — in a sprint, over distance. Jax is a machine. But the result of our friendship is that I can run harder and faster than I ever thought possible.

I dig in deep — heedless of how far we've come, how I'll get back when I've burned all my energy. I'm closing the distance, not asking the important question of who am I chasing — or why.

I stumble; my right knee hits the ground hard. But I get back up. Branches whip at my face. Just like my recurring nightmares, the memories I can't release. I've been here before. I've never stopped being here.

Soon, the only sound is me. There's no shadow ahead any longer. Whoever I was chasing is gone. Silence has settled all around, thick and eerie. Starlight makes its debut of the evening above. I stop, my breath hot and fast, a vein in my throat throbbing.

"Adam!" I call. My voice is desperate and wounded, an animal crying. No answer comes. "Why are you *doing this*?"

The final syllables are just a girlish shriek. I'm sick from exertion. I hope I don't puke. Breathe, breathe, breathe.

Is it you? Why would you follow me if you wanted to get away from me? Why would you stand on the edge of my life, then run when I came to you?

The obvious answer is: it *wasn't* you.

It was no one, nothing. Like the form in the office window.

Like Robin.

I see the things I want to see.

A barred owl hoots, mocking, its rhythmic call sounding all the world like: *Who looks for you?* The forest and its residents, how they must laugh at us, all our folly of wanting and trying, wasting, and burning energy.

Or possibly some drifter. Or some freak who hangs around a cemetery, smoking over a dead stranger's grave for kicks.

I touch a stinging spot on my face and pull back fingers wet with blood. I use the cuff of my shirt, sticking out of my jacket, to try to stop it. But it's a bit of a gusher. The white of my shirt-sleeve looks black in the dark. I press harder hoping to stave the flow, lean against the nearest tree and sink down, feeling its rough bark against my back. There's something comforting and familiar about the tree, about even the wet, cold ground. Nature's embrace, however cold, is a comfort. It's where we belong, my father would surely say.

Here I begin to weep, a deep, ugly sadness welling up, a tsunami of emotion. Every loss evokes the loss that formed me. I know the slick walled abyss of losing someone, losing everyone, even myself. Which is maybe why you're the first person I've risked loving in a long, long time.

Yes, I loved you. Still, I love you. It's not a switch that gets turned off.

I let it all out, great heaving sobs. The flow becomes an eddy; I'm caught there awhile. Then it releases me. I breathe, feel cleansed as the sobs subside.

When my name echoes on the wind, at first I think it's my imagination, just the call of a bird, or something carrying from far away as sometimes happens in the woods at night. Sound bounces around and winds up in all kinds of weird places.

"Wren! Wren Greenwood!"

Not the name I was given. But the name I gave myself. But maybe that makes it more real than the name my mother gave me. It's the name of the person in the story I tell myself about myself. The girl who was born from ashes and formed herself from what remained.

"Wren Greenwood!"

The voice comes from the direction of the graveyard, back where I need to be, in the opposite direction of the person I was chasing. Who is it? Who knows I'm here?

"Wren Greenwood!"

It's a stupid name. A name that a child would make up. Of course, that's the truth of it. I was a child when I gave myself that name, cobbling together pieces of myself to

265

make a patched-up whole. A rag doll stitched back together.

I pull myself to standing, spent emotionally and physically, and walk in the direction of the voice. The night has grown frigid, and after the heat of exertion I am shivering, sweat having dampened my clothes, my butt wet from sitting on the forest floor. I'm ready to go back to the inn and sleep. For a week.

A figure moves toward me, this one real, the white glow of a flashlight bobbing up and down. I turn to look back behind me in the direction where the dark form disappeared, but there's no one, nothing.

When he calls my name again, he's close enough that I can recognize his voice.

In the story of my life, I'm not often surprised. I've lived through too many twists and turns of my own, heard too many tales of woe from those reaching out to Dear Birdie. Sometimes I think I know people and the way of things too well. I ache for unpredictability.

But I *am* surprised when the man comes close and drops his light.

Bailey Kirk.

"What the hell?" I say, some uncomfortable combination of angry, embarrassed, and relieved. "Are you *following* me?"

266

"Are you hurt?" he asks. He touches his own cheek, in empathy for the lash he must see on mine. "You're bleeding."

His voice is soft, a little breathless from the trek out here. He shines the light in my direction, and I shield my eyes, must be a wreck — face bleeding, leaves in my hair, jeans dirty at the knees.

Yes, I want to tell him. *I'm hurt in about a hundred different ways.*

He shines his flashlight around, scattering the darkness that has fallen around us. Then back to me. He moves in close, puts his hand on my arm.

"Are you okay?" he asks. His eyes search my face, as he puts his thumb to my eyes, wipes away tears. Something about his heat, his strength. When he pulls me in, I let him. I sink into him, let him wrap me up in strong arms. Finally, embarrassed, I pull away, stare down at the ground.

"Wren, what are you thinking? Coming out here alone?"

Just like a man, right? Imagining that he knows best what should and shouldn't be done. About to deliver some lecture.

"I could ask you the same," I say.

I can't read his expression. He looks past me into the darkness, and I turn to look, as well. Still nothing but winter trees, the

267

ground starting to glow with the rising moon.

Into the silence between us, I admit, "I saw someone. Maybe. I thought —"

I'm going to stop talking because it sounds too much like what I told him the other day. I saw a man in the building across the street and I gave chase, and then he was gone. No one else had seen him — not Bailey Kirk, not the many office workers at their desks. Just me.

In fact, no one has ever seen you, have they, Adam? Not even Jax. I wasn't ready to introduce you to my friends, my life. I didn't want to tell you about *Dear Birdie*. But I didn't want to lie about it either. And now you're gone from my life, and no one else has ever laid eyes on you.

"Yeah," he says in answer to my first question, I guess. "I'm following you. I followed you here."

"Why?"

Stupid question, right? He thinks I'm looking for you, or that you're going to come back for me with some nefarious intent. He's right about me. Maybe he's right about you. Either way, and I don't plan to admit this, I'm glad to see Bailey Kirk. I don't want to be alone in this dark place anymore, chasing shadows into nothing, feeling my way out.

"Because that's what detectives do," he says, holding out his arm. "We follow. It's usually pretty dull. A lot of times, we just sit and wait, and nothing ever happens. So far that's not the case with you. You're keeping me busy."

In spite of myself, I take the help he's offered, grab on to him. We start moving back in the direction of my car. I'm limping a little, my knee aching from the fall.

"But you're not getting any closer to Mia."

He offers a thoughtful dip of his head. "We'll see. The night is young."

We exit the forest and step out into the clearing, the moon on the rise. It's fat and white, looking down impassively.

"Who were you visiting?" he asks.

There's no easy lie, nothing quick to say to deflect the question. So, I opt for silence. But we have to walk past the graves to get to our cars, his parked behind me, lights burning, engine running.

"What do you know about me, Detective?" I ask, stopping at Robin's grave.

She loved the cemetery, which is essentially a wildlife sanctuary. Centuries, in some cases, of mainly undisturbed trees. A place of quietude and peace, birds find safety among the dead — warblers, thrushes, and, of course, robins.

"I'm sorry," he says. He rubs at the crown of his head.

I take this as an admission that he knows everything I have tried to hide. I hate him for it a little. And yet, there's also a wash of relief, a tension that dissolves from my shoulders and my neck. It takes so much energy to lie, to hide, to be someone else all the time. The weight of it never occurred to me, how it would grow and become heavier over the years, a great hump on my back, bending me down low.

"Want to get out of here?" he says.

He looks uncomfortable, keeps glancing back at the trees. City boy. Like so many of us, he's forgotten that we are one with nature, with death. That one day we'll be trees and grass, wildflowers, lichen on headstones, stars in the sky.

"I know a place," I say.

"I'll follow you."

"Yeah," I answer. "I'm getting that."

In the dark of my car, I start the engine. Just as I'm about to pull away, my phone pings.

A text from an unknown number.

Welcome home, little bird.

Little bird. The only person on earth who ever called me that was my father. But the text must be from you, Adam. Did I tell you that he used to call me that? How do you know I'm back here? Was it you in the woods watching?

I feel like the world is spinning, past blurring into present, a great spinning wheel. You. This place. The girl I was. The woman I've become. And my father.

Just as it is with you, when I reach for him he slips away, like all the mysteries of childhood. He comes back to me only in snapshots, yellowed and faded with age, grainy. Always a stranger, like the boy in the photograph I found.

I am always chasing him.

TWENTY-FOUR

Then

"Little bird. Get up."

My father's voice, his touch on my shoulder, drew me up through layers of deepest sleep. When I woke, he stood over me, dressed, a heavy pack on his back.

"What's wrong?" I asked, feeling the jangle of alarm.

Jay stood over by the door, also dressed, also burdened by a heavy pack. He looked dead on his feet, hair sleep tousled, eyes blank.

"If they come," my father said, eyes shining, "they'll come in the night."

"If who comes?" I asked, looking past him. The bright full moon washed in through my window, casting him in an eerie white glow. "Where's Mom?"

Behind him, Jay shook his head quickly. I read his thoughts: *Shut up. Do what he says.*

"Get up," my father said more sternly. "I

272

need you to be strong."

I climbed out of bed, pulled on my jeans over my nightgown, grabbed my sweatshirt — a hand-me-down of Jay's that I wore pretty much daily. I slipped into my sneakers.

"Where are we going?" I asked. I knew I could push him further than Jay could. Too many questions could earn Jay a crack across the face. The youngest, the girl, my father's clear favorite, I had more leeway. But he didn't answer me.

Out in the hall was another big pack, smaller than those that Jay and my father had on their backs but still huge. "When they come, you grab this pack. See? It's red. Mine's blue; your brother's is black."

I shifted it on.

"What about Mom?"

"Your mother has another job to do when they come. She knows what it is."

What was in these packs? Where had they come from? Where would I find mine when "they" came in the night? There were always big plot holes in my father's stories. Better just to go along. Especially when he had that tension coming off him like electricity, when his tone was pulled taut and excited.

He helped me heft on the pack, and I nearly buckled under the weight.

Where was Mom? *Luke,* she'd say, *it's too heavy for her.* But their bedroom door was closed. I felt tears start to well from a place of helpless anger and deep fatigue.

"Let's go," said my father. "We won't have this kind of time. Keep up."

Outside, he took off in a jog, Jay following suit. I could barely walk, the pack was so heavy. I moved as fast as I could along the trail trying to keep up with Jay, who I could tell was purposely slowing his pace for my benefit. It was more than a mile from the house to the bunker. And by the time I got there, I was breathless, every muscle in my back and legs screaming. The moonlight was so bright, washing everything in blue-white.

Resting a hand against the concrete wall, I leaned over and threw up.

My father lifted the pack off me. "You're going to have to do better than that. You need to get stronger. Faster."

I nodded, always eager to please, willing myself not to get sick again. "Okay. I will."

As my father unlocked the bunker door, I recognized the look on Jay's face. It was just like my father's — a mask of buried rage, just waiting for a moment of ignition. Jay's eyes were dark with hatred, but it was that terrible hatred undercut by fear and longing we can only feel for the parent who is abusing us.

"When they come, you bring those packs here. I'll either be with you, or I'll be waiting."

"When who comes, Dad?" asked Jay, voice sizzling with anger. "Who's coming? I mean really. *Who* is *coming*?"

But my father didn't answer, just unlocked the door and pushed inside. We followed him down the staircase to the interior door.

"You lock the outer door behind you," he said. "Then when you get to the bottom, you unlock this door."

Inside my father shifted off his pack, and Jay did the same; they sagged heavy on the floor. What was in them? I didn't even know. The orange lantern light flickered. I wanted to lie down on the old plaid couch and fall asleep, but I stood, pushing my body in close to my brother's, taking his hand. I expected him to push me away. But he didn't, squeezing my hand tight.

How would the world end? I wondered. Disease, my father said sometimes. Global financial collapse. Famine. Climate change. There were myriad ways, and we'd survive them all, isolated as we were, able to live off the grid.

"And this is where we'll stay, all of us.

Until it's safe."

"Safe from what?" I ventured.

He rubbed at the crown of his head, looked around wildly, and there was a shattering moment when I realized that he was scared. Scared and trying to figure out how to protect us against an unnamed threat that was on its way. One we couldn't identify but had to prepare for just the same.

I think Jay had the same realization, but instead of feeling pity as I did, his face registered disgust.

"Dad," Jay said, his voice holding a pleading quality. "Oh, my God. You're fucking crazy. You're completely nuts."

The slap came so fast, it was like the strike of a snake. Jay reeled, stumbling back into the wall, knocking his head hard. He sank to the ground, my father moving in. I raced between them, standing in front of Jay and holding my arms out wide. Jay edged back, pushing himself against the wall. Head in his hands. My father took a big step toward us, arm raised. I raced over to him, pushing him backward with all my strength.

"Don't! Don't!" I yelled. "Stop!"

My father lowered his arm, stared at me, anger and sadness doing battle on his face.

"Stop," I said again. "He didn't mean it. He's just — *scared.*"

276

Because that was the truth, wasn't it? We were all scared of different things.

My father took a step back, shaking his head.

"Man up, son," he said, voice soft. "This is the world."

The silence expanded, my brother softly crying behind me. When he rose, there was a big skein of blood from both nostrils down the front of his shirt.

"This is *your* world," he said.

When my father moved toward him, I ran and wrapped my arms around his slim waist, holding him, holding him back. "Please," I whispered. "Please."

Jay left the cellar, footfalls echoing up the steps. I wanted to go after him, but something kept me rooted. My father, he never hit me. I wasn't physically afraid of him, not really. That's why it fell to me to protect Jay.

I stayed behind, still holding on to my father. I felt his arms drop around me. The air was silent, the energy taut.

"Women are always stronger," my father said finally, pushing me back to look at me. "Survival won't just be about might. It will be about endurance, fortitude, courage. Those are female qualities."

He walked back to the weapons cache,

unlocked the door and stepped inside.

The dank of the cellar made my sinuses swell as I stood watching his light traveling over rows of weapons.

"Next week, I'm going to teach you to hunt with a crossbow."

He put his hand on one; it was black and curved like a snake, a strange hybrid of bow and gun. It terrified and intrigued me.

"I don't want to kill anything," I said. He smiled, put a hand on my head.

"But you'll eat a hamburger, right?" he said. "What about those chicken fingers you used to like? Where do you think they came from? Somebody killed the cow, the hen."

"That's different."

"It's not," he said. "It's not different at all except that you'll understand what it means to eat meat."

The logic of it was undeniable. I felt it in my nerve endings.

"Don't worry. It will be a long time before your aim is any good. You'll be lucky to hit the side of the barn."

Back in the outer room, I stared in dismay at the packs. Jay had left his. I did not want to carry mine back.

"Why not just leave them here," I suggested. "If this is where they need to be."

Fatigue had seemed to settle on him, too.

He nodded his agreement and we trudged home.

Outside, I followed him out into the dawn. Even now I can see that strange golden light.

That afternoon, while I was reading in the study, I saw her again through the window, the girl with the wild hair and torn jeans, the too small flowered blouse.

She stood still inside the dark space between the trees. We stared at each other for a moment, then she lifted her hand in greeting. I waved back and she motioned for me to come. I rose from my perch and went outside with no hesitation. I hadn't seen another kid in so long; I was so lonely.

She disappeared into the trees and I followed, finally catching up to her by the creek. She crouched over a big rock, ran her fingers gently over its surface, whispering like she was talking to a pet.

"Do you know what this is?" she asked me. The surface of the rock was covered with a patina green layer.

"Moss?" I ventured.

She shook her head. "It's lichen," she said, looking at me. "It's alive."

She said it with a kind of wonder. I leaned in close to see what she saw; it just looked like paint on the gray surface of the rock.

"It's two things," she went on. "It's fungus and algae. They work together to survive."

I touched it gently; it was soft and papery.

"They're tough," she said. "Some lichen has been around for hundreds of years."

The creek babbled and somewhere a woodpecker knocked. I looked around for its bobbing red head, but I didn't see it.

When I looked back, the girl was staring at me, her eyes twinkly and smiley.

"Where did you come from?" I asked.

She pointed over to the east. "Way over there," she said.

I hadn't ventured to the edge of our property. But I knew there were other homes, other people. Some of the men came to meet with my father now and then; they played cards and talked late. My brother, and some of the other older boys, were allowed to sit with them, but I was sent to bed. Which was fine because they smoked and cussed, and the things they said didn't make any sense to me anyway.

"What's your name," I asked.

"Robin," she said.

"That's my name, too," I said, surprised.

"That won't do," she answered. "We can't have the same name if we're going to be best friends."

That made sense. She looked at me, finger to her pink chin. She was a sprite, pug nose and pouty mouth, skin translucent, wisp thin, fast and agile as a rabbit.

"I'm going to call you Wren."

I liked that. I was happy to have a new name, a new friend.

TWENTY-FIVE

Now

I'm still shaken when we wind up in a bar
just outside town, grab a booth in the back
at a place called The Juke. I've been here
before and it seems eternal, unchanging.
There's a pool table where no one's playing, a silent jukebox, a lone bartender shooting the shit with a couple of guys who look
like off-duty cops with buzz cuts and big
shoulders, tired eyes. A football game plays
on the television hanging on the wall, sound
down. An occasional half-hearted cheer
goes up from a group I can't see from where
I'm sitting. I find myself staring at the
screen, though I have no interest in sports,
or television for that matter.

Welcome home, little bird.

Only one person has ever called me that.
My father. My nerve endings tingle.

Bailey Kirk hasn't said a thing since he
ordered his bacon double cheeseburger with

fries and a large root beer. I ordered the same from the waitress who I think was working this shift the last time I was here years ago. Or maybe it's just a type that works in a place like this — buxom, hard miles on the face, a certain shade of maroon lipstick and blue fingernails. Her T-shirt reads affably: Don't like my attitude? Dial 1-800-F*CK-YOU.

I know Bailey's game. He's waiting for me to talk. But I'm waiting for him to talk. Let's see who wins.

Finally: "So, what brings you up here?" he asks.

"Look," I answer, leaning across the table, "can we stop this? I've told you everything I know about Adam. Truly. Why don't you tell me what you think you know about me? Everything out on the table. Okay?"

The waitress comes with our food. Its greasy aroma wafts up and I'm suddenly ravenous. I can't remember the last time I ate.

Oh, it's good — hamburger juicy, fries crispy. I feel myself perking up a bit. The root beer sends fireworks of endorphins through my system. The magical restorative powers of fat and sugar cannot be overstated.

"I'm not trying to unearth all your secrets," he says, after taking a big bite. "It's just that there are four women, three of them missing. I'm looking for the place where you all intersect. The only way I can do that is to look at your lives."

"That's easy," I say, mouth full. "I mean it's obvious, isn't it? Torch. That's the thing we all had in common. That we were desperate enough, or lonely enough that we all got online looking for love."

I wipe at a drop of ketchup I can feel on the side of my mouth. I flash on our last visit to the Shake Shack in Madison Square Park where you reached over with your napkin and wiped some mustard away, an amused smile lighting up your brooding face. I've always been a sloppy eater. *You weren't raised by wolves!* my mother used to lament. If only.

"I think there's more to it," he says.

"What if there isn't anything else that connects us?" I say. "What if he's just a predator, and like any predator he has an appetite for a specific kind of prey. Torch is his hunting ground of choice."

Bailey is quiet a moment as he goes to town on those fries. He's an unapologetic eater, too. I can tell by his build that he works out, the definition of his muscles, the way he carries himself, the solid strength of his arm back in the woods. But he's got that softness to him of the person who loves food. He's not the guy counting calories and opting for the vegan plate.

"But none of you look especially similar," he says finally. "Same age, I suppose. All of you beautiful, but in really different ways. Not like you all have dark hair, or the same color eyes."

Heat rises to my cheeks at the compliment. But it sounds like a throwaway line, so I don't acknowledge it.

"Maybe it's a kind of energy he's picking up on, rather than anything physical," I say. My root beer is gone. Should I have another one? I lift my glass to the waitress, and she gives me a thumbs-up. "Do you have pictures of the other girls?"

He takes out his phone and slides it over. He's created a layout with all four women, including me in one image. It's my Torch profile picture, which Jax took. It's not the worst shot of me. She told me to think about getting laid — which made me laugh; that's when she took the picture. My eyes glitter with mischief.

"All women of means," he continues. Then more gently, "All suffered extreme childhood trauma."

A painful ache has settled behind my eyes.

I rub at my temples, push my plate away.

"Maybe it's just coincidence that they all dated him? Maybe he has nothing to do with what happened to them?"

"Possible," he says. "But highly unlikely. I'm not a big believer in coincidence."

The waitress brings my second root beer. I sip at it. It's not as good as the first one, for some reason. Now it tastes sickly sweet. My stomach protests a little at its greasy contents.

"What brings you up here today?" he asks again.

I focus on my burger, which is almost gone, rather than look at him. He must have seen me kneeling at the graves. He knows my history. This place, as much as I wish it wasn't, is a kind of home.

But that's not why I came. I came because of the article I found. Because of Melissa Farrow, who also had a connection to this place. There are answers here maybe. Maybe the answers have always been here.

"I just come here sometimes. To manage things. The graves. The house."

That's true, too. I don't want to admit that I'm here looking for you. We're both looking for you, but for very different reasons. If he finds you first, I may never get what I want.

286

What I also don't say: when I come back here, I'm overcome with homesickness for a place that never existed. A word I read comes to mind: *solastalgia,* a miserable tangle of solace, desolation, and nostalgia. Glenn Albrecht defines it as the distress of seeing a familiar environment bitterly transformed by drought, fire, flood, war. But it describes perfectly how I feel about my childhood.

"When I mentioned this town last night, you didn't say anything."

"Didn't I?"

Again, with that unreadable expression, a blink of his icy eyes.

"I get it." He polishes off his burger, glances at his phone. "You don't trust me. We all have things we don't want to talk about, or even remember. I just wondered if you were trying to follow his trail. You know, playing amateur detective. Maybe looking for Melissa Farrow."

"No," I lie. "Nothing like that."

"Do you know her?"

"No," I say. "I don't."

"But you grew up here. So did she."

I shrug, my eyes drifting back to the television where the game continues. Someone scores. More cheering.

"I wouldn't say I grew up here. After my

father came back from his deployment, he moved us into the house he'd inherited. It sat on twenty acres, and I was home-schooled. My dad — he wanted to move away from modern life. The world of men, as he called it. We weren't part of the community in that way."

He's doing this slow nodding thing. It's oddly comforting, as if he was perfectly present in the conversation. "I understand."

"So we were here, but apart. My dad — he wasn't well. I know that now. He had untreated PTSD, was self-medicating, a heavy drinker. There were problems even before he went overseas, I think. Some history of bipolar disorder in the family."

I'm not sure I've ever said these things before, not even to Jax, who knows more about me than anyone. I never talk about the details, the logistics of what happened. How things unraveled. It all exists as if in a nightmare, not connected to the real word of my present life.

"It was common back then for PTSD in soldiers to go largely untreated," Bailey says. "Only more recently is it better understood, more treatment available."

"If they seek it," I say. "And often they don't. There's still a lot of shame. Still a lot of men who come home and try to tough

288

their way through it. That was my father. He fought a war he didn't understand, only to come and fight one he understood even less. He lost."

Bailey goes inward, a sudden shift in the light of his eyes. I wonder who he's thinking about. Not himself. He doesn't have soldier's eyes, that look they get when they've seen things that they can't unsee, know things about life and the human body that they shouldn't know.

Someone has started up the jukebox. Jim Morrison wants us to roll baby roll.

He touches the phone between us, and it glows with the images of the four women you've encountered. Four that I know of. Are there more?

"I didn't know Melissa Farrow," I say. "I didn't have any friends here."

He looks like he's about to push. His mouth opens; he puts his forearms on the table. Close up, there are violet circles of fatigue under his eyes, tiny lines around his mouth. He has strong arches for eyebrows, a few grays in the stubble growing on his jaw. He presses his mouth closed, leans back. Whatever he wants to say, he keeps it to himself.

"How did you find out about *Dear Birdie*?" I ask, eager to move on from the topic of my past.

"A magician never reveals how his tricks are performed."

"You're no magician."

He does that thing with his hands, puts one fist in the other palm, squeezes. His knuckles crack softly. "It wasn't hard. You dug yourself a pretty shallow grave."

The analogy stings, brings to mind those white orchids, already wilting on the graves of Jay, Robin, my mom. I imagine the snow-white petals against the black earth, slowly sinking in, buried by falling leaves.

"Once I had your name, address, and cell phone from my contact at Torch, I ran a couple of background checks, including a criminal check. Those revealed other names you have used, including the one on your birth certificate. You legally changed your given name to Wren Greenwood when you were still a kid."

I thought I was hidden, safe behind my made-up name. But only because maybe no one was truly looking until now.

How did you know that I was someone else once upon a time, Adam?

Bailey steeples his fingers. He thinks he knows everything but probably he doesn't.

"Your secrets are safe with me," he says. "I'm the vault. What you tell me, stays between us, okay? I'm not here to blow up your life. I only care about finding Mia, and making sure this guy doesn't hurt anyone else, including you. I promise you that."

Promises. We break them so easily, don't we? But when I look at him, really look at him, I see he means it.

"What if there is nothing else?" I say again. "What if the only thing we all share is that we were stupid enough to think we could find true love in a digital wasteland?"

He polishes off his burger, drains his root beer. The paper lining the plastic basket is translucent with grease.

"Then Mia's trail is cold. She's gone. Your friend?" A muscle works in his jaw. I noticed that particular tell back on the train. What is it? Frustration. Determination. "He's gone, too. And I have to go back to my client and tell him I failed him, failed his child. That he might never know what happened to his daughter."

It strikes me as a heavy burden, one with which I'm familiar in my capacity as Dear Birdie. When you endeavor to take on other people's heartache, it becomes your own in some ways.

"And I don't want to do that yet," he says. "I'm not ready to let go."

Me, neither.

"So now what?" I say.

"I have a couple more tricks up my sleeve yet."

"Sticking with the magician analogy?"

He reaches across the table, as if for behind my right ear. I flinch away, no idea what he's doing. When he brings his hand back, he's holding two twenties, offers a big grin.

At some point our waitress has brought the check, a paper slip with her scrawl on. Forty dollars is more than enough to cover it with a large tip.

"I'll be in touch," he says, rising.

"Great." I watch him go, some combination of annoyed and relieved.

The waitress comes back to my table.

"Friend of yours?" she asks. Which is odd. Because I don't know her.

"In a way," I answer.

"He's been around awhile," she says. She picks up the check, the money, slips it into the pocket of her apron. "He's staying at the Motel 8 just outside town."

"How do you know that?" I have to ask. What I don't ask: And why are you telling me?

"That big fancy truck he drives. Seen it around town. Seen it there. He's not from around here."

Neither am I, I want to assert. But it's not really true, is it?

"I'd watch out for that one," she says. "He's trouble."

Okay, I'm about to say, with just an edge of attitude. Thanks.

But when I look up at her she's already walked back behind the bar. The bartender leans into her as she says something to him. They both turn to look at me.

As I pick up my things and exit into the dark, I can feel their eyes on me.

TWENTY-SIX

Then

The morning dawned wild with birdsong, waking me from the uncomfortable bed I'd made on the porch swing. Jay sat sentry in the old rocker, shoulders stiff and face drawn in the new light. My father had started drinking after dinner the night before, and what began as a peaceful evening, with him playing the guitar and my mother knitting, had soured.

Soured. Not the right word. That implies the slow turning of something good into something rotten.

Ignited.

My father's rage was a fuse that took any excuse to light. It transformed him, made him huge, and cruel, brutal. Since the late-night trip to the bunker, things had been worse than ever. He never hit me, not once. Maybe because I made myself small, shrank myself down to nothing, hid. But my mother and Jay, they fought back.

The makeshift ice pack I'd put together from a bag of frozen peas and a dishcloth sat on the arm of the rocker. Jay rubbed at his jaw. Even in the dim light, I could see that the side of his face was purple and swollen.

He'd come out here last night to be ready if my father came back. I'd stayed with him; my mother cried herself to sleep in my bedroom. What had made my father so angry? I didn't even remember. I thought about the garden we'd planted, the lunches I'd shared with him, his quiet in those moments, his strength, the way he understood the land.

"Put it back," I urged Jay. A blackbird landed on the porch rail, cocking his head back and forth at me.

Jay had taken a handgun from the weapons cache the night before. It lay in his lap.

"He's passed out somewhere now, probably in the barn," I went on when he said nothing. "He won't even remember what happened when he wakes up."

Jay turned his head slowly to look at me. His voice last night, it had been high and desperate, childlike. *Leave her alone,* he'd wailed. My father hit him so hard that I felt it in my own jaw, started to cry.

The blackbird flew off.

"Don't love him," Jay said. "Even though he's nice sometimes, and he's our father. Don't love him. He doesn't deserve it."

"I don't," I said quick, defensive. But I did. The man he was during the day, just like my mother loved the man he was "before." The man in the photographs — young, brave, strong in his uniform, face fresh and eyes bright. Thank you for your service. The boy in the photograph, wearing his best suit. The man in the garden, with the sweat on his face, hands in the earth.

"Put it back," I said again.

As long as Jay had that gun, I knew something bad could happen, something worse, any second. We'd both been learning to shoot, aiming at cans my father lined up on a rusted-out old tractor that sat in the clearing.

You're a deadeye, son, he told Jay. My brother hit every can, every time.

I got a pat on the head. *Keep at it, girl.*

Girl. He didn't mean it as an insult. But it felt like one. I vowed to get better.

Jay and I locked eyes now. The sun was breaking the horizon, painting the sky pink. He nodded, just slightly and rose, the rocker beneath him groaning. He stepped over the porch and took the path that led to the cellar where the guns were kept. God forbid, my father should find it missing.

I waited for him to return, listening to the morning cacophony, that sun salutation — chickadee, warbler, thrush, starling, northern cardinal. Back "in town," in our other life, I never heard their song, not really. In the quiet, birds thrive. Noise is a kind of pollution; it silences nature.

Finally, Jay returned, walking by me into the house without a word, letting the squeaky screen door slam hard.

I sat, listening to the birds. When I looked into the trees, I saw Robin standing there. I walked off the porch to join her.

You have to do something, she told me. *Or things are just going to get worse and worse.*

TWENTY-SEVEN

Now

Back at the bed-and-breakfast, I turn on the fireplace, put on my sweats and check my computer. No word from my mysterious contact. I didn't expect him to be fast. In fact, I wouldn't be surprised to never hear from him again. There *is* an email from Marty, my accountant, confirming the Bitcoin transaction and asking if I need to talk. I don't.

No more texts from you. But I feel you, shadowing me. Where are you?

Was it you out in the woods tonight? Or am I losing it? If not you, then who? And those cigarettes by Jay's grave. Do you smoke? I doubt it.

That text. *Welcome home, little bird.*

It confirms that you know way more about me than you have a right to.

I turn off all the lights except the one by my bed, which is dim. I'll sleep with it on, its pink glow keeping the shadows at bay. I never liked the dark.

As I settle into bed, my phone rings, Jax's high cheekbones and wide smile on my screen. It's a picture I took of her ages ago, still stored in her contact file.

"You're not coming home," she says when I answer. "I can see your little blue dot blipping on Find My Friends. Up in the middle of nowhere and nothing."

"Not tonight."

She sighs.

"Want me to stay at the house?" she asks.

"If you want," I tell her. I like the idea of her and the house keeping each other company. My favorite human and my favorite place. Maybe she should just move in. It's a big house. Her Chelsea rent is obscene.

"Don't worry," she says. "I'm not gonna blow up your iTunes, your UberEats, your grocery delivery account."

"But it seems like you're well on your way."

I've been getting text notifications all day — pizza for lunch, Chinese for dinner, binge-watching Christmas romcoms. This is a very typical postbreakup day for Jax.

"A girl has got to eat."

Truth.

"What happened with the mauler?" I ask.

"Ghosted."

"Good."

"He's not the last Coca-Cola in the desert, right?" She must have talked to her mother.

"Hell no."

I don't know. Maybe he is. I'm not feeling very optimistic about love at the moment. Or anything. A pall has settled over me — this place, the search for you, the missing women, my strange relationship with Bailey Kirk, my unbidden memories. It's one ugly twist that I can't seem to untangle. But I don't need to drag her down with me.

"You don't sound right," she says. "Just come home. You know you get depressed up there. Sell that damn house. Forget about the graves. What are you holding on to, Wren?"

She's right. I know this. What *am* I holding on to?

"I'll come home tomorrow." I nestle down into the soft sheets and covers, watch the flames in the fireplace.

"Promise?"

"Promise."

"What about *Dear Birdie*?"

"You can do her, Jax. I trust you. I'll pay you."

She's chewing. Must be Chicken Lo

Mein, her Chinese go-to. "I think you already did — in takeout and movies."

"Just bill me."

"I don't know how you do it, Wren."

"Do what?"

"Dear Birdie. Don't you get tired of other people's problems?"

I think about Bailey Kirk for some reason. The fatigue under his eyes, the burden he seemed to shoulder. The weight of other people's sorrows is often far less than the idea of examining your own. I wonder what *he's* carrying. Those eyes are full of secrets.

"Someone has to help people in this cruel world," I say, only half kidding.

"Yeah," she says, drawing out the syllable. "But does it have to be you?"

The fire crackles, and the room is bathed in the pink light coming from the lamp by the bed. I feel safe, ensconced. That's the other thing about The Hollows. I may not like it. But there's something comforting in its familiarity. Like I could just stay. Or like I *should.*

"Maybe," I answer. "I don't know."

"Because I was thinking that you could just sell *Dear Birdie.*"

"*Sell* her?"

"Yeah, you know, like Princess Bride. Dread Pirate Roberts? It was just a name, right, someone else slipping into the role, then handing it off to the next person who needs a cover."

"You've been watching too much Netflix."

She blows out a breath. "It's a *thing.* For real. People do that shit. How many dead authors are still writing books from beyond the grave?"

I never thought about that, the idea that I could shed Dear Birdie like a shawl, put it on someone else's shoulders. The thought is equal parts comforting and frightening. Who am I without *Dear Birdie*? I don't even know.

"Do *you* want to be Dear Birdie?" I ask.

When she stops laughing: *"Heeellll* no. You must be out of your mind. I've got my own problems. I can barely handle the nonproblems — *my boss won't promote me, what is my purpose, am I following my bliss* — I'm dealing with day to day on my own blog. *Dear Birdie?* Some of those troubles are *dark."*

It's true. Jax's blog is a bit lighter, the problems more existential, the issues of people who are standing on solid ground. I wonder . . . could I, *would I,* shed Dear Birdie?

"What would I do about the podcast?"

"Just find someone who sounds like you,"

302

says Jax. "That Dear Birdie voice isn't your real voice anyway. It's like you're channeling someone."

"You've given this a lot of thought."

"Some," she says softly. "Wren, I just want you to find a little joy, take a little time for you. Can you do that when you're tethered to your past? When you spend your days listening to everyone else's heartbreak?"

We don't find many true friends in our lives. Everyone's always looking for love, right? That perfect soul mate. The candy, flowers, trips to Paris, romance. No one ever talks about the power and comfort of a true friendship that endures years. The friend who worries about you, is there when you call, brings soup when you're sick, camps out on your couch when you're sad. There aren't many friends like that. If you have one, be grateful. I know I am.

"Don't worry about me," I tell her. "I'm okay."

"Okay," she says. "We can keep talking about it. In the meantime, I'll cover her tomorrow. But then you need to take her back."

"Deal."

"Oh, hey. There's a message — not spying on your email but something forwarded from the old account. You know — the one from the blog where you used to get the *Dear Birdie* letters. I couldn't log in to see what it was."

Sometimes people email their letters to that old address. It's still floating out there in the eternity of the internet. I should close the box. But I hate the thought of someone reaching out and just getting an error message. I check it periodically.

"I'll take a look."

She draws in and releases a deep breath.

"Let him go, Wren. What I said about taking back your power, finding justice. Forget it. Just move on. Let *that place* go. Come on home to the life you've made. It's a good one."

"Tomorrow. I promise."

Silence, then, "Love you."

"Love you more."

I try to sleep but I can't — every time I start to drift off I'm chasing Robin, or chasing you, waking with a start as I trip and fall, or catch a wrist and find myself holding on to a ghoul.

Finally, I give up on sleep and open my laptop, I log on to the old account. There's only one message from a strange address, just a number and an unfamiliar server.

I open the message.

Dear Birdie,

I didn't think it was possible but I've fallen in love. Crazy love. The kind that makes you question all your choices, makes you want to be a better man. I've made mistakes. Terrible ones. In fact, the kind of mistakes some people would never be able to forgive. Regret is a burden I carry, day and night. It sneaks up on me in blank moments. It wakes me from sleep. I know it will never leave me.

I was about to share myself with this woman. She shared herself with me, bared her soul without fear. But just as I was about to open up to her, my past came back to haunt.

There's someone at my heels, wanting me to pay for the things I've done. And maybe this is right. Maybe I don't deserve to love or to be loved after the things I've done. But I just wanted my chance to show myself to this woman, to let her judge me, so that I can know whether I could ever be truly worthy of her.

I had to leave her, suddenly, and without explanation. I know it broke her heart. But I didn't have a choice. There are people looking for me, and they are catching up fast. And, now, if I reach out to her, I risk my life, my freedom. I'll be asked to pay a price that I'm not sure I'm willing to pay. The world is harsh and cruel, but without my freedom I will die. I can't live in a cage.

So, my question is this, Dear Birdie. If I ask her to come to me, if I find a way to ask her to meet me, so that I can share myself with her, do you think that she would come? Or would she turn me in, open the door to the wolves waiting outside. Would she want to hear the awful things I have to tell her? Could she ever forgive me? Could she possibly still love me?

Whatever you tell me to do. I'll do.

Sincerely,
Unforgiven

The words swim on the screen, and I'm shaking from deep inside. It's you, Adam, it must be. Asking for my love, my forgiveness. And something else, you always knew I was Dear Birdie. All my layers, the ones I thought I'd hidden were exposed long ago. Buffeted by anger, sadness, fear, I answer now, my fingers quaking over the keyboard.

Dear Unforgiven,

We can never undo the things we've done. We can't turn back time and right wrongs. All we can do is move forward wiser for our mistakes, vowing never to make the same mistakes again. We can make amends to those we've harmed. And we can face our punishment, if that's what's called for by the law.

If you love this woman, and she loves you, she deserves to know everything about you. Even the things that sound like they are very dark, maybe things she can never understand or accept. Still, if she has given herself to you and you have given yourself to her, there can only be honesty now. The truth is the only way forward. Otherwise, she'll never really know you. And she'll never have the chance to love you. Can I promise that she'll accept you? Can I promise that she won't force you to pay for your crimes? No. But if you don't reach out to her, you'll never know if the love you shared was real. And you will remain unforgiven.

Sincerely,
Dear Birdie

I send the letter and wait, refreshing the

screen every few minutes.

No answer ever comes.

I drift off into a dreamless sleep.

When I awake, the sun is streaming through my window and my screen has gone dark. I touch the keypad, my heart racing.

But the inbox is empty.

There is however a text on my phone. Hey, it reads. I heard you were in town. Come see me. We need to talk.

TWENTY-EIGHT

Then

Robin taught me how to track, how to follow signs, detect a game trail. How to determine if it had been a rabbit or a squirrel or a deer nibbling at the vegetation. How if you saw crows circling in the sky, there was likely a fresh kill — coyotes or less common wolves — and they were waiting their turn to pick the bones clean. The land spoke to her. And she was my translator. Or so it seemed to me at the time.

But it was my father who taught me how to hunt.

"Killing a thing," my father told me, "is a sacred act."

We'd been trekking through the woods for what seemed like hours, the vegetation thick, the crossbow heavy on my back. I was tired already, though the sun was just rising. And dread was thick in my throat. I was no hunter. I knew this, and I wondered how my father was going to feel about me when he figured it out.

"It's nature's way that we must kill to survive."

Was that true? It sounded true but it didn't feel right.

I'd seen enough nature shows — impalas felled by lions, seals taken by killer whales, bunnies carried off by eagles — to know that death was part of life. But animals act on instinct. They have no choice. Some animals kill to survive; others are born prey. Humans, supposedly, are elevated by their intelligence.

"Like war?" I asked quietly, knowing to keep my voice low.

My father looked back and down at me, eyes startled, deeply sad. "No," he said. "Not like war at all."

How is it different? I didn't dare ask.

"When you kill an animal to feed yourself and your family, it's part of an agreement you have with the planet."

I didn't say anything. There was only our breath, the sound of our movement through the woods. "Now, people take and take. They've taken too much. The bill will come due. And those of us who know how to survive when civilization crumbles will keep our contract with the planet. Take what you need to survive. Not more."

I stayed quiet as we moved slowly on. The world we'd left behind had swiftly fallen away. Without phone or cable or internet, everything I knew and thought was real seemed as distant as a dream. Even the faces of my friends were fading.

The first sign of the deer was her scat. A pile still-warm, berries visible through the muck.

A few feet later, a nibbled branch, the end left rough and torn from her bottom incisors, frayed. Rabbits make a bite that looks like a knife's cut from their sharp teeth. But deer munching leaves a ragged edge.

My father touched the frayed branch and gave me a slow nod, raising his fingers to his lips.

Soon enough, there she was. A doe, peacefully crunching on viburnum leaves. Her tawny fur and shining black eyes punching a contrast against the verdant green of the leaves. I watched her, overcome with a sense of peace — the wind, the birdsong, the quiet whisper of her eating.

My father's eyes stayed on me as I took the crossbow from my back. I'd been practicing for months, and the weight of it was familiar. I slipped an arrow from my quiver. I had grown practiced at loading, took it to the ground put my foot on the bow and drew back the rack, slid the arrow down the flight track. He didn't move to help me.

I lifted the bow to peer through the sight.

Jay had already refused to hunt. *I'm not killing for you,* he told my father.

Then don't eat, my father had answered. It was the rare argument that didn't end with violence.

I'm a vegetarian.

My father scowled. *Since when?*

Since now.

I was my father's last hope if we were going to survive the end days, which no one but my father believed were coming. Meanwhile, the freezer was full of hot dogs. We could probably live on those for a year if we had to. My mother brought fresh groceries from town every week; personally, I could live on boxed macaroni and cheese and toaster waffles. So, we didn't *actually* need to kill to survive. Were we still acting within the contract we had with the planet?

I watched the doe, nibbling. She had not detected our presence.

All I would have to do was step on a branch and crack it to send her running.

But I felt the tension of that cocked bow, the pressure of my father's expectation. My arms had grown strong, my aim steady. I had her in my site. My breath was so slow and measured. It almost happened without me. The arrow released, slicing the air, and found its mark solid and sure, sinking deep into her flesh. Her body jerked, eyes wild with fear and pain.

The doe went down, silent.

My father turned to me; his eyes filled with proud amazement.

It was both the worst and the best moment of my life.

Something inside me shifted and changed. There was a powerful rush of despair. I had taken the life of an innocent creature, a thing that could never be undone. I could never go back to the person I was before that action. Once the arrow left the bow and found its mark, I was forever altered.

But, deeper, there was also a calm that came with a new knowledge of the world, the way of it. That life and death existed together in one inextricable tangle. The scope and depth of that understanding came with a terrified awe. I sank to my knees, silently weeping.

My father stood beside me, his hand on my head, kept it there until I looked up at him. His face was drawn, haunted.

"I know," he said softly. "I'm sorry."

TWENTY-NINE

Now

I leave the inn and head into town. The sky is sullen gray, threatening weather.

After a short drive, winding through the picture-postcard square, a few turns on pretty tree-lined streets, I pull in front of a carefully maintained house with white shingles, maroon shutters, and a matching front door with brass knocker. The shrubs are neat, the flower beds empty for winter. Some poinsettias sit on the stoop, a vibrant red and snowy white. It's as I remember it, warm, welcoming. A safe house.

I'm triggered, as they say in modern trauma speak, heart racing, anxiety mounting, that familiar feeling that the world is unsafe and I am not in control of what's happening to me. I breathe — years of therapy and it really is that simple. Breathe. Ground yourself in the moment. Be here now. After a few deep inhales and exhales,

314

my nervous system settles.

I park and pick up the article from the box of your belongings, hold it and peer into the past, force myself to read the headline:

Local Police Discover Cache of Arms on Doomsday Prepper Compound

The faded black-and-white pictures bring back visceral sense memories. The sound of gunfire. My mother, so still and bleeding, on the floor. My brother screaming. My father's enraged roaring of my name. Running, terrified through the woods, branches whipping at my face.

That cop in the article is a man named Jones Cooper. He stands grimly beside a row of assault rifles.

As I step out of the car, the air seems to be growing colder, a biting northern winter chill. That burger from last night is sitting in my gut like a concrete block, and my terrible sleep has me jumpy, edgy.

I find myself glancing around for you, a shadow who might emerge from behind the trees, a dark form in my periphery. I think that Bailey is right; you're not done with me. These texts and emails. You're teasing me. I feel you nearby. What do you want?

A northern cardinal perched in the bush flies off in a startling flash of red, as I push through the picket fence and follow the small white arrow sign that reads: Jones Cooper Investigations. Long retired from the police force now, he has hung out a shingle. According to his bare-bones website, he specializes in finding missing persons just like Bailey Kirk. It doesn't say anything about how he helped a traumatized girl disappear. That's our little secret.

Ghosting.

It means one thing now. But once it was used to describe the event in which a person takes the identity of another person of about the same age who has died. The living fraudster then slips into the life of the deceased person and takes on that identity. One person becomes another person.

It helps the enterprise if the deceased person has no living family. If he or she was born in one state and died in another, died young, without debt, never earned a paycheck. All of those things make it easier to slip into another skin.

It's not identity theft as we know it now. The point isn't to use someone's information for illegal financial gain. The point is to disappear. To shed an old life, one that's not working for you, and move into another.

It's harder now than it used to be. Government databases — birth and death registries, criminal records, fingerprint and DNA gathering — are computerized, and states can communicate with each other in a way that they couldn't in the past.

But back when I was just a broken, abused kid who had survived a nightmare and needed to leave my ugly legacy behind and start fresh, I had help. I wouldn't have been able to do it alone.

I knock on the door and after a moment, it opens.

Jones Cooper has barely aged, still tall and powerful, square jawed and thick through the middle. Maybe his hair is a little thinner, maybe there are a few more lines around his eyes and on his brow. But mainly he's the same, as comforting and familiar as an old oak.

"Look at you," he says, extending his hand. "You're all grown up."

We shake; he's not a hugger.

"Am I?" I ask with a smile. "I'm not sure I feel like a grown-up."

"No one ever feels like a grown-up," he says, patting me on the shoulder. "We're all just figuring it out as we go along."

"Good to know," I say, as he ushers me inside.

The room is sparsely furnished, as I would expect it to be knowing him. The only nod to decor of any kind is an oil landscape on the wall, a dark and haunting stand of trees.

"I know you stay in touch with Maggie," he says. "She tells me that you're doing well."

He motions for me to sit, and I sink down to the gray couch that looks as if it will be stiff, but is surprisingly soft as he takes a seat in the chair behind his desk. There's an ancient computer, a landline, a big Rolodex. Time has not advanced here in Jones Cooper's office; it's like the late '90s.

"I have been well. Thanks to everything you and Maggie have done for me."

Dr. Maggie Cooper, therapist, mentor, friend, she helped me put the broken pieces of my psyche back together, and remains my go-to when I'm overwhelmed by memories, when Dear Birdie is out of her depth. If this was any normal breakup, maybe I'd have called her for a session to manage my feelings of loss, which for trauma survivors are always layered. But this is not a normal breakup. This is something else.

"So we have a problem," he says, not one to beat around the bush. "There's a private detective asking questions."

He glances down at his desk and picks up

a card, hands it over.

"A guy named Bailey Kirk employed by a big, wealthy, high-tech firm called Turner and Ives. They've unearthed some of our secrets, it seems. He came here. I missed him but he left this. Later we traded messages."

I look at the simple white card, feeling a rush of anger, undercut by fear. *I'm not trying to blow up your life,* he said last night.

"He's not the only one who's digging into the past," I say.

The whole story comes out in a wild, disjointed tumble. Torch, your disappearance, the storage unit, Bailey Kirk, the missing women, the cigarette butts at Jay's grave, the man in the woods. It must sound crazy, rambling, but he rubs at his chin, smoky eyes focused on me, making all the right affirming noises.

When I'm done, I rise to hand him the article. He unfolds it and looks at it for a few moments, a frown darkening his brow. The chair creaks beneath his weight.

"Seems like such a long time ago," he says.

It feels like a hundred years ago, and five minutes ago, like I never left, like I'm still there. Time, memory, it shifts and twists, a kaleidoscope, different in every change of light.

"Where did you get this?" he asks, glancing up.

"It was in the belongings Adam left behind. He knew my past somehow. Must have known before we met. But I don't understand how. I've been so careful."

Jones tilts back in his chair, stares up at the ceiling as if it is all playing out for him there.

"I made a lot of mistakes," he says. "We should have done things differently. I'm sorry."

"This is not about blame, all these years later."

He draws in and releases a deep breath. Then he gets up and walks over to a free-standing cabinet and withdraws a thick file, brings it back to his desk. It has one word scrawled on it: *Greenwood.*

I'm shaking. And there's a volcanic brew in my center.

That night. It was buried so deep. A blessed amnesia can set in after trauma. You move away from the event and it takes on dreamlike qualities. It recedes from the day-to-day. But it's not gone, just submerged. When it surfaces, it brings up powerful emotions. Rage. Terror. Sadness like a well with no bottom.

"I'm trying to piece things together. That's

why I'm back here," I say. "Can we talk about it? About what happened?"

He opens the file, flips through the papers there. From where I'm sitting, I see some official records, some copies of newspaper articles, some photographs. But I don't move in for a closer look.

"What we did — it wasn't protocol. It wasn't *legal,*" he says, voice low. "We should have called Child Protective Services, but I just couldn't see my way to that. You were so young, seemed so fragile, catatonic with grief. You'd lost everything."

I'm back there, but the memories are disjointed, in pieces. Jones Cooper held me up, a strong arm around my shoulders, ushering me away from the sounds of people shouting. Shock had me disoriented, unable to piece together the things I'd seen, done, lost. My ears were ringing, breath tight in my chest. He wrapped me in a blanket, put me in the back seat of a big SUV, made a call. His voice was muffled; I couldn't hear his words.

My brother, I said when he came back to me. *My mom.*

He rested a heavy hand on my shoulder, his face grim but kind. *Hang in there, kid. We're going to take care of you.*

I don't remember anything until Maggie

came for me, sat beside me in the back seat, then ushered me to another vehicle.

This is the worst night of your life, she said. *But you're going to get through it.*

There was a drive away from my family, my home. I wept and wept and wept. *Please,* I remember begging. *Let me go home.* I thought it was a nightmare, that I would wake up. I didn't.

"Our plan was to call CPS in the morning, after you'd had some rest, some time in a safe place," Jones went on. "But later that night when I saw the list of the dead, your name was on it. A mistake."

I don't say anything, just listen to the sound of my memories: gunfire. The screaming. My father roaring my name. The sharp scent of smoke and cordite.

"I had an idea. I wondered if we could do better for you than to have you go into a cold, unfeeling system. Both Maggie and I have seen too many kids get lost that way."

He shrugs, as if he's not sure now that it was the right thing, knowing that it's far too late to change it.

I remember the next morning, sitting at their sun-drenched kitchen table, a bowl of oatmeal uneaten before me. The day outside was cruelly blue and beautiful, and my life was in ruins. I was stunned, stoic, out of

322

tears, sadness hardened into a shell.

Jones Cooper sat at the table and gave me a choice. Keep my name and be taken away into the foster care system. Or change my name and the Coopers would find me a safe home, and help me heal and create a new life. I chose to stay.

I know now that it was only possible to do this because of how isolated my family had been. I wasn't known in The Hollows, nor were the other people up on the property. In town they called us hill people, strange, mysterious, to be avoided.

"Maggie disagreed but she went along with it," Jones says now. "*We can never hide from the truth,* or some such. You know Maggie.*"

Outside the wind has picked up, rattles the window frame.

"The girl whose body they mistook for yours, she was the same age, her whole family gone. No one in town knew her or her parents. So I called in a favor with a guy in Records."

He says it like it's nothing. Truly, it was fraud. Maybe it couldn't have happened anywhere else.

But this is The Hollows and the usual rules don't apply. This town takes care of its own. Sometimes the wrong thing is the right thing here. The Hollows will keep your secrets.

"We gave you her birth certificate, her Social Security number," says Jones. "We let you choose your own name, and we legally changed it. We never filed a death certificate for her. But we filed one for Robin Carson. So Robin Carson died that day."

"Doesn't a minor need a guardian to change her name?"

He gives me a look. I take his point. I don't ask for any more details about how he did what he did.

It strikes me as terribly sad. A girl, just like me, gone without a trace. We illegally erased her name and it's as though she never existed. Funny how our whole identity comes down to a few sheets of paper, how a sleight of hand, a forged document, can erase an existence, create a new one.

"I chose Wren Greenwood." A bird name, like my mother would have wanted. The name my imaginary friend gave me. And the image that gave me the most peace, green trees moving in the wind.

He offers a thoughtful nod. "It suits you."

"What was her name? The girl who died?"

He hesitates. More details he doesn't want to discuss. Maybe it's better for him if the past stays buried. Maybe he doesn't want to say her name. Finally, he hands over the file.

"Everything is in here."

"Does anyone else know what we did?" I ask.

"The man who helped me in Records has passed on," he says, a note of finality to his voice. "Miss Lovely is gone, too."

Miss Lovely, the woman who took me in, gave me a safe and comfortable home.

"I guess that leaves Joy Martin."

Joy Martin. The librarian at The Hollows Historical Society, and Miss Lovely's closest friend. She knows everything about this town; but she is a keeper of secrets.

"Sometimes it's better to leave old selves, old lives, old mistakes behind," he says.

"I tried. It's caught up with me."

He looks down at the article.

"What did you tell Bailey Kirk?" I ask.

"I told him what was in the public record. Nothing about you or what we did. But I got the feeling he already knew. What we did, maybe it only could have happened in a small place like this, without the eyes of the outside world on us. If the ATF or the FBI had been involved, it would have been impossible. But the case was small; it never made national news. Still, if you looked closely, dug through paperwork, it probably wasn't hard to figure out."

"He's looking for connections between me and the missing women. His trail to Mia Thorpe is cold."

Jones offers a thoughtful nod.

"And what do you think the connection is?" he asks.

"Loneliness, a dating app we all used called Torch, trauma in our pasts. One of the missing women also lived here, Melissa Farrow. Did you know her or her family?"

He squints into the middle distance.

"The name rings a bell. Was there a fire? Yeah — that was it. Her parents were killed. She went to live with her grandparents. Tragic — a long time ago."

"Do you have access to any of the old files from the incident?"

"I can ask the chief. He might let me take a look. There's only one other person alive who knows the whole story of what happened there that night. Who knows about you, and what was done to protect you."

My throat goes dry, and I can't find my voice.

"Your father."

My father.

Out the window, that northern cardinal perches on the fence. I focus on his bright red body. I wish I was a bird and could fly away.

My father is alive. Dead to me. But still drawing breath.

"Have you talked to him?" he asks when I say nothing.

I shake my head. My father. The man who killed my brother and my mother. The man whose actions are responsible for the deaths of so many others, including a nameless girl who, thanks to me, was neither born, nor died, but who existed just the same.

My ghost. Or am I hers?

"There's nothing to say." My voice sounds tight and small.

"I understand," he answers, letting the silence expand. Then, "My father wasn't a good man either. We were estranged for most of my life."

"But *your* father wasn't a monster," I say. "A killer."

"There are all kinds of monsters. People inflict all kinds of pain."

That's very true. I know it well.

"Anyway," he goes on when I stay silent. "I went to see my father before he died. In my mind, he was this behemoth, you know. This giant pain giver. A towering person, with hands like paddles and this face distorted in rage. I was scared. Even though I was a middle-aged man, had a son of my own, I was shaking when I went to see him."

He walks around from his desk, and sits heavily on the other end of the couch. I turn toward him.

"But in the end, he was a tiny sliver of a man, barely a bump in the bed, pale and bald, with just this whispery voice. I sat next to him — for a while. I looked through this photo album he had by his bed. Weird. He left my mom when I was a kid. We never heard from him again. But this album was filled with pictures of me — in my football uniform, at my police academy graduation. There was even a wedding picture. Turns out Maggie had been sending him pictures of me over the years. You know what he said?"

"What?"

"He said, 'I've made mistakes. I'm sorry.' "

We both sit a moment, the words hanging on the air.

Jones clears his throat, leans forward onto his thighs. "Too little, too late, of course. But still. There was something healing about that. That he was just a man who made mistakes, who didn't know better, whose own father probably beat the crap out of him."

I look down at my hands. I don't want to

see the pain on Jones Cooper's face.

There's music coming from somewhere above us, a heavy rock riff through the floor. "Your father. He was — sick," Jones says.

"I know."

"I'm not saying that you can or even that you should forgive him. I'm just saying that he might have some words for you that would help you not just run from the past, but resolve it. Understand it. Come to terms."

"That's not what this is about."

"Isn't it?"

What would I say if Wren Greenwood wrote to Dear Birdie?

Dear Birdie,
I can't forgive my father for killing my mother and my brother. I've been hiding from that horrible night, from him, from myself ever since.

I'd tell her to face down her demons, including her father. I'd tell her to confront the past and take back her name. Funny how I can never take my own advice.

"I hear he helps other people now," says Jones. He rises and walks over to the window, plays with a latch that seems loose.

"What do you mean?" There's a constriction in my throat, my chest.

"He's like a prison preacher now."

"You're telling me that he's found God."

"He's found something," he says. "He gives a mindfulness and meditation class. He advises. He counsels death row inmates."

The idea of this twists in my center. *He* should be dead. My mother and my brother, they should be alive. He shouldn't have this chance to redeem himself by helping others.

"How do you know this?" I ask.

"I keep tabs on the people I help to send away, the people I help, my clients. I like to know how things unfold."

"Do you keep tabs on me?" I ask.

"Of course," he says.

He turns to face me with an easy smile, folds his arms around his middle. The light coming in from the window reveals how he's aged more than I thought at first glance — the lines on his face a little deeper, a slight sag at the jaw. He's still good-looking, though. For an old guy.

"My judgment in your case," he says. "Maybe I didn't make the right decisions for you. We broke the law. We stole a girl's identity. We forged paperwork. It was wrong."

Regret. It comes for all of us sooner or

later. What might have been. What we might have done differently.

"You did what you thought was right. I know that. And it *was* right. I wasn't dogged by media, or stalked by fans of mass murder, or hunted down by true crime podcasters. As far as everyone knows, I died that night. And in a way I did. Anyway, I chose. I *wanted* a new name, a new self."

"But you were just a kid. You weren't really able to make an informed choice."

"So, if you'd followed protocol, then what? I'd have gone to foster care. An uncertain fate if ever there was one."

He bows his head, keeping his eyes down.

"Instead, you gave me a new way forward and helped me to choose a new name and took me to Miss Lovely."

Miss Lovely, the proprietor of The Blue House Inn. Back then she ran a group home for kids.

After my world exploded, she offered me a safe place to live, homeschooled me until I took my GED, helped me apply to college. There were other kids, too, over the couple of years I was with her, who came and went. A runaway she found at the bus station who stayed a few nights, then left with all the money Miss Lovely had hidden in a jar in a high kitchen cabinet. There was

331

another boy whose mother had passed, and whose father was in rehab. He was quiet, read a lot. He wasn't there long, didn't say much.

I barely remember him or anything about that time. I was in a fog of grief. But Miss Lovely took care of all of us with kindness and laughter. She taught me to cook, to sew, how to make a bed like a soldier. She's gone now, too. Her daughter, who was already grown when I went to live with Miss Lovely, owns the inn now, hires out its operation and management. She never sets foot in The Hollows.

"She was good to me. Miss Lovely. And Dr. Cooper, too. They helped me to heal, build a life."

"Yes, but Maggie was right. You can't hide from the truth."

He walks over to the article on the desk, holds it up to me.

"Maybe not," I concede, taking it.

"What else can I do to help now?" he asks.

Jones Cooper is a native son of The Hollows. He knows how it works, its history, has access to all its dark passages. Maybe that's why I'm here. He's the guide I need to this place. If what's happening now is in any way connected to what happened to me then, Jones Cooper is the one to ask.

I tell him about the dark web, about the man who helped me create Wren Greenwood online, and bury all traces of my past, how I reached out to him to see what he knew, what he could find. I tell him about the money I paid, and how I'm waiting now. He doesn't like that, gives me a frown.

"The dark web," he says. "Is that a thing? I thought it was an urban legend."

"It's very real."

"I don't get it."

There's a deep gulf between our generations. I'm a tech native; he's a late and reluctant adopter. His desktop is ancient with a huge screen and a hulking CPU on the floor. There's a flip phone on the coffee table.

I explain it to him. "It's a part of the internet that's untraceable. On the conventional web using servers like Safari or Chrome, you leave a digital trail that anyone can find. But on the dark web, accessed by Tor, no one can detect your activity. It's a black market for — anything. Guns. Drugs. Hired killers. Identity change. There are people who can get you anything, help you do anything."

He raises his eyebrow, the skeptic.

"And this guy Adam — you met him online, too."

"Right."

"I'm seeing a pattern here. The further you get from the real world, the darker and more dangerous it all gets."

He has a point.

"It's the way of it now, though."

"Doesn't have to be."

"Now you sound like my father. He wanted us to escape technology, the world of men. He told us that their world was about to implode, that global collapse was around the corner. And that we would be safe on our land, living as we were intended to live in harmony with nature."

He nods, thoughtful, leaning against his desk, hands dug in his pockets.

"But the world of men still stands," I say. "It was *we* who imploded. It was *our world* that collapsed."

He gives an easy nod, taking it in, considering.

"So," he says finally. "I'll go back over my case notes, and I'll talk to the new chief. I'll do some digging."

"Looking for what?"

"I guess I'll know it if I find it."

This makes me smile, that kind of practical two feet on the ground idea of things.

He looks at his watch. "I think Maggie is expecting us both for lunch."

"I really should go," I say.

"Stay," he says. It's gentle. A kind nudge. "Your problems will wait until after a meal with old friends."

The world slows down here. That's what my father loved about it. When you cross over the city line, you draw a breath, release it slowly. The frenetic pace of our modern world shifts away.

There isn't always cell service, many dead spots, calls just dropped or never come through at all. Voice mail lags. My phone has gone strangely quiet. I have to go back to my computer to check email. For some reason, it won't download to my phone here.

There are no big roads, no horns, no sirens, no shouts. Instead, there's a heavy quietude. I don't want to feel the tug of this place and all its promises. But I do. I know why my father loved it. Why he thought we could find a different way of life here.

Rewilding.

I give him a nod of acceptance. "Of course," I say. "I'd love to."

After all, what's the rush? If that was you who wrote to me last night, Adam. If you are Unforgiven, then I am sure I have frightened you away by not offering you any promises. You're probably long gone, and all this chasing I find myself doing will probably just end as it started, with me alone, a ghost, hiding behind a fake name.

Jones pats my shoulder in approval. "Everything is more manageable with a full stomach."

I know you would agree with that.

My head swims. You, my father, my past, the dead girl whose name I stole, Bailey Kirk, his missing Mia, Melissa Farrow, Dear Birdie. But instead of chasing after you or them, I follow Jones Cooper down the long hallway.

There's always time for lunch.

THIRTY

I'm still buzzing after my conversation with Jones, the past and present a spinning wheel in my mind. But lunch with the Coopers has me feeling more centered, calmer. Jones's practicality, Maggie's wisdom, grilled cheese and tomato soup — I am nourished and stronger for my time with them. And one thing is clear — it's time to figure out everything that Bailey Kirk knows.

The Motel 8 is a flat, tidy place, a typical roadside establishment with a big sign and a vacancy light that has never been dark, a row of gray doors and square windows, curtains drawn inside.

I've passed this place many times and always wondered who might find occasion to stop here. Truckers, I guess, or outdoorsy types on their way to or from campsites, fishermen come to try their luck on the river a few miles away, hunters perhaps come to cull the burgeoning deer population. Private investigators chasing missing girls, following a trail that somehow led them to this isolated place. The waitress described Bailey's truck, but I don't see it, a black shiny thing, she said. The parking lot is mostly empty, just two other cars — a white Toyota, and a beat-up vintage VW bus.

What am I doing here? This whole errand has taken on a dreamy nonreality. Your disappearance, my conversation with Jones, thoughts of my father, this place, all of it on a Tilt-A-Whirl in my mind. I am untethered from the world I left behind.

My phone vibrates on the seat beside me.

Jax: On your way back?

She must be tracking me, seeing that I've left town.

Not just yet, I type.

The little gray dots pulse. Then: You promised.

I know. Soon.

Call me.

Wren, I mean it. Call me.

I exit the car and approach the office. A

little bell rings and announces my arrival and a wizened old man peers up from a paperback book. His face looks like a catcher's mitt, a lifetime of ignoring warnings about the sun damage. He pushes up his black-framed glasses and peers at me. His eyes are cartoonishly big behind his thick lenses.

"Help you, miss?"

"I'm looking for a friend," I say.

He puts down the book, military fiction I'd say by the bold colors and the shadow of a soldier on the jacket. Its binding is creased, cover ripped.

"You're pretty enough," he says. "I bet you don't have any trouble making friends."

This is an example of a thing men shouldn't say these days, somehow solicitous and insulting all at once. But I smile anyway, because he's older with a big belly, and few wisps of gray hair on his head. This probably counts as charming in his book, his very old book written long ago in a language most of us would like to forget. It might be too late to school him; old dogs, new tricks and all of that.

"Actually, I am looking for one specific friend," I say. "A man named Bailey Kirk."

He points at the ledger on the counter and I follow his finger to Bailey's name, written in a wobbly cursive.

"Hasn't been here long," says the old man. "Might be around for a while, he told me. Quiet. No trouble. Gone most of the day." He nods over to a drip machine that has seen better days. "Early riser. Comes in for the coffee."

So much for privacy protection.

I am about to push my luck and ask which room he's in, but then I notice the board of keys behind him. There's only one missing. Number 12.

"What time does he usually get back?" I ask instead.

"Hard to say." He nods to the phone I have in my hand. "Aren't you kids in constant touch these days? Can't you send him a text or something? If he's a friend of yours."

Kids.

"Good idea," I say with an easy nod. "I'll do that. Thank you."

I'm about to leave when he speaks up. "Nosy one."

"Oh?" I turn back.

"He asks a lot of questions." This does not surprise me.

"What kind of questions?"

"About people and places, things most of us around here would rather forget. Nobody likes to dredge up the past."

I walk back to the counter. The wood paneled walls are decorated with all manner of fishing gear — poles and nets, lures and reels. There are photographs of outdoorsy looking men, holding up trout and bass, hanging in foggy, crooked frames. I recognize the man behind the counter in one, many years younger looking virile and happy with his big catch.

"Such as?"

"That group we had up there years ago, the doomsday preppers. That mess with the guns and the police. People died. A tragedy."

He shakes his head, walks around the counter and pours himself some coffee, holds up a foam cup to me and I nod my acceptance just to be cordial, bite back another wave of nausea. I usually have an iron stomach.

"What did he want to know about it?"

He hands me the cup, black. It smells bitter and burnt but I take a sip anyway, just to be polite. Predictably, it's absolute swill. My stomach lurches.

He sits on the pilled plaid couch that comprises the lobby lounge and I sit in a stiff chair across from him. I'm still waiting for him to answer my question, am about to nudge. Finally, "He wanted to know who lived up there. Did I remember any names? Did I know what happened to the people who left after the incident, were there any children? Did anyone still live in town?"

"What did you tell him?"

He rubs at a knee with his free hand. His knuckles are thick, fingers bent with arthritis.

"That land has been owned by the same family for generations."

This much I know. It belongs to my family. Well, it belongs to me. Because my family is all gone.

"It's empty now. But the people up there then were just looking for a different way of life, the old way, you know, where you lived off the land and you only took what you needed."

My phone keeps vibrating. I glance at it to see a row of texts from Jax.

What is the Motel 8 and what are you doing there?
I feel like I'm going to be interviewed for a true crime podcast when you go missing.
Call me or I'm coming up there after you.
Wren. I'm serious.

I shove the phone in my pocket. Look up to find the old man watching me. I haven't

342

asked his name and it seems awkward to do so now.

"The land is owned by the Carson family. The other people up there weren't from around here, so I don't remember any names. They scattered after the raid. There's no one left here from that time."

"How many families were up there?" I ask. I honestly don't remember who was there. I had a child's view of the world, utterly myopic, consumed by my own needs, fears, likes and dislikes. I remember other people, but not names. Faces have faded. Even my mother and Jay, I have to dig deep into my memories to recall their eyes, their voices.

"The Carson family and two others, maybe," he says, rubbing at his chin. "They kept to themselves. They were pretty self-sufficient up there. Not a bad way to live, I suppose. It was the guns that got them in trouble.

"Someone reported them," the old man said, snapping me back to the moment, the strange motel office. Outside the sky is a startlingly cheerful blue, the green pines sway. "That's what got the police up there. Then when they tried to search the property, someone started shooting, and the whole thing went haywire. FUBAR they used to say in the military. Fucked up beyond all recognition."

He points to an installation I hadn't noticed, up above the mounted television that stands dark. A dark blue uniform in a shadow box, another display of medals, dog tags hanging from a nail.

"Luke Carson, the man who owned the land." He puts a finger to his temple, makes a slow circle. "War. It makes you crazy if you let it. Sometimes, some men, never come home."

The man who left never came home, my mother whispered to me on one of the nights she slept in my bed. *I thought I could heal him.*

"They say he killed his family but it's hard to believe."

"You knew him?"

"I knew him when he was a kid. He was a real ray of sunshine, always smiling, always polite. Parents were good people."

I never knew my grandparents. In some ways, I never knew my father.

"Mother was a seamstress, father was a carpenter. They lived off the grid though, up there, farming and hunting. Luke went to school with my boy. After high school, he left this place. I heard he joined the army. When I saw him again, all the light in him had gone out. I think he just wanted to go back to that place, to that life. The world wouldn't let him."

I feel a rare glimmer of compassion for my father — a sunshiny boy who went away with ideals and dreams and came home broken, diseased — but hammer it down hard. His face as I last saw him, bloodied and monstrous with rage, swims. That sunshiny boy this old man remembers is not known to me.

"Did you tell all of this to Bailey Kirk?" I ask.

He shakes his head. "I told him the truth, which is I didn't remember much and that there was someone else who might know more."

"Who's that?"

"Joy at The Hollows Historical Society. More than her job, it's her calling to keep the record of this place. Maybe you should pay her a visit."

"I didn't get your name," I say, rising to reach over for his hand.

"Bob Shaw." We shake; his grip is surprisingly strong. A clean, fresh scent of his laundry detergent wafts into the air.

"I'm Wren."

"I hope you find what you're looking for," he says in the silence, and returns to his spot behind his desk, where he picks up his book and goes back to his reading. I stand, and stay there stupidly for a moment, all my questions jammed up in my throat.

Didn't I come here looking for you?

Or am I looking for something else?

Outside, the sky has suddenly shifted darker.

My phone is a catalog of missed texts and calls, most of them from Jax, one from my accountant's office. There's one from an unknown number with this:

I'm slipping, I'm slipping away/like sand/ slipping through fingers. All/my cells . . .

Rilke.

Drawing in a breath, I stare at the words, and then find myself looking around. The motel rooms, the trees across the street, the parked cars. Are you here? Are you watching me? My whole body is cold, nerves frayed and tingling. Maybe your tall, dark form will slip from the trees or come from behind the dumpster.

A red car races past, kicking up dirt and leaves.

I am alone.

How to answer? I could answer with a Rilke verse of my own:

Extinguish my eyes, I'll go on seeing you./
Seal my ears, I'll go on hearing you.

Don't go. Come back to me. Let me see
all of you.

Instead, I don't respond at all, my heart
racing, my hands shaking.

You are slipping away. And I should let
you go.

But I can't and I don't. I walk to room
12.

THIRTY-ONE

I have some gifts. Gifts I don't generally employ. I can use a gun. I can dissemble, clean, and reassemble a number of firearms. I can hunt with a crossbow. I can plant and raise a vegetable garden. I can fish. I can scale and clean my catch. I can build a fire without a match. If called upon to survive in the world my father imagined, I'd probably be okay.

It's the modern world I've had the most trouble with.

I can also pick a simple lock — the type on this motel room door — with a credit card. I move in close and slide my American Express platinum card, a thick heavy thing, in between the door and the jamb. Finding the latch, wedging in the card and pushing it back into its home, the door eases open for me. Not every lock, but this kind might as well not be on the door at all.

The room inside is dark, the curtains

drawn. I shouldn't be here. This is wrong. Regardless, I step inside and close the door behind me, hoping Bob wasn't watching me and then called the police.

Bailey Kirk's suitcase is open on a chair next to a small table. The case is compact and black; inside, things are perfectly folded into tight rectangles of gray and black and blue, the only color palate I've seen him wear.

The bed is neatly made; there's a stack of books on the end table, one about the dark web, a thick volume on identity theft, and the *Complete Works of Sherlock Holmes.* Which makes me smile because most PIs are very *into* their thing, imagining themselves as the hero of an ongoing detective story. Not Jones Cooper, though. He's a rare breed, into the work, the people, doing the right thing. He's never thinking about himself from the outside in. I kind of got that feeling from Bailey Kirk; that they might be cut from the same cloth. But the Sherlock Holmes tome makes me wonder.

In the bathroom, there's a tidy Dopp kit, with a toothbrush, toothpaste, razor, deodorant all precisely placed inside. Surfaces are wiped clean. There's no trace of grime, or disorder. I noticed that about you, too, Adam; nothing out of place, everything carefully arranged. I know most men are slobs, but my father was meticulous like that, my brother, too. I am drawn to order, the careful arrangement of the objects that we possess. I don't touch anything.

Bailey's computer and a stack of paper files sit on the desk.

I sit in the chair and open the lid of his laptop, only to find it, predictably, password protected. I don't know him well enough to hazard a guess at his password. So, I thumb through the files. There's one on each missing woman, all with a name on the tab, and a picture on the front of the file. Mia is on top. And I am on the bottom. Mine has two names written in the tab. Wren Greenwood. And my real name, or anyway, the name my parents gave me.

Robin Carson.

We all have different parts of our self, different aspects. We're kaleidoscopes. I am Robin Carson — that's the name I was born with. I am Wren Greenwood, the name I gave myself. I am Dear Birdie, the name I hide behind as I give others the benefit of my hard-won wisdom.

You know all about this, don't you, Adam? You know all about that shifting around of pieces of yourself. I did it to survive. What's *your* game?

I open the file with my name — names — on it. I don't feel even a little bad about breaking into Bailey Kirk's room and rifling through his personal belongings, his carefully gathered data. Why should I?

Robin sits on her haunches in the corner of the motel room. She looks out of place here, her auburn hair picking up the light streaming in from between the drawn drapes.

I'm real, she tells me, eyes accusing.

"You're more real than most," I assure her.

She seems satisfied, fades into the light.

Bailey's files are as orderly as his personal possessions.

Inside mine, there's a tidy stack of copied documents. On top sits a copy of my original birth certificate. I hold it in my hand. Robin Anne Carson. She's just a trick of light now, a shadow that's gone when you turn to look at it. My father, Luke, my mother, Alice — their names are neatly typed in the appropriate boxes. Two people who loved each other once and made a baby. Just a few months later, he'd go off to the Middle East to fight. When he came back, he was someone else.

There's another birth certificate, with a name I don't know. Emily Stone. That must be her. The girl in my grave. I stare at it a moment — her birthday, same year, just a few days later than my own. Her parents are listed as Wyatt and Melba Stone. I dig deep into my memory of the other families who lived up there, but there's nothing. This girl, her parents — they're gone, too.

I stare at Robin Carson's death certificate. That version of myself died at the tender age of fifteen. There's an autopsy report that says she died of a gunshot wound to the heart. I put my hand to my own chest.

Next, I find a document that certifies a name change — Emily Stone to Wren Greenwood. Did you know that anyone can legally change their name to anything? That you can just discard the name you were given and pick a new one if you want? Wren, because it was the name that Robin gave me. Greenwood because it made me think of that magical moment when you're lying on the forest floor and the high sun beams through the canopy, how fingers of buttery light break the leaves, making them glow a verdant electric green. How the air is moist and smells of vegetation, and sunshine dapples the ground.

A copy of Wren Greenwood's Social Security card and driver's license. And then my tax records from the *Chronicle*, essentially outing me as the "author" of *Dear Birdie.* A shallow grave, Bailey had said. And so it is, if you're paying attention. I can see how he easily connected the dots. But the truth is, you can't hide from yourself. No matter how hard you try.

And people broke the law and worked very hard to hide Robin Carson from the world.

Next a raft of articles about the raid on the property. I flip through without really reading. I don't like to go back there. It still feels like a knife in the gut. But a grainy image catches my eye: a black-and-white picture of the armory, that big rack of guns, ammunition, and explosives in the back of the bunker.

I browse the article. Jones Cooper, who was the chief of police back then, is quoted as saying: *We received an anonymous tip about a weapon stockpile and other illegal activity.*

My heart thumps, mouth dry and sticky as glue, remembering the sound of gunfire. This memory is a dark doorway. If I walk through, it swallows me.

I close the file and focus on my breath to bring myself back to the present. *The past is gone. The future is a fantasy. There is only the breath, the moment.* It's a mantra Dr.

353

Cooper gave me. Sometimes it even works.

You never have to go back there, she told me. *The night is gone forever if you release it.*

But it comes back for me, a haunting.

At the bottom of the stack of files is one Bailey Kirk has labeled as "The Ghost."

If I dug myself a shallow grave, you must have dug yourself a pretty deep one. In your file, there are only a few pictures that I have already seen. Different versions of you, younger, maybe happier incarnations. There are printouts of your Torch profiles with different names but all virtually identical verbiage.

There's no birth certificate, no driver's license, or any official documents. There's a printout of the Airbnb listing. There are some handwritten notes on this page, I assume by Bailey Kirk. His handwriting is tight and precise, each letter carefully formed. "Two messages left for Joe, the host, at the number obtained from RC/WG. No response. Likewise, email not returned. Will follow up in person."

There are other notes about your company Blackbox. "Cybersecurity. Owned by a shell corporation, all accounts offshore. Another ghost lead."

I scan through the rest of the files, one for Mia, one for Melissa, one for Bonnie — a

354

raft of pictures, official documents, news-paper articles, emails, social media profiles, statements from friends.

But I can see why Bailey Kirk is frustrated. When I'm done, I have a sketch, a sense of each woman, but there's nothing obvious that connects them. Melissa and I have The Hollows in common, so maybe that's some-thing. But she and I never met.

Abandoned apartments, cars, cell phones. All of them stepped away from her life, or were taken, not leaving a trace behind, or even a digital trace to follow. They all dropped off the grid.

I am the only one left.

I was probably days away from knowing what happened to the others.

What were you going to ask me?

Adam, if you had asked me to fold up my life and walk away leaving everyone and everything behind. Would I have done it? Would I have followed you, like my mother followed my father? If you had said to me, like he did to her, the world is broken, let's leave it behind and create another kind of life, would I have gone with you?

I don't know.

There's Jax and her family. There's Dear Birdie and all the people who need her.

My conversation with Jax rings back. *Any-*

one could be Dear Birdie. There's a certain amount of relief in that idea. Is it true? Maybe anyone can be anyone. Robin Carson can be Emily Stone. Emily Stone can become Wren Greenwood. Wren Greenwood can become Dear Birdie. I have not so much dug a shallow grave for myself, as woven a tangled web of lies and false identities. Am I the spider or the fly?

"Find what you're looking for?"

His voice moves through me like an electric shock. I turn to see a dark form filling the doorway. For just a second, I think it's you. And a tsunami of anger, sadness, fear rushes through me. But when he steps closer, I see that it's Bailey Kirk — bigger and broader than he seemed to me the first time I met him. I hold my ground, won't give him the satisfaction of a flustered apology.

"No," I say. "Not at all."

He moves into the room and shuts the door behind him. He seems unruffled, a slight smile on his face. I don't suppose, as a PI, you can muster much anger for someone invading your space and rifling through your stuff.

"Yeah," he says. "Welcome to my world."

I close the file in my lap, shutting out your face, and look at Bailey. He seats himself on

356

the edge of the bed and rests his hands on his thighs. There's something solid about him, something comforting and good.

"You know everything there is to know about me," I say.

"Not everything," he says gently. "We never know everything about each other, do we?"

Based on what I read in those files, he knows more about my past than anyone. I am seen. Revealed. There's a kind of relief to that, a tension sheds.

For the first time, the feeling I thought might be love, the weight of my sadness and loss, the sharp edge of my disappointment have all shifted to anger.

"I'll help you," I say. "I'll help you find him."

THIRTY-TWO

The sun is setting outside, the room growing darker. But neither of us gets up to turn on the light. He stays on the bed, and I sit uncomfortably on the stiff desk chair my arms wrapped around my middle.

In the dim of this cheap motel room, I tell Bailey how my father came home from war, moved us from our happy "city" life and out to his family property. How Jay, my mother, and I left everything and everyone we knew behind, because my father wanted us to live off the grid, away from the world of men.

"So, he was a doomsday prepper," Bailey says.

It has a load, that phrase, a kind of joke inherent in its syllables, evoking crazy people who erroneously predict the apocalypse, who have gone mad because they shed all the things we hold to. But there are all kind of madness. And my father could be forgiven for thinking that the modern world was failing.

"He called himself a 'collapsist.' "

"A collapsist?"

"He wasn't preparing for some distant event. He believed the world was already in decline. He said that he joined the army as an idealist and returned as a realist. War, famine, disaster, pestilence — the four horsemen of the apocalypse. According to my father, they'd already arrived."

Bailey nods, rubs at his chin. "That must have been frightening for a kid, to be waiting for the end of the world."

"Lots of things are frightening when you're a kid. My dad — he was a scary guy when he drank. I think I was more afraid of him than I was of the end of the world."

"So how did you cope?"

I tell him about "Robin," the girl who came to me in the woods and taught me everything I needed to survive, to become the daughter my father wanted me to be. What was she? An imaginary friend, I suppose. Dr. Cooper says that in the case of childhood trauma, it's not uncommon for a young person to create a presence, something or someone who comforts and soothes, who eases loneliness, who protects. As we grow older, stronger, we need that presence less and it fades.

"But really it was just the books in the study," I admit. "And him, my father. He taught me a lot about survival. And I was a decent student. I learned the things he wanted me to know, how to be in on that land. I even wanted to learn it."

"And what about your mother?"

I close my eyes and conjure her. Her golden hair and kind smile, her indulgence of my imaginary friend who she knew was real to me and an important feature of my adjustment to our new life, her laughter, her warmth.

"She loved him. She thought that the house, nature, the retreat from the madness of modern life would heal him. That he would become again the man she used to love."

"And *did* it heal him?"

"It might have," I say, though I'm not sure I believe it. "If not for the raid."

"There were other families up there, right?" says Bailey. "Do you remember any of them?"

"Not really," I say. "In the article, I recognized the names — Stone, Wilson. But some of those folks had been up there all their lives. Many of them wouldn't have reported the birth of their children at all, or the deaths in the family."

"I'm getting that," he says. "This place. It keeps its secrets, doesn't it?"

I find myself smiling. It does.

"Did you go to The Hollows Historical Society?" I ask.

"Every time I go there, the door is locked. The woman who apparently runs the show there, Joy, she hasn't returned my calls."

That makes sense. Bailey Kirk is an outsider, an interloper. He's been snooping around, and the folks up here have noticed. She won't open the doors to the past for him unless she's sure of his intentions. That those intentions are in line with what The Hollows wants.

"That was going to be my next stop. I know Joy," I say.

She was Miss Lovely's oldest friend. She came to the house every Thursday afternoon for coffee and cake, always had a story about this place, a memory, an anecdote. One of the few people who knew my secret, she was always talking about the property that my father's family owned. *Take care of it. You don't want to go back there now. But someday you will. It belongs to you and you to it.*

Honestly, I thought Joy's obsession with this town and its history was a bit much.

361

And I had no plans to go back to my father's house, not ever. But it turns out she was right; I do have a sense of ownership. And I haven't been able to let it go.

Bailey gets up from his perch and walks to the window, looks outside. The fading light washes his face. Maybe that's a PI thing, always wanting to know who's coming and going. I want to ask him: Were you always a curious kid, the kind who asks too many questions? I like to know what makes people tick. And Bailey, aloof, cool, is a bit of a mystery to me.

"What do you think you'll find at The Hollows Historical Society that you don't already know?" he asks. "I mean you were there. Who knows better than you? And what does this have to do with the ghost?"

"The ghost?"

"Adam Harper."

"Is that what you call him?" I ask.

"What else? He is a man I've never seen, who doesn't have a name. The closer I get, the more quickly he slips away."

"Why did *you* come here?"

"Because it's a place that you and Melissa have in common. And I'm out of leads, out of time. This is the last solid thing I have."

"Same."

He turns to regard me, gives me a kind of

up and down assessing glance. Is he looking at me? Or trying to decide if I'm telling the truth? "Fair enough."

I walk over to his bedside and pick up the book he has there about the dark web. It's a floppy paperback, looks self-published with bad art and unprofessional looking typeface.

When Bailey speaks again, his voice has gone soft.

"Time is running out. She's slipping away. Time is a kind of distance, isn't it? It's a road you can't turn back on."

Maybe he's fallen in love with Mia, I think. Or the ghost of her, his idea of her — since they've never met. Maybe he's been chasing her so long, tracking her, that he's formed a kind of attachment. There's a tug to him, a kind of sad understanding.

"My firm," he says. "My boss, Nora, she wants to pull the plug and tell the client our case is cold."

"Is it?"

"I haven't found a single thing that brings me closer to her. Except for you."

I tell him about the email message I received. The texts on my phone. They are lures on the end of a line. All I have to do is bite and he'll reel me in.

"This is not a game," he says when I'm done. He moves closer to me, his face dark with worry. We stand a foot apart in the middle of the room. "He's a dangerous man. A predator. What do you think he wants from you, Wren? Why is he reaching out?"

"I don't know."

But I do. I feel the pull of that darkness, a deadly riptide. It reminds me in a weird way of my father, how the things he said about the world, and nature, and mankind both frightened me and made a kind of sense. How I wanted to get away from him and get closer to him all in one complicated twist of the heart.

"Because he knows you're hooked into him," Bailey says. "He knows you'll go to him. And then what do you think will happen?"

In tracking, it's a known quantity that your quarry may, will probably, elude you. You can follow the sign — the prints, the broken branches — but you may never find the creature that left little pieces of himself behind. Even when he's in your sights, one wrong move and he will dash away. Every good hunter knows that nature is smarter, faster, more sensitive than he will ever be. If you catch what you're stalking, it's a gift, something that's been offered, not something taken. But you still hunt if you want to survive.

"Do you have another plan?" I say, already knowing the answer. "Another way to find him? To find out what happened to Mia?"

The frown he wears deepens, he rubs at his temples with a thumb and forefinger.

"I don't." He sounds weary with the admission.

A photograph falls out of the book I'm holding. When I bend to pick it up, I see that it's a portrait — a man who looks like an older, thicker version of Bailey, a woman with dark hair and kind face, a younger girl who looks like her but slimmer. All of them wind whipped and smiling, a beach behind them. I'm guessing it's his family — parents, a sister. Something about that makes me like him a little more. I remember that he mentioned a brother and wonder why he's not shown. It seems rude to ask. So, I slip the picture back in the book, and say nothing.

I walk back over to the desk, put down the book. From the stack of Bailey's files, I take the one labeled Greenwood. He nods to acknowledge that it belongs to me. Then I walk out the door, and climb into my car. He comes out after me right away, climbs into his own truck.

As I pull out of the lot, Bob waves to me

from the office window. And Bailey Kirk
follows me back to town.

THIRTY-THREE

Then

My mother took me to town the next day, a rare thing. She had a bruise on the side of her face; she'd done an artful job of covering it with makeup and styling her hair in a way that it was barely noticeable, nothing more than the faintest shadow. If you didn't know it was there, maybe you wouldn't see it all.

In the cab of the old pickup truck, we bounced down the rural road. We were headed out to find the ingredients for Guinness stew, my father's favorite. A way to appease him maybe, to make him happy. She was always looking for ways to make him less angry.

I know a lot of people grow to hate their abused mothers for never standing up, for never fighting back, for not leaving. I never felt that. I know she was in love with a ghost. She was haunted, waiting for that

367

man to come home to her and rescue her from the one he had become. I was waiting, too. She had so much faith, it was contagious.

"He's going to kill her," my brother told me the night before.

I was lying beside her in the bed, and he sat on the floor of her room, his back against the door. He'd held my father off until he'd stormed from the house. We were waiting for him to come back, but he didn't.

My mother was sleeping, fitful, sighing.

"Don't say that," I whispered, panic constricting my throat.

"We have to leave this place," he said. He was just a shadow by the door; his baseball bat lay beside him, his hand resting on it.

"She won't leave," I told him.

"Then I'm going to wind up killing him."

"Stop," I said, a sob rushing up my throat. "Stop it."

"That's how these things go, you know. The violence — it just escalates. Until."

"He's getting better," I said, not believing it myself. There would be days, even a week of peace, where my father worked hard during the day, slept well at night. Where he was happy. There was laughter, and home-cooked meals, music from my father's guitar in the evening. Prior to that night's explosion, things had almost been *good.*

"You sound like her," said Jay, voice heavy with disdain. "I told you not to love him."

His words rang in my head, knocking around in my frightened child's brain. My father would kill my mother, or my brother would kill my father. This was what I carried into town with me. It burned in my center, burned like acid up my throat.

In the big grocery store, I wandered the colorful aisles. It had been a while since I'd been off the property. And I'd forgotten, maybe never even noticed before that day, the wild, Technicolor plenty of an American supermarket. The rows and rows of snacks in glossy, crinkly bags, the bubbling bottles of soda, the fat, waxy produce, and the bloodless meat in neat packages. I grabbed the royal blue package of Oreos. My mother took them from me indulgently and put them in the cart.

"Go get the beef," she told me, and I obeyed her, walking off. The other shoppers glanced at us askance. Why? Maybe we were a little raggedy, hair too long, clothes past worn. I think they called us hill people, those of us that lived off the grid out of town. Energetically, there was something different about us now.

We were just like you, I wanted to tell

them. Not long ago, I never dreamed of killing a living thing, or growing my own vegetables.

My father said that they — the worldly ones, the people still dwelling in the modern dream — were all sleepwalkers. So it seemed, all of them lost in their own thoughts, maybe casting a glance in our direction but nothing more. They didn't care, that's what Dad said. They didn't care about anything except their own desires, fears, and cravings. They didn't even know there was anything else besides the movie playing in their minds.

Was he right?

There was what seemed like a mile of chicken, turkey, hams, different cuts of beef, all tightly wrapped in plastic, neatly on yellow foam trays. Not a drop of blood, no odor, clean and prepped.

After I'd killed the deer, my father and I had hauled it back to the waiting truck. Later he hung it from a tree to bleed it. The blood ran from the doe like a viscous river, collecting in a bucket. I threw up twice.

People should know what it means to eat meat, my father said. *Someone has to do the slaughtering, the cleaning, the butchering. There's always pain and fear and blood. That's life. That's death.*

Above the tidy, bloodless packages, I caught sight of myself in the reflective side of the meat case — a feral girl in dirty jeans, and a too-small shirt, hair wild, soil under her nails.

At first, I thought it was Robin, turned to look for her. Then I realized it was me.

Help them, she whispered, inside my head. *Help your mom and Jay.*

That's when I saw it, the pay phone over by the bathrooms.

It was fast; I knew I had to be. I called 911.

What's your emergency?

I talked quickly and clearly, telling the operator that my family was in trouble, that my father was unwell. I told her about the weapons on the property.

Where, honey, where does your family live?

With a sinking feeling of terror I realized that I didn't know our address.

"It's out of town, up the road."

"That's not an address, honey. I can't help you without an address."

I saw my mother moving up the aisles, craning her head to look for me.

"What's your name?"

"My name is Robin Carson."

I had to hang up, running to grab the meat and head my mother off before she

371

saw the pay phone. My whole body tingled with relief.

I'd saved us. I'd saved my mother from my father. My father from Jay. I had saved Jay from himself. Killing a deer had cut a valley through me, opening a dark hollow of despair I could barely stand. Imagine what it would be to kill your own father.

The police would find us, and take my father to the hospital. And then my mother would be free. We would all be free.

That's what I believed as we drove back home.

"Things are going to get better and better," my mother said in the truck as we turned onto the property.

"You'll see."

"I know, Mom," I told her. I took her delicate hand. "It's okay."

But weeks went by, and things got worse and worse, and no one came.

Thirty-Four

Now

Now
Dear Unforgiven,

Maybe I've frightened you. Please show
yourself to her. All of you. True love sees
past the ugliness, past the disease of
what it means to be human in this dark
world. If she belongs to you, and you to
her, nothing you've done, nothing that
you are will make her turn away from
you. I promise.

Yours,
Dear Birdie

Will you buy this, Adam? Or will you see it
for what it is?

"Do you think that will do it?" Bailey asks.

Bailey Kirk is sitting in the wingback chair
by the fireplace in my room at The Blue
House Inn, on his own laptop. We've fallen
into a kind of reluctant partnership, each of

us with things the other needs.

I've given him everything I gave the internet fixer — all the information I had on Adam — and he's submitting it all to his team at Turner and Ives. He knows everything about me now, and he knows everything I know about you.

"Maybe."

You're no dummy. Maybe you'll see this missive for what it is. A trap.

"Is it true?" asks Bailey. "Do you think that real love forgives all things?"

The question makes me think of my father. The war hero. The monster. The murderer. The prison preacher, according to Jones Cooper. The damaged man who asked for forgiveness from his daughter and was denied.

"I don't know the answer to that either."

"I don't think it is true," he says, answering his own question. "Maybe in an idealized sense. Or maybe a mother's love can forgive. But love — grown-up love — has to be conditional, right? Otherwise it means you don't love yourself."

I'm only half listening, trying to convince Jax via text not to come up here, assuring her that she can do *Dear Birdie* without my help for one day, I'm sure of it. Please, Jax. Just one more day.

"That's awfully deep, Detective."

A shrug. "I have a lot of time to think about these things."

He's staring at his screen, his angular face washed in its white glow. I cannot figure this guy out.

"Anyway, it doesn't matter if it's true," I say. "It only matters if he believes it."

A blink, a glance up at me, then back to the screen.

"It matters if *you* believe it," he says, voice deep.

Now, he's watching me from over the lid of his own laptop. He shifts his weight, puts one leg up on the hassock. I notice that he keeps his shoe off it, though. That means he had a good mother, one who taught him about the value of things, how to keep things clean.

"Do you mean could I love him if he really hurt those women?"

"Could you?"

I find the question insulting, don't even bother answering. *Fuck you, Detective,* I think but don't say. He must see it on my face, lifts his palms.

"I'm just asking."

I've managed to quiet my phone. Jax seems to be satisfied. I told Marty I'd call him tomorrow. No more Rilke verses.

Maybe you're gone. Maybe that last message was goodbye. Maybe we'll both have to let you go.

Bailey snaps the lid closed on his laptop, stares into the fireplace.

"It's all vapor, isn't it? All this information we have — fake names, digital images, profile pages, ghost email accounts, a company that may or may not exist."

"That's why you call him the ghost."

"What it lacks in originality it makes up for in accuracy." Then, "Do *you* have any pictures of him?"

I scroll through my phone. You're camera-shy, which I kind of liked about you. Of course, I understand it better now. There are two photos, compared to the hundreds of Jax and me, in all manner of misadventure — nightclubs, a weekend getaway to Miami, in the studio. Of you and I, Adam, there is a selfie of both of us you let me take on the Brooklyn Bridge. We're cheek to cheek, smiling like idiots in love which, speaking strictly for me, we were. Another, I took of you outside my house. You stand on my stoop, tall and dark in a long black coat. I edited it to an artfully grainy black-and-white, your skin ghostly pale against the ink of your hair and eyes. Cutting the figure of a crow against the gray scale of the buildings, you look off into the middle distance, your hand on the railing. Looking at it now I think, *I was always going to lose you.* A clutch in my solar plexus.

Does true love forgive all?

My mother would have said yes. She believed in him, right up until the night he killed her and Jay, and would have killed me, too, if I hadn't run from him.

I hand the phone to Bailey Kirk as my email alert pings.

The strange address of the internet fixer, the number and a server I don't recognize. I open it eagerly, heart thumping in anticipation.

I'm sorry, it reads. Your friend. He does not exist; he's covered his tracks very carefully. So carefully I'd say he was expert. Even the company is owned by a shell corporation with all accounts offshore, information inaccessible.

Bailey comes to look over my shoulder.

Just a thought. Are you sure this guy doesn't work for the CIA? Not a single one of the names you gave me leads to anything authentic. Certainly not an address, or any way to find his actual location. No previous address attached to a credit card, parking ticket, nothing.

Disappointment is a weight on my chest.

I'm usually pretty good at following digital trails. But this one is cold. I'm keeping your deposit because I've basically been obsessed since you reached out, but keep the rest. I hate that I couldn't find him. I feel like he won. I'll loop back if anything surfaces.

"Who is this guy?" Bailey wants to know.

"He's a guy who can create an online identity for you, basically construct a history in social media, so that people only find what you want them to find when they search your name out on the internet."

"Because that's the first thing people do now, is search you out on the web, visit your social media profiles."

"That's right. These days, your whole history lives on the internet — where you grew up, went to school, anything that's ever written about you, any post you're tagged in. You can create your whole persona online."

"When did you do this?"

"After college. Jax knew someone. It was her idea. A way to make sure no one ever connected my past to my present."

"You buried Robin Carson."

"Again. Just not deep enough, I guess."

"Pretty deep."

He puts a hand on my shoulder and my whole body tingles. "Your secrets — they're safe with me. *You're* safe with me. I don't want to blow up your life."

His voice is low. I don't turn to look at him.

"Maybe it needs blowing up. There's a forgotten girl in my grave."

"That's your call," he says. "But just know this. You *deserved* to move on back then, to have a good life after what happened to you. You did that. Not everyone could have."

"I had help." Miss Lovely, Jones and Maggie Cooper. They were the real fixers. They helped me stitch myself back together.

"That's good," he says, staying close. When I rise, he takes a step back, but puts a hand on my arm.

"I'm sorry," he says, voice thick.

"For what?" I ask. He takes my hand and I don't pull away, let him draw me in closer.

"For what you went through, for what you're going through now. I'm sorry that this is how we met."

His hand moves up my arm, comes to rest on the back of my neck where it's strong and tender at the same time. I put my palm to his chest and feel his heat, the rise and fall of his breath. The draw to him is irresistible, and when he puts his lips on mine, the kiss lights a fire inside. What is gentle, inquiring at first, grows urgent, his arms tightening around me. His lips move down my neck, and when he whispers my name, I can hear the pitch of his desire.

"Wren."

I want to pull away, but I don't. I really don't.

My phone starts ringing then, startling us both, breaking the trance. We both stare at each other, awkward, embarrassed. What just happened?

The caller ID reads: The Hollows Historical Society.

He moves away from me, goes to stand by the window, and I feel the loss of his heat against my body.

"Joy?" I answer.

"Miss Greenwood." The clipped professional voice of a historian more comfortable with textbooks than people.

"Yes. Thank you for getting back to me."

"I received your message and have been doing some research. Would you like to come in to review the documents I've found?"

"When's a good time?" It's getting late. I'm worried she'll put me off until tomorrow.

"No time like the present, Miss Green-wood."

"I'll be right there."

THIRTY-FIVE

Then

Every time I killed a thing, it hurt a little less. I grew accustomed to watching the light die in eyes, to bodies growing slack and still, those final shuddering breaths. My body grew stronger, my aim more precise. My tracking skills became elevated — more than just seeing and following signs, I could feel the energy of my quarry.

"You're a natural, little bird," my father said, with something like awe in his voice.

He became a silent assistant, the muscle required to lift and carry. He did the dirty work of bleeding, gutting, skinning, preparing meat for curing, salting, and smoking.

Those days with him, spent mostly in nature, mostly in silence, often catching nothing, eating our packed lunches as we sat against a tree or perched on boulders by the creek. I hate to say it. Those were happy days. It was in the night that the demons

came for him, mainly when he'd been drinking, but not always. Something about the
sun setting. He was two different men. During the day as we worked, when he homeschooled me, when we took off our shoes
and waded in the creek, he was at peace. In
those moments, I regretted what I'd done,
calling the police.

The weeks wound on and no one came.

My mother grew more silent, withdrawn.
She wore one arm in a sling, favoring it, but
didn't dare go to the doctor. Jay got angrier
and angrier, the fuse between him and my
father quicker to ignite.

My mother took Jay into town to take his
GED. Of course, they never said so, but I
sensed that she was trying to help him leave.
That one day they'd go to town and she'd
come back without him. I knew she would
never leave me and my father, but Jay was
old enough to go. He could have joined the
army and my father wouldn't have been able
to do anything.

But he didn't leave us.

I wish he had.

I was sleeping the night they came. I was
deep in the woods of my dreams, tracking a
doe through the brush unarmed. When I
came close to her, I sat and watched her
graze, relieved that I wouldn't have to kill

her, that I could just let her be.

Jay roused me with a rough hand to my shoulder, the green light of the woods fading into the darkness of my bedroom.

"I need you to go to the tree house and stay there until I come to get you."

Two crisp, sharp shots rang out, shouting voices carried on the night. I knew in my bones what was happening. Jay pulled me from the bed, threw my tattered jeans at me.

"Get dressed."

"I called them," I said, shifting out of my pajamas and putting on the clothes. I didn't even care if he saw me in my underwear.

"Who?"

"The police. I called the police, told them about the guns."

He froze. I thought he would explode like my father. Instead, he put a hand on my head.

"That's good," he said. "That was smart. Now go hide. I'll get you when it's over."

I wanted to hug him. But I didn't. We just didn't do that. My brother was stiff and distant, maybe all boys were. He wouldn't even let my mother kiss him, and I knew how much he loved her. I should have grabbed him and wrapped my arms around him. That's a thing I'll always regret.

"Go."

Robin was waiting for me on the porch. Together we ran along the narrow path to the big oak where my tree house sat and scrambled up the ladder. Above us, through the slats, there were stars. Voices and shots rang out through the night. We were frozen, silent, my heart thumping.

I knew Robin wasn't real. But she was real enough. I've done a little research since then, into the theories of the imaginary friend. It's a function, often of the traumatized childhood psyche, a survival mechanism. Sometimes it comes in the form of an animal, sometimes it might be a spirit or an angel. Robin was everything I was afraid to be — at one with the woods and that place, brave, unafraid of the dark, and my father's rages, my mother's weakness. She observed it all with the equanimity of the wise.

My breathing was shallow, my heart an engine. I knew I couldn't stay hidden while Jay and my mother might be in danger.

I looked at Robin.

She said, *Where's your crossbow?*

Joy is waiting for me at the door when I walk up the path. She is a slim and angular woman with a steel gray bob. She smooths her pencil skirt, tugs at the collar of her crisp white blouse, every inch the elegant librarian. But as I approach, she softens and opens her arms. She smells like Miss Lovely; they wore the same perfume, L'Aire du Temps, floral and light. Her embrace is solid, strong, where Miss Lovely was soft and ensconcing. But I still take comfort in it, hold on to her longer than I would hold on to most people.

"I take it you two know each other."

Joy pulls back and peers over her glasses at Bailey, who comes up the walk behind me. Her expression leaves no doubt that she is not impressed.

"You don't return calls," he says into the silence that follows.

"I do," she says. "In time."

She loops her arm through mine and brings me inside. I wonder if she'll shut him out, but she lets him enter, too. The interior of the building smells of hardwood and old paper, a comforting smell that makes me think of Miss Lovely and her library of books. The more digital the world becomes, the more I find myself craving wood and paper, solid, simple things.

"I knew you'd have questions one day," she says. "These things have a way of rising up as we come of age, grow older, find new perspectives."

386

"It's more than that."

"Tell me."

I sit at the long wood table that stands in an open area between the shelves and shelves of books. I've been here before and know that this historical library houses books and records, primary documents like letters and diaries. Everything from the town's founding documents, to files of old newspapers. There's a microfiche room, and a computer lab, a nod to the new way records are kept. Here in this library, Joy Martin has amassed as many pieces of town history as exist. The place has an energy, like a thousand voices whispering their piece of the story of this town.

I tell Joy about everything that's happened, and she listens carefully, foot tapping. Bailey stands by the door, arms folded. Something about the expansiveness of the room, the silent presence of recorded moments in time, the ticking of the clock on the wall over the desk, I feel lifted away from the world outside. My words seem to float on the air, soft and dissipating like a breath. When I'm done, I take the newspaper article from my bag and put it on the table.

She reaches for it, regards it for a second with a frown, then stands to sort through a stack of red, hardbound binders that sit on the table. She opens one labeled Carson Family Murder and starts shifting through the pages. When she finds what she's looking for, she opens the book to me. Bailey moves in closer, standing over my shoulder.

The space in the book is blank. She places a protective hand on the newsprint.

"That article came from this book."

I stare at the empty page, trying to make sense of it.

You were here in this room, digging though my past? How? When? *Why?*

"Was someone here, asking about this event?" Bailey wants to know.

"When?" I ask. "Why didn't you call me?"

Joy raises a hand.

"Hold on," she says. "About a year ago someone did make an appointment to come in and search through old records. One of the local Realtors was searching for a history on a property a client was looking to buy. Your property."

"You still own the property?" asks Bailey.

I nod my head, but find I've lost my voice.

"It's been in the Carson family for generations," says Joy. "Luke Carson signed it over to Robin, well, legally Wren Greenwood, when he went to prison. He's serving two life sentences without possibility of parole."

Yes, she's right. The property is mine, and it's true that Realtors do often call with offers on the place. City people looking for their little piece of nature, their escape from the modern world — for the weekend anyway — make huge offers to raze the house and put up some gleaming monument to their wealth. And anyone with half a brain would have sold it years ago. But I didn't. I've held on to it because some piece of me still lives there. We used to think that the house was haunted. But really it's *our* ghosts that roam that land. It's their home, and though I should chop off that part of my life like a gangrenous limb, I find I can't. In my dreams, I still live there roaming the woods and listening to the birdsong, even if in my waking life I can't stand the thought of stepping foot on that property.

"Who was the Realtor?" asks Bailey. He's still running his agenda, while I've veered off course some, drifting into the past. All of this is not so much about you as it was at first. I feel like I've stepped into quicksand.

"I keep a log of visitors," she says, rising. She walks over to her desk at the end of the room, her heels clicking purposefully. A few taps on the keyboard and she looks up, over her glasses.

"Rick Javits," she says thoughtfully.

The name rings a bell; he was probably one of the Realtors who called me and whom I ignored. There's a woman, too, Barbara something or other. She called only recently. Maybe I should call her back.

"Did he come alone?" asks Bailey.

"No," she says. "He had his client with him, wanted to show the place off. You know how people like to think they're buying a piece of history."

"Do you have a name there?" I can tell he's getting annoyed, having to drag every piece of information out of Joy.

"I'm sorry, no," she says stiffly. "I entered Rick Javits and client."

"That seems odd," says Bailey. "You're so meticulous about everything else."

He sweeps his arm around the library to make his point.

Joy peers at him over her glasses, annoyed, imperious. "If I thought he'd be moving into town, I might have paid more attention to him."

"But he was looking to buy property, so wasn't that a reasonable expectation?"

"No."

"Why not?"

"Because the Carson property is not for sale and never has been. Robin won't sell that land."

Won't I? How does she know that?

"Is there a way for us to reach Rick Javits?" asks Bailey.

"He's a Realtor, Mr. Kirk, I promise you that he'll be easy to find. You *have heard* of Google, right?"

"Wow," he says. "What's your problem with me?"

"I don't like people who ask questions thinking that they already have the answers."

Bailey raises his eyebrows and blows out a breath. "You're a librarian, right? Aren't you supposed to *live* for people who have questions?"

"When they're honest, when the agenda is clear."

I'd wonder what Joy has against Bailey Kirk but I already know. Joy is the keeper of history, of the story of this town and how it is told. Bailey Kirk is an outsider and an interloper. He doesn't speak the language of this place. As someone with a foot in both worlds, I can see why the two would never be compatible. You can't be a part of the world out there, and understand people like my father who wanted to leave it behind.

Joy comes to sit beside me.

"This is about you right now," she says, taking my hands. "You've been through a lot. What have you come home to find?"

What *have* I come home to find? I thought I was looking for you. But maybe I am really looking for myself.

"Can you tell me what you remember? About the property, about my father, about the raid? Not just what's here in the records. But what you know to be true about all of it?"

She regards me over her glasses for a moment with stormy gray eyes. She nods to Bailey, indicating that he can take a seat, which he does with a sigh.

Opening the first of the binders, she tells me what she knows, and she starts at the beginning.

■ ■ ■ ■

Part Three:
I Am the Storm

■ ■ ■ ■

You are the future,
The red sky before sunrise
Over the fields of time.

Rainer Maria Rilke

THIRTY-SIX

BONNIE

Even though we can't always have affection for every person we meet, we can always treat every person with kindness.

How many times had Bonnie's mother said that? A hundred. A thousand. And that was the reason why Bonnie never made fun of Doug. The other kids in their class, when they weren't actively teasing him — an enterprise usually reserved for lunch or PE when supervision was light — kept their distance.

The truth was that poor Doug wasn't always clean; often he smelled, and his hair hung greasy and stringy over his eyes. He wasn't always nice; he had a bad temper and when he got frustrated, he turned an awful shade of red. Even though he was smart, no one wanted to be his lab partner in science class.

But Bonnie kind of liked him, in a strange way. She always made a point to choose him, when it was left up to the chemistry class to pick their groups. And even though Jessica and Evie, her two best friends, were in the class, too, and they were a ready-made group, and they groaned and rolled their eyes when she picked him, Bonnie hated how sad he looked when he thought no one was watching. And he was a good lab partner, even Jessie and Evie admitted that. They were nice to him, too. Bonnie and her friends were the opposite of the "mean" girls — which always seemed like kind of a silly thing. She didn't really know anyone who was mean all the time.

Anyway, Doug was gentle and quiet when he was part of their group. He took good notes. And he understood things. When Bonnie was struggling with something, and she often was, she went to find him in the library where he spent most of his study halls, and recess, and after school because his older brother always picked him up late in a beat-up old pickup that looked and sounded like it was going to shake apart. He always helped her.

On Valentine's Day, she made sure that he was one of the people who got the little bags of candy she handed out. And at the end of each grade, she'd signed his nearly blank yearbook. Have a great summer, Doug! You're such a good friend!

She'd known Doug since kindergarten. She

would say he was a school friend, not an outside-of-school friend like Jessie and Evie. He didn't go to the movies, or the games, or the fair with her group. Sometimes she saw him at those things, but he was usually alone or with his brother, who everyone knew smoked and sold pot.

One afternoon when Doug was helping her with algebra, he said out of nowhere, "My brother has a gun."

Something about the way he said it made her uncomfortable. She shifted away from him a little; they'd been sitting kind of close together so she could see his notebook.

"Oh, yeah? Wow."

"He took me to the range and taught me how to shoot."

She knew that boys did that sometimes. Lied or exaggerated to make themselves seem cool. Her brother did it all the time — saying he made a goal in soccer when he'd really only assisted, or pretending a girl liked him when she obviously didn't know he was alive. She figured that's what Doug was doing.

She changed the subject, back to algebra, and he didn't bring it up again. Probably if she had seemed impressed, he would have talked about it nonstop, since boys also seemed to do that.

She was in English class when it happened. Jessie sat beside her and Evie was out sick with her period. The sound, like a loud crack, made everyone freeze. Her teacher, Mr. Brennan, stopped writing midsentence on the board.

Another sound, louder, more like a bang.

When she looked back on that moment, she knew. Even though it was so far from anything she'd ever imagined. She knew what was happening. She knew it was Doug.

"Okay, guys," said Mr. Brennan, his voice tight with a false brightness. "Don't panic. Just get under your desks, okay?"

Get under our desks? She and Jessie looked at each other, and Jessie started to cry.

Bonnie grabbed her friend and pulled her down to the ground. Mr. Brennan walked over to the door and turned off the light. She saw him try to lock the door, but it wouldn't latch. She heard him swear under his breath. He heaved a table in front of the door, with the help of Bruce, who leaped up to assist. Then he put his finger to his lips, and everyone was stone still. Except Jessie who was whimpering so softly into Bonnie's shoulder.

When Doug came to the slim window in the door, his eyes seemed to find hers right away. She was in a direct line from the door. He was so pale, and his dark hair was wild, his eyes glassy and strange, like he wasn't Doug at all, but some monster in a Doug shell. She forced herself to offer him a sad smile, her whole body shaking, her mouth filled with cotton.

"Ohmygodohmygod," Jessie whispered. "Ohpleaseno."

Bonnie gave him a slight shake of her head. *Please don't do this, Doug. It's not right,* she thought. Trying to send the message to him with her mind.

He pushed the door, was stopped by the heavy table. She saw him redden. She heard sirens, very faint, way, way too far away.

That's where he did it.

Holding Bonnie's eyes, he put the gun to his own head and pulled the trigger.

The sound. The sight. That moment. It burned into her brain, into her soul.

She would never, ever stop seeing it. It would invade her dreams, her thoughts.

Whenever there was a loud sudden noise of any kind, it would come back. From that day, she would be plagued by migraines. Doug killed five kids, Becky Johnson, Amy Watson, Chad Markus, Martie Doyle, and Will Jones, and two teachers, Miss Carol and Mr. Beech, and then ended his own life. Bonnie thought he sought her out on purpose, looking for the only one who had ever seemed to care about him. Someone who would bear witness to his tragic end.

Jessie said that Bonnie screamed and screamed, but Bonnie didn't remember.

Later there were funerals, and a long investigation. Some of the parents brought a lawsuit against the school because so many of the doors had failed to lock, and the police seemed to think that would have saved lives. Not everyone had been as fast thinking as Mr. Brennan in moving obstacles in front of the door.

There was a payout, a big one, to all the families who had lost children, or been affected, like Bonnie for mental trauma, or James Smith, who Doug shot in the leg. Her parents put the money in an account for her education. It was invested well, and it grew into a sizable nest egg by the time she graduated college.

But it didn't matter. Because Doug had ruined her life that day.

And it was her fault that all those people had been killed.

Because that day when he told her about the gun in the library, she never said a word about it. In fact, she promptly forgot about the conversation and about Doug as soon as she climbed into Jessie's mom's SUV to head to their house for pizza, movie, and a sleepover.

The truth was that she didn't think about Doug at all, before, unless he was right in front of her, or unless she needed his help with something. And she was only nice to him because her mother had taught her that it was important to be nice to everyone.

And maybe it was. Maybe Doug would have killed her, too, if she hadn't been. He only had one bullet left in his gun, and he used it on himself. Or maybe it was just because he couldn't open the door. Maybe it was because he, too, heard the sirens.

But he killed a part of her. The part that believed that the world was a good and safe place, that people most of the time were helpful and friendly, that her future was bright with possibilities. And even though she went on to college, to grad school, to become a college English professor at the small private school not far from where her parents still lived, part of her never moved on from that day, from the moment. It was a weight she carried forward, a dark cloak that seemed perpetually wrapped around her. Her parents worried, she knew that, as her friends all partied their way through their twenties, met "the one," got married, had babies. Not Bonnie. She stayed back there in the English classroom, watching Doug shoot himself in the head. Over and over.

Of course, there had been a battalion of

therapists. Medication for a time. She'd even written into her favorite advice columnist once. It helped; it all did — a bit. She healed some, moved on, was productive enough. Still, she had trouble joining life, building friendships, dating. That was why Jessie, who was still her best friend, forced her to join Torch. And it was on Torch that she met Shawn.

"You know darkness," he said to her that first night. They'd left the bar where they agreed to meet and found their way to a park bench, sat while the full moon glistened on the lake water and talked. "I see it in you."

The statement startled her into telling the truth.

"I do," she admitted. She told him, in broad strokes, about the school shooting.

"I do, too." He'd had a violent childhood, he said. He'd lost a sister. He didn't offer details and she didn't press. "It's part of life. You don't have to fear it. To accept it is an embrace."

He quoted Rilke. " 'You are not surprised at the force of the storm . . .' "

And something inside her relaxed and felt known for the first time since the day she watched Doug die. All this time, she'd wondered how she could live knowing what darkness awaited. With Shawn, she realized all of it, light and dark, life and death, was one terrible, beautiful mingle, and that the whole point was to just live well, while you could.

She disappeared into him. He was her first everything — her first love, her first real mature kiss, her first nongroping, nonawkward, and vaguely unpleasant sexual encounter.

Her parents had worried before that she was too lonely. But they didn't like Shawn.

"He seems controlling, Bonnie, brooding," said her mother gently. "Are you sure he's for you? You've always been such a bright spirit."

She loved her parents. But they smothered. She needed a break.

Now, she drove, hypnotized by the night and the winding of the road. It wasn't much farther now, she didn't think. She'd left her phone, cleared out her accounts, followed the map he'd left for her. She hadn't told anyone where she was going. It was like an adventure.

"There's a place where we can go," he told her. "Not forever. But for a time, where we can disconnect from the madness of the modern world. You can write. I can do my work from anywhere. Think of it as a retreat. When you return to the world, you'll be stronger, more able to face the madness and not be swallowed by it."

It made sense. The world had gone mad — social media had turned people into narcissists, there were more school shootings than ever, the planet, long abused by corporate greed, was angrily unleashing fires and hor- rific storms. Maybe it was time to retreat for a while. Once upon a time she'd dreamed of writing — poetry, maybe a novel.

She felt bad about her parents. But Shawn was right. "You're an adult," he said. "You own yourself. You're not their child anymore."

When she felt stronger, she'd write to them. They'd be angry, hurt, but maybe they'd understand that this was what she needed to finally heal.

Bonnie came to the final turn. A tilting mailbox with three red reflectors on a twisting rural road. He would be waiting here for her, he said. He went early because he wanted the house to be perfect when she arrived.

She hesitated.

Her life, her parents, her job, her friends. Why did she feel like if she made that turn, she might never be able to go back to any of it, not really?

She felt the beating of her own heart in her chest. Maybe this was a mistake. Maybe she should at least go back to that last gas station and call her mom.

But then she thought of him — his warmth, his gentleness, the way he knew her heart and her body. She put on her blinker though there was no one there to see her make the turn, and drove toward her new life.

THIRTY-SEVEN

Then

We kept the crossbow in the barn near the house. The night had grown quieter, but I heard the crackle of gunfire off in the distance, the sound of shouting through the trees.

I took my crossbow down from its place, loaded it, and made my way toward the sound of my father's voice.

I was just a kid that night, but I was older than my years in many ways, stronger than I would have been had we stayed in the life we had before my father returned. I was scared, but I was used to fear, knew how to push it deep, to focus on my breath and force away the chaos of my mind. He had taught me how to do that, when he taught me how to kill.

"Which one of you called them?" I heard my father roar as I climbed the porch steps. "After everything, after *everything*."

His voice was a wild pitch of rage and sadness; my nerve endings sizzled as I made my way down the long hall to the kitchen. My feet were bare, the wood hard and cold beneath my soles. I was careful to keep my step light, not to make a sound.

"Get away from her." Jay's voice was a wail. "Get away from us."

The scene revealed itself in pieces as I came to the door.

I know Jay saw me, but he didn't move his gaze in my direction. My father's broad back was to me, heaving with his rage. My mother was motionless on the floor, a pool of blood beneath her. Her head was at an unnatural angle against the hearth.

My mind distanced. It didn't seem real. Her stillness was impossible; I knew that sight too well. Jay's face was red and streaked with tears.

"Which one of you?" my father roared.

I lifted the crossbow, its butt against my shoulder, the red of my father's shirt filling the sight.

"It was me," I said. "*I* called the police."

He spun at the sound of my voice, turning to face me. There was a gun in his hand, that flat black semiautomatic he favored for target practice. He, like Jay, rarely missed his mark. I felt the heat of his aim in the center of my chest.

"You?" he breathed. In the single syllable I heard amazement, anger, sadness. "Why?"

"Put down your gun, Dad," I said. I had my stance, my aim. But did I have the will to shoot my father? I wasn't sure; the crossbow quaked in my grip.

"Don't you know what will happen to you now?" he said. "They'll take you from this place and you'll belong to *them,* to their government, to this sick world they've made."

"Put the gun down."

He started to cry, then, and my heart broke into a thousand little pieces in my chest.

He moved toward me. "What have you done, little bird?"

The room spun, my brain grappling with a moment that was too awful, too ugly.

"Dad. Put down your gun." My voice didn't even sound like mine. It was the voice of a young woman, someone powerful, someone who knew she could kill if she had to. "I don't want to do this. Please."

That's when Jay tackled him from behind, issuing a warrior's yell. As he knocked my father to the floor, the gun careened out of reach. I stood frozen, my bow aimed as they tangled on the ground.

"You killed her," screamed Jay. "She's *gone.*"

My eyes fell on my mother, her golden hair around her like a halo, her robin's-egg blue eyes staring, the black-red of her blood spilled. She lay as beautiful and lifeless as that doe I killed.

There's a peace to it, most people don't know. A release, but not then, not for me.

A terrible scream of pain exploded from me, just as my father got the gun, and he and Jay struggled for it. He raised himself high, away from my brother. And I pulled the trigger to release my arrow, just as the gun fired, filling the air with sound and the acrid smell of cordite, making my ears ring.

There was a long moment where Jay and I locked eyes, and my father wobbled in place, the arrow in one side of his back, its green feathers vibrating.

Here, the whole world took and released a breath.

My father fell heavily to the side with a groan, dropping the gun. I raced over to kick it away from him. That's when I saw the flower of blood blooming on Jay's white shirt. I dropped the bow and ran to him where he lay, put my hands to the flow, right over his heart. I tried, tried so hard to press it all back inside of him, to reverse the flow, the passage of time.

"Please," I whispered. "Please."

He grabbed my wrist, urgent, his eyes wild with fear. But he never spoke another word. And I lay my head upon his chest and listened to his last breath leave him, looking up in time to see all the light drain from his gaze.

And all I could do was scream with rage and sorrow. The sound bouncing around the room, around the inside of my head.

My father grabbed hold of my ankle, and started pulling me toward him. He was so strong, even then, with the arrow sticking horribly out of his back. I kicked at him hard, hitting him in the jaw and getting him to release his grip. I didn't want to leave them but I had to, grabbing my bow, backing toward the door.

"You did this," he said. With one hard pull, he yanked the arrow out of his back, howling in pain. He rose, pitching, unsteady to his feet, drunk on rage and pain. "*You* did this."

Even then I knew it wasn't true.

"No," I told him. "You did."

He lunged for me, his face contorted. With him at my heels, I ran.

Robin was ahead of me like the white rabbit showing me the way. Around us the

410

sound of shouting and gunfire, just like I imagine war must be. It *was* a war, a battle anyway. One I'd already lost and was just trying to survive. Above us, the swaying trees and the starlight.

This way, she kept calling back to me. *This way.*

I heard him calling my name over and over. *Robin. Robin. Robin.*

I ran straight into Jones Cooper, who caught me against the great barrel of his chest, in the expansive strength of his arms. He pushed me behind him, and pointed his gun at the darkness. We both heard him coming, crashing through the trees. He came to a stop when he saw Jones, the gun aimed at him.

"Stay where you are," said Jones. "Get down on your knees and put your hands in the air."

He didn't yell.

But there was the unmistakable volume of authority, a righteousness to the command. And my father, winded, injured, defeated, suddenly and abruptly complied, as if all the life had drained from him. He sank to his knees, then fell to the ground weeping. He was a big man, physically formidable. In that moment, he was a child, damaged and broken by the life he'd lived, the things he'd seen and done. None of it was my fault. But it wasn't all his fault either. I sank to my haunches and leaned against the big tree as Jones Cooper put handcuffs on my father. I held his eyes and saw all the depths of his pain and rage and deep sorrow.

I saw it all. And still I hated him. And I never forgave him.

The rest of that night, and most of what followed in the weeks after, is blur of grief and the profound misery of unimaginable loss.

"This is the worst night of your life," Maggie Cooper said as she wrapped me in a blanket and took me stunned and in deep shock away from that place. I remember the back of her car vividly, the velvety softness of the upholstery, the light scent of something floral, the cool of the window. There were no words in my head, just a siren of misery. "But you are going to get through it."

It was more of a command than an assurance. I remember thinking that I didn't want to survive. That I wanted to go where my mother had gone, and my brother, and that first doe I killed. I wanted to go to the place where you go when the light dies.

I'm trying not to go back to that night as

Joy talks, but the sights and sounds and smells come back to me vividly. Some things you can never forget, hard as you try. It's all well and good to say that the past is gone and all we have is the moment. But for me, the past is a haunting.

Bailey is antsy, his knee bouncing as Joy takes the scenic route to the night I lost everything. There's a tension, an awkwardness between us now. I try to ignore it.

"There were three families on that property. Your family who owned the land, and the Stones and the Wilsons who rented other structures on the property. Both pretty bare bones, an old barn which the Stones converted into a relatively livable place, drawing from the well and building a septic."

She has the property survey out in front of her. On it I can see the main house, the barn, the well, the septic. I didn't know the other families were our renters. Did they pay? Or was it a barter arrangement? I ask the question of Joy but she shakes her head. She doesn't know the answer.

I think of the bunker, packed with food supplies, big bins of rice, flour, sugar, canned fruits and other goods, the guns, ammunition. It never occurred to me to ask where it all came from.

413

"The Wilsons lived here." She points to a clearing where no structure is shown on the survey. "They built a cabin. No permit was obtained, of course, but I've been up there and seen it with my own eyes. It's a solid, well-built structure. There's a generator, some solar panels."

I've been to the main house a time or two since that night, but I've never wandered the property again even though Robin always begs me to follow her, to go back to the tree house.

"They were all off the grid?" said Bailey.

"There was a power line to the property if that's what you mean. But Luke Carson built a pretty sophisticated system using solar panels. There were a couple of generators. There are two septic tanks on the property, running water from wells."

"But they were self-sufficient up there."

"More or less. Robin's mother worked in town at the grocery. Lovely lady, always with a smile. But the Wilsons and the Stones, they were real 'hill people' as folks in town here like to say. Lived off the land almost totally. Homeschooled kids. Failed to report births, buried their own dead."

"Doomsday preppers," says Bailey. He seems to like this phrase; I suppose it's a kind of shorthand that makes the lifestyle

414

choice easy to understand.

Joy shakes her head slightly, pushes up her glasses. "These folks thought that society had already collapsed. They had dropped out, walked away from —"

"The world of men," I finish. "That's what my father always said. That the end was already underway."

"Some days it's hard to argue with that," says Joy.

I think of the fires raging, the virus that's spreading, the category five hurricanes that have been ravaging coastlines, war all over the world, famine, drought. Maybe he was right.

"Anyway, they were up there peacefully enough," Joy continues. "Living off the land, not really bothering anyone and no one bothering with them. Then the local police got the call about guns and ammunition being stored."

"Law enforcement doesn't like to hear about private weapons stockpiles," says Bailey. "Generally it comes to no good. I'm not surprised that they raided the property."

Joy shook her head.

"It wasn't meant to be a raid. I don't get that sense. It was meant to be an investigative call, hoping for transparency and cooperation. But apparently, word got back that the cops were coming, and the men up there armed themselves."

"How did word get back? A leak in the department?"

"I'm afraid I don't know," she says with a sigh. "But violence erupted. A tragedy."

"Who died that night?" I ask.

"Your mother and brother." She reaches for my hand. "The Stones — Wyatt, Melba, Emily, and Joseph. The Wilsons fled."

"How many Wilsons were there?" asks Bailey.

Joy opens another binder and flips through the pages.

"Jessup and Lina and as far as I can recall there were two children, whose births were not recorded in The Hollows. But there might have been more children born at home."

As hard as I try, I can't remember any of them. I have vague recall of the men who gathered with my father sometimes, one with dark hair and a scar on his face, the other with a shaved head, lots of tattoos. Maybe there was an older boy around Jay's age, sullen and silent. I don't know that I ever saw the women, or Emily, the girl whose life I stole. I suppose it's the typical myopia of youth; you only see what impacts you directly.

"Any idea where Jessup and Lina Wilson might have gone?" Bailey again, looking for that thread he hopes to pull.

Joy Martin shrugs. "I imagine they found another place to live off the grid. When strangers leave this town, we let them go."

The comment is more than a little pointed. I hold back a smile, wondering what Joy has against Bailey.

My gaze falls on Bailey's phone; he's recording the conversation. I wonder if he's recorded other conversations, those between us, and that's why he never takes notes. I don't say anything but he sees me looking, gives me a lift of his eyebrows like: *Yeah, so what.*

"Do you think that what happened to you and your family has something to do with what's happening now?" asks Joy gently.

"I wouldn't have thought so if not for this." I rest my hand on the article. She's already placed it back in the binder where it belongs. "I didn't think anyone knew about me."

I flip through the binder, glancing over *The Hollows Gazette* articles, the survey, the copy of the property deed. There's an unexpected surge of protective pride — my history, my family, my land. However ugly and unwanted, it all belongs to me.

417

My phone is silenced, but when I feel it buzzing, I take it from my pocket. There's a text from an unknown number.

I am the dream you are dreaming.
When you want to awaken, I am that wanting:

Rilke's poems in *The Book of Hours* are a kind of prayer, his love letters, his one-sided conversation with God. I stare at the words, feel their meaning in my bones. I hate to admit it but I pulse with longing for you.

Then: Lose him and I'll come for you. If you don't get rid of him, I'm gone for good.

The room is spinning, but Bailey and Joy don't seem to notice.

"What about the Farrow family?" asks Bailey. "Were they connected to any of these families?"

Joy shakes her head, thoughtful, seeming to search her memory.

"Mr. Farrow was a math teacher at the high school. Mrs. Farrow taught kindergarten. When they were killed in that house fire — an accident — their daughter went to live with her grandparents just a few miles away. But she left after high school and did not return here to live."

"It seems odd though, doesn't it? Two

women connected to this case came from this town. Both with tragedy in their past, both become involved with the same man."

"Might just be coincidence."

"I don't believe in coincidence."

"I'm sure there are lots of things you don't believe in that exist all the same," she says. "Meanwhile, you don't understand The Hollows, its strange ways. Maybe it was just a hook, a way to bring Robin home."

A smile teases at the corner of Bailey's mouth. "It's a place, not a person."

"Some places have power, energy," she says. I don't argue because I know it to be true. Even Robin has something to do with that, the little piece of The Hollows that never leaves me, always nudging me to come home. If you don't know this place, you can't understand.

Joy doesn't like Bailey but I think he likes her, or she amuses him anyway. I keep my eyes on him, remembering that kiss, how it felt to be in his arms. Your text. My pull to you. I shake it away.

He gets up and walks the perimeter of the room, looking at the photos hanging on the wall — pictures of the town founders, the old church, the first school. The town's founding documents sit under glass on a velvet bed.

My phone vibrates again: Tonight.

"So this is your life," said Bailey. "To record what happens in this town."

I don't think he's being flip or disrespectful. Bailey Kirk is a person who wants to know and understand things.

"That's right," she says easily. "We all have our calling. You want to find lost things. Miss Carson wants to help people find their way through the darkness in their lives. And I want to keep the history of this little town in the middle of nowhere."

He smiles at her, gives her a respectful nod. There's something else beneath the current of their antagonism, a kind of understanding. It's weird.

"I guess we don't always choose," he says.

"No," she says, stiffening a little. "Not always."

He keeps his place by the door. Maybe he's decided that there's nothing here to help him, just dusty old documents from a night long ago, my personal tragedy, but nothing more. A trip into the past, but not a thread into the future where he finds Mia.

"It's all here for you," says Joy. "I'll leave you to look through it if you like. Let me know if I can help."

She rises and disappears behind a door that closes with a soft click.

"Did you get a call?" He nods at my phone.

"Just Jax," I lie.

He wears a thoughtful scowl, which might be his default expression. But I feel like he knows that I'm lying. If he does, he keeps it to himself, walks over to the stacks, takes a book from the shelf and opens it.

Though I feel a powerful pull to him, can still feel his arms around me, I am going to blow Bailey Kirk off. Hard. I know it's wrong, and that just hours ago I've agreed to help him find you, using myself as bait. And that there's no way I should be planning to meet you alone.

But the truth is that I'm not going to blow my chance to see you one last time. I can't. I need to understand you and the things you've done. The need is dark and deep, twisting at my insides. If you disappear now, I know I'll never see you again.

"I'm going to go through these documents," I say, keeping my voice light.

"Okay," Bailey says. "I'm going to go look for Rick Javits, find out about his client."

I'm no detective but that does seem like a lead. "Go for it," I say.

His eyes linger. It seems like he wants to say something. He shoves his hands in his pockets. "Do we — uh — need to talk?"

"About what?" We do need to talk. Of course we do. But not now. I can't let whatever feelings I might have for Bailey Kirk deter me from my goals.

He offers a slow nod. Then, "Stay in touch, Wren."

It sounds like a warning as he exits and leaves me with my past. I stare at the door, fighting the urge to go after him. I could tell him what's happening. Ask for his help. But no. This is my errand alone.

When Bailey's truck rumbles away, I text back the strange number.

He's gone.

The response comes right away, an error message. I try again but only get the same. I scroll back through the texts, searching for a meaning I might have missed. But the words are stripped and bare, offering no trace of you. Frustration is a taste in the back of my throat. These games. You dangle the line. I reach. You yank it away.

I open one of the binders and travel back in time, looking for — I don't know what. Me. You. Some piece that connects then to now. I get lost wandering through my family's past — old photographs, birth and death records, marriage certificates. All the little pieces of paper that mark the passage of a life, all the images of moments frozen and preserved. There are even some letters from my grandfather to my grandmother while he was off to war. *Every day there's horror, but every night I dream of you.*

I don't know how much time has passed when my phone vibrates again.

It's a series of directions and simple commands: Write this down. Delete all traces of me from your text messages. Destroy your phone.

My skin tingles as I scribble the directions on to a pad of paper Joy has left for me. There's something quiet about it, final, that placing of pen to paper. I tear the sheet from the pad.

Then I leave without saying goodbye to Joy, get in my car and start to drive.

THIRTY-EIGHT

"I want you to come in, Bailey."

Nora was annoyed with him, and he could understand why. He'd failed her. Failed his client. Failed a girl who had, in all likelihood, fallen victim to a predator.

"I have a lead. A solid one."

"Tell me."

He told her about the Realtor, about the client looking to buy the Carson property, about how he had an address and was sitting outside the Realtor's house that very minute, ready to go knock on the door.

"It's almost midnight."

"Since when does that matter? There's a missing woman, a ticking clock."

She issued a sigh. "Look," she said, her voice tinny over the car speaker, "Thorpe fired us. He's hired someone else. So you're officially costing me money right now."

She didn't care about that. Neither did he.

"Just one more day. Twenty-four more hours."

Silence.

"I'll take it as a vacation day."

The neighborhood he'd stopped in was modest; tidy houses, well-kept, tree-lined. Nothing special, no grand McMansions, no run-down shacks. Basketball hoops and late-model cars in the driveways. It had the look of an organized neighborhood — block parties and coordinated decorating, maybe candles in brown bags at the curb on Christmas Eve. What did they call those things? Luminarias, that was it. It reminded Bailey of the way he grew up — a kind of all-American, ride your bike out to meet your friends, home when the streetlights came on, soccer on Saturdays, picnics, vacations to the beach upbringing. Rick Javits's house was a neat little Craftsman with a picket fence and postcard-sized front yard.

Nora was talking again.

"You know, sometimes we get wrapped up in these things for our own reasons. It stops being about the client, and becomes about something inside us that needs resolving. And when that happens things get murky."

"We've had this talk." Whenever he talked to Nora late at night, which was often, he always imagined her in gray silk pajamas and a cashmere robe, drinking a glass of wine. He wasn't sure why; he'd certainly never seen his boss in her pajamas.

"How much does this have to do with Wren Greenwood?" she asked.

A jolt of annoyed embarrassment. "She's in danger."

"You don't know that."

"He's going to come back for her. He wanted something he didn't get, and men like that don't give up."

"Have you developed feelings for her?"

"It's not like that."

Not like he'd been watching her for a while, digging through the layers of her life. Not like he couldn't stop thinking about her. Not like he felt a kind of thrill to find her in his motel room. Not like he felt a deep and abiding urge to make sure nothing happened to her. That she didn't slip into whatever black hole this monster had opened in the world.

"Then what's it like?"

"She's a good person. She deserves to have someone looking out for her right now. She — doesn't have anyone else."

More silence.

"You know, she lived through a nightmare, right?" he went on. "Then, instead of letting it ruin her life, she took on a role —

426

the whole Dear Birdie thing — trying to help people. She doesn't deserve this."

"She's not our client."

"What about the lab? Anything on those items I sent in?"

"There was some DNA from the sweater, but it doesn't match anything on CODIS or NDIS."

He deflated a bit. He had high hopes for the items Wren had retrieved from the rental property.

An old man walked his little white dog up the street, didn't glance in Bailey's direction.

"Just one more day," he said. "If he comes back for her, and I'm there, maybe we find Mia, too."

"Did I mention we've been fired from the Thorpe case?"

"You did."

"The job is no longer yours. Come in."

"Okay."

"Bailey."

"I said okay. I'll come in."

Obviously, he had no intention of going back in. It just wasn't going to happen, and Nora would let him get away with it because she didn't have a better detective in her firm. All of this was unspoken between them. Because Nora was like Bailey. The work wasn't about cases and fees; the work was about people. And when you took on someone's case, *those* people became *your* people and you cared about what happened to them. Nora's partner, Diana, was a different story. She was the money woman; she balanced the books. And right now, in the case of Mia Thorpe, the numbers didn't add up. Honestly, Bailey got that, too.

And then there was Wren Greenwood — wild, delicate, stubborn, kind. A fire to her, a softness. He thought about her. Too much.

"Never fall in love out there," Nora said, maybe reading his mind as she sometimes seemed to. "I warned you about that early."

She had warned him, and he'd scoffed. He'd never really been in love then. He didn't know what it was like to give yourself to someone and then lose them. The loved child of good parents, older brother to a devoted sister, he knew only about the kind of love that lasted, sustained, nourished. He didn't know about the kind of love that was like wildfire, burning everything to ash.

"That's not what's happening here."

"It's okay to care, as long as you're on solid ground, not ready to jump off the cliff after someone."

"I'll see you tomorrow, Nora."

"Good night, Bailey."

He checked the clock on the dash. It was late. Probably too late to do this; he wasn't a cop after all. And that ticking clock — no one but Bailey and Henry Thorpe could still hear it. But he *was* running out of time. He killed the engine, exited the truck, and approached the house.

A black cat sat on the porch swing, and the red door stood ajar. Inside, Bailey heard the sound of a television. He paused, listening.

This weird little town was one of those places where people still didn't lock their doors.

Which he always found idiotic. Hubristic. Especially since, statistically speaking, lots of bad things seemed to happen here — arson, child abductions, disappearances, murders. He was looking forward to packing up his stuff and getting out.

He knocked and the door swung open easily, and even though it was pretty rude, borderline illegal, Bailey stepped inside onto a creaky hardwood floor.

He knocked again, this time on the door that had swung wide open.

"Mr. Javits, excuse me. Investigator Bailey Kirk."

Not a lie. Just because he was a private investigator, not a police officer, didn't mean he had to clarify that every time. He worked with people's assumptions. People usually assumed he was a cop, and he just went with that.

"I have some questions about a client of yours."

He stepped farther down the hallway, toward the sound of the blaring television. It sounded like the news, which was all bad these days.

A deadly virus rages out of control in China. Officials say it's only a matter of time before it spreads to Europe and the United States. Are we prepared?

A puffy balding guy lay in a recliner, head tilted, mouth open in a snore that Bailey couldn't hear over the television. He knocked again, this time on the door frame to the living room. It was a tidy little space, comfortable with a big sectional, a fireplace that was dark, family pictures on the mantel, some Staffordshire dogs on the hearth. The big-screen television mounted on the wall showed images of rows of patients in hospital beds, a woman weeping, people of indeterminate sex in hazmat suits spraying down a city street.

Bailey raised his voice. "Mr. Javits."

Bailey recognized Rick Javits from his website, though the picture where he was impeccably coiffed, besuited, and unapologetically airbrushed bore little resemblance to the sleeping middle-aged schmo in the La-Z-Boy before him.

He thought he saw something move behind him, but when he turned to look, there was nothing but a dark doorway. People were armed these days, more than you'd think. You have to be careful, wouldn't want the wife coming in terrified, with her revolver drawn shooting first and asking questions later.

He moved toward Rick Javits. As he grew closer, Bailey's skin started to tingle. The angle of Javits's neck wasn't right. Drawing closer, Bailey realized it wasn't a shadow he was seeing on the other man's chest; his pajama top was soaked with blood. His eyes were not closed in sleep but wide open and glassy.

"Fuck," whispered Bailey, reaching for his phone.

"Mr. Kirk."

Bailey spun to see a tall, dark man dressed all in black seem to leak out from the darkness of the doorway. He knew him right away from the pictures he'd seen online.

He'd wondered what all those beautiful women had seen in the frankly kind of ugly guy he saw in pictures with the big nose, and the wide mouth, the hulking frame. He saw it now. There was a kind of power, a raw virility to him.

"You just can't let this go, can you?"

Bailey had been chasing this man for so long that he didn't even seem real. He wore a long black coat and held a gun with a silencer.

"Let's talk," said Bailey, lifting one palm and moving his other hand toward the gun in his shoulder holster. He could tick off at least three mistakes he'd made in the last hour that had led him to this moment that practically sizzled with bad possibilities.

"Let's not."

Bailey Kirk didn't even hear the gun go off, just saw the muzzle-flash, and then nothing.

THIRTY-NINE

Firewood. The smell of leaves on the ground. A black crow feather glinting in the sunlight. The sound of bees on wildflowers. Fireflies luminescent, languid, on summer nights. Robin's tinkling laughter.

I'm back there as I drive away from town, taking the back roads you have in your directions, seeming to weave further and further away from my life, from the city, from Dear Birdie.

For the first time in a long time, I am aware of the call back to that place, to that kind of life — its peace and quietude, its simplicity. Just you and the day, only the tasks of survival, of living — cooking and cleaning, gardening and hunting. No television to suck away the hours, to invade with the misery of the world news. No ringing, beeping devices; no noise pollution.

There are all kinds of words to define people like my father — prepper, hoarder, recluse, survivalist. To those of us dwelling in the modern world, with every convenience, all the abundance of the first world taken for granted, hyperconnected to each other and to the consumer machine that is our society, they seem strange. These people that want to go live out in the woods, return to subsistence living, working to grow and kill their own food. Why would anyone want to live that way? But maybe they're not the ones that have it wrong.

But really I think he was just trying to quiet all the chatter — the ceaseless demands, the soulless selling and buying, the constant messages of who he should want to be. He was tortured by what he'd seen overseas, what he'd done. I think he wanted to go back, to the last safe, happy place he knew, to the person he was there.

But I brought the world back to him. And it destroyed us all.

What are we doing?

Robin sits small and faint in the passenger seat, looking out at the darkness.

Where are we going?

I don't answer her. To be honest, I am a little embarrassed by her presence. By how real she is to me, how constant. Most people leave their imaginary friends in childhood where they belong. But Robin has stayed with me. She's still that feral girl, raggedy, wide-eyed with wonder at the world all around her. In happier times, when I'm busy, engaged with my work and my life, she's barely around. It's in the darker moments, when memory comes to visit and stay, or I'm lonely, or the weight of Dear Birdie is too much to bear, she's as real as Jax.

But the only person who knows about her is Dr. Cooper. I had a session with her a couple of years ago during a time when Robin seemed to be everywhere I looked.

"Robin isn't so hard to understand," Maggie said during that session. I'd driven back to see her rather than talk to her on the phone the way we sometimes did. "In your childhood, she was all the things you needed to be to survive your new life. She was a teacher, someone to show you the way of the land. She was a friend, when you'd been wrested from all yours back home. In adolescence, our friends are very significant. They help us to define who we are, who we want to become. She was a comfort in the instability of your home."

"I get that." I sank into the softness of Maggie's couch, grateful for the warmth of the room, the sun streaming in through the windows. "But why is she still with me?"

"Had you not experienced life-altering trauma, she probably would have just faded as you found your way in your new life, as you grew and started to make decisions for yourself. She would have gone the way of all psychological formations of this kind."

I wonder, is there a place where all the imaginary friends go, some kind of heaven for these "formations" of the troubled young mind. A place where they go and play with each other. I hope so.

"What's unusual about her," mused Dr. Cooper, "is that she has remained the same."

"Why?"

"Because often these friends, if they stay on to adulthood —" she paused here, looking at me in that serious way she has "— sometimes they become darker, in some cases they become a tormentor, possessive maybe, controlling — like an unseparated parent who can't let go."

Robin wasn't dark. Never that. She was all light. I told Dr. Cooper as much.

"Does she ever ask anything of you? Something you don't want to give?"

I had to think about it a moment.

"She wants to go home, to go back to the land, to the tree house. In some ways she'd be happier living the way my father wanted to live."

"Is that what you want?"

"Do I want to go back to the place where my father killed my brother and my mother and live there? No."

"And yet here you are, back in town. Why?"

"Because I needed to talk to you."

"About Robin," she said pointedly.

"Yes."

Maggie nodded thoughtfully. "You have to do some soul-searching here. Who is Robin to you really now? What does she represent? She's a formation of your psyche. What is she trying to tell you about yourself?"

Robin fades as I drive until there's no one beside me.

When the phone rings, I answer it via the button on my steering wheel.

"Don't worry," I answer. "Everything's fine."

"Really." Jax.

No, I did not leave my phone. I'm not in your spell the way those other women seem to have been. I'm not cashing out my accounts and walking away from everything I've built to follow you through whatever dark doorway you're offering. I think you know me better than that. I saw them, their faces, their shining eyes. Those girls — I'm sorry — but they were broken. I'm not. I'm a survivor.

I'm not worried that you'll know. Or that if you discover I haven't followed the rules, you'll disappear. You're as hooked into me as I am to you, I think. Otherwise you'd be long gone, wouldn't you, never looking back and on to your next victim.

"You know," Jax says, "I asked Siri to let me know when you were leaving that place. Since I track you I can do that."

"Jax."

"But it looks to me like you're not heading back this way. It looks to me like you're heading in the other direction. Tell me I'm wrong."

"You're not wrong."

A sigh.

"Talk."

I tell her everything. And I mean everything about my past, about Bailey Kirk, about the other women who have disappeared, about your text. There's a leaden silence when I'm done. I think maybe she's hung up, or that we were disconnected and I failed to notice because I was rambling on.

Then, "Am I hearing you right? You've

ditched the good guy, and you're chasing after the bad one. Why would you do that?"

The question brings me up short. She has a way of cutting through all the bullshit, getting right to the beating, red heart of the matter. I find myself at a rare loss for words.

"He dangles the line, a little bit of Rilke, a little bit of intrigue, and you go running? What would Dear Birdie say?"

"Uh," I say stupidly. I'm so far from my Dear Birdie mind. I didn't even read the letters Jax sent. I just told her to forward them to Liz. It's freeing in a way I wouldn't expect, not to have those voices in my head. I feel like I can hear my own for the first time in a while.

Do you hear that?
No, I don't hear anything.
What you hear is silence.

"She'd say that you need to check your impulses. She'd say that when your actions put you in harm's way, you need to unpack that. You need to sit with it and ask yourself why."

"That's not what I'm doing. I'm not chasing after him."

"Then what?"

I don't answer because it sounds too dark. But the truth is I'm hunting you.

What happens when I catch up with you

depends largely on what you've done with those women. But Jax doesn't know that side of me. Even my closest friend hasn't seen all the facets of Wren Greenwood, and she's never met Robin Carson.

"I'm going to go," I tell her gently. "But I'll be okay. And I'll be in touch soon."

"Wren."

"Don't worry," I tell her. "Just take care of the house and *Dear Birdie* for me."

"I really don't like the way you sound right now."

"I love you."

"Wren, don't you dare hang up this phone."

I do, though. And then with one hand, I disable her ability to follow me and I turn off the phone. No more distractions.

When tracking a creature, focus and silence are critical.

The darkness fans out before me, dancing at the edges of my headlights.

I make the last turn on the directions you gave me. There is no final destination, no address, just a series of turns and road names, markers to look out for — an old barn, a rusted pickup up on blocks in the drive of a red farmhouse.

The road is rocky and dark. The moon

dips behind the clouds.
I keep driving.

441

FORTY

Bailey Kirk didn't believe in an angry God, one who punished and raged. His father was an atheist, but his mother believed that God was in everyone and everything, and that was why you had to treat yourself, and the planet, and each other with love and respect. As a family, they did not attend church, but his mother had a kind of spiritual practice that consisted of meditation, long walks in nature, good deeds, and some various rituals involving a sage stick and singing bowl.

Mom's smudging again, his sister would say, with an indulgent roll of the eyes.

The smell would fill the house, cleansing it, she said, of stale energy or negativity, or inviting positivity, or expressing gratitude for some blessing. That smell of burning sage brought him right back to his childhood, to the warmth and safety of that place and time in his life.

It burned in his nostrils now, strong and

442

tangy on the back of his tongue.

Open your eyes, Bailey. His mother's voice. *Wake up, son.*

He followed the scent up through layers of darkness, only to find himself on the floor of a strange living room, definitely not his mother's house. A man he'd never seen — or wait, *had* he? — knelt beside him, wearing a worried frown. When Bailey tried to move, a violent pain in his shoulder radiated down his arm and he cried out with it.

"Okay," said the older man. "Take it easy."

There was no smell of burning sage now, and that feeling of warmth and safety was long gone as the man, surprisingly strong, helped Bailey over to the couch. He leaned in to inspect the wound.

"You're lucky. Looks like the bullet passed right through. Lost some blood, though."

He was feeling a lot of things — lucky wasn't one of them.

Rick Javits still lay in his recliner, pale and growing stiff, his final resting place, staring blankly. Okay, yeah, Bailey conceded to himself. Lucky.

The older man who was tall and broad, wearing jeans, work boots, and a barn jacket, walked over to the body, shook his head.

"Rick was a good guy. Who did this?"

443

The world pitched and tilted, and Bailey vomited on the floor, causing another bottle rocket of pain to shoot down his arm.

Stars danced in his peripheral vision. He was going to pass out again.

No. No. Pull your shit together, Bailey Kirk.

He dug in deep to his center, forced his breathing to slow. He focused on the pain until it became manageable. Pain was just a program. It could be hacked. Or so the man who taught him to fight had advised. Press it down. Compartmentalize it. Ignore it.

"Son, who did this?"

Son? Really? Who was this guy? Then he realized. He recognized the man from the articles about the Carson property raid. He was thicker, grayer but Bailey recognized him as the cop that led the team. They'd traded messages but never talked seen each other in person.

"A man I've been chasing. I don't know his real name. Some people know him as Raife Mannes, or Adam Harper. He's a ghost."

"A ghost with a gun," said the big man. "I'm guessing you're Bailey Kirk. The private detective."

"That's right," said Bailey. "And you are?"

"I'm Jones Cooper," he said. "I'm a friend of Wren's. My wife got a call from one of

Wren's girlfriends in NYC, a woman named Jax, of all things. Kind of hysterical. Said she thought her friend was in trouble."

"Okay," said Bailey.

Jax, the best friend. Bailey knew that women didn't like being called hysterical, and they didn't like men who called them that. But this guy was obviously running on an old operating system; maybe he hadn't downloaded the new software.

Cooper went on, "Then I got a call from Joy Martin of The Hollows Historical Society saying she thought you were headed here, maybe together. She also thought Wren was in trouble."

"Where is she?"

"That's the thing. Her friend Jax said that she and Wren track each other, and that Wren blocked her. That the last Jax saw Wren was headed out of town but not back to the city. Farther north."

"Why?"

"Jax seemed to think she was chasing your ghost."

"Goddammit." Bailey rose, then sank back, weak with pain. He steeled himself and rose again, determined to make it to his car. He had a first-aid kit there, some pain pills. He'd patched himself up and soldiered on before.

445

The old man looked at him with a mildly amused frown. "What do you think you're doing?"

"I put a tracking device on her car," said Bailey. When he saw her vehicle at the hotel, he took a moment and stuck one on the inside of the wheel well. All he had to do was open the app on his phone. "I'm going after her."

"You can't drive."

The old guy had a point.

"Can *you*?"

Jones Cooper was that kind of guy, wasn't he? You could always recognize them — the cop, the soldier, the first responder. He was the guy at the scene, who knew instinctively what was right, and what to do, did it without question or regard for himself.

"I have to call this in and stay until someone comes to secure the scene," he said. "But, yeah, let's go. I have a first-aid kit in my car."

Of course he did.

The police arrived just as Cooper had finished expertly wrapping up Bailey's shoulder — tight but not too tight. The pressure gave a relief from the pain, and the two Vicodin he popped had him less than sharp mentally, but at least functional. In the passenger seat of Cooper's car, he opened the app on his phone and saw the little blue dot that was Wren Greenwood, creeping north.

Cooper seemed to know the two officers who exited the squad car. They had a quick conversation, nods all around. Then Cooper walked to the car, climbing into the driver's seat, making the car pitch with his weight.

"I agreed to bring you in for questioning later tonight."

"We made a mess of their crime scene."

Jones Cooper nodded. "I told them where we were in the room, what we did, and we didn't touch Rick. I texted the chief with the suspect's names, details, and told him we'll loop back. This department is on a shoestring. They'll be happy for the help with this."

"You were the chief here once."

"That's right," Cooper said, putting the car into gear and pulling away from the drive. "Just a private investigator now."

"I read about you."

There were a lot of articles about Jones Cooper in *The Hollows Gazette,* not all of them flattering. He'd "retired" from the department in scandal, hung out a shingle, worked with a psychic at some point.

Jones Cooper gave him a flat look, didn't seem interested in what Bailey had read or what his opinion might be. "Where are we headed?" he asked.

He held up the phone to Cooper who squinted in to look at the map. "Rural road 181. I know where that is."

He nodded and peeled out, surprising Bailey. He'd had the older man pegged as a slow driver. The big SUV must have been souped-up. It ate the dark road ahead of them, engine growling.

Bailey didn't love being in the passenger seat, but it was that or the hospital where he surely belonged. He forced himself to sit up straight and keep his eyes on the road ahead, fought back waves of pain, anger, fear.

He flashed on the ghost standing there, a black form in the dark, a gun in his hand; the orange of the muzzle-flash. God, so stupid — careless. He'd let Nora distract him. He hadn't checked his surroundings.

And Wren. How did he not predict that she'd go after him alone?

Bailey watched the blue dot pulse on his screen, surrounded by nothing, just the green that signified trees. If he was in the driver's seat, he'd be pushing his foot to the floor, trying to close the distance faster, faster. He leaned forward, the seat belt pressing uncomfortably on the wound.

"We'll get to her," said Cooper, probably reading his body language. "We'll find her." The other man picked up speed; Bailey leaned back.

"Tell me about your case," said Cooper. "Start from the beginning."

Bailey Kirk didn't like lost things. And he wasn't going to lose the ghost again, Mia — and Wren — with him.

FORTY-ONE

The road, a great unfurling black ribbon, the engine, a low hum in my brain. It's hypnotic and I fight to stay awake. My phone is off and stowed, a nod to your request — demand? Maybe you won't show because you know I've disobeyed. Or maybe this is just a game you are playing with me. How far can I get her to run? How long will she chase? Will she follow me wherever I go?

My mother told us over and over about the night she met my father. How she was a waitress in a diner, and he came in with a group of his friends, many of them coworkers on the same construction site. They were a rowdy, funny group, bawdy, flirty but not disrespectful as groups of men can sometimes be. They ordered a ton of food — burgers, big subs, fries, onion rings, and milkshakes mostly.

As a kid, I liked to imagine it. In my mind

the diner was a sunny, glossy place, colorful, and kitschy with red booths and big menus, a pie case with desserts circling slowly, vintage ads and a sizzling grill. Probably it was nothing like that; it was just a dump at a truck stop. But in my imagination, it gleamed with shiny surfaces, the Beatles playing on a jukebox.

My mom, Alice, she was in a bad place that day. She'd run out of money and had to drop out of community college, was taking care of my grandmother who was sick. She never even knew her father; he'd left her mother before Alice was even born. She got the occasional Christmas card from him, which she tossed right in the trash. Alice wasn't prone to depression or dark moods, but she was feeling lost, adrift in her life — not sure what was coming next.

"I saw him right away," she said. "There was just this one second when they all walked in, crowded into a couple of booths, and our eyes met. I swear, I knew right that second. Felt it right here."

She'd always put her hand to her heart.

While she served the tables, the men joked with her and hit on her, and all the while she just smiled and kept to her work. When one of the guys got handsy, wrapping an arm around her hips when she came to stand beside him, my dad stepped up.

"Show some respect," he told his friend, who tipped his baseball cap and apologized to my mom with a sheepish grin.

Show some respect.

It was those words that moved Alice, who said that she rarely felt respected as a young woman with no money, a struggling student until she couldn't even afford to be that anymore. Just a waitress then, working for tips. *Respect* was for other people. She blushed, was embarrassed for herself and even for the handsy guy who probably meant no harm.

After a while, my father rose to talk to her when she was at the register.

"Sorry about my friend," he said. "They're good guys. It's just that — they're guys."

"It's fine," she said. It was fine. There were good men, and bad men, she thought then. Bad men who hurt you, left you, broke you — like her father. But Alice had my dad and his friends pegged for good men — maybe rowdy, silly, but not dangerous, not cruel.

"So I'm not hitting on you, but —"

"But?" She smiled at him, and he blushed like a girl, his cheeks turning pink. He looked down shyly, dug his hands into his pockets.

"When does your shift end? Can I take

452

you for an ice cream?"

Rocky road for him. Chocolate chip mint for her. A proposal with his mother's gifted ring not even a month later. A backyard wedding with family and friends, wildflowers, and tears of happiness. Then she was pregnant with Jay — not planned but they greeted the news with joy. Then my father was deployed for the first time. That's how the story went. Later, when he was home between tours, I was conceived.

It was no fairy tale, but it was their story.

She always told it after a bad night with him, when we were all shaken and he was sleeping it off. It was like a prayer, a reminder that there was good in him somewhere and that she had seen it once. That she'd loved him.

As a kid, I loved that story — imagining them, who they were before us, before he went overseas. And toward the end I hated it. It was a fantasy about a man who no longer existed. And no matter how badly she wanted him to come home, he was gone. And when I think of it now, anger lodges in my throat. I think if she just gave up on who he was, maybe she would have seen who he had become. Maybe she could have saved us all.

Instead, we all followed him, and didn't

leave even when he hurt her again and again.

What would Dear Birdie say?

She'd say to forgive the past, forgive my mother for loving someone who hurt her, for not taking us away. Because she could only do what she knew how to do.

It's cold comfort.

There's no moon, no stars. Just the trees and layers of dark. Up ahead I see it. A tilting wood post with three red reflectors. Here, I should turn right. I stop, idle a moment. I haven't seen another car for an hour; the road I'm on is completely deserted. I roll down the window, hear only the wind, smell the scent of pine.

What is this place?

Did Bonnie, Mia, and Melissa come to this fork in the road and make the turn, never to be heard from again?

Maybe she wanted the pain, says Robin. She's talking about Mom. *Maybe she thought that's what love was.*

There's a twig stuck in the tangle of her hair. She's frowning. *Maybe you do, too.*

"No," I say.

Didn't you see it in him? she asks, holding a glistening black crow feather.

"No," I lie.

Here is where I should go back and find Bailey Kirk, call the police. It's clear that my actions are hubristic, foolhardy. But it's as if there's a gossamer strand from my heart to yours, a tug at my solar plexus leading me forward, no turning back.

Making the turn, the night gets darker still. I keep driving.

I was living with Jax in a Lower East Side two-bedroom, four-flight walk-up when my father reached out to me the first time. Cobbling together a living writing book reviews for *The Village Voice,* working as a temp at a poetry magazine, and waitressing at a busy restaurant on Avenue A, I was running ragged, tired all the time. But happy. I owned my life. My blog was taking off, more and more followers every day.

And even though I was trying to live on what I made, I did have family money — my mother had managed to save quite a bit, enough to pay for my education and Jay's. She had a small inheritance, as well, from her mother's life insurance payout. There wasn't a ton, but there was a comfortable buffer that allowed me to cover the rent when earnings were lean, especially since Jay's money came to me, too. Like the property, my father signed all the money over to me, Wren Greenwood. His way of making penance, I guess.

We had a landline in the apartment back then. Jax's mother insisted that we needed it to call 911 in an emergency. Jax came from a big Brooklyn family — a loud, funny, loving cast of brothers, cousins, aunts, and uncles. Her mother would stop by unannounced with food, but really just to check up on her. Over the years, they basically adopted me into their clan and it was with her family that I spent all holidays. Jax informed me that her mom thought we were a couple, in spite of her efforts to convince them otherwise. When I moved out, they thought we broke up. Her mother called me.

"You're part of our family," she told me. "I want you to know that."

I tried to explain how Jax and I were best friends, always would be.

"I know, I know," she said. "It's all good, honey. You understand? There's always a place at our table."

Jax was out the night the landline — which never rang — woke me from sleep.

I answered it, groggy. A collect call from the Highwater County Correctional Facility.

I was jolted awake, heart threatening to leap from my chest. I accepted the charges, just in a daze of confusion.

"Robin."

I hadn't heard that name in so long it felt like a lie. My eyes filled and my throat closed.

"You call yourself something different now. That's probably a good thing. As long as you don't forget who you are."

"Dad." The word was thick in my mouth, tasting of sorrow and betrayal. *Don't love him,* Jay warned. *He doesn't deserve it.* But I did. Even after everything. Tears fell like a river. I sank to the floor, legs weak. I was back there with him in the garden, walking through the woods.

"Are you safe? Are you well?"

"Yes," I managed to say.

"There are no words for what I've done. There's no road back. But I wanted you to know that I found a way forward. That I think of you all every day. And that regret is my constant companion."

I couldn't find my voice. But a sob escaped my throat.

"Be strong," he told me. "And that place is always there for you. When the world of men fails you, it will open its arms."

Anger rose up. I wish my aim had been better, that I hadn't lost my nerve — that my arrow had found his heart.

"You're the one who failed me, Dad," I said. "Not the world."

"I know it." His voice was just a whisper. "Forgive me."

We stayed on the phone in silence, not sure how long, hatred and love and longing and grief a desperate mingle. Dr. Cooper always said that forgiveness was for me and not for him. That it was a way to release the pain in my own heart, not a condoning or an acceptance of his wrongs. But I couldn't find my way there then, though I understand those words better now. I'm still not there.

Then, "Goodbye, little bird."

He hung up, and I sat in the same spot until Jax got home from the clubs. We stayed up almost until the sun rose, talking about the things I'd never shared with anyone else — until I met you.

This road has no end. The urge to call Jax is strong. She'll know what to do. But I just keep driving, following your trail.

FORTY-TWO

The blue dot pulsed. Cooper, who was driving fast and sure, eyes ahead, hands at two and twelve, had hardly said a word the whole ride. Bailey appreciated a man who didn't feel the need to make small talk, especially as Bailey fought off waves of nausea, pain, held on tenuously to his consciousness. He'd told Cooper everything about the case, and Bailey could tell the other man was processing it all like a machine. But he'd said very little, except to admit that they'd made mistakes the night of the raid. That if they'd handled it differently, things might not have spun out of control.

"You carry that, you know. When your mistakes cost people their lives."

"I know it," said Bailey. "When you fail at this job, it hurts — and not just you. People get hurt."

Cooper flashed him some kind of look, an

acknowledgment of the truth, an acceptance.

Bailey tried Wren's phone again. Where was she going?

He'd called multiple times. No answer, straight to voice mail. *Wren Greenwood, what the hell are you doing?*

The dot came to an abrupt halt, kept flashing.

"She's stopped," he told Cooper. The other man nodded as if this didn't surprise him.

"There's a gas station up ahead if I remember correctly," Cooper said.

But the road was dark and empty — they hadn't seen a house or a business or another car in an hour of driving. Bailey always lived in cities, where everything was a crush and you were never really alone. He craved the buzz of people and culture, food and energy, architecture. Say what you want about the modern world and all its evils. But the emptiness of the area was starting to press on him. He couldn't imagine anything appearing out of this darkness.

But there — just up ahead on the right, a glow, a distant lit sign.

Bailey felt a rush of relief. Everyone had to stop for gas sometime. Gas stations and toll booth security cameras were the best things to ever happen to law enforcement and private detectives. Though it hadn't helped him with Mia. Once she'd left her apartment, her image wasn't captured anywhere within a three hundred mile radius — not a toll road, not at a pump, not at a motel. She'd made no charges on her credit card. Her phone was left behind. She'd slipped off that electronic grid that existed now to keep people findable.

Lost stays lost, when it wants to stay lost.

There were still holes. You could still slip through with a little effort.

Not this time. This time Bailey had thought ahead by placing that tracker in Wren's wheel well.

They closed in on the dot, tires crunching as the road turned gravelly on the shoulder.

"Just up here on the right."

Cooper slowed the truck and pulled into the gas station. It was closed, the little market shuttered and dark. The lights still shone over the pump island, the metal gleaming.

A single vehicle was parked over by the pay phone, an old Mustang that had seen better days, its paint job just black primer.

"That's not her car," said Cooper.

"No," said Bailey.

Cooper pulled up close and climbed out.

Bailey sat, staring at the dot. She was here. She had to be. But where? He scanned the property, the surrounding trees. He climbed out of Cooper's car and approached the old black Mustang. Cooper had his hand on the hood.

"It's still warm."

They peered inside, tried the door, and found it open. It was empty, clean.

"Pop the trunk."

Bailey walked around and took a breath before pressing the latch and lifting it. Mercifully, it was empty except for a spare tire. His body tingled with relief.

Bailey walked around the perimeter of the gas station, heading for the restroom, looking for the black Range Rover to be parked somewhere they hadn't seen right away.

Maybe the ghost followed her here in that Mustang — had Bailey seen that vehicle somewhere before? At the motel? On the street in front of Rick Javits's house? His head was swimming, his shoulder and arm a wildfire of pain. He wasn't sharp. He wasn't strong. And he shouldn't be here. He knew that.

When he rounded the building, he leaned over and threw up again — quietly so that Cooper wouldn't hear. Never ideal to show weakness in front of a hard-ass like Cooper, and he'd already thrown up once. He rested against the cool concrete of the building for a moment, then kept going, circling the entire property.

Her car. The big, shiny, outrageously expensive Range Rover was not here.

The restroom door was locked. See Attendant for Key, read a faded sign. It was a solid, heavy door. He banged on it pointlessly. Silence echoed back. Frustration was a taste in his mouth.

Where are you?

When he returned to the Mustang, Cooper was inspecting the wheel wells. He came back from the rear right with something in his hand.

"Is this your tracker?"

Bailey took it from the other man and held the small black device in his hand. It *was* his tracker, obviously taken from Wren's car and placed on this one. It rested dark against his palm.

"She's gone," he said, a rush of anger, pain had the world around him pulsing again.

Jones Cooper looked down the road that seemed to lead to nowhere.

"Goddammit," he said softly.

"I lost her."

FORTY-THREE

How long have I been driving? The drive has started to feel like a dream. And Robin has abandoned me to this insane errand.

Finally, the long driveway ends at a tall, chain-link fence. A faded sign hangs, tilted, unreadable in the glare of my headlights. But clearly — with its red border and exclamation points — it's a warning to stay away.

I sit, engine idling, wondering what to do next.

Another good moment to turn around and head back to the world, look for some help, get far away from you. Just as I've decided that's what I'll do, the gate slides open, rattling and squealing, obviously by remote control.

The night expands. Instead of leaving, I drive through the open gate and it rattles closed behind me.

Tires crunch on the gravel road, headlights

cut a swath of light into black. Soon, a house rises into view. It's known, familiar. Where have I seen it before?

Maybe in one of the few photographs from your childhood? It has a low profile, a flat roof, big, angled widows, a tall front door. It cuts a modern shape, nestled in the trees. Off to the side of the drive sits a raft of solar panels. Everything looks new, the landscaping wild and unbothered as if just space for the house, the panels, and the drive have been cleared. No lawn, no shrubs, just a house nestled in the woods. Flat stones act as a walkway to the front door.

There's a light on inside.

Kill the engine. I lean across the passenger seat, to open the glove compartment where a revolver rests silver and menacing. Heavy, cold, it fits into the pocket of my jacket. I exit the car to walk toward the house, hand resting on the butt of the gun.

I've been here a thousand times. That's how it feels, like a kind of home.

My heart is knocking in my chest.

Then the door swings open, slowly. And first there is darkness.

Then there you are, Adam, waiting.

Your form fills the doorway and when you step into the light, that crooked, dark smile, the gleam of victory in your eyes. We stand a moment, what feels like a great distance between us, though it's only feet.

The call of a barred owl, ghostly, asking, *Who looks for you? Who looks for you?* Then the answer of another bird, this time a low moan.

You think I'm here to forgive you.

That I've come to let you reveal your darkness to me.

But that is not why I have come.

In one swift movement, I draw, aim, and fire. The sound vibrates through the night, wings flap from the trees. Your eyes widen in surprise, mouth dropping open. You fall heavily to the wood.

As I move closer, your hand reaches up to stanch the flow of blood, a terrible blossom on the white of your shirt, just like the night Jay died. I stand over you and watch the light drain from your eyes as you reach for me. Then I look more closely.

It's not you at all. It's my father.

I wake up screaming as my car jerks off the road, careening into the ditch and coming to a hard, jarring stop. My airbag deploys, filling all my senses and pushing me back against the seat. I must have fallen asleep at the wheel, just lucky I veered to the right, no other cars on this dark road.

My God. What is wrong with me?

Breathless, disoriented, I stumble from the car into the cold darkness. Your face, my father's face swim. All my fury, all my fear, all my frustration, it claws up my chest and releases in a wail into the black, absorbed by the uncaring trees and the distant sky. I lean against the hot hood and scream and scream into the silence of the night until I'm spent.

My head aches from the impact of the airbag, the whiplash of the stop.

Now what? Now *what*?

Okay, breathe. Orient.

I walk a few feet and around the bend. I see that fence, the one in my dream. Chain link with a sign of warning, faded and hanging by a single link. I approach.

Reclaimed Land. Private Property. Do Not Enter.

I know about this, a movement to repair lands that have been damaged by corporations, contaminated, and abandoned. Some private citizens have sought to buy those areas and restore them, heal them and make them livable again.

This metal fence with the hanging sign was in your directions. Maybe that's why my addled mind wove it into my dreams. I should go back to the car, get my phone and my gun. But I don't.

Already, the world I belonged to is slipping away from me. There's something about the air, the trees, the quiet that's calling me, its pull irresistible.

I'm in a trance. Maybe I hit my head. Maybe I'm still dreaming.

The gate will not be locked. Pull it open and follow the path. It's not far now. Leave your car and come on foot.

Robin is waiting on the path. She doesn't have to ask me to follow her. She knows I will. She races away, finally set free. She's always so confined in the town house, aching to get back to the place she came from. She disappears from view, swallowed by the dark and the trees.

I like the idea of this, the reclamation of damaged lands. I know my father would have, too, the idea that you can take a piece of the planet that has been destroyed and heal it. Make it habitable again. Even the most devastated regions, like Chernobyl, heal with time — animals return, vegetation reforests the abandoned structures, wildflowers growing up through floorboards. After the enormous fire that destroyed almost 30 percent of Yellowstone, it is healthier than ever. The planet repairs itself, heals itself. I like the idea that we, the perpetrators, can help it, clear away debris, use abandoned structures to create sanctuaries for animals, birds, native plants. Build homes that cooperate with the planet, don't scar it.

The house is waiting around the next bend.

It is not the place in my dreams, but similar, and again I have the feeling that I have been here before. It's low and modern, with big windows and a tall, double front door. I step onto the stone walkway, and then up the shallow steps to the porch. The wood is reclaimed, distressed, and etched with character. The doors, too, look as though they are pieces of another structure, maybe a barn. My hand on the knob, the door swings open and I step inside.

A great room with an open plan. From the foyer, the kitchen, the living room, the dining table and chairs are all visible. The back wall is a row of glass doors. It's dark outside, but I imagine they open onto a deck surrounded by trees.

It looks like you, Adam.

Simple, elegant — the couch modular, low profile. The tables, the benches, all have the look of materials that have been repurposed, rescued. The walls are a soft dove gray. In the kitchen — marble countertops and a

469

restaurant-grade stove and oven. A giant gleaming stainless-steel refrigerator. There's a simple white card near the sink. It reads: *This is where we'll make our meals.*

The lamplight is dim, casting everything in a soft rose. In the living room, a coffee table is stacked high with books — big, cloth-bound books about art, architecture, furniture. By the stone hearth, another card. *This is where we'll spend our evenings.*

All my nerve endings are screaming.

Sane voices in my head — mine, Jax, Miranda — are a siren, trying to wake me from this dream, urging me to get out. *Unarmed, no phone. What are you thinking?* But I keep walking, down the long hallway that glows from lighting in the baseboards, and push into the first room.

It's a library with floor-to-ceiling shelves, lined with volumes and volumes of books. A lifetime's collection of literature and poetry, textbooks, journals. The bindings are smooth and soft — some leather, some cloth, some paper. I don't look at the titles, the authors — there are too many. A single window acts as a mirror in the darkness behind it. I watch myself approach a simple pale wood desk and ergonomic chair standing in the middle of the space.

This is where you'll write, reads the note

card there. I imagine myself sitting there with my laptop open among all these words, in all this quiet. Yes, I see it.

At the end of the hall, I push through the farthest door.

Here, there's a simple platform bed in the bedroom that, like the rest of the house, has one wall made completely of glass. A white oak floor. An Eames chair in the corner, a simple three-legged table beside it. On the downy comforter, yet another card reads: *This is where we'll make love.*

Your handwriting is precise, perfectly inked black letters on the thick paper. The card stock is heavy in my hand. The bed soft as clouds as I sink onto the mattress. I imagine your hands roaming my body, your flesh against mine, the tender power of your desire.

That's when the front door opens and closes with a final thud. Its sound moves through me like a wave. My senses come alive with a jolt.

And in this moment I realize far too late, that this has been your plan all along.

Mia, Bonnie, Melissa. You didn't take them, didn't wrest them from their lives. You lured them here. And they followed, willing. Just like this. You didn't take their money; they gave it to you. Just as I would have.

Just as I have, they followed all their own darkest impulses.

I am not the hunter after all.

I'm the doe.

FORTY-FOUR

You.

You almost don't seem real. Over the last few days — few days? — you have been lover, leaver, mystery, demon. You have been a wraith slipping away, back through whatever shadowy doorway you used to enter my life.

And now, here you are, just a man standing before me. Breath and flushed skin, hands open at your side, eyes — hopeful.

"Wren," you say in the doorway to the bedroom. The syllable of the name I gave myself vibrates.

I know your face — or thought I did. How it looks when you are thinking hard — a little furrow between your eyebrows makes its debut. When you are sleeping — the muscles around your eyes and mouth release, leaving your expression as soft and open as a child's. When you are hungry with desire, those black eyes sear into me —

473

searching, searching. I haven't ever seen you angry; you are cool, placid as slack tide. Though, yes, I know there is rage in you. I see it now. It was always just beneath the mask you wore. I don't want to think that your darkness, your disease, was the thing that attracted me most of all.

"Or should I call you Robin?"

I haven't moved an inch since I heard the door open and close. I am wise enough to know that I am trapped. There's no back door. The windows don't open. I freeze, a prey animal assessing the environment.

I don't say anything.

"*Or* — do you prefer Dear Birdie?"

My phone. My gun. My car. I left it all behind. Why?

"I'm not the only one who lied, am I?" he continues on into the silence, voice deep, a growl. "I'm not the only one with secrets."

I feel my breath in my chest, my lungs fill and expand, blood rushing in my ears.

You offer me a gentle smile. "Are you wondering about these things?"

From your jacket pocket you retrieve my phone — in pieces. "I told you to leave it. These things are like little spies, aren't they? They know everything about us."

You let the parts clatter to the floor — the shattered screen, the cracked casing, the glittering innards of copper and wires.

"Or this?"

My gun looks small in your hand. You press the latch with your thumb to release the cylinder, which falls open. Six bullets fall like flower petals, clattering and rolling every which way as they hit the hardwood. One rolls and comes to rest against my foot. I look down at it; the bullet catches the light, glints.

"And these?"

You hold up my keys — my car, my home, my office. Those you shove into your pocket. The unloaded gun you place on the table.

"You won't be needing any of these things. You're home now."

No, I think. *Home is the place you choose.*

But I know better than to argue. And I did choose — in a way.

Instead, I rise and move slowly forward. You look startled, but hold your ground and reach out a hand to me, which I take. Electricity moves from your body to mine with the touch of our fingers.

Your heat. It still calls to me. You pull me in, and not a single part of me resists you. I flow into you and then you are devouring me, your mouth on mine, on my neck, your breath on my collarbone, behind my ear. The tension that has found a home at the base of my skull, in my shoulders, between my eyes, dissolves.

I release myself into the powerful hold of your arms, I know every muscle, every hill and valley; into your kiss, I know every note, every layer. Your hunger moves through me awakening a fierce desire. Your touch is desperate.

You lift me and carry me to the bed, where you ease me down, your weight on top of me.

"I know everything about you," you say, eyes shining. Your voice is a growl in my ear. "All your dark layers. All your secret selves. I want it all."

And then we're only skin, our clothes a careless heap on the floor. I climb on top of you, roam your body with my hands across your broad chest, through the silk of your hair. You never take your eyes off mine, holding me with that gaze.

We go deep and true, make love in wide, slow circles of pleasure until there's nothing left of either one of us. You're right. It's a homecoming.

Later we lie in the dark, all my nerve endings buzzing.

"What happened to them?" I ask.

"Who?"

"Bonnie. Melissa. Mia."

Their names hang on the air. Were they all here once? In your arms, in your bed? Did you want each of them the way you wanted me? Would your appetites be sated by any willing prey?

But you don't answer me. The air grows thick.

"You never told me about *your* ex, not really. The one in college," he counters.

The memory comes back, violent, leaving me cold. I pull the covers over my bare skin. Another layer pulled back.

"There's nothing to tell."

"That's not true though, is it?"

The silence expands all around us. It's never totally quiet in the city, even with good windows. There's always street noise, or the rumble of trains beneath you, car horns, someone shouting. Here, silence has a pitch and vibration that fills the darkness.

I guess we're baring all.

"Jackson. I met him in economics class. He asked for help with an essay, and we started seeing each other."

Do I hear something, the distant rumble of an engine? Hope surges. Maybe Bailey Kirk is still on my trail, even though I ducked out on him, and my phone is in pieces on the floor. Maybe he's found a way to follow. Do you hear it, too? Then silence again.

"Was it love? Did you love him?"

"I don't know," I answer. "He was the first person I let get close to me — after I lost my family. After leaving the safety of Miss Lovely's group home."

"What was it about him?"

I was attracted to his light, to his clean scent, to the ease of someone who has never known hardship or loss. His hair was spun gold, his eyes a rare sea green. Like Jay's.

"Maybe he looked like my brother a little. He was outdoorsy."

"He took you back to the woods."

Yes. We drove out of the city, and hiked trails upstate. I didn't even know that my body ached for the green, for the whisper of leaves in wind, the birdsong, the smell of the forest floor.

"Yes."

"Did you love him?" you ask again.

"I'm not sure I knew what love was then. But, yes, maybe. I felt something for him that I hadn't felt yet. Something more than desire. But I held myself back. Sexually."

"You were a virgin."

"That's right," I admit. "How do you know?"

"It's not hard to figure out. After what

478

you endured, I imagine that you wouldn't give yourself over easily."

Or at all. Our fooling around had reached a desperate pitch, each of us aching. But I couldn't give myself to him, show myself that way. I — just couldn't offer him that part of myself. Later, I'd give it over to people I cared about far less, wanted less. But back then I guarded everything that was precious to me.

"He got drunk one night," I continue. "We were at some party. Back in his apartment, he got aggressive. Said I'd been teasing him, toying with him. I didn't even know him in that moment. He was strong, and so angry. He was someone else when he drank."

"Like your father." It's so easy with you. You understand me.

"Yes."

"What happened?"

"We struggled. I thought I was strong, in shape, fast. But he was stronger by far. I was a child in comparison."

Your heart is beating in your chest; I can feel it pulsing.

"What did you do? Did he rape you?"

"He would have."

"But."

"Something primal rose up, a rage I didn't know lived inside me. It was raw power. I reached out for any weapon, my fingers found this bookend, a geode — sharp and heavy. I hit him with it, in the head. I hit him hard. I thought —"

Your chest rises and falls. I liked it, that feeling of rage. It was better than fear. Fear cowers and begs. Rage raises her sword and stands her ground.

"I thought —"

"What?"

"I thought I killed him. He was so still. One minute he was all power, and the next he was as soft and quiet as a sleeping child."

"And then what did you do?"

What might I have done? Called for help, reported his assault, waited for the police. It was a clear case of self-defense. My shirt was ripped; already his grip on my arms was marked by bruising.

"I gathered my things and I left him there to die."

The memory has come back vividly — the dark of the room, lit only by the streetlamp outside, the stale smell of alcohol coming off his skin, his breath, a black skein of blood on the side of his head. The green glow of his digital clock. It's a time and place I rarely visit because of what it says about men, boys who take what they want, what it says about me. How remorselessly I left him there, not caring if he lived or died. When the rage dissipated, there was only apathy, a kind of kill or be killed resolve.

"But he was fine," you say. You've done your homework, I guess.

"He left school, went back home, I heard. I hurt him, a fairly serious head injury. He recovered though, yes. He's married now. We follow each other on Facebook."

"I noticed that. Wouldn't that be awkward? He tried to rape you. You tried to kill him. Not exactly the stuff of a lasting friendship."

No, not the stuff of friendship. Jackson is an accountant now, apparently happily married — but you never know. Social media is such a lie. He coaches his son's lacrosse team, takes his wife to Cabo for their anniversary. That night between us, so primal and bloody, is stitched somewhere into the underlay of our lives, there but mostly untouched.

"You know how it is. He either doesn't remember what happened, or doesn't want to. I don't really want to remember it either. Loose tie connections, right? It's all very distant, almost a fiction, isn't it?"

"All modern relationships are a kind of fiction. A story we tell ourselves in curated, filtered posts on a screen. The truth, real relationships, are gritty and messy and complicated."

They're all here; their specters hover. Over the last few days, I have come to know well the stories of Mia, Bonnie, and Melissa — I know their faces, their favorite books and smoothies, their chosen Instagram color palates. Brightening Claredon for Mia, dramatic Ludwig for Bonnie. Melissa favored the calming Lark. I could feel Mia's desperate search for the light in her earnest blog, her gaggle of friends on Facebook, her pastel colored, inspirational memes. Bonnie clung to childhood — unicorns, bubbles, adult coloring books. She was a loner, lots of nature shots and quotes about solitude. There were no girls' night out posts, no cheerful selfies, no boyfriend shots, romantic dates for Bonnie, plenty of sweet images though of other people's children. Melissa was online far less than the other two. It seemed that she couldn't find her voice in social, wasn't as adept as the other two in creating her avatar.

All of them were flesh and bone. And now gone.

"What happened to them, Adam?"

Is that your name? I don't even know. I don't want to know you, what you're capable of. Not really. Part of me could stay here with you like this forever, in this limbo of not knowing. In the fiction of us.

"I offered this to them. This safe space, away from the modern world. It's so ugly out there, so fake. Here, this place, it's freedom."

"And what happened?"

"They didn't want it."

Your voice has gotten tight, the first sign of your anger. Robin wanted to know if I had seen your darkness. I think I did. I think I saw it first — in that grainy image, in your Rilke quotes. Worse still, I think it's what drew me to you.

"So what did you do?" I keep my voice light.

The air expands. I have a mental model of the room. The gun on the table, the bullets on the floor, the keys still in the pocket of your pants that are in a heap at the foot of the bed. Will the car still run with the airbag deployed? I have no idea. That's a thing I'd instantly Google — but my phone is a junk pile.

My head is still on your chest, the way it was the night I shared myself with you. I know if I were looking into your eyes that they would reveal nothing. "I let them go."

"You let them go."

"That's right." You lift your palms, then drop your hands back to where they'd rested on my hip, on my shoulder. "What else? Love lets go, Wren. It doesn't hold on."

But the brand of love I know from men is one that holds on tight. It strangles. Of course, I don't believe you.

"They're all gone though," I venture. "No one ever heard from them again."

"I never heard from them either," you say. "They left me. They didn't want this life. They thought they did, at first. But eventually the world, their ties to it, pulled them back. Not everyone can walk away. You know that."

"So you let them all leave," I say.

"You can't make someone stay where they don't want to be. You can try, but they'll just hate you for it. Didn't your mother hate your father at the end?"

The mention of them stings.

"I don't know if she did hate him," I answer. "I don't think she *ever* stopped hoping that he'd be the man he was when she first loved him. Even in those final moments, I think she still saw him for what he was deep down."

"But the world. It destroyed that man, left a monster in his place."

A monster. A raging ghoul wailing my name.

"He wasn't a monster," I whisper, though

484

I've called him that myself. "He was broken, not evil."

"What the difference?"

"Is this a philosophical discussion?"

"Isn't everything?"

I don't answer you, because I know when you get like this the conversation can wind on for hours, diving deep into perception and reality, that house of mirrors.

"Wren?" you say into the silence. "You wanted to know what I planned to ask you."

"Yes?"

"Will you leave the world behind and stay with me?"

I let the part of me who wants to, that dark, secret part of me, answer.

"Of course," I say. "Of course I'll stay."

Your arms tighten around me. You believe me. I almost convince myself.

"You won't be sorry, Wren. I love you."

"I love you, too, Adam."

The words have the ring of truth because, sadly, they are true. I know what it is to love darkness, to love the pain someone can cause you, to crave the person you see beneath the ugly. It's a familiar feeling, a home I have chosen.

We lay there until you're softly snoring, until your arms have fallen slack and you release your hold on me. You seem deeply

485

asleep, but I know you wake easily.

Quietly, I rise. In the dark I gather my clothes, the gun, the one bullet I can find quickly. I slip my keys from your pocket, careful not to jingle. In the hallway, I wiggle into my clothes, and move softly down the hall. A floorboard creaks but I keep moving. Across the great room, shouldering into my jacket as I go. My feet are bare, no time to find my shoes. Doesn't matter.

I reach the door and find it locked. Dead bolted with a lock that needs a key. And my heart, which has been a caged bird in my chest, sinks deep into my belly. I lean against the door and feel how solid it is, how heavy, how cold from the air outside.

I reach around the door frame; maybe there's a key on top. No, of course not. You're not that type. I have to go back to the room where you're sleeping and find it in your pocket. If it's there.

Back down the hall, I sidestep the squeaky board, edging along the wall, measuring my frightened breathing, which is expanding my chest, wheezing too loud in my nose. You're still sleeping, still and peaceful. I crouch down and crawl to your clothes. The gun sticks out of one of my pockets, the bullet is in the other; I haven't had the chance to load it. If I find the key, I won't need to.

There, a single cold key in the pocket of your jeans. I clutch it in my palm.

I could kill you while you sleep. The thought comes unbidden. A single shot to the head or the chest.

If I leave here while you live, will you chase? Will you follow me through the dark alleys of the web — steal my money, reveal my secrets? Will you shadow me like the predator you are? Will I always live in fear? Or will you let me go?

Still crouched at the foot of the bed, I take the gun from my pocket, slip the bullet in the chamber, make sure it's aligned with the firing pin. Can I do it? Can I kill you in cold blood while you lay, arms wide, trusting?

I already know the answer.

I rise, lift the gun, and find the bed empty.

Then I sense you behind me. How?

I don't have time to fight; your hands close over my wrists, squeezing hard until I drop the gun where it falls with a dead thud. Then your arms are around me. I can't even struggle. You're so strong.

"Wren." I hear all the notes of your sadness, disappointment, anger. It brings to mind my father's face the night I shot him with my arrow. "I trusted you. You betrayed me. Just like they all do."

"Let me go," I whisper. Your face is right next to mine, eyes dark with anger.

But I don't remember your answer. Because in a single motion, you release one of my wrists and there's a painful prick, a heat rushing down my arm. The world falters, going dark around the edges.

Robin cowers in the corner, watching me with wide eyes. She's crying.

I'm sorry, she whispers. *I'm so sorry.*

And then there's nothing.

FORTY-FIVE

Bailey Kirk waited in the plush lobby of the accounting firm, nursing a headache brought on from his own stupidity and lack of self-control. He felt the eyes of the receptionist fall on him occasionally; he'd been there awhile. When he turned his gaze back to her, she was answering the phone. Gleaming, flame-red hair, dark blue eyes, glossed lips, full-bodied; she was a pinup girl, a beauty of a bygone era. The electric blue frames of her glasses highlighted her eyes, her lips. She didn't look up at him again.

His arm, healing slowly but throbbing from the physical therapy session yesterday, was still in a sling, six weeks after the gunshot wound.

The pain, though dull, was persistent, constant, a white noise in his awareness, reminding him of all his mistakes and failures.

Since that terrible day, he'd lost his job — well, technically it was a medical leave. He'd failed his client Henry Thorpe, who was no closer to finding his child. The ghost was gone. He'd taken Wren Greenwood — and Mia, and Bonnie, and Melissa — with him. Whatever hole the ghost had opened in the world and slipped through had swallowed them all.

And since that day, Bailey Kirk had been drinking too much. Taking too many pain pills. His mother was worried. She'd lost one child to drugs and alcohol; she knew the signs of someone in trouble.

"Come home," she told him. "I don't like the way you sound. Let us take care of you."

The temptation was strong. His room was just as he left it — lacrosse team pennants on the wall, navy blue bedspread over a twin mattress, the desk where he'd done — or hadn't done — his homework, a shelf of old yearbooks. When he went back to that room — during visits, on the holidays — he went back to his teenage self with his mom doing laundry and making his breakfast. It was a good thing, a soothing thing. A blessing to be loved by parents who took you in when you were low, let you go again when you were strong enough to pick yourself back up.

But no. He'd been on his own since college, never had to go back, not like his sister, or his brother. Never asked them for anything, not a dime.

"You're persistent." The voice snapped him from his thoughts.

Marty Friedman, Wren's longtime accountant, was not easy to reach, not willing to talk about his clients. Now, the small old man stood before him looking more like a character out of *Lord of the Rings* than a financial adviser, with a smart suit and round spectacles, a cloud of wild white hair, ears too big for his head, a bulbous nose. Bailey's calls had gone unreturned, and this visit was unannounced. He told the receptionist that he'd wait until Mr. Friedman could fit him in. This was important. He wouldn't leave until they'd spoken.

He supposed she could have called security, or the police, and Bailey would have had no choice but to vacate the private premises. But she didn't, gave him a look with those deep blue eyes, and asked him to wait.

"I called your firm," said Marty, rubbing at his chin. "Turner and Ives. They say you're on medical leave. That the case you're investigating is no longer your responsibility."

"Is that so?"

The man dug his hands into the pockets of wool pants. That suit probably cost more than Bailey made in a month — crisp lines, elegant drape. Bespoke, Bailey guessed for a man that size. Bailey by contrast wore jeans, a distressed leather jacket, a gray T-shirt that had seen better days. In fact, he'd slept in it — as much as he slept these days. He was going to be asked to leave; that was obvious. And if he didn't go politely, he'd be escorted out. Not the first time that had happened.

"You're not looking well, young man," Marty said finally into the silence that was probably only awkward for Bailey. The other man had been sizing him up. "Can I get you some water, some coffee?"

"I have some questions about Wren Greenwood," he said.

"I told you over the phone, I'm not at liberty to discuss my clients."

"She's *missing,* Mr. Friedman. She's left her home, her friends, her job. She has disappeared."

"So you say."

"Do you say something different? Have you heard from her?"

The other man regarded him behind the round lenses of his glasses that picked up

492

the light coming in from the window and obscured his eyes. Bailey saw the receptionist rest her hand on the phone, anticipating a call to have Bailey escorted from the building.

But Marty surprised them both.

"Come to my office," he said. "Beth, honey, will you get Mr. Kirk a glass of water?"

What was this, 1950? But the receptionist, Beth, gave a quick, officious nod. "Of course, Marty."

Bailey followed Marty through thick glass doors, over a plush navy blue carpet, and into an office that looked more like a study in a grand old house.

Family man. Avid reader. Philanthropist. Scholar. Bailey liked to visit a person in the space they'd created because it spoke volumes. An elaborately detailed model of a sailboat under a gleaming glass case. *It All Adds Up* from Long Island, New York, read the script on the stern. Pictures of various big-eyed, round-cheeked children in matching silver frames of different shapes. A shelf of industry trophies and prizes, a certificate acknowledging a huge donation to a home for abused women and children called Safe House. A large standing globe, a painting of a chocolate Labrador retriever. Charley

Beth glided in with Bailey's glass of water in a tall glass tumbler, embossed with the firm logo. He took it, thanked her, and drank it, feeling better almost instantly. She closed the door behind her, flashing him a polite smile before she disappeared.

"Have a seat," said Marty.

Bailey joined him in the comfortable sitting area. The couch was plush, so Bailey sat forward on the seat. He couldn't afford to sink in; he was too tired. He needed to stay alert.

"I know you have a duty to respect your clients' privacy. But when was the last time you heard from Wren Greenwood?"

Marty removed his glasses, and took a handkerchief from his pocket — monogrammed of course — and cleaned the lenses.

"I can tell you what I told the police. I had been trying to reach her for several days. She'd made a couple of strange withdrawals, cash, a Bitcoin transfer. I wanted to discuss with her the long-term health of her portfolio. As you know, due to recent global events, the market has taken a hit. She'd sustained significant losses."

Yes, a virus in China had spread, several countries in Europe were going on lockdown, borders closing, airlines failing, the cratering of the stock market due to a stark decrease in oil prices. The news was all panic and chaos. Bailey was barely paying attention. He didn't have any money in the market. He didn't believe in it, kept all his money in a savings account that seemed to grow and grow because he never did anything but work. Until now, when he mainly just lay around brooding, and searched the web for some hint of Wren and the ghost.

And the way he saw it, there was always something dark on the horizon. If you fell into a panic every time the world news was bad, you'd have to be locked up.

"We had a scheduled time to talk," Marty went on. "And she called me at that time." Marty took out his phone, offered Bailey the day and time of the call.

"The day after I last saw her, lost my track on her car."

"If you say so," said Marty. "At that time, she asked me to transfer available cash to an account that was not in my control and provided an account number. I gave the transfer paperwork to the police."

"Can I have a copy of that?"

Marty rose and went to his computer, did some tapping on the keyboard.

"I can give this to you but it won't help

495

you. This account is a Bitcoin address. It's totally untraceable. There's no way to source it back to a company or individual. In fact, that is the point of Bitcoin. It is the anarchist's preferred form of currency."

He came back with a piece of paper that had been spit from a printer near his desk. Just some numbers on a white page. Meaningless.

"Generally we discourage our clients from dealing in Bitcoin since as a firm we don't invest in those funds. But we have to honor our clients' wishes, of course. It's their money. But this is part of the problem, and why the government doesn't like it. That money is gone for good, except to the person who has the password to that account."

Bitcoin. He didn't know anything about it — what it was, how it worked. It brought to mind some hacker in a darkened room, hunched over a laptop screen.

"Did you talk to her again after that?"

"I have not heard from Ms. Greenwood. Even under normal circumstances, she's very hard to reach. She told me, and I think a close friend of hers, according to police, that she needed time away. Time off from work, from the pressures of the modern world. That she'd be in touch, and that I could manage the rest of her money as I saw fit."

"The rest of her money."

"She asked for her available cash. Her long-term accounts that can't be touched without penalty, remain intact."

"Does anyone know she has more money?"

"Only I, Ms. Greenwood, and the people she's told know how much she has."

"And if she wants the rest of it?"

"She'll have to call me."

"Not email or text."

"No," he said. "I'll need to hear her voice."

"How did she sound when you talked to her?"

"Do you mean did she sound as though she were under duress?"

"Exactly."

"She sounded as she always does — cool, calm, maybe a bit distant. I even asked her if there was a problem. Was she in trouble? And she said that she just needed some space and time. Not like her, admittedly. She's never taken time off, as long as I've known her, never withdrawn anything but the expected sums for expenses."

Bailey took a card from his wallet and slid it across the wood coffee table to Marty.

"If you hear from her again, will you call me?"

The older man looked at the card, but didn't reach for it.

"I'll tell her you were looking for her, Mr. Kirk."

They sat watching each other for an uncomfortable moment. Was he hiding something? Or just protecting Wren's privacy?

"You're not concerned about her?" asked Bailey.

"I am," said Marty. "But I'm not able to betray her confidence in me."

"Four women all met the same man on a dating site. All four of those women have disappeared through some rabbit hole that closed up behind them. They walked away from their homes, their family and friends, their lives, and all their money is gone."

Bailey took out his phone and opened the picture he had of the ghost, slid it over to Marty Friedman.

"Do you know this man?"

Marty leaned in and pushed up his glasses, squinting at the photo. Was there something, some glimmer of recognition?

"No," he said. "I'm sorry. I've never seen him before."

Marty leaned back and his phone issued a

little chime. "I have another meeting. I'm sorry I couldn't be of more help."

Dismissed. Bailey rose, folding the paper and putting it in his pocket.

"I'll see myself out," he said.

"You know, you asked if she seemed off? I guess if I was going to say that anything was different, that she seemed happier, more relaxed than I've heard her before. Maybe you just have to accept that she's gone because she wants to be. People walk away sometimes. They just get — tired of it all. Haven't you ever felt that way, Mr. Kirk?"

Uh, yeah. Like right now.

The receptionist wasn't at her desk. But outside, she stood near the corner of the building, smoking. She made it look good in her short black raincoat and high heels.

He gave her a wave, and headed toward the subway.

"Mr. Kirk," she called, stubbing out her cigarette and chasing after him.

"Ms. Greenwood's friend, Jax Morris? She calls every day. Marty won't talk to her anymore, but she's worried. She doesn't think Wren just took off either."

She handed him a folded slip of paper. "This is her number. Call her?"

"I will." He was in touch daily with Jax;

they were an unofficial team in the hunt for Wren.

He grabbed his phone, called up that picture again. How many times had he done it?

"Do you know this man?"

Beth looked at the phone a moment, bit at her lip and cocked her head. "Is he on Torch?"

A little adrenaline blast of hope. Was the ghost trawling again?

"Have you seen him there?"

She squinted at him. "Maybe?"

"Recently?"

"Yeah, like in the last couple of days."

"Was he one of your matches?" He wasn't really thinking of using her as bait, was he? Yes, yes he was. Nora would say this was because his judgment was clouded. But he and Nora weren't speaking at the moment.

"Noooo," Beth said, lifting a palm. Her nails were perfect opalescent squares.

"Why not?"

"*Not* my type. I'm not into dark and brooding. Truth? I like them pretty and vacant, up for anything — raves, weekends away. For now anyway."

Up close he could see how young she was, a smooth freshness to her skin, a kind of mischievous innocence gleaming in her eyes. She didn't know what kind of men were out there, lurking in the digital sphere, hiding behind palatable avatars, modern predators, just waiting for the right kind of prey.

"Girls just want to have fun, right?" she added when he didn't say anything.

Did she even *know* it was a song from the eighties?

"Well, be careful," he said, sounding like the grouchy old guy.

"Always," she said breezily, like she knew the world, all its pitfalls and hard consequences. She didn't. "And, Mr. Kirk, if Wren calls Marty, I'll call you. People are not always nice, you know. Especially to a receptionist. She was always kind to me, remembered my name, sent me chocolates at Christmas. I hope — she's okay."

He handed her his card, earning a smile and a raised eyebrow. "Bailey Kirk, private investigator. That sounds pretty cool."

Then she spun away, disappearing through the glass doors.

The fatigue he'd been carrying around seemed to lift some. He almost jogged to the subway, heading to Brooklyn.

FORTY-SIX

"The world of men. It's a trap."

The day is clear, sky a violent blue above the evergreen treetops, air cool but not cold. We sit beneath the tree, eating the cheese sandwiches he'd packed that morning before I even woke up, drinking water from a metal canteen we're sharing. Here, with me among the trees, he's calm and centered. He has a boy's eyes — hazel today, sometimes bluish, and thickly lashed, wide, three days of growth on his jaw, golden in the sunlight. He slouches. His hands are as big as paddles. He never hurt me. But he hurt Mom and Jay all the time, so I feared him as much as I wanted to love him.

"It turns you into a slave. They teach you to want more and more and more. Encourage you to go into debt to buy the bigger house, the bigger car, a certain type of clothes. Then you have to work more and more for their companies to pay for the things you must have. You spend your life on a treadmill. You never get where you're going. It's never enough."

I want to agree with him, but I don't understand his anger, which I can see settled into his jaw, his shoulders.

"When all you really need is this, enough food, water, shelter, time in nature."

The world of movie theaters and video games, slumber parties, friends, school, pizza delivery — it was such a distant memory that it was almost a dream. I, like him, like Robin, was one with the land, with our life there.

"When I'm gone, this place will belong to you and your brother. Not that he'll want it. It will probably fall to you to care for it."

"Where are you going?" I asked.

"I mean when I die."

The words send a shock through me. He sees it on my face.

"Not now, but someday."

"Someday."

"Everyone dies, kid. Your time comes and you return to the earth. Make sure you put my ashes out here on the land. Okay?"

"Okay."

As hunters, we were close to death. I knew, theoretically, that everyone died. But the conversation opened a pit in my stomach all the same.

"And don't sell it. Don't let some rich fuck come in and build a McMansion on it, or some corporation use it for their needs. Promise?"

"I promise."

We sit a long time. Maybe I doze. Because then I hear his voice.

Come on, kid. You gotta get up, been sleeping too long. We've got to get out of here. We won't make it home before dark. Wake up, little bird.

I ascend through layers of sleep and find myself in the dark, head throbbing, body aching. Can't move. My hands are bound behind me and I lie on a hard cold surface.

Oh, God, where am I?

My throat is so raw it's like breathing fire. Still, I find my voice. And my situation comes back to me in a rush.

"Adam," I scream. "Adam, *what* are you doing?"

I writhe against my bindings and find that they have grown tighter, cutting meanly into the delicate flesh of my wrists.

Oh, God. How long? How long have I been here? A sob crawls up from my belly into my throat and I weep, fear and desperation an acid in my gullet. When I'm spent, I lie still, breath rasping. I summon calm, intelligence.

My eyes adjust to the light and I see a cot, a rocking chair, a standing shelf of books, a round area rug. There's a light source somewhere, a covered window, maybe?

The room evolves from black to a midnight blue. I shift, trying to get myself to a seated position. As I do, my gaze falls on something on the wall, down low near the ground. Words carved into the stone.

I am the storm.

Those words. At once, fierce and desperate, brave and doubting, are the exact pitch of hope. I've heard them before. Where? Where? It comes back to me. Mia's Instagram, one of her inspirational memes. The Universe whispers to the warrior, "You're not strong enough to defeat the storm." The warrior's reply, "I am the storm."

Sadness is a gut punch. Tears threaten again, but I bite them back.

I am the storm, I say to myself, then say it again, *I am the storm.* The words infuse me with a new strength, the distant light of hope. I'm still alive. Still ready to fight. It's something — Mia's message through time to me. I cling to the faint glimmer it offers.

Finally, a thin sliver of light opens in the darkness, grows wider, an opening door. Then I see you fill the light, your dark form a cardboard cutout of menace. You climb down a creaking staircase.

I want to reach for you, begging, the man I thought you were. And then I think of my mother. Was that how it was for her? Always reaching for someone who was long gone, who perhaps was never there at all. Just a fantasy.

"It doesn't have to be like this, Wren," you say at the bottom of the stairs, voice heavy with sadness. "Can we talk? Work this out?"

The question is so innocuous as if we've had a minor disagreement that we need to get past. This question has earned a different response from me; that's why I'm here, beaten, bound, and helpless. I ache with desperation now.

"Yes," I say, too quickly. "Let's talk."

"Good. That's good." Relief. "I don't want to hurt you anymore."

You approach, give a disapproving shake of your head as if this all could have so easily been avoided, then lift me easily as if I am a child, carry me up the stairs into the light. I squint against it, my headache raging. Down the hall, to the bedroom, my eyes adjust. You've let your beard grow. Your hair is longer, wild. You look bigger; your strength is impossible. You're barely breathing harder after carrying me up the stairs.

Gently, you lay me on the bed where we made love — when? The time here has no beginning and end, no day or night; it's a terrible warp, a carnival ride of pain.

You snap my binding with a pair of wire cutters you produce from your pocket and my arms are free, but so numb and sore I can barely move them. You leave me on the bed, and I hear the water from the shower start to run.

When you return: "Can you stand?"

You offer me a hand, and I take it to help myself back to my feet. I am wobbly, unsteady, completely naked. You've taken my clothes and I don't know where they are. You help me to the bathroom.

"I'll give you your privacy."

What a funny thing to say. You've taken everything since I arrived here.

Before I can respond, you shut the door and I am alone in the bathroom that grows warm with the steam from the shower. In the mirror there's a woman I don't recognize, her dark hair wild, skin bruised, eyes frightened. She's folded her shoulders in, wrapped her arms around her middle. Her ribs and collarbone press through pasty skin.

I step into the shower, let the warm water wash over me, use the bar of soap in the teak dish to clean myself slowly. It smells of

507

coconut, reviving my senses some. But my body feels heavy, my mind cloudy, thoughts crowding, then taking flight like frightened birds. Leaning against the white tile, I summon my strength. Tonight will be the night that I escape this place, one way or another.

I am the storm.

But those are just words. My body and mind are weak.

Robin crouches in the corner of the room, and I sink down onto the gray stone floor of the shower, let the water beat on my back. We regard each other.

"How do I get out of here?" I ask her.

She whispers the answer, but I already know it.

I have to kill you. If I had done it that first night, I wouldn't be here. If I had let Jay kill my father, they'd still be alive. Some people are predators; all they do is harm. Sometimes it's kill or die.

The key to the dead bolt is on a ring in his pocket, Robin says.

I heard it jingling as we walked down the hall.

The gun you brought is loaded in the drawer beside the bed.

It's just a guess. A hopeful one.

You push into the bathroom, and find me crouched on the shower floor. You enter

508

through the steam, reach in to turn off the water, and help me from the floor. There's a towel folded on the wooden shelf beneath the wide marble sink. You wrap it around my shoulders and lead me from the room. So strong. So gentle. Your touch sends waves of revulsion and fear through my body now.

There's a dress on the bed, a simple black wool shift, camel cashmere wrap because you know I get cold, some lacy underwear that no doubt will fit me perfectly.

"I'm making dinner. Join me when you're ready."

"Thank you," I whisper.

"Let's make a fresh start tonight."

"Yes."

Your eyes linger on me as you close the door. When it's closed, I head straight for the table by the bed. But, of course, it's empty. I look for Robin but she's gone. She's out of her league here, just as I am. Neither one of us knows how, or if, I'll survive you. Poor Robin, she's only as strong and smart as I am. I guess I always knew that, even as a kid.

I dress slowly, my body aching, my heart pulsing. The lace of the undergarments you chose is sexy but soft. The dress slips over my shoulders and fits perfectly, clinging to and glancing off all the right places. The wrap is heaven. A velvety pair of flats slip onto my feet; I don't recognize the designer but they'll be pricey. You despise the flashy brands — Jimmy Choo, Louboutin, Chanel, Valentino. *People without style buy those things to communicate wealth, nothing to do with beauty or art. Just, Look at me and what I can afford to buy.*

I step out into the hallway and walk toward the great room.

I already know that there are only two doors, both dead-bolt locked, no windows that open. That those windows are double-paned, argon-filled, impact glass and will bear two hundred mile an hour winds and most things that wind might hurl at them. They won't be broken by a chair, or desperate pounding. Another lesson I have learned the hard way.

I know that there is no other property for miles. That there is no way for anyone who might be looking to track me here. I am only a few hours from The Hollows, but I might as well be on the moon. You have disposed of my car. The gate is locked. This property, this home is utterly off the grid.

And now I know what happened to Bonnie, Melissa, and Mia.

I know because it's happening to me.

I sit at your table and you bring two glasses of wine, place one before each plate. The liquid is bloodred, the crystal gleaming. Aromas from the kitchen waft, heavenly, and my mutinous stomach rumbles.

I resist the urge to break the glass against the table and lunge for you with the sharpened edge. You are far stronger and faster than I am. You don't trust me anymore and you're on guard. This is yet another bitter lesson I've learned — over and over. It's finally sunk in. I am as obedient as a schoolgirl.

My hands are shaking.

You light the candles, glance at me with dark, loving eyes.

You favor Chopin Nocturnes and, suitably grim, the music plays softly in the background.

Anyone peering in through the window would think we were an elegant, loving couple sharing a beautifully prepared meal. I could post this moment on social media, filter it: #romance #datenightathome. I'd be the envy of all my followers.

When you return to the table with our plates — a beautiful filet and delicate sliced roasted potatoes, brussels sprouts cooked with bacon and drizzled with aioli — you place the food before me and take your seat.

"To a fresh start for us, my love," you say and raise your glass.

"Yes," I breathe.

We drink.

I pray.

FORTY-SEVEN

Bailey rings the bell, and Jax opens the door looking cored out and frazzled — her cloud of dark hair piled high, fastened by some mystery of scrunchie and hot pink headband. Her black T-shirt slips off her defined shoulder. A bit of a *Flashdance* thing going on, Bailey thinks.

Jax doesn't say anything, just tugs at her violet leggings, moves aside so that he can pass into Wren's town house.

Ben and Jason, the Dear Birdie zen master and PI respectively, are at the dining room table. Jason lifts a hand, and Bailey nods. The three friends have turned Wren's dining room into a war room, every surface occupied by a computer, a spread of photos, property surveys, newspaper articles, police reports. The search for their friend has been long and exhaustive. And they all look a bit frayed, a bit red around the eyes, defeated. *Welcome to my world,* he thinks.

"What did you find out?" Jax asks, taking a cross-legged seat on the couch.

He runs down his conversation with Marty, with Beth, then the news that the ghost was back on Torch. It lands hard; Jax's eyes go wide, she seems to shrink.

"What does that mean?" she breathes. "Does it mean that he's — moved on?"

Bailey shakes his head, feeling the weight of the question. "I don't know. But I have an idea."

"An idea."

"Let's make a match for him."

Jax gasps, then releases a long slow breath. "I'll do it," she says. "I'll swipe."

"No," say Ben and Bailey simultaneously.

The two men regard each other. Bailey likes all of these people — Jax is a staid and reliable friend; Ben is a good-hearted hard worker. Jason is a young, tech-savvy PI. They all love Wren. Together they've been managing *Dear Birdie,* the media storm that followed Wren's disappearance, and have launched their own investigation. They have become Bailey's unofficial team since Turner and Ives pulled the plug on his case, on him.

"I'm not *firing* you, Bailey," Nora had said during their last conversation. "You're the best investigator I've ever had. I'm trying to *help* you. There's always one case in every career, you know. I've had mine. Diana hers. The one that hurts too much, that destabilized the process. This is yours. Recover and come back. Work on something else."

"You're telling me I care too much," he'd said, injured, angry, frustration lodged in his solar plexus. "That's bullshit."

A breath drawn and released.

"I'm telling you that your judgment is off. That you're not the man for this case."

"Who is?"

"Whoever Henry Thorpe hires next. Did you forget about the client? The one who's paying the bills? That's my point."

He *had* forgotten about the client. All he thought about was the ghost. And Wren.

"Get over this and come back home," Nora said, then hung up in the silence that followed.

But he hadn't stopped. He'd tracked down Jax, agreed to help her gratis. Now, here they were, six weeks later.

"Not you," Bailey says now. "He'll know you. Obviously, he knows everything about her."

Ben comes to sit beside Jax, takes her hand. They're mismatched, Bailey thinks. She's all wild energy, high passion, ass-kicking. Ben is mellow and pale, graying —

515

khakis and sensible shoes. She reacts, hot, fast. He's all slow nods and chin rubbing. But something works. Yin and yang.

"Then what?" asks Ben.

"We create a person, one who fits his criteria — young, gorgeous, rich, and tortured by some childhood trauma. If he takes the bait, we set a date. When our fake person doesn't show, we follow him from there," says Jax.

"What are the odds something like that even works?" says Jason from the table. He's a tall, skinny guy with a mop of dark hair and a beard, bespectacled, pasty and slouched from too much screen time.

"About as good as our odds just going over all the same information we've been looking at for the last week. We have nothing. Well, almost nothing," says Bailey.

He fishes the folded white paper from his pocket, hands it to Jason.

"What's this?"

"The Bitcoin account where Wren had her money transferred. Can you do anything with it?"

"The whole point of Bitcoin is that it's untraceable." Jason nods thoughtfully, looking at the mostly blank page. "Maybe. I'll need to see a guy."

He rises, moves quickly toward the door

with a wave. "I'll call you later."

"Be careful," Jax says, eyes following him. It's what she says to everyone when they leave the town house. Ben rubs her shoulder, and she leans into him.

"How do we create a person?" she asks.

"I know someone who can help. Who might help. We might not have to do it from scratch."

"Do it," says Jax. She is the unofficial client, the ringleader of the team that has been assembled to find Wren. "Do it fast. We're losing her. I can feel it."

Bailey nods, pretends not to notice that she's crying. He walks away to make the call.

"Hey," a smoky voice answers. Sabrina. "You are in the shithouse around here."

"I know."

"Let me guess. You've gone rogue. And PI work is not as easy as it is when you have a whole tech team at your disposal, a bank of millennials who live for the screen. Some of whom will sleep with you when they've had too much to drink after the office Christmas party."

"Sabrina."

"And who you casually hook up with from time to time."

"It's not like that." He makes his voice

soft, smiles.

"And then don't call for months."

"Stop."

"Until you need something."

"Wow."

"Am I wrong?"

"No," he admits. "You're not wrong except that you left out the fact that we're friends. That we go to the movies, we play pool, we had a picnic that time. It wasn't just hookups."

She clicks her tongue twice. "There's always a polite preamble to hooking up. True. You're good like that. I never *feel* used."

He can almost see her twirling at a strand of her hair, which was violet the last time he saw her but could be any color now. Those heavily lidded eyes, that knowing smile of glossed lips. She's almost twenty years younger than Bailey, lush and full, funny, sexy, smart-ass.

"How are you?" she asks. "Really."

"I've been better."

"Are you hurt?"

"No, I'm okay."

"That sounded like a lie. I'd have thought you'd be a better liar."

"What's that supposed to mean?"

"Nothing, just you know, there are all

518

these layers to you. You're complicated. Anyway, let me guess. You found out our guy is back on Torch."

"You knew."

"Of course, I've been watching for him. I want him as bad as you do."

"I need you to create a profile."

"Way ahead of you." His phone pings; there is a link in his texts that he clicks with his thumb. A grainy image of a girl with big eyes and ombre hair, bleach blonde with copper roots. It's Sabrina's face, but the name is Angel. Likes: solitude, darkness, rain storms; Dislikes: stupid people, haters, litter; Favorite band: Bauhaus; Favorite Film: *The Cook The Thief, His Wife and Her Lover;* Poet? Rilke, of course.

"She already has a history. I gave her an Instagram — fuck Facebook and Twitter, they're for tools and oldsters."

"What's her background trauma?"

"Parents died in a car crash when she was thirteen, picking her up from a party that she wasn't supposed to be at. I found some news articles first, about a real incident. That's how I created her. If he hunts for info on the Torch Angel, that's the background information he'll find. Also, the real girl is loaded; and she looks *a lot* like me. I copied her hair. If he doesn't look too closely, dig too deep, it would be easy to think that Torch Angel was the real girl from the articles. The character of Angel, bait for the ghost."

"Is the real Angel on Torch?"

"She's not," says Sabrina. "I already checked. This is a hack job, by the way. If he digs deep, he might figure out that Torch Angel and real Angel are not the same girl."

"Okay. Good enough. Nice work."

"I swiped on his profile. Now we just wait and see if he likes me back."

"When he does, set a date to meet. Move it along fast."

"Nora isn't going to like this."

"Nora isn't going to find out, right?"

"I like my job."

"She won't fire you. She wants him as bad as we do. Trust me. She's just giving herself plausible deniability with Diana."

"She fired *you.*"

"I'm on medical leave."

She offers a snort. "Oh, is that what they told you?"

Bailey ignores her. He doesn't think he's fired. But even if he is, it doesn't matter. It's nice to have all the toys and, yes, the bank of millennial techies, but he'll always find his way. And it would be nice to work without a tether. "And then when you set the date, let me know."

He can hear her tapping on her keyboard, voices in the background, a ringing phone.

"I'll go," she says. "I'll be the bait."

"No way. No one has to show. I'm going to follow him when he leaves."

"But what if he gets suspicious? What if he suspects a setup and gets spooked. And you lose him for good."

She has a point. "We'll talk about it if you get a match."

There's silence on the line. Then, "Hey, Bailey."

He likes Sabrina. They've had some good times. He doesn't think he uses her. He doesn't want to be the kind of man who uses women. Their thing — it was just *what it was,* right? Light, fun, a friendship of sorts. "Yeah."

"Be careful. I feel like you're out on a limb."

He feels like that, too. Way out. It's Wren. He's reaching for her, dangling over the edge of what's smart and she's slipping further and further away.

"I'm okay," he says, not sure if it's true. "Hey, Sabrina, you don't really feel used do you?"

She laughs and it's throaty and full, making him smile, too. "As if. If anything, I'm the one using *you* for sex."

"I'm okay with that."

"I bet you are." Her laughter rings on the line as she ends the call.

It's not even an hour before she texts him: I have a match. I'm meeting him tomorrow at a dive in the East Village, WCOU Radio Bar. He chose it.

Don't go there, he texts her back. I'll take care of it.

But she doesn't answer. And he knows he can't stop her from doing what she wants. In fact, he can't stop *anyone* from doing what they want. Hard as he tries. Not his brother. Not Wren. Obviously not even his millennial "friend." Maybe there's a life lesson in it. Maybe one day he'll learn it.

FORTY-EIGHT

The night is cold and a light snow falls on First Avenue. There used to be a grit, a smell to the East Village. But these days, it's all tony boutiques and fancy food shops, vaping hipsters, and stylish bars, restaurants. Bailey liked New York City better before its Disney-fication, when it was still messy and dangerous, full of style, outrage, art, underground clubs. When you might easily get mugged on the Bowery, or offered drugs on Tenth Street, or propositioned in the Meatpacking District. Now things were homogenized, gentrified. Safer, prettier, Instagrammable. Better, some would no doubt say. But not real, somehow. Somehow packaged and sold. The idea of New York City, the dream of it.

"Is that her?"

Jax sits beside him in his SUV; he had not invited her, did not want the distraction and the responsibility of a civilian in his car.

He'd, in fact, point-blank asked her not to come. But she was not the kind of woman who took no for an answer. He'd read her blog. *Take what you want from this life. Don't ask permission. Don't make apologies for being yourself.*

The woman walked the walk, he'd give her that.

"Yeah, that's her," he answers.

"What's she wearing?" asks Jax. "Is that like a leather catsuit?"

"Looks like it," he concedes. What about "be subtle" did Sabrina not understand?

High heels, big bag, some kind of dramatic red wrap. She hustles up the street, looking around, lips painted so red he can see them from where he sits half a block away.

All wrong.

Not the type of woman the ghost liked, too flashy, too confident. Not that it mattered.

Maybe it was better if he lost interest fast and got on his way. If he showed up at all. So often, too often, things just didn't work. That was a dirty secret of detective work — lots of sitting around, nothing happening, reports back to the office that took hours and said nothing. At least he didn't have to fill out any reports at the moment.

Though Nora had called him three times

today; he declined her calls and hadn't listened to the voice mail messages.

Bailey watches the light snow fall; finally his phone pings.

Sabrina: I'm here.

He clicks on the surveillance app that turns her phone into a camera and listening device. It's an app for parents to track their children, spy on their activities, watch all their texts and phone calls. Total high-tech spyware, once the thing of science fiction, now commonplace and available for $19.99 a month.

It activates and he's in the bar. The music is low jazz, the lighting dim. It's packed, but she seems to have a quiet table in the corner.

"What if he doesn't show?" Sabrina whispers, knowing he can hear her.

The angle of the phone camera catches the curve of her neck and chin, the red of her lips.

He texts her: Shh. Don't talk. Just wait. Look — vulnerable.

"I am vulnerable," she whispers, winking to reveal a glittered eyelid.

"This is a really bad idea," says Jax, leaning annoyingly over Bailey's shoulder. "She's like a kid. I mean — how old is she?"

Jax is right of course. "She'll be fine," Bailey assures her. "She's a professional."

She's not really. She's a tech geek with no field experience.

"She doesn't *look* like a professional."

They wait, Jax shifting every few seconds, fidgety, eyes trained on the door to the bar. Ten minutes to the appointed meeting time. Bailey guesses he won't be early or late. He'll be right on time. He tries not to think about the muzzle-flash, the figure moving out of the dark. His shoulder aches.

"Why are you doing this?" Jax asks. "Why are you helping us? When it's not your job. When you're not getting paid."

She has dark eyes trained on him, a slight frown that seems to be a semipermanent expression. He thinks about it before he answers.

"I've been on this case for the better part of a year, chasing this man, who seems to be the connection point between four missing women. The job is over, my firm fired. But I can't let it go."

She keeps that stare on him. "The real reason. The reason *under* the reason."

He knows what she's getting at. Everybody wants something and acts out of that desire. What they *think* they want, what they *say* they want, might be very different from what they're actually craving.

"I don't like questions without answers,"

he says. "I don't like lost. It doesn't make sense. Everyone is somewhere."

The sounds from the bar — music, a peal of laughter — are tinny over the phone between them.

"And Wren?"

Wren. He thought about little else these days. She seemed to have invaded even his dreams. Yes, as Nora claimed, clouded his judgment. He was chasing her as much as he was the ghost.

"I — care about her."

Jax's eyes, big and thickly lashed, smart, seeing, search his face. Whatever she finds seems to satisfy her, and she offers him a quick nod like he's confirmed something she already knows.

"She's my family," says Jax, eyes filling. "Some friends become like blood. She has holidays at my mother's house. She's *never once* not answered when I called. A lot of people who have been through the things she has — they go crazy, get ugly, depressed, angry. But she *helps* people, gives everything over to the people who write to her. Strangers."

"We're going to find her," says Bailey, putting a hand on her shoulder. He believes it. He has to.

"It's my fault," says Jax, tears falling now.

She bats at them with manicured fingertips. "*I'm* the one who made her go on Torch."

"Everyone's on Torch. He's a predator. *None* of this is your fault."

She wraps her arms around her middle, stares out the window toward the bar. "I need to bring her home, okay?"

"Okay."

She nods, looks at him sideways, another nod, a breath released. "Okay."

Bailey sees him first and he swears his arm starts to ache in response. He'd ditched the sling, just to stop looking like a goddamn invalid. But the arm is weak and stiff; he's not up to a fight and he knows it. Reason enough not to be in the field.

"There he is," he says.

Right on time. His hair is longer; he's grown a beard. He seems bulkier, like he's been working out and packing on calories.

It's everything Bailey can do not to leap out of the car, run up the street, and tackle the guy, beat the answers out of him. He breathes through the rage, feels it coil up into his middle.

The ghost moves, unhurried up the avenue, a tall figure on the nearly empty sidewalk. It's a quiet, cold night, not many people out. There's a homeless man huddled on a stoop, a couple rushing by, pressing close to each other, giggling. The snow is not sticking, but the road is slick and wet. In front of the bar, he stops, seems to pause, peering in the window. Bailey tenses. Does he sense something? Is he going to leave?

No.

He walks inside.

"He's here," Sabrina whispers from her phone.

FORTY-NINE

"You look different from your picture."

"Do I?" Sabrina's voice, low and throaty, is easy and light. "Better or worse."

"You're beautiful," he says. "You know that."

"It's always nice to hear."

"What can I get you?" A young male voice. A svelte waiter with slicked back hair and some artfully groomed stubble appears at an odd angle on the phone camera, which must be on the table.

The ghost, his profile name today is James Lowry, orders a Blanton's bourbon on the rocks. Sabrina asks for a dirty martini, extra olives. Bailey hopes she doesn't plan to drink it. When the waiter is gone: "Do you date often?"

Mentally, Bailey wills Sabrina to move the phone so he can see the other man better.

"Not at all, really," says Sabrina with a laugh.

Finally, she shifts the phone just a bit. There he is. He looks huge, ghostly pale, big jaw and intense dark eyes. His nose his large, crooked. Not handsome. Not the kind of man you would think could lure women away from their lives. But maybe it's not about looks. Maybe he offers them something else, something they crave but don't even know it.

"So why Torch?" asks the ghost.

"My friend, she thought it was time for me to meet someone. And this is the way everyone's doing it these days. Right?"

The music is a little too loud. Bailey strains to hear.

"Seems so. Don't meet people at work?"

"No," she says. "It's kind of a small place. And that can get messy, right? Dating people you work with — not the best idea?"

"Researcher."

"Hmm?"

"That was your job description."

"That's right. I do research for authors. And you're in IT."

"Right."

The conversation is flat, uninteresting.

"He doesn't like her," says Jax. "She's not damaged enough. He can sense it. Men like that, predators, they have a sense."

"He doesn't need to like her. He needs to

leave so that we can follow."

The drinks come, the conversation drones on. Where he lives, where he's from. All lies probably. Sabrina is laughing too much, obviously nervous.

"Family?"

Sabrina bows her head, makes a not very convincing stab at looking sad. "All gone."

"I'm sorry."

"I — try not to dwell on the past. It's gone. I'm all about the moment."

It comes off too light, the throwaway sentiment of a person who's read too many memes but hasn't done the work.

"I see," he says. "That's wise."

"Is that a scar?" she asks. "There on your throat?"

Bailey watches his eyes darken, his hand go to his neck.

"I don't like to talk about the past either," he says.

"I get that."

"Then let's talk about the future," he says. "Should we get out of here?"

"Where to?"

"Just walk awhile. I love a snowy city night. Find another place that looks good."

"Sure," she says.

"What is she *doing*?" hisses Jax, gripping the dash.

"I have no idea," says Bailey.

He puts a fifty on the table, then helps Sabrina into her coat. The connection falters as Sabrina sticks the phone in her pocket. Their voices become muffled.

"Shit."

Then they're on the street, moving uptown, the ghost with his arm around Sabrina's shoulders.

"Can you drive?" Bailey asks.

"Of course I can drive," says Jax, annoyed. "What am I, twelve?"

"Follow me."

"Wait! What?"

Bailey exits the car to follow the couple on foot, jogging across the street and catching them just as they turn onto St. Marks. The connection on the phone is still live, but he can't hear anything, just the city noise, the siren of the ambulance that passes them by, a shout, some music from a bar.

The couple comes to an abrupt stop and Bailey ducks into a doorway, but not before the ghost turns and their eyes meet, a shock of recognition passing between them.

The moment blurs and warps, as Bailey watches, then breaks into a run. The ghost pulls Sabrina close, a tight embrace, then pushes her away and backs up, his gaze still on Bailey, a slight cold smile playing at his lips.

Bailey just gets to Sabrina as she falls, legs buckling, head tilting back. He's there to keep her from hitting the concrete, catching her soft weight in his arms. He sinks with her to the ground. When he looks into the faceted depths of her blue eyes, he sees pain, and fear; a terrible gush of blood from her mouth as she tries to say his name.

"Oh, God. Sabrina, please."

She's too young. Pleasepleaseplease.

He takes his phone from his pocket and dials 911 as Jax brings the SUV to a screeching halt beside them, leaves it in the street to run to them. Horns start blaring at the blockage; drivers roll down their windows to yell.

"What happened?" Jax's voice is a shriek of despair. "Oh, my God, *where is he?*"

When he looks up from Sabrina's terrified gaze, the ghost is gone again.

FIFTY

My father is an old man now, wizened and thin with a white beard and drawn cheeks. His eyes have a hollow look; it's not sadness exactly. It's too much seeing.

"I made mistakes, Robin. Too many. I was wrong about so much."

We sit on an outcropping of rock, bare feet dangling over the rushing creek. I can't breathe, my chest heavy, the air too thin. I want to tell him but I have no voice.

It's an old conversation, one I can't have right now. There's something I need to do. I'm just not sure what it is. Panic flutters in my chest.

"You should have killed me when you had the chance."

"I tried," I rasp. "My aim was bad."

"You choked."

"It was too late. They were gone."

"Don't fuck it up again."

"Too late."

535

"No," he says, taking my hand. His gaze is urgent to the point of being desperate. "Not quite yet."

I wheeze, hear my own breath in my throat.

"Little bird," he says, reaching for my hands and squeezing hard. "Get up and run."

When I open my eyes, there is nothing, just gray. The air around me is tight; my breath ragged. I push out into the murk and feel plastic. Panic is a wave that washes up and I start thrashing, using all my strength, my lungs growing tighter. I'm a dervish, kicking and scratching, not enough air to even scream.

Ohgodohgod. It all comes back.

No. No. I don't want to go. Not now, not like this. The world. My life. Jax. Dear Birdie. *You built a life. A good one. Come back to it.*

There. A point of light. I calm myself enough to poke a finger toward it and feel the teeth of a zipper. It takes all my strength, all my focus to push, push until the zipper starts to move. Blessed air rushes in, then more. Light. Stars. The tops of trees swaying in bright moonlight, just like the tree house.

I burst out of my cocoon with a wail,

536

drawing gorgeous air into my lungs. I scramble out of the body bag I'm in, and feel the dirt beneath my palms.

You.

You left me for dead. I put my hands to my throat; it's bruised and painful. I remember your hands squeezing, your eyes staring into mine, as I thrashed and struggled for breath. You an impossibly heavy weight on top of me.

We could have had everything, you whispered, as the light drained from the world. White stars danced in front of my vision. I stopped trying to pry your fingers from my neck. Your grip was a vise, your eyes blank with the pleasure my pain and fear gave you. *But you threw it all away.*

Robin is crouched beside me.

He's gone, she whispers. *He's left. This is your chance.*

She's crying, shaking.

The day will come when you won't need her anymore, Dr. Cooper said. *And on that day, you'll let her go. She won't go away; she'll just become a part of you on the inside.*

Lungs aching, I crawl to her and move a wild strand of hair out of her eyes.

I'm sorry, she says. *I don't know what to do.*

"It's okay," I tell her. She is only air and light. "I do."

There's a rustle of leaves, a mournful call in the night; the moon moves out from behind the clouds. And I'm alone in the darkness of the woods. A homecoming of sorts. An awakening. I was always alone out here. And it's okay, even right.

The bag I was in gapes like a mouth and I sit shaking, still wearing that thin black shift, feeling my body, which is savaged and broken, every movement marked with pain, but whole and alive.

Beside me are three makeshift graves, each marked with a simple wooden cross, each carved with a name — Mia, Melissa, Bonnie.

I sit weeping for them.

I offered them the gift of freedom, you said. *And no one wanted it. I thought you were different. I thought you were* the one.

The wine, and whatever was in it, had the room pitching. *It's only freedom if you choose it for yourself.*

That earned me a blow across the jaw; I lift my hand to touch the ache. I crawl over to their graves. I want to offer them each something — a flower, an apology, a rescue — though I have nothing left to give. It's too late for them. But not for me.

That's when I see the headlights of a car moving up the drive.

You're back.

I could make my way back to the road, find my way home. But I don't. I owe us all more than that, more than just an escape where I spend the rest of my life looking over my shoulder. But one that brings justice for us all.

Now I just have to get there before you do.

I marshal every ounce of strength I have and run.

FIFTY-ONE

The bitter taste of failure and loss crawls like reflux up Bailey Kirk's throat. It's a taste in his mouth, a pounding in his ears. He holds on to Jax as they exit the car in front of the town house. She has not stopped crying — not at the hospital, not at the police station. Ben rushes out of the town house doors and takes Jax from Bailey, and she falls against him, holds on tight.

"I'm so sorry," he says. The street is empty; the snow that fell earlier has stopped, some of it collected on branches, the parked cars. The air is frigid.

Ben helps Jax inside and Bailey follows.

Jason sits at the dining room table, and Bailey looks at him, hopeful. But the younger man just shakes his head.

"There's no way to track the number. I'm sorry. That's the whole point of Bitcoin. No trail. I thought I could find a way. But — no."

"What about the internet fixer she hired?"

"Another ghost," says Jason. "I used her computer, the one she uses to access the dark web. But he's not responding."

Despair sits in the room, a ghoul in the corner, sucking up all the air.

"She's gone. Like all those other girls," says Jax from the couch. "Just gone. You never found them. How are we going to find her now?"

He doesn't answer. He can't. He doesn't have any answers, just keeps seeing the fear in Sabrina's eyes. He rode with her in the ambulance, Jax following in his truck. They sat in the waiting room until her parents arrived, Nora on her way. Now, he keeps reading the text his boss just sent:

She's lost a lot of blood. But she should pull through. This is on you, Bailey.

He needs a drink. He needs to drink until the whole world goes black.

A hard knock on the door startles them all. Both Bailey and Jason rise, Bailey instinctively resting his hand on his gun and heading toward the door. A dark form stands on the stoop, thick and still.

"Who is it?" asks Jason behind him.

Bailey knows him right away, reaches to

open the door.

Standing there in the cold is Jones Cooper wearing a parka and a wool cap. He holds a thick envelope under his arm.

"Your boss said you would be here. I think she's tracking your location."

That makes sense.

"Probably. The car belongs to the firm."

"I've been going over some old files. I think I found something."

They gather around him as he sits at the dining room table and spreads out some photographs and old newspaper clippings, a few printouts, what looks like a survey and a property deed.

"On the Carson property, the night of the raid, there were several families there. One who got away that night. This young man was among them."

He points to a photograph in a newspaper clipping. The boy there is slim, with dark hair and eyes. "His name is Adam Wilson."

"Adam," says Jax. "She believed it was his real name."

"The family stayed off the grid for a number of years. There are no records of any of them — taxes, employment, educa- tion. But he pops up a few years later. It looks like he went to MIT on scholarship. He was homeschooled, but took the SAT, making an almost perfect score. He got a full ride."

He offers the school records, printouts with the school seal.

"Later he started his own company, an internet security firm called Blackbox."

There's a document registering the business with the IRS. Another piece of paper, taking them a step closer.

"That company lists this as its registered address."

Bailey stares. He should have found this piece of information. It strikes him hard that Nora was right. He'd lost his focus; his judgment was off. He'd missed something critical. He'd let an inexperienced colleague almost lose her life.

Jones shifts the paper aside to show a property survey. "It's off the gird, a piece of property that was pretty much destroyed and abandoned by the chemical company that was housed there originally. It was part of a project that sold damaged lands to private owners who wanted to work with the government to heal it, essentially, make it livable again."

Bailey feels a surge of hope.

"It is not on the electric grid, the city water and sewage doesn't reach it. But from these aerial photographs, there does seem to be a structure on there."

He slips out some photographs showing acreage of trees. There's a red circle around what looks to be a roof beneath the green. He points to other circles. "Looks like a generator, some solar panels. There's probably a well, but I haven't been able to find a permit pulled in the area for water and septic."

The digital world had failed them. But this paper trail, pieces carefully connected by a retired cop who cared about Wren, had given him the only solid lead he'd had in months. A real place, an actual destination.

"Let's go," says Bailey.

"I had a feeling you'd say that," says Jones. "I've already turned this information over to your boss and to the police."

"Let's *go,*" says Jax, grabbing her coat and drying her eyes. She's already at the door, turns back to look at both of them. Jones Cooper bows his head a moment, then lifts his eyes to them.

"She's been missing a long time. Are you prepared for what you might find?"

Jax's eyes fill but she sets her jaw into a determined line, juts out her chin. Bailey rises. Jones gazes back and forth between them, then stands with a resigned nod.

"I'll drive," he says.

FIFTY-TWO

You can't help but register your surprise when you see me, sitting at your table. You literally draw up, step back toward the door through which you've just entered the house. After all, you left me for dead in a body bag beside the graves of other women you have kidnapped and killed. Yet, here I am.

Talk about awkward.

Why didn't you bury me beside them? Why didn't you finish the job you started? Did you get distracted? Grave digging *is* hard work. Maybe you're running out of energy. Maybe you didn't have the heart to kill another woman who loved you. Maybe you're tired.

I know I am.

There's a deep furrow in your brow, a pallor to your skin. It looks like you've had a hard night.

"Wren."

"Adam."

After a little searching, I found my gun in the cabinet over the refrigerator. It's fully loaded. And my father was right. My aim is good. I *did* choke that night so long ago. It's my heart that gets in the way. It won't happen again.

You stand in the doorway, collect yourself. Are *you* armed? It's likely, I imagine.

You must feel it, as I do. Your luck is running out.

I sit at the head of the table, the gun before me, my hand resting on it. I flatten my other palm against the wood grain.

"Is your name Adam?" I ask. Stupid question, I guess. But still I find I want to know.

You offer a shrug of surrender. Though I imagine you could run for the door. Maybe you could be gone before I could catch you. Maybe not. We all want to be seen, don't we? No matter how we conspire to hide ourselves, don't we all secretly want to reveal our true selves?

"It is. Adam Wilson."

The name sounds familiar. I dig through my memory banks but come up empty. Did he write to Dear Birdie? I've found that other elusive connection that evaded Bailey Kirk. Lying around in the dark, bound and naked, you think about things. You dig through the recesses of your memories and your thoughts. Each girl — Mia, Bonnie, Melissa — each of them wrote to Dear Birdie.

And I answered each letter, offered them advice on moving on, finding a way through grief, pain, self-blame. Were you in the audience? Reading the blog? The newspaper articles? Listening to the podcasts?

"Don't you know who I am?" you say. "You still haven't put it together."

"Tell me."

"My family rented property from your father. We lived on the north end, in a house my father restored with his own hands. We were there the night of the raid."

The revelation hits hard. Of course.

"The family that fled. The Wilsons."

"That's right," you say, stepping closer. I lift the gun and you stop moving. "Fled with nowhere to go. We were homeless after that night, living out of our van. We traveled, moved around the country, wherever my father found work — mostly on farms. He drank. My parents split. Finally, my sister and I were left in Florida with my grandparents."

I don't feel sorry for him. At all.

"You really don't remember us," he says. "I saw you. Working in the garden with your father, climbing into your tree house. I would come with my father when the men met to talk about plans for the end."

I shake my head. I was lost in my own world, and the only friend I remember was imaginary. The property was vast. We didn't mingle with anyone. If he was really there, I never saw him.

"What happened to your parents?"

"Deaths of despair," he says. "My father died in a bar fight. Can you imagine anything more ignoble? My mother overdosed on oxy."

He wrinkles his nose in disgust. I notice with a shock that there's a skein of blood down his shirt. "I don't talk to my sister. Haven't seen or heard from her in ten years. Sometimes I look on her social media feeds. She seems solid enough — husband, kids, stay-at-home mom. Normal. Bland."

"Is that so bad?"

You shrug, eyes glassy. Just another broken man who resorts to hurting women to ease your pain.

"Maybe not. Comparatively."

The metal of the gun has warmed in my grip.

"I remember those days on your family's land as a kind of paradise. Peaceful. Easy. My mother was a good teacher. Homeschooling came easily to her. My father loved working the land. We had some sheep, sold the wool. A vegetable garden, fruit trees. It was beautiful there, wasn't it?"

"I remember it differently. For my family, it was far from heaven."

"Not always though, right?" he says. "There were good days, too."

"There are always good days, too," I concede.

You draw and release a breath, move closer still.

"I wrote to him," you say. I see the hint of smile.

"Who?" I ask, already knowing the answer.

"Your father. After I went to MIT, found some venture capitalists to invest in my cybersecurity software, and was making a go of it, I wrote to him in prison. To thank him for that time and space in my life."

A letter, to thank him for all he'd done. My stomach roils with disgust.

"He killed my brother and my mother. He's a murderer."

You lift your palms. "He's sorry for the things he's done. I am, too."

The ease with which you forgive him and yourself stokes my rage, which is burning bright in my middle, growing hotter by the second.

"How nice." The words feel like poison on my tongue.

"Sarcasm doesn't suit you."

"Don't tell me what suits me," I say mildly. "I'm the one holding the gun."

A smile, the easy turning up of the corners of your mouth; it's mirthless and cruel.

"It was you," he says. "You called the police."

"That's right," I say.

I have taken the journey of self-blame, only to realize if the choice played out before me again and again, I'd do the same. I thought that I was saving my family. I was calling for help. That it went another way does not rest with me. It rests with my father. I have Dr. Cooper to thank for that bit of mental clarity.

"You destroyed that place. If the police hadn't come, your brother and mother would still be alive. Maybe my family wouldn't have been destroyed. Maybe we'd have met sooner, been together."

You sound petulant and young, a child to whom someone has broken a promise they were never able to keep in the first place. You are living in a fantasy of what might have been had we all remained in that place.

"We don't get to go back," I say. "We can't change the past."

Your frown deepens, but you stay silent.

"How did you choose them?" I ask.

You raise your eyebrows in surprise at my question. "*Dear Birdie,* of course. I was just out of school when I stumbled across your blog. I was one of your earliest fans."

You shift forward just slightly. I close my hand more tightly around the gun.

"With my skill set, it didn't take long for me to put the pieces together, to figure out that Dear Birdie was Wren Greenwood. And once I found you online, I knew you right away. Your father didn't tell me you were still alive. He protected you. You should know that. But I figured it out."

"Unforgiven."

"That was my first letter to you. After all those years of reading."

Your eyebrows do the dance of sadness; your eyes fill, jaw tensing. Do you think I'll find compassion for you? I'm only not dead by your hand out of sheer luck. I was inches from my own grave. Three other women just like me were not so lucky. Still, I try to stay neutral. There's so much I need to understand before this comes to what can only be an ugly end.

"What came first, Torch or Dear Birdie?"

You're still slowly moving toward me. Maybe you think I don't notice.

"Dear Birdie, of course. It's so easy to track people down with the little details they don't even know they're giving, find their social media, their Torch profiles, craft a persona for yourself that appeals to someone craving darkness, even if she doesn't know it herself. Even when they think they're anonymous, people give so much away, little details that tell the story. It's not magic. Just algorithms."

I let my finger slide over the trigger.

"So a *Dear Birdie* letter, a Torch profile. And if there was no match?"

You lift your palms, another step closer. "No match, no connection."

"Were there some that slipped through your net?"

"A few."

"And what about Melissa's connection to The Hollows?"

You raise your eyebrows, impressed with my research, I suppose. "That was a surprise. I thought it was a sign actually that we were meant to be. You know how tricky The Hollows can be. But it turns out that she hated that place. She was — *difficult.*"

I see your anger now.

"In fact, each of *my exes,* they all thought they wanted to live off the grid, find a simpler way. They all *said* that they wanted

552

to leave the world behind. But when it came down to it, no. None of them were really cut out for it."

A chill moves through my body, thinking of them. You lured them here, kept them here when they tried to leave, finally making sure they stayed forever.

"You tried to convince them."

"Yes."

"And when you couldn't?"

You're inching ever closer.

"It wasn't supposed to go like this. I never *wanted* to hurt any of them. I loved each of them, in my own way. I never wanted to hurt you, Wren. I love you."

"Why me finally?"

Now you laugh a little. "It was *always* you. I was always trying to find my way to you, back to that land."

I think about the article.

"It was you. You were Rick Javits's client. You're the one who wanted to buy the property."

"But you wouldn't sell." Your face has pulled sad. "I thought you'd stay here with me, Wren. I thought *you* were ready to leave the world behind. It's so dark out there, so cold, so devoid of life and hope. You of all people must know how broken we are. Those letters day after day. The modern world with all its digital malice, its soulless flash, how it takes, how it separates us from what's real. I believed you were ready for the life your father wanted for you. I thought I could hear it in the tone of your letters. I thought it was time for us."

I am still silent. There's nothing to say. You've created me, thought I was someone else.

"Your father — you called him a collapsist," you go on. "He believed the world was already ending. Look around. Was he wrong?"

Was he wrong?

"No," I admit. "He wasn't wrong. He wasn't wrong that the world is in chaos. That it's dangerous and cruel. That the planet is dying."

"This land," you say, still slowly moving closer.

My hand closes tighter. I lift the gun again and your eyes fall on it.

"I've healed it," you continue. "Spent hundreds of thousands to dig up barrels, leave the land raw to repair itself. It took years. Then I built this house on the restored acres, just like your father's place. You can hunt. We can grow our own produce. It's paradise *repaired,* a reversal of crimes against the planet. Far from the damage done by the world of men."

There it is. My father's mantra.

But this is what I have come to understand.

The world *is* in chaos. It's not about that. The world has *always* been on fire. Now, it might not be about saving it, as much as it is about helping each other through it all. Holding each other up, helping, fixing, working together, loving, forgiving. You don't get to *just leave*, just make a space and hide there waiting for everything dark and frightening to go away.

The world of men — and women — it's my world. I want to stay. I want to help.

But it's not a thing someone like you can understand.

You who takes what isn't given. You who breaks and destroys, lies and kills.

It's *you* who needs to go. Not the world. Not the rest of us.

When you find your moment, take it, my father said when he was teaching me how to hunt. *If you hesitate, wait even a second too long, he'll be gone. He'll sense you, your intention. You'll telegraph your fear with a breath, with an uncertain step. And he'll disappear into the trees.*

My father's lessons. Some of them I have learned well.

So, it's swift when I make my move.

Just one fluid motion, then a flash of light, and burst of sound.

There are always a few tense seconds where you're not sure if you've hit your mark.

In that space our eyes meet. There's fear, and relief, always relief. There's love. You loved me and I loved you, even if it was only just a part of you.

I have hit my mark. A bullet to your heart.

You fall to your knees. I move closer, as I would to my quarry. Your mouth is open, then closed. You tilt to the side and I am there to catch you, to ease you to the ground. You try to speak but can't, your own blood mingling with whatever blood was already on your shirt. Who else have you hurt tonight, Adam? She'll be the last.

Your hand closes around my wrist, and I see the depths of your pain. That's over now.

Watch the light leave, my father said. *Be present for that. It's the least you can do.*

And I am. I hold your eyes and in their darkness I see the whole universe, the glittering galaxies, and swallowing black holes, the bloated red giants, and all the mysteries not yet revealed. I watch you return to that place. Heavy in my arms, eyes staring.

And I feel no sadness. No guilt or remorse.
I am not the hunter.
Or the doe.
I am the storm.

FIFTY-THREE

I run from the house and down the path to where I was supposed to die. There's a shovel there beside the bag, heavy, well-used. He would have used it to dig my grave I guess, when he got around to it. I use it to try to find Mia, but the ground is hard and cold and I don't make much progress before I hear the sirens.

I want to know the end of their stories — Melissa, Bonnie, and Mia. What he did to them, how they each died. But I may never know, only that I escaped the same fate, by luck alone. And some skills I learned from a man as dark as Adam, one I loved in spite of all his failings. My father.

Around me the trees sigh. Nature, impervious as ever.

In the movies, there's always a battle — epic and bloody. Terrible losses and a darkening sky. There's always a moment when it seems that evil triumphs and the hero has fallen. And then in that moment when all appears lost, reinforcements rush in to save the day.

But in life, you have to save yourself. And there are still a million battles large and small ahead. And that's the beauty of it all, the blessed, terrible mingle of good and bad, right and wrong, bliss and agony.

That's where Jax, Jones Cooper, and Bailey Kirk find me when they come bursting through the trees. I'm on my knees beside the grave of a girl none of us could help, after having saved myself from my own dark impulses, and the man who saw them more clearly than anyone else.

Bailey gets to me first, drops down beside me, gathers me in his arms. I wrap myself around him as he buries his face in my neck.

"Oh, my God, Wren, I thought I lost you," he breathes, holding me tight. "Thank God. Thank God."

His eyes are full of stars — joy, relief, fear, sadness, love. All of it, everything. Not blank like yours. Not black holes sucking in life and light. How did I not see it? Or maybe I did and it's what I wanted. But not now. Not anymore.

"You're hurt," he whispers. "Wren."

I am, I want to tell him. But I'm the best

I can be after all of it. Alive. Strong.
Ready to fight another day.

FIFTY-FOUR

Dear Birdie,

My father was a sick man. Mental illness ran in our family. He was unstitched by his experiences in the military. He self-medicated with alcohol and he was a violent drunk. My mother, she loved him, even though he was not the man she married, even though he was broken, addicted, and coming apart. When he told her that he wanted to take his family — her, my brother, and me — to the land where he grew up, she agreed. The plan was to return to nature, to live off the grid, and away from the modern world.

She agreed.

The drive has been long and gray and I am tired. It has been mostly flat for a while now, the scattered trees just black line drawings against a silver-gray sky, a light dusting of snow on the ground. When it looms into view, a tall white wall, a red-roofed tower, the building looks more like a castle keep than a prison. My hands, my shoulders are stiff with tension, my stomach fluttering with nerves as I park. I almost turn around and leave. Must happen a lot. People arrive here to visit, to confront, to forgive, and lose their nerve.

But I find a spot and park, sit a moment, staring at the guard turrets, the large gate. There's an aura of pain and desolation. This is a maximum security facility, housing some of the most dangerous criminals in the state. Many people who walk though these doors will not walk back out.

Why have I come here?

In my childhood memory, there are so many different versions of my father. There's the handsome young soldier in uniform, a picture in a frame beside my mother's bed. There was the stranger on the video calls that we took on my mother's old laptop, cuddled together on the bed. There was the hulking, exhausted man who came home and was either in bed, or slouched in front of the television most of the day. He had haunted eyes, looked at me with a kind of despair. He frightened me. There was the man who taught me how to hunt, how to fish, how to garden, how to prepare food for winter, how fire a gun, use a crossbow. He was quiet and careful, gentle, wise. I loved him. There was the monster who hurt my brother, and mother — beat them, screamed at them, and finally killed them. I hated him. I still do. In my heart, he remains unforgiven.

I endure the questioning and search, the pat down by a young female prison guard who is way too pretty and young for her uniform and her job, the hunt through my bag. The process is rote, done a thousand times. The space is gray and cool, my journey punctuated by the sliding and clanging of heavy metal doors. The deeper I go, the more I want to turn around.

This was a mistake.

Shit.

Jax was dead set against it. She's all about cutting off the dark past — *don't go back, don't look back.* Maggie declined to offer an opinion, said the decision was mine alone. In the end, it was Jones Cooper who urged me to do it. *Monsters only have a life in our imagination. The light of day reveals us all as the same flawed, broken soul trying to survive in this world.*

Finally, I am escorted to a booth where the seat across from me is empty, a thick glass divide separates the two spaces.

I don't blame myself, not anymore. But I do take responsibility for what happened that night. I called the police, reported the stockpile of weapons. I was a child and I set unforeseen events in motion, though really I was just trying to save us. I thought that they would come and take him away. I didn't know how things would unfold — none of us do, even as grown-ups.

There were so many other things that might have happened, though. I could have let Jay kill him; I could have killed him — in the woods while we were hunting. It would have been simple enough. He trusted me. I could have killed him that night, but my aim wasn't true and my heart was weak. And so because of a call I made, my brother and mother were killed, our home, such as it was, was destroyed, my father went to prison to serve two consecutive life sentences, and another monster — Adam Wilson — was born. I went to stay with Miss Lovely. More violence in college with a boy I thought I loved. Finally I found Jax and her family. I built a life. Found a calling, a way to heal through helping others.

For a moment, the man in front of me looks like a stranger. I think there's been a mistake, that they've brought the wrong man. He's so slim, I can see the knobs of his elbows, the press of his cheekbones. He's clean-shaven. But then I look into the eyes of this old man and find my father. His gaze is clear and kind, a stormy green-gray that evokes my brother. Off him wafts the unmistakable aura of peace. He picks up the phone beside him, a warm smile on his lips, as if he's been waiting for me all his life but is not surprised to see me. I hesitate before I pick up the phone. The receiver smells of disinfectant.

"Hello, little bird." His voice crackles over the line.

"Hi, Dad."

"It's been a long time. You're beautiful. The most beautiful thing I've ever seen."

I don't know what to say. I'm not embarrassed when the tears come. I let them fall.

"I don't expect your forgiveness," he says, leaning forward. He is nothing like the man

I remember; he is frail, eyes knowing, with the quietude of a monk.

I haven't come to give him my forgiveness. But sitting here in a glass box, I find something within myself I didn't expect for my father who did so much wrong, whom I have hated and feared. I'll never touch him again — never feel his arms or hold his hand.

Dear Birdie, I can't find my way to forgiveness. Because how can I forgive what he has done to others? He robbed me of my family, my childhood, my happiness. But he robbed Jay and my mother of their lives. It's not my place to absolve him of his crimes. To know that he's found peace, a path forward, does not comfort me. Because why should he have that when Jay and Alice are gone, when I have suffered so much because of his actions?

He presses his hand to the glass. And it takes me a second, but I do the same.

We are separated by the things he's done. But I can see his journey. How he, too, has suffered. How damaged, how broken he was by the world of men, by war, by his own

566

inadequacies as a husband and a father, as a man.

"I never meant to hurt them," he says. "I want you to know that. I was in wild, red rage, separated from reality."

I get that. I do. But.

"I can't forgive you. I love you, Dad. But I can't."

He bows his head and releases a deep breath. When he looks up, a single tear trails down his face. "Love is enough, Robin. That's more than enough."

Don't love him, Jay said, speaking from his anger. *He doesn't deserve it.*

But the truth is that we all deserve that, even the most damaged and twisted among us. It's the least we deserve. And if there was more of it, there would be a lot less pain in this world we share.

I place my hand on my belly, which has just started to swell to the point where my clothes don't fit. I was barely able to squeeze into the dress I'm wearing.

"Something you need to tell me?" he asks gently.

I tell him everything. About my memories of our land, of him and the things he taught me, how they stayed with me, my journey from that horrible night. I tell him about you, Adam. About how you stalked me and

567

would have killed me, and killed three other women like me, Bonnie, Melissa, Mia — those carrying the burden of guilt, shame, and anger, but looking for love. How I couldn't help them; how I was far too late for them, as I was for Jay and my mother. How you were a monster, a ruthless predator. And that I ended you.

My question is, Dear Birdie, how do you move forward in life without offering forgiveness to those who have wronged you? How can you forgive yourself for your own failings and dark deeds? Can you find health, happiness, and wholeness without it?

But I don't need Dear Birdie — that wiser part of myself — to answer my question.

And then I tell my father that I am carrying your child, Adam. And how I know in my heart that this child will be well and good, and that she will have a safe place in this world.

One that I have created.

I pull the sonogram printout from my pocket and press it up to the glass. If he is unsettled by any of this, it doesn't show. He accepts it all.

"What will you call her?" he asks.

"I'll call her Emily, the girl who is in Robin's grave."

"That makes sense," he says. "A rebirth."

"That's right."

"The past is gone, little bird. Go forward, don't look back."

Funny. I think that's exactly what Dear Birdie would say.

FIFTY-FIVE

In the end, all we have is each other.

The drive home is long and hard, and I am exhausted when I return to the town house. The door swings open when I get to the top of the steps, and there's Jax waiting with open arms. I fall into her, my best friend, and as of this week, my roommate. She smells of patchouli and lemongrass; her arms are soft and strong.

"You didn't call," she says. "You promised you'd call when you were on your way home."

"I needed the time to process."

"I tracked you."

"I know."

She's leasing out her apartment and has moved into the town house. We're not getting married, our long-standing joke, but she's going to be my family, our family. She's going to help me raise this baby. I am going to help her write her book. She's going to be a regular guest on my *Dear Birdie* podcast. And sometimes she's going to *be* Dear Birdie — a tougher, more kick-ass version of my Dear Birdie. She and Ben — are seeing each other, a lot. How is that going to work? We have no idea. One moment at a time.

I find Ben at the dining room table, going through the *Dear Birdie* letters for our podcast tomorrow. He rises to embrace me.

"Need to talk?" he asks. He has a way about him, something gentle and yet strong, quietly present, easy. He's Jax's opposite, but also her match, in every way.

"Not right now," I say, squeezing him and releasing.

"Anytime."

"Uh," says Jax, lowering her voice to a whisper, "*he's* in the kitchen. Were you expecting him? He brought groceries? And he just looked so — *eager* to be here? I couldn't turn him away."

Bailey Kirk. I was expecting him. *Hoping* to see him.

"I think he's — cooking?" she says with a smile.

Something about that guy. I return her grin.

When I move back over toward her, she

rests her hand on my belly. "How's our girl?"

I put my hand on hers, our fingers entwine. "Good." I'm talking about the baby and about myself. "Healthy. Whole."

If my best friend thinks it's strange that I want to have your child, she hasn't said so. Her mother gave me the side-eye, but then she started stocking the freezer with all manner of soups and stews, lasagnas, casseroles.

Life wins.

Love wins.

Love and life *always* win.

In the kitchen, I find Bailey at the stove. I didn't have him pegged as someone who could cook. But I didn't have him pegged as someone who would stay on a case after he was fired, and come after me with Jones Cooper and Jax.

"What are you making?" I ask, seating myself at the kitchen island. My back is aching and I just want to go put on my pajamas and crawl into bed.

"Spicy white bean soup with pancetta." The wafting scents of garlic, onion, olive oil fill the air.

"Sounds like heaven."

"Heaven in a Dutch oven. It's done. Just needs to simmer for a while."

He wipes his hands on a dish towel and comes around to me.

"How was it?" he asks.

"Strange, sad," I say, feeling the tug of sorrow. Love doesn't always feel good. "But I'm glad I went. It was past time. I've been running from him for so long, from that night, from that place. Time to stand and hold my ground."

Bailey and I have been dancing around each other since the night he found me. He stayed. Rode in the ambulance with me, was always there when I opened my eyes. Was in the room with Jax and I when the doctor told me I was pregnant. He helped us get back to the town house. He's come for dinner, twice.

Every morning I get a text from him: Has the world ended yet?

Not yet, I answer.

That kiss, it's on my mind. The feel of his arms, the sound of my name on his breath.

When he quit Turner and Ives, he and Jason decided to form a partnership and open their own agency. A nice combo of old- and new-school detective skills; I think they'll learn a lot from each other.

He never questioned my decision to keep the baby either. The other day, he touched my hand when I walked him out to his car.

We both drew back as if there was an electric shock. And I've been thinking about that touch ever since.

That boy's in love, warned Jax.

Stop it, I told her.

What, are you blind, my friend?

Please. I'm damaged goods.

Jax got mad. I really got the riot act. *Don't you dare say that. Not ever. Truly. That's so fucked on so many levels. You are who you are because of everything that made you and that's beautiful. You're a survivor.*

I am the storm?

Damn straight.

"I hope you don't mind that I came by," Bailey says now. We're both as tense and awkward as tweens at our first dance.

"I'm glad you're here," I manage to say. "I realize that I haven't thanked you for everything you've done. Or said that I am so sorry about Mia. And about Sabrina. She tried to help me, and Adam nearly killed her."

He bows his head. "The conversation with Henry Thorpe was a heartbreaker. But Nora was right, he deserved closure, deserved to grieve his loss. I could give him that at least."

He lifts his head.

"And Sabrina — she's doing okay. But

that was my fault," he says. Regret pulls his features tight. "My judgment was off. I'd lost you — and I was in a dark place. I didn't stop her from inserting herself into a plan that was flawed from the beginning."

"You did your best," I say. "*I* ditched *you.* If I'd stayed with you — you wouldn't have been shot, I wouldn't have played into his plan, Sabrina never would have been hurt."

Bailey shakes his head.

"Maybe we never would have known what happened to Mia, Bonnie, and Melissa if you hadn't followed the ghost. Their families would have spent a lifetime wondering, unable to let go."

I let his words settle. Yes, we all have to let go. It's the hardest thing, isn't it?

"We blame ourselves, always," he goes on into the silence. "But really there's only one person to blame for what happened."

"And he's gone," I say.

You're gone.

Bailey is dangerously close; I feel his heat. He offers me both his hands, and I pivot to face him. His gaze is clear and true, a slight smile at his lips. There's mischief there, and light. I put my hands into his waiting palms, and the electricity races up my arms. He steps in closer, pulls me in, and I rest my head on his chest. He wraps his arms

575

around me, closer.

"This isn't going to be easy," I whisper.

He laughs a little, soft and throaty without much mirth. "Nothing worth it ever is."

I close my eyes and see the expression on your face as I last saw it — anger, confusion, fear, relief.

A day will come when I don't see the light draining from you, feel the weight of you in my arms as the life leaves your body.

A day will come when my injuries heal, and my grief abates, and I don't jump at every shadow and loud noise. There will be a time when I don't see you in every crowd, find you in the shadowy alleys of every street. And I know this, because I have survived horrors before. And life grows over damage, covering it with new growth, and there will be all new storms, and fires, and broken pieces, and healing again. That's the way of it.

When I open my eyes, I see Bailey's smile — full of life and promise and laughter. He does look like Jay, a lot. And that's a comfort.

A day will come when I give birth to your child. She'll come into the world in a wash of blood and pain, a flood of tears, just as you left it. And I will weep with joy.

I will love her without fear or worry of

who she will become, or how much of you is in her. Because I will give her all of myself and the people I have gathered in my life. It will be enough.

I, too, come from darkness, and have found a path to the light.

I'll show her the way. *We'll* show her the way.

Love is the way.

ACKNOWLEDGMENTS

Interestingly enough, writing your nineteenth novel isn't any easier than writing your first. In fact, in some ways it's harder. And that's okay. Nothing worth doing is ever easy. And I guess if I ever sit down and think, *No problem. I've got this,* that might be the day that I decide to hang it up. But even though the *writing* of each novel is a journey I must make alone — at least the first draft — luckily, *publishing* is a team effort. And I am blessed to be supported by some of the best people I know.

Every book I write is for my husband, Jeffrey, and our daughter, Ocean Rae. They are the home team, bolstering, supporting, making me laugh, keeping me sane, and filling my life with love. It's not easy living with a writer — lots of ups and downs! I'm sorry! I love you guys more than anything. Thank you for being on this crazy Tilt-A-Whirl with me and making it a blast. And of course, my beloved labradoodle, Jak Jak, is always at my feet or by my side, reminding me to get on with it so we can play ball.

My deep and heartfelt thanks to my compassionate, thoughtful, and wise — and oh wow let's not forget patient! — editor, Erika Imranyi. I think the books I have written for her are the best of my career. Thanks, Erika, for your steady and guiding hand. Meanwhile, HarperCollins/Harlequin/ Park Row Books is a dream publisher. My most profound gratitude goes to the amazing team members in the US, Canada, and the UK, from the stellar copy editor to the brilliant art departments to the intrepid sales teams. Special thanks to Loriana Sacilotto, executive vice president and publisher, and Margaret Marbury, vice president of editorial, for their tremendous leadership and passion. And I'm so grateful for publicist extraordinaire Roxanne Jones.

My agent, Amy Berkower, and her assistant, Meridith Viguet, of the stellar Writers House agency are my tireless champions and fearless navigators of the big waters of the writing life. I am so grateful for their support, wisdom, and good humor.

I am blessed with a wonderful network of friends who cheer me through the good days and offer a hand through the bad. Erin

Mitchell is an early reader, tireless promoter, inbox wrangler, voice of wisdom, and pal. I am in an ongoing text conversation with Alafair Burke and Karin Slaughter about all things life, writing, and business. It's a constant source of comfort and laughter. The #authortalks team of J.T. Ellison, Heather Gudenkauf, and Mary Kubica are truly a powerhouse group of stellar writers and sage voices. Love our talks about craft, creativity, and the writing life. Heather Mikesell is forever bestie and eagle-eyed reader. Nothing feels done until she's read it. My dear friend Jennifer Manfrey is always standing by to "give me a session" or talk through some obsession. Thanks for not hanging up every time I say, "So, I've been doing a little research . . ."

My mom, Virginia Miscione, a former librarian, gave me my love of story. And she remains one of my very first and most important readers. I made a change for her in this book — she knows what it is! And I'm so glad I did. My dad, Joseph, and brother, Joe, are captains of Team PA and Team VA, tirelessly flogging, facing out, and giving away books. Their ongoing support means everything.

As always, research is a big part of my process. A number of books were very important in the writing of this one. *Trauma and the Soul: A Psycho-Spiritual Approach to Human Development and Its Interruption* by Donald Kalsched is a deep dive into the psychic response to trauma. There's a deep well of wisdom here, and I return to Kalsched's work again and again for inspiration and understanding. *Tracking and the Art of Seeing: How to Read Animal Tracks and Sign* by Paul Rezendes is a practical, but also philosophical, look at being present with, understanding, and respecting nature. *The Bumper Book of Nature: A User's Guide to the Great Outdoors* by Stephen Moss is really a child's activity book, one which my daughter and I spent years exploring. But there are so many little jewels of knowledge, such a deep appreciation of the natural world, that I often find bits of it coming back to inspire my work. As always, all mistakes, liberties taken, or fictionalizations of inconvenient truths are mine and mine alone.

Finally, I am so grateful to my readers, many of whom have been with me from my very first book. I hear from you via email, on my social media accounts, at events — live and virtual. It means so much to know that my stories, my characters, my words have found a home in your hearts and minds. Thank you for buying, checking out from the library, reviewing, sharing with friends, and spreading the word. A writer is nothing without her readers. I am so thankful for each and every one. Happy reading!

ABOUT THE AUTHOR

Lisa Unger is a *New York Times* and internationally bestselling author of eighteen novels. An award-winning and acclaimed writer with millions of readers worldwide, Lisa is widely regarded as a master of suspense. Her books are published in twenty-six languages and have been voted "Best of the Year" or top picks by the *Today* show, *Good Morning America, Entertainment Weekly,* Amazon, IndieBound and many others. In 2019, her novel *Under My Skin* and her short story "The Sleep Tight Motel" were both nominated for the prestigious Edgar Award. Her nonfiction work has appeared in the *New York Times, Wall Street Journal, NPR* and *Travel + Leisure.* Lisa lives on the west coast of Florida with her family.

The employees of Thorndike Press hope you have enjoyed this Large Print book. All our Thorndike, Wheeler, and Kennebec Large Print titles are designed for easy reading, and all our books are made to last. Other Thorndike Press Large Print books are available at your library, through selected bookstores, or directly from us.

For information about titles, please call:
  (800) 223-1244

or visit our website at:
  gale.com/thorndike

To share your comments, please write:
  Publisher
  Thorndike Press
  10 Water St., Suite 310
  Waterville, ME 04901